REDDEVIL 4

REDDEVIL 4

Eric C. Leuthardt

A TOM DOHERTY ASSOCIATES BOOK
NEW YORK

This is a work of fiction. All of the characters, organizations, and events portrayed in this novel are either products of the author's imagination or are used fictitiously.

REDDEVIL 4

Copyright © 2014 by Eric C. Leuthardt

A Forge Book
Published by Tom Doherty Associates, LLC
175 Fifth Avenue
New York, NY 10010

www.tor-forge.com

Forge® is a registered trademark of Tom Doherty Associates, LLC.

Library of Congress Cataloging-in-Publication Data

Leuthardt, Eric C.
    RedDevil 4 / Eric C. Leuthardt. — First edition.
        p. cm.
    ISBN 978-0-7653-3256-1 (hardcover)
    ISBN 978-1-4668-0098-4 (e-book)
    1. Artificial intelligence—Fiction.   2. Murder—Investigation—Fiction.
I. Title.   II. Title: RedDevil 4.
    PS3612.E922R44 2014
    813'.6—dc23

                                                    2013024043

Forge books may be purchased for educational, business, or promotional use. For information on bulk purchases, please contact Macmillan Corporate and Premium Sales Department at 1-800-221-7945, extension 5442, or write specialmarkets@macmillan.com.

First Edition: February 2014

Printed in the United States of America

0 9 8 7 6 5 4 3 2 1

To Ellie and Melissa

ACKNOWLEDGMENTS

There are numerous people that deserve a lot of credit for helping make this book a reality (but none of the blame). To all my friends in the academic universe of neuroprosthetics, I have a deep gratitude to all of you for challenging my imagination for what the world could look like. Whether this occurred across podiums or over beers, the community that studies and advances the field of brain computer interfaces is one of the most vibrant and interesting groups of people I have had the pleasure to meet. First and foremost among them, I need to thank my close friend and mentor, Dan Moran, who gave me a chance by letting me work in his lab when I was a neurosurgery resident. Additionally, I would like to thank Keith Crutcher and Jeff Ojemann for their mentorship in my life and career. My chairman, Ralph Dacey, deserves credit for his leadership in giving me a position that enabled me to pursue my vision for brain computer interfaces within the Department of Neurosurgery at Washington University in St. Louis.

The book would never have approached reality if it wasn't for the good nature of some friends, John Lauria and Don Reardon, who eventually led me to my agent, Adam Chromy. It is hard to give Adam enough praise. His brass-knuckle honesty always kept me on track and focused. I would also like to thank Patrick Lobrutto, whose insight into books and early editorial diligence not only raised the caliber of this book, but also elevated me as a writer.

I want to give a special thanks to Bob Gleason, Lee Lawless, and Kelly Quinn at Tor/Forge Books. Whether it be at a bar in Harlem, doing karaoke at TGIF's, or tracking satellites with high-powered lasers at Goddard Space Station, it is an absolute pleasure to work with you. They welcomed and shepherded me into the writing world with such kindness, generosity, and enthusiasm.

Finally, I would like to thank my family—my wife, Melissa, my daughter, Ellie Claire, and yet to be named son on the way. They are my foundation and my joy.

REDDEVIL 4

"Have a seat, Hagan." The man gestured toward the black leather sofa in front of his desk. He was tall and bony and wore a white coat that was impeccably ironed and creased. With his broad bald dome of a head and small pallid ice-fleck-colored eyes, he had an annoyed look that suggested an irritable impatience. His chin was barely distinguishable from his thin neck, his face was small and pale, and the residual hair of his eyebrows and thin mustache were all a white blond. To Hagan, he looked more like an asshole than usual.

Sighing to himself, Hagan sat down. The pitch of the seat always tilted him slightly back so that his knees were higher than his buttocks. He never could position himself to sit up straight and always had to lean to the side or with his legs bowed out to lean forward, making him feel like was sitting on a toilet. Like he was a kid in the principal's office, the conversations always began with "have a seat." He prepared himself for the usual preamble.

"Hagan, I have been looking at your numbers, and they are not good." Hagan's chairman put his fingertips together and touched the tip of his nose for a long pause. "You are not generating the revenue you ought to be, either in clinical fees or in grants. Some things are going to have to change, Hagan."

"Simon, you and I both know the market is down. Elective surgeries are always the first to take the hit. It's a small downturn, *and* cases are sure to pick up in the spring."

"Are you giving me excuses, soldier?"

Hagan rolled his eyes. Simon Canter, his boss, loved to take on military lingo when they would argue. Hagan knew Simon thought it made him sound tough or commanding or something. To Hagan, it just sounded silly.

"Simon, Jesus, no. What am I supposed to do—pull people into the OR against their will?"

"Market or no market, if it takes more work beating the bushes to get patients, then that's what you gotta do. Less time in that little closet and more time out in the community talking to the primary care docs. If there is less water in the towel you gotta wring it harder, got me?"

"You know that's more than a little closet, Simon." Hagan could feel the heat rise on the back of his neck.

"To me, since your research isn't generating any research dollars from Uncle Sam, it may as well be a closet."

"I'm close, you know that, you've seen it, for Pete's sake. I just need to take it a little further, and we're not going to have any complaints about money for this department, I promise."

"You promise, you keep saying, 'its gonna happen, its gonna happen.'" Hagan watched as Simon put up his fingers to form the annoying quotation marks. "I need more than empty air—I need results. I need you to say to me, 'mission accomplished.' You keep saying neuromorphic artificial intelligence is the future; well, I need to pay bills in the present."

"Dammit, Simon, do I really need to spell it out for you? If we were having this same conversation thirty years ago, you would be arguing against all the work that went into neuroprosthetics. Look what changed—every human's mind is connected and augmented in every way possible. You and I, and about ninety percent of the human population, have a neuroprosthetic implanted. We can use our thoughts to engage the world beyond the limits of our bodies, brain-to-brain communication has changed the way humans interact, we can fix almost any brain injury, *and* the virtual reality—it's changed the way we do everything. It's what fucking built this city."

"Do you also want to tell me about how my car works? I already know all this. What's your point?" Canter asked snidely.

Hagan sighed. "Creating truly artificial intelligence based on the human brain's architecture is the next step. After three decades of implants we have the data—all we need to do is apply it. Again, Jesus, you *know* that. Once we get there, we can make armies of virtual scientists to solve every problem in medicine. We can have enough intellectual resources to answer pretty much every question that the human species can't currently figure out. It's worth the sacrifice."

"Show me the money, Hagan, show me the money. We are living in the here and now in 2053—not thirty years in the past, not thirty years in the future. And here in the present, no grants, no science, no cases—no salary."

The old man looked down at the gravestone. Tall and thin in a rumpled suit, he stood there for a few moments in silent contemplation, holding a handful of pink flowers.

"Hello, April, I brought you some daisies today. These are the pink ones with yellow centers. The lady at the flower shop called them Strawberry Blushes." He slowly kneeled next to the headstone and carefully placed the bouquet in the adjacent basin.

"Thought you would like them—not your typical yellow or orange ones. Something a little different this time." He sighed as he looked at the silent stone.

"Gonna cut the grass tomorrow. The yard is looking pretty good, though not much in the way of flowers the way that you used to like it, but I'm still keeping it tidy." As he spoke, he brushed the letters and the runners free of pebbly dirt and bits of bark. He let his fingers linger on the words—APRIL G. KRANTZ, 4/23/1985–11/4/2050. *God I miss her,* he thought to himself.

This was his Friday ritual. He had kept it for the several years since her death. Every Friday after work he would bring her flowers. It was what she had always loved, bright colorful flowers.

"So, typical stuff this week. Young punks broke into some ninety-four-year-old Asian guy's home and beat him senseless. Guy died a few days later. Apparently stole about two hundred dollars. Tragic—got DNA traces on all of 'em. Probably bring 'em in on Monday. The forensics guys are telling me they are probably fifteen by their epigenetic markers—whatever that means.

"I know I've said it in the past, but God, how young are criminals gonna get . . ." As the old man continued to recount the week's events, blue letters appeared across his field of view.

DETECTIVE KRANTZ, COMMUNICATION REQUESTED. CONFERENCE CALL WITH SERGEANT ORTIZ IN 10 MINUTES. MATTER CONSIDERED URGENT. PLEASE CONNECT WITH DIVISION HUB 3. THIS IS AN AUTOMATED MESSAGE.

Krantz sighed. "Honestly, April, I don't know how you convinced me to get these things put in." The lawn, stone, and flowers remained silent in response. He could still hear her voice in his head. He remembered how she browbeat him into getting these neuroprosthetic implants—"Nobody is using cell phones or laptops anymore," she had said. "How are we going to communicate with people? How are we going to shop? We need to keep up with the times," she had said. *She was always the modern one. Change was always exciting for her.* Finally he had acquiesced, and after about thirty minutes, a few patches of shaved scalp, a little bit of lidocaine, and a brief pinching sensation, his mind and the outside world were forever connected—his thoughts were accessible—for better or worse.

"April, how are we gonna get any peace? That's what I say." He felt the small lump behind his ear where the power source was. He was almost tempted to turn it off for a few moments of mental silence.

MEETING IN 5 MINUTES. MATTER CONSIDERED URGENT. PLEASE CONNECT WITH DIVISION HUB 3. THIS IS AN AUTOMATED MESSAGE.

"Well babe, looks like I may have to cut this visit a bit short. Work is work, no escaping it. I'll be back to see you next week." The detective lifted himself up and walked toward his car. Amid the trees and shrubs and carved stone, blue-lettered highlights, names, and advertisements all floated in the air. Today it bothered him more than most; he reached behind his ear and pushed on the small bump. *I need a break, just for a few minutes.* He felt a click and all the images disappeared.

Scuffling along the large marble hallway, a young man slowly limped his way forward. The end was highlighted with large windows framing a large mountain vista. His left foot slapped the polished surface with an echoing clack, and the right followed in a slow scratching drag. With each clack and drag, his body would rise and fall with the imbalance of his gait. He slowly made his way to the large steel doors of his room. A large plump woman came up behind him quickly.

"'Ello, Trent." Startled, the young man straightened slightly. He turned on his good leg, pulling the other, paretic limb along like a compass. The inverted foot rasped against the ground in a wide circular arc. His maid stood looking at him with plain-faced enthusiasm and said, in her singsong Bosnian accent, "Sorry, I no mean to scare you. Your fadder wants you to join him for dinner."

"Hey, Jasmina, I already ate, I'm meeting some friends in a bit." His words were lisped and contorted by a facial paralysis. Spittle accumulated at the corner of his mouth with each word. Though in his mid twenties, he could easily pass for a prepubescent adolescent teen. He was small and thin and lopsided in his stance, his right shoulder held far below the left. His thin atrophic right arm was held rigidly bent against his body as if he was holding a book against his chest. The hand was a nonfunctional clump of knuckles and thin fingers bundled into a fist. Knotty and jagged scars on his scalp pushed through patchy, thinning chestnut-colored hair.

None of this bothered his maid, who had known him since he was a child. Ruddy and round-faced, she exuded a simple indomitable pleasantness that he greatly appreciated. In her broken English, she spoke to him as she would anyone else. "Trent, you spend too much time in room, come join for dinner."

"Can't, Jasmina, I'm gonna be late. My friends are waiting."

"Who is in room?" Her voice took on a higher pitch. "Nobody in room—nobody—you need be with people, *real people*, boys your age."

"I'm meeting with them virtually, in the SIM, like I always do."

"Dees nothing for me, dees tings in head, I no understand. I know your fadder make for many years, but for me I still like see people. You too, you should see people."

Knowing he wasn't about to convince her, Trent held his hand up in acquiescence. "Jasmina, really, I gotta go." He directed his attention to the doors of his room, and watched as the pieces of polished metal slid apart with a mechanical whisper.

"Alright, alright, I tell Dr. Devron you no come." She rolled her eyes. "Fadders and der sons, always de same."

Trent walked into the room and the doors hissed behind him. He thought about Jasmina as she went bobbing off to clean another one of the domestic quarters. He could see her plump arms pumping as she cleaned some forlorn corner of the house. He always enjoyed her enthusiasm. The little things always made her happy.

My closest human relationship is probably with a maid who barely speaks English, he thought with a sigh. He didn't like lying to her. The happening was not for another thirty minutes, but spending it with his father would have been a misery. The whole scene would play out as it had for years—sitting in that cavernous dining room, watching as the members of the household staff silently moved in and out like well-dressed zombies. He and his father would have forced one-sentence exchanges with long uncomfortable pauses, and finally, when it was all over, he would walk away hungry because he had been too anxious to actually eat anything. *No thanks.*

He looked out his digital window.

Another fake reality brought to you by Devron Incorporated.

Trent climbed into his bed. *System. Log on to Nexucist.* The room began to dissipate into a snowstorm of blue flashing lights. As images began to emerge, he felt his body begin to relax. *This is the way things should be. These are the lies I want to believe.*

"OK . . . Now tell me . . . what a 'stitch in time saves nine' means."

Hagan's mind was connected to an artificial intellect he was pushing toward consciousness. Human thoughts raced and analyzed to coax awareness out of a compilation of data bits and electrons where there was none. *I can get him there . . . true consciousness . . . it can be done.*

The man sat motionless at the table looking into the space before him. Slate eyes stared intently forward beneath slightly furrowed brows. He had dark hair, short, wavy, and brushed back with hints of gray dispersed throughout. The slightly rounded jaw and Roman nose suggested a certain old-world European quality. A solid figure in a white coat, he sat still and erect on a high-backed ebony chair with a frame of vertical lines. His elbows rested lightly on the polished gunmetal gray surface with crossed hands. Around him were walls paneled with the same iridescent adamantine material as that of the table. A soft white light diffused from the seamless surface of the ceiling. The only overt activity in the ascetic and sterile room was a small flashing green light on the table to the left of the man's arm. This was the neurosurgeon Dr. Hagan Maerici, and this was his lab.

To the outside observer, there was only a still man and the quiet buzz of hidden electronics. To Dr. Maerici, he was looking at a semi-transparent bluish child sitting cross-legged in front of him. Superimposed on the minimalist environment, the walls were covered with an assortment of blue-lined squares with numerous diagrams, graphs, and various anatomic pictures of the nervous system. In the air behind the blue cherub-faced child were various bar graphs and waveforms, all fluctuating dynamically with each thought that went between the solid multitoned figure of Hagan and the azure boy before him. The boy, the graphs, and the images were all the conjured result of innumerable miniscule electrodes stimulating various neurons within Hagan's brain.

The boy shook his head. *"I will require more data to perform adequate assessment."*

"Alright, Omid, access cortical information from subjects ten and forty-two." Data wirelessly streamed to hidden data banks—the recorded compilation reflecting billions upon billions of neurons of

human subjects attempting to understand a proverb entered into a computer, pushing the furthest limits of physics.

Voice audiograms bounced and adjusted to the pitch, timbre, and volume of the projected thought that Hagan was directing to the figure. The young boy looked placid and calm. With the appearance of a baroque marble angel held under a neon blue light, he had a certain statuesque presence—solid, immutable, and imperturbable.

The ghost child never blinked. His gaze was fixed on Hagan with a quiet thoughtfulness.

"Calling subjects ten and forty-two. Frontal lobe sets." The boy's voice, the synthetic product of Hagan's stimulated cortex, sounded profoundly unchildlike. He had the unwavering and focused delivery of a soprano Zen master.

"Processing." Waveforms were fluctuating rapidly, and a small sliver of a pie chart behind the boy widened slightly. *"Download complete."*

Hagan was anxious to begin. *"OK . . . go ahead, tell me what 'a stitch in time saves nine' means."*

"Processing." For the first time the boy closed his eyes and his head tilted back. Nothing else about his face changed. Wire graphs jumped and bobbed.

The bar histograms again returned to their basal level and the flowing line charts reduced to a slight quiver. The boy opened his eyes.

"Small efforts now reduce larger efforts in the future." Omid said in even and measured tones.

"That's correct." Hagan's pulse quickened—*progress. Did he really get it?* Now to make sure he wasn't just using verbal parity from the downloaded experiences, just imitating the experience from humans who had answered the proverb questions by using alternative words. Researchers called it the "thesaurus trick." Artificial Intelligence Reverse-Engineered from Neural Signals—AIRENS—were getting better and better at the trick, but it still didn't represent understanding. Omid, perhaps arguably one of the highest engineered AIRENS to date, was the best at it.

"OK, lets try this one—'a rolling stone gathers no moss.'" Hagan gripped the edge of the table in anxious expectation.

A flashing orb suddenly appeared to the right of Hagan's field of view. It looked like a white golf ball winking in an out of sight. Someone was attempting to call.

"Ignore," he commanded. *"Not now."* The phosphene ball winked

out. He again returned his attention to Omid. Looking beyond him, he could still see that the processing function indicators were maximally engaged. *Why is he struggling with this so much? Machines just don't understand context. Why is that so difficult?*

The flashing orb appeared again . . . *"Dammit . . . Ignore and disengage external communication."*

"Dr. Maerici, I believe that it is your wife calling. Shall we pause?"

"No. She can wait."

"Multiple attempts at communication can sometimes indicate urgency."

Hagan waved his hand as if he was trying to shoo away a fly.

"Unlikely, lets proceed."

Hagan was close—he felt it. Frustrated at the interruption, he tried to refocus. He held his attention on the boy and the sterile graphs and charts—solace from a chaotic and emotional world. He took a deep breath.

"Lets try again. Tell me what 'a rolling stone gathers no moss' means."

His tense expectation was fractured with the presence of a new flashing orb. Distinct from the previous call, the flashes had a checkered pattern indicating an emergency communication. Regardless of receptor status, the indicator was put through.

"No, no, no, NO! Not now. Disregard."

"Dr. Maerici, this appears to be an emergency call from your wife. Shall we conclude?"

The flashing orb increased in size and brightness. Hagan knew it wouldn't relent until he answered it.

"Hello." His tone was flat.

"Hagan, what time are you coming home?"

"Anna? That is the emergency connection. What time I'm coming home—is that really an emergency?"

"Its eight o'clock at night. It's not unreasonable, since it's the only way I seem to get through to you."

Hagan sighed. *"I'm finishing up, I'll be home soon."* His shoulders bowed, already exhausted from what was now becoming a routine conversation.

"Soon?"

"Soon—I'm in the middle of something right now, and I'll be there as soon as I can."

There was a long silence. Hagan couldn't hear the muffled sniffs as his wife stifled tears.

She sometimes just didn't understand, he thought to himself—careful not to project his internal reflections to her.

"I'll see you whenever, then—" Their thoughts were disconnected. The conversation had ended as abruptly as it had started.

Hagan felt a heavy ball in his stomach, tight with frustration. She was throwing him off his rhythm. He just wanted to get a little further tonight. He had to. If he didn't make progress, Simon would significantly reduce his research time. *Between my wife and my boss, hard to believe I get anything done.*

He refocused his gaze on Omid. The boy met his eyes with a muted calm. *"Alright, where were we—right—'a rolling stone gathers no moss.' Tell me what it means."*

The opalescent child again closed his eyes. The multiple graphs and charts did their dance. Moments later the boy opened his eyes.

"Movement impairs growth of vegetation."

Maerici shook his head. *"No, that is not correct."*

"Are you dissatisfied, Dr. Maerici?" said the boy in the same even, composed manner, his unblinking gaze never deviating from Hagan's face. *"There are increased high gamma frequency power fluctuations in multiple limbic regions. As you know, these often are associated with emotional processing and response. This is in conjunction with your parietal P300 response, often an indicator of surprise. Can I infer that my incorrect answer has created an emotional response of surprise and dissatisfaction?"*

"That is correct, Omid. I am disappointed and frustrated on many levels tonight. Why do you think I am disappointed?" He again pushed the AIRENS to abstract an answer. He was pushing him to process the why of the situation, to move beyond correlation.

The two, human and synthetic, were communicating without firewall. All the information within each system was completely transparent. Hagan could see everything that was going on as Omid processed information, and so too did Omid have access to the full panorama of electrical signals produced and recorded by Hagan's neuroprosthetic implant.

Hagan turned his gaze to a blue-lined window in the far corner of the lab. His attention brought the image closer. Lines of iridescent white script scrolled past the square aperture, pausing momentarily as Hagan's attention lifted or focused on a title or subheading. As files of interest appeared they would then get diverted to another empty window that appeared next to the original one Hagan was observing. Hagan began following a thread.

I'm getting closer, he thought. Lines, connectors, and windows all flitted and bounced throughout the room as the intense and driven mind of Hagan Maerici pursued its goal.

A spinning orb again appeared in his visual field. The man slammed his fist on the table.

Trent looked at himself in the still waters of the expansive pool. The brackish water smelled of saunas and indoor swimming pools. Small wisps of steam arose from the clear surface, suggesting the water's deeper warmth. All around him were the bluish and silvery tones of his synthetic world.

The motif for this Friday night was Rome. The large bath was an enclosed square with ornately carved thick slabs. Diving fish, mermaids, and astrological symbols of the sun, moon, and stars ran along the edges. Surrounding the large mere was a colonnade of Corinthian columns supporting carved friezes in various arrangements of conflict and adoration. The water was a semilucent mirror. He stood approximately six feet tall with a shock of silvery spiked hair that angled back from his smooth forehead. His eyes were a crystalline blue. The transient haze of emerging vapor occasionally obscured the high cheekbones and angled jaw that belied a Scandinavian appearance. A straight nose with soft nasal creases divided the symmetric face. A distinct cleft beneath the narrow lips accentuated the prominence of his squared chin. Underneath the Roman sway of a cloth tunic, he could see the broad shoulders and well-defined chest of his avatar. His surroundings were interrupted by the distant sound of a gentle wind blowing through unseen trees.

He looked at himself—his avatar, really. His chest tightened both from admiration and loathing. He felt more real here than he did at any other time.

This is the way I should be, he thought to himself.

A brief look of dismay crossed the statuesque features. Though a solace, the avatar was also a prison—it reminded him of the part of his life that no amount of carbon nanotube, silicon, and grafted stem cell could ever rebuild.

He was always the first for a *happening.* These were the parties held in the azure monochromatic world of SIM, the synthetic immersive metaverse. It was a virtual cosmos that contained every time and every place. An endless digital expanse that one could explore for a lifetime—separated and removed from the vicissitudes of a decaying and degenerate reality, a pulsing, thriving macrocosm consisting of oscillating qubits, memory banks, and connectivity. Everything existed.

From ancient Rome to the aesthetic fields of Mars to the whimsical and surreal speculations of programmers, drug addicts, religious fanatics, and geniuses; it was all in here, a rainforest of the mind. Layer upon layer of sensory experience packed to an infinite density and racing out to the limits of imagination. In the moment it takes an electron to switch its quantum state, a photon to move along a nanotube, or the oscillation of a neuron's field potential, he could shift and morph into a new world. Here, in any place and in any moment in time, one could be whoever and whatever he or she wanted to be.

He, however, didn't change. Trent had worked and crafted his avatar for years. A David of the virtual world; every detail had been attended to. From the wrinkles in his hands, the cadence of his walk, to the slight bend in his eyebrows, all had been defined. Here he could be whole and strong. Others changed their personas like clothes. Trent's appearance was more solid and convincing than most people appeared in the real world. His visual bit resolution was denser than what was normally perceived by normal sight. He was resplendent with solidity and detail.

As he looked at himself a shimmering sphere appeared over his shoulder, beneath which was the caller's name—Father.

His well-crafted mouth pinched to a thin line. *Connect.*

Before he could hear a word from his father, he cut in. *"What is it? I'm busy right now."*

"Wondered if you wanted to join me for dinner. I'm taking a break from work, and the staff members are preparing a meal. Would you care to come up to the fourth floor?"

"Not now, meeting friends."

"Very well, enjoy your outing. I will be dining for the next hour or so; please attend if you can."

"'Kay—bye." Disconnect. The sphere and his father's presence disappeared.

Was it guilt? Probably. He thought about his father—eighty-two and still working late into the evening on a Friday night—the eminent Dr. Marcus Devron. *We could never connect.* His avatar shook its head. Focused and indomitable, his father was a social monolith Trent could never know, could never understand. He was never Dad, Daddy, or Papa—never something personal. He was Father, very proper, nothing causal or intimate about the relationship. Even before his accident Trent had been an uncomfortable and awkward teen, never of the "go-get-'em" stock his father was.

The accident . . . a stinging discomfort splintered through him as he broached the recollection. He quickly drew away from the painful abscess of memories.

It was the reason for the gifts. He was a pariah. His father would never admit to it, but he was. He knew it. His father had given his son an exit—an enticing solace of being someone else. Beyond the premium visual, auditory, and haptic constructs, he also had the exotics—the olfactory, taste, and synesthetic transforms. For the average man's lifetime of income, he had the best olfactory and gustatory constructs placed so that he could experience virtual reality with all five of his senses.

More real than reality, he thought to himself.

The sounds of the approaching avatars distracted him from his reverie. Emerging from the misty surrounds were figures of all shapes. Intermingled in the nondescript figures approached the serious revelers. A figure that looked like a fat man with an elephant head was closest. As the portly outline got closer, Trent could see that the creature had four arms with flowing baggy pants and a shawl that seemed to flit around the heavyset head. The avatar's elongate proboscis bobbed and flipped upward randomly. The eyes were small and dark and peered at Trent with a certain twinkling gaiety.

The elephant man gave a nod of acknowledgment with a quick flap of his large ears. *"What eez up, Nordeec."* His voice was thick with an Indian accent. He always called Trent Nordic for his avatar's blond hair; the nicknames and the monikers, however, changed as easily as the avatars—everything varied in this world. For this guy, at this moment, he was Nordic.

"Hey, Ganesha, been a time, how are you? Still with the elephant head, huh?"

"Coming from blondie, who doesn't change a ting, not one to criticize. Suits me, though, don't you think? Ganesha head—that god always loses his; that's how it come to be an elephant. Most appropriate for happening, no? G-net gonna lose his head tonight, Nordeec, lose it big time. Got some code you wanna share?"

"None right now, you know people will be dealing though, just wait. It's always clickers with the decked avatars."

More figures and shapes were winking into existence. Behind him was a floating orb that burned with a silvery fire. In the center was a wildly grinning face. More creatures and personas emerged. Coincident with the Roman theme, a Bacchus avatar enwreathed in grapes and carrying two inordinately large chalices marched forward with exaggerated steps of excitement.

"*G–net, over there—the goat-dude, the satyr, the one with the chalice and all the gems. He's your man. That is pleasure code if I have ever seen it.*"

The elephant-headed avatar wagged its giant nose with enthusiasm. "*Let us find some mental treats, my friend.*"

"*Check it, elephant man, check it.*" The two walked into the emerging crowd toward the code dealers. Trent walked with Ganesha while lithe nymphs clothed in garlands and reeds flitted about. There were several butterfly-winged pixies floating above. A large wolf loped among the crowd. Some of the figures shifted and morphed. *Here I am a normal guy, a person people hang out with.* He relished the comraderie of two dudes trying to get high.

More and more figures began to appear. Some winked into the middle of the crowd, others walked, floated, or flew from the peripheral mists. The menagerie of avatars intermingled and engaged in various forms of communication in a multiplicity of languages. Trent smiled to himself. The group was highly tailored. The crowd was gaining a good energy—he could feel it.

He removed himself from darker thoughts.

This was going to be a good night.

"*I'm about halfway home.*" Hagan sat back in the black leather of his car seat and took some slow silent deep breaths. A fight was building and he wanted to avoid it. With his car on autopilot, he could feel the stop and go of traffic that occurred invisibly beyond his frosted windows. The images and equations that had been projected on the opaque windows were still from their momentary neglect.

"*I am hungry and sick of waiting.*" Anna's voice had that familiar edge to it, that overenunciated quality that meant a powder keg of dissatisfaction was lying out there somewhere in the interaction.

"*Won't be more than fifteen minutes.*" Hagan worked to keep his voice casual. "*Go ahead and eat, seriously, I'll eat later.*"

"*I am tired of eating alone, Hagan.*"

Hagan paused. He could smell the gunpowder.

"*Hello . . .*"

"*Look, Anna, I don't know how you want me to respond. I am coming home as soon as I can. Canter spent the better part of the afternoon skinning me alive about not having results from the lab. He's threatening to shut me down if I don't do more cases and produce more results. I'm doing the best I can here.*"

"*Don't use him as an excuse, you'd be there anyway, Hagan.*"

Hagan felt the car jolt to a halt. "*Anna, hold on for a second, something's going on with traffic.*" He directed his attention to the windows—*street view*. Like steam dissipating, the windshield cleared to reveal a tangle of traffic all around him. To his surprise, he was barely a mile away from the hospital.

"*Looks like a bad traffic jam. Crap.*" Hagan directed his attention to the console. "*System, perform traffic analysis and reroute.*"

"*Hagan, don't change the subject.*"

Blue words emerged at the periphery of his view.

EVENT: CHURCH OF EVANGENLICAL MISSION—CONVENTION CENTER. SOUTH AND WEST ROUTES CONGESTED. REROUTING . . .

Hagan regained his focus. "*I'm not, look, I have a hardworking job—the clinical and research stuff—it takes up time, you know that, you've always known that, and right now it's more difficult than usual because of Canter. You know how close I am with everything. I'm almost there with getting Omid to consciousness. It could mean a Nobel Prize, for Christ's sake. This is important, really important— you know that.*" Hagan watched as his car tried to navigate between an old van covered in shiny bumper stickers asking WHAT WOULD JESUS DO? and a car full of white-haired old ladies.

"*So is a marriage, Hagan. Something you seem to fail to understand.*"

Hagan could feel his heart beat faster. "*Jesus, Anna, I'm late for dinner—I'm sorry—why does everything have to mean something bigger? I'll be home soon; let's talk about it then.*" He knew he was slipping into an unpleasant place. More cars with religious icons and slogans were boxing him in.

"*A million little things can add up to a big thing. It's not just about being late for dinner—are you ever going to take my perspective into consideration, ever? Is what I am telling you that foreign?*"

"*Anna, we are not getting anywhere here.*"

"*I've known that for while.*"

"*You mean since about April—that was quite a big thing—don't you think?*" He knew he just lit the match.

"*Of course you would bring that up wouldn't you. You just have to keep opening that wound.*"

Hagan clenched his jaw. As his wife's voice continued to reverberate in his head, he was quickly growing a new appreciation for God's intervention at slowing his arrival home.

Reverend Franklin Elymas could feel the fervor rising. The pews were full and people were still coming in. His flock, he thought to himself. Old men with walkers, mothers pulling their toddlers by their sticky hands, vagrants, they all paid their fees and packed into the auditorium. They lined the aisles and stood against the walls.

Even today when it could all be virtual they still came, he thought.

He looked through the one-way mirror of his dressing room as he pushed his platinum cuff links through the shirtsleeves. The music from Worship Network reverberated off the walls of the aluminum building. Gospel arias and choir praises penetrated his enclosure like sparrows flying though the room. What he was doing was good. He knew that. It was the Lord's work. He looked at himself in the mirror and smiled. A broad row of impossibly white teeth shimmered back.

"I am the Lord's messenger," he said to himself.

It was almost time. Elymas always enjoyed the buildup. The preacher put a pill into his mouth and felt it fizz under his tongue. Moments later the effect was upon him.

His head rolled back and he looked to the ceiling. "Come, Lord, fill me with your power—my heart is open." Shimmers and sparkles swirled above. The glint of diamonds floated and encircled him, in moments they popped with small phosphors of light. A burning warmth grew within his chest.

The feeling of the Spirit roiled and frothed within and through him. He felt the full effect of the power and glory. Words and sounds bubbled from his mouth that he had never heard before—he was speaking in tongues, the hidden language of the divine. They issued with the intensity and convictions of a true believer. He was ready. Ready to spread the good word, to lead the righteous out of the desert, to turn his flock of sheep into warriors for the faith in the final times. His body began to sway. Beads of sweat formed on his forehead. His hands shook with the power of it. His actions didn't matter—it was the message. He was a vessel ready to pour forth that which the people needed. He would deliver the word to them. That was his mission.

The music was beginning to crescendo.

"In five—Reverend," a voice from a hidden speaker announced. "Five, four, three, two . . ."

The silver-haired man in a shimmering white suit ran out onto the stage. Arms raised, Elymas felt the roar of adulation engulf him. The lights were upon him and made him glow with an angelic haze. The audience shifted, cried, and called out hallelujahs. Elymas looked around. He saw their faces—he felt as if he looked into the eyes of each and every one. In the air he saw angels. Not the plump cherubic type, but muscular figures with sinewy arms and thick condor-like wings. He could hear the *thumb-thumb* of their flight as they slapped their immense wings in the air like great feather-covered cymbals. He drew in his breath.

"Abomination!!!" he called out. The roar of the crowd came to a sudden and immediate stillness. He drew out the palpable silence for maximal effect. The angels held themselves in the air still and waiting.

"We are at the end times, and abomination is around us everywhere. The time is coming for the Lord to sweep the devil's work from the world." Hallelujahs and amens from the crowd punctuated each of his words.

"YOU are his chosen people. YOU are his children in faith that will be saved. YOU will be his warriors that will cleanse this world that is riddled with sin." His arm swept out over the crowd emphasizing who the "you" was.

"YOU here today are PURE! Unlike your neighbors, your coworkers, those who have abandoned the faith, who have marked and sullied themselves. They pretend that their thoughts, that their minds can be read, they believe that the seat of the soul is open for business!" Elymas let his righteous indignation build.

"Man CANNOT know that which is the property of God. He CANNOT control that which does not belong to him. Our minds and our souls cannot be—THEY MUST NOT BE—the playthings of the devil. What people hear and see when they place pieces of metal in their brain are not facts, they are not the thoughts of another human, they do not make us better or stronger—NO—they are delusions. They are deceits from the Great Liar. Do you know of whom I speak?" The angels circled and fluttered their large gray wings in agitation. They bent and shook their arms in holy angst. The musty animal scent of their feathers filled his nose.

An angry roar emerged from the crowd. "Devil!" "Lucifer!" "The Antichrist!"

"That is right, my children. It is the mark of the Beast. They have identified their place in this holy conflagration. It is time to choose sides. They have made their choice and we are making ours. Rather than hear the words of the Lord that I am speaking tonight, they would hear the lies whispered by the devil in their heads!" Open hands held aloft fell together at his chest to form tight fists. Again he fell silent. The crowd swayed as if in a trance, waiting and expectant. Some held their arms aloft, eyes closed and calling out in religious rapture.

Elymas's arms again shot forth with a volley of words. Like a soldier trooping across the stage, he moved around with exaggerated steps, knees lifting high, he stomped and stomped to deliver his message.

"We must not cower, we must not fear. Those that would attempt to take that which is the Lord's must know that there are those who say NO. We are those sources of light. WE in this room are the ones who will stare into the eyes of the deceiver and demand truth. Go, my children, speak the words of Jesus and watch the sinners tremble." The divine muse spoke through him like a vessel. He let the power of the crowd take him.

"Go to their homes, go to all houses of evil, and evangelize the truth! March as God's holy warriors, conquer for Christ!" A hail of raucous cries engulfed him.

Like hungry hawks the angels swooped and lifted people out of the crowd. Some vanished into the rafters. *Those must be the souls that are saved,* he mused, as words continued to issue forth. Others were dropped—*the damned.*

Soon the divine creatures became more angular, more broken, and disconnected. Elymas saw wings flying by themselves. Feathers were all around him. The dander tickled the back of his throat. The audience became a kaleidoscope of fractal images. Angels, supplicants, lights all began to melt and bend. His voice began to quaver. He knew it was time to stop.

The girl tried to hide the bluish circles beneath her eyes. Her hands shook from the effort—the glittered mascara went on in thick messy strokes. She looked at the person in the mirror. The emerging sobriety brought her appearance into an uncomfortable focus. Her face was pale and gaunt, pretty in a starved model sort of way. There were lines around her mouth and crow's-feet creasing her eyes that hadn't been there before. She had spikey silvery hair that gave the high cheek bones and small features of her nose and mouth a pixie-like appearance.

She splashed water on her face. It didn't help.

God, where am I? Her last concrete recollection was a modern beach home in San Diego. She had been sitting on a wood bench. She remembered the pills. How the world seemed to bend and shimmer. She remembered how the guy, she didn't remember his name, the guy with the short hair and piercings, had put a small sticker over the small divot in her arm. It had bubbled and dissolved into her vein. How the world had changed.

How long ago was that? She couldn't tell. The world had become a shifting kaleidoscope of scenes. Parties, buses, streets, people, all sorts of people, sex, sex with boys, sex with girls, they all seemed so strange, but she had loved it, maybe not loved it, but felt compelled to go along with it. There was too much movement, too much inertia that pushed her along. Moved her from place to place, room to room. Now she was here.

Where is this? she asked herself again. She felt a rising tide of panic. Not from being lost, but from the absence. She was becoming more sober and the expanding emptiness filled her with a blackness and self-loathing that pulled at her insides.

Outside was an old man who could fix it. He sat there waiting like a vulture because he knew that she needed it. He had something new. Something that would bring her back to a better place. She wore a sheer dress. She lifted up the hem and removed her panties. She knew what was required. She walked out to meet him.

He sat there at the edge of the bed smiling lasciviously. "Come on over and have a seat here next to good ole Cyrus." He made no pretense about the parts of her body that he was looking at.

"There's something I think that you are gonna want?" The dirty sweet smell of cigarettes filled her nose. She nodded her head.

There was a small silvery pill in the palm of his hand. His fingernails were yellow and caked with grime. As she reached out for it, he pulled away.

"Ahn-ahn, sugar. There's something I want first. This is the way we do business, isn't it?" She shivered as he put his hand on her shoulder.

The party began to take on a new intensity. The avatars were morphing into more and more human forms. The speed and volume of the music was increasing. His friend Ganesha was lost in the crowd. The personas were now dancing and cavorting. They touched and caressed one another with labile abandon. Each figure danced not only to the music that coursed through their environment but to the internal music of their brain rhythms and that of whoever it was they came into contact with. The group became a collective organism that jumped, twisted, and pressed with the music and thoughts of the throng.

Trent approached the crowd in excited anticipation. His senses were ringing like tuning forks.

Curving, writhing, twisting, and touching, the digital crowd mixed and intermingled with a growing fervor. Their crafted humanoid figures touched and shared haptic stimulus. With each brush, push, and caress there were brief glimmers of the individuals' thoughts. *Hey . . . I'm so high . . . who's that . . . nice avi . . . wanna fuck . . . crush . . . Ken?* The music was loud—a heavy bass-driven syncopated beat escalating in speed. The light was dusky and the steam from the pool was now a shimmering fog intermingled amidst the crowd. *BOOM . . . BOOM . . . BOOM . . .* There were now hundreds present. Everything was monochromatic tones of dark navy and prussian blues punctuated by the lustrous argent light from the rising moon.

BOOM BOOMBOOMBOOM CHK—CHK—CHKBOOM . . . BOOM

With nerves like quivering needles, Trent began to push his way into the periphery. The avatars had transformed to more recognizable figures. He could see that Ganesha had shed the elephant head and was now a heavy-featured Indian with long hair instead of big ears. He wore the same flowing pantaloons over his stolid frame. He was between lithe women with iridescent skin. He nodded to Trent. The girls on either side of him also smiled. The touch of the partygoers was electric—a shock and a tingle to his code-enhanced senses.

Trent felt alive, exhilarated, far, far away from the broken body that was sitting on a couch two hundred feet below the earth. Swaying hips, rounded thighs, arms held aloft, he was surrounded by women of every real and imaginary type. The music coursed through him.

Arms swayed and moved to the music like a crowd of frenzied fla-
mingo heads. He heard the echoes and glimpses of the thoughts of all
the women around him. The allure and promise of some virtual interlude reverberated everywhere.

It was then that he saw the impossible—red.

He saw the red eyes of a woman standing near him. She stood there
immobile amid her nubile dancing peers, staring. Her eyes penetrated
Trent like spotlights shining through smoke. He felt something deep
within him—a yearning, a need, a pull, something viscerally emotional, something forgotten and nameless.

"Ganesha, do you see that?" He grabbed his shoulders. The senses
of the two intermingled. He could feel the press of the women's bodies against him. "Do you see those eyes, those red eyes? Have you ever
seen that before?"

His friend's head rolled toward him, he saw both an Indian face
and his own. "It's the code, man, it's the code. Probably some bug. All
I see is blue. Everything here is blue, so blue, always blue." Ganesha
pulled and jumped as the waves of music moved through him.

Trent looked back. Her back was to him now. The primal sensations were gone. He had only gained a glimpse, but he was sure that
he had seen a trace of red. There was an irregular bumpiness to her
skin as if she were covered in brail. Black hair was pulled back and
held tight in a straight tubular ponytail.

How could she have red eyes? I am sure I saw it. He tried to move
closer. The press of the bodies slowed him and pushed her farther away.
I have got to see . . . it can't be possible. Color was the only thing this
world lacked. Everything was painted in the various monochromatic
shades of blue, black, and white. It was known as the "phosphene barrier." Stimulating the visual cortex only produced one color—blue. You
could alter how bright or dark it was, but blue was all you got. Color
perception was the largest mystery in neuroprosthetics.

I have to see those eyes. It was more than the color. Trent struggled
to comprehend. For a brief moment he felt like a toy that had been
finally plugged in. Lights turning on and wheels rolling—for a brief
moment he felt alive, really alive, whole.

He pushed further. He was closer now. He could almost touch her
shoulder. The music was deafening, avatars were moving with frenzy.
The pitch of the music was getting higher and higher. She turned to
him, again the glowing ember-red eyes—silence. Everything slowed,
the people, the sound, everything was deafeningly slow and quiet.

Her gaze filled him with a hot liquid; perfusing though every capillary, wakening every cell in his body. She was closer now. Again a glimpse— silence, followed by the abrupt return of the booming cacophony.

What is going on here? Is anybody else noticing this?

She continued to move farther away from him. A frictionless, supple creature, she effortlessly passed through the tangle of jerking, agitated bodies. Her skin shimmered in irregular metallic steel tones.

Trent was now pushing and shoving. The mystery of her red eyes drew him in an incomprehensible way. As he shoved through the press of arms and legs, the thoughts and feelings of the fellow revelers, once symbiotic and intoxicating moments, were now intrusive. He jumped to catch a glimpse of her. She was outside the press. Strolling along the bank of the pond twenty yards away, she bounced slightly with each step keeping a subtle rhythm in her stride.

Fuck, where is she going, is she going to log off . . . Trent was becoming frantic. He needed to see those red eyes. His yearning wasn't rational. Losing her would deny him some deep-needed purpose, some revelation, insight; something meant for him and him alone.

"Ouch. . . . Motherfucker! . . . Asshole."

Trent pulled and tugged his way forward. His single-mindedness was a stark intensity, uncomfortable to those he came into contact with. Finally free, he captured a fleeting glimpse of the woman walking between the pillars into darkness.

He sprinted in pursuit. In this world he could move quickly and tirelessly. His bare feet slapped against the old Roman stones and up the steps. At the top, beneath the column-supported architrave were dark vaulted passages. She was gone.

Did she log off? Trent felt sick with anxiety.

In the distance he heard a brief peal of laughter. A light echoing sound as if canaries had just been released. He ran into the dark passage. The indigo light fading behind him, he again heard the trace sound of footsteps. At the end of the corridor he saw her pass though some curtains. Racing forward, Trent ran toward the veiled aperture.

Leaning forward, arms outstretched, he launched his body past the cloth passage.

In the same moment, his face abruptly distorted against a smooth surface. His body bounced back and he lay flattened on the cobbled Roman floor.

"What the . . ." His head stung from the impact. Raising himself up, Trent slowly approached the curtains, which still swayed slightly from the collision. He held his hand out and pushed the heavy velvety fabric aside.

"A mirror . . ." Trent looked at himself. His whitish eyebrows were knitted together in a shallow V. The mouth was a pinched straight line. *I lost her . . .*

He reached out and touched the mirror. The glass was smooth and cool. Leaning against the glass and looking down, his heart felt as empty as the large corridor behind him. *Gone . . .*

After several moments of misery, he finally exhaled and looked up. With his hand still against the mirror, the reflection looking at him was not his own. *It was her.* The cerulean woman with the ember-red glowing eyes stared back at him, smiling. Her hand emanated from the spot where he touched the mirror in perfect symmetry.

Trent jumped back in astonishment and surprise. With the same stumbling clumsiness, his mirror image faltered back into the reflected corridor with eyes wide and mouth agape. *What is going on here?* He was again looking at himself.

Trent approached the mirror with slow and careful steps. Head cocked to the side, walking sideways with careful steps, he took in every motion and aspect of his reflection's movement. He padded carefully toward the mirror, preparing himself for another surprise.

Shaking from both hope and fear of disappointment, he reached with tremulous outstretched fingers toward the mirror. With the very tips of his index and middle fingers he made contact.

She's back! The inner exultation was mirrored by the large beautiful smile of the woman looking at him. Her eyes never left his. He was transfixed by the burning magenta orbs of her gaze. Those eyes filled him with warmth. He pressed both hands against the mirror. The woman matched his movements. They now stood together forming an arch. As he looked into her eyes they seemed to grow. They were dual sunsets, blazing furnaces; they occupied the full field of his vision. All was the lambent orange-red of her eyes. In those eyes he saw things. Wonderful things. He was safe. Whole. Absolved. They were his dreams, his fantasies, his heart's desires fulfilled.

Hagan walked stiff-legged and bleary toward his car. The evening hadn't been a good one and he was eager to get back to work. He quickly sipped from a small shot cup of espresso. He directed his attention to his Mercedes, a sleek black affair, and the car powered up. Light emerged from the hidden headlights in the front and a holographic three-sided star appeared over the hood. As he approached the door opened. Burning the back of his throat, he hurriedly finished the last remnants of the overbrewed stimulant and pressed a button on the cup. It quickly evaporated in his hand. Hagan eased himself into the crafted inner sanctum of leather, black mahogany, and brushed steel.

"Engage," he projected to the car.

Recognizing his prosthetic and cortical signature, the car came to life. *"Good morning, Dr. Maerici."* The resonant voice of a sultry woman with a slight German accent echoed in his mind. Holographic displays and subtle highlights came to overlay on the highly crafted interior. Above the seat and dash, what initially had been a small enclosed windowless space transformed to a full virtual panoramic view. The electric engine whirred in anticipation.

"Initiate Autonav—destination Barnes Hospital. Parking spot thirty-two. Please link to office workstation."

"Satellite linkage achieved, beginning trip, estimated time—twelve minutes. Office connected." Hagan watched as the car pulled out of his driveway. He moved past his Tudor-style home and went down the tree-lined street.

"Please change driving view to office." The view of old three-story homes and hundred-year-old oaks flitting by faded and were replaced by a virtual view of the brushed metal space of his lab. He felt himself relax. He didn't want to think about the last twelve hours. The emotionally barbed exchanges with his wife left him upset and off-balance. He just couldn't think about what all of it meant—it was just too much . . . too messy.

"To-do list," he projected. Neon blue panels materialized before him. Bullets and subbullets of the numerous tasks he had assigned himself scrolled before his eyes. His patient list and the ongoing plans of care also came into view. He focused hard on his tasks, more so than was necessary. He needed to maintain attention on things within

his control. The ritual of organizing his day gave him solace. Surgeries, research projects, and strategies for tests he was planning with Omid all shifted and reorganized as he evaluated their priority.

"Contacts," he thought to himself. A list of names with their associated pictures came into his view. He always started his day by talking to the chief resident, his right-hand man who helped manage his patients.

"Initiate link with Reid Vestin." The shell of a half-empty white sphere rotated in front of his field of view. After a few moments, the ball became a solid white and he heard Reid's familiar voice in his head.

"Good morning, sir."

"Hey, Reid, how is everybody doing?" The two began exchanging facts and details and the plan of care for each of the patients. With the concrete and unemotional exchange, the muscles in Hagan's neck began to relax.

The calm, however, was to be short-lived. *"Warning, there are pedestrians blocking the path."* As the German woman's voice began to register, the images of Hagan's office vanished and he was again seeing through the windows of his car. He was stopped at the gates of his neighborhood. Standing in front of his car was an obese woman holding a sign saying Abomination. Below it was a grainy picture of an electrode array on the brain. Each time she bobbed the sign, her fish-white belly would jiggle out from underneath her lime green shirt. She looked to be about three hundred pounds and was holding hands with a thin little man that probably weighed in at about a third of that. He had a thin, anemic mustache and with his other hand was holding onto a Bible that he proffered as a shield to the oncoming car.

"Oh you have to be kidding!"

"What's the matter?" Reid exclaimed.

"Oh, a bunch of protestors at my neighborhood's gates. I should have known—that evangelical nut job Elymas was in town last night. It happens almost every year. Let me call you back."

"Sure, good luck." With that, the spinning orb disappeared.

"Disengage Autonav." Hagan took over control of his car and slowly maneuvered past the protestors. Fortunately, they couldn't see who he was. Signs exclaiming Marked by the Beast, with more twenty-year-old pictures of bloody brain surgeries; My Mind Is Holy; Repent; and Hagan's favorite, Maerici=Evolutionist=Antichrist, all bounced and bumped against one another as he slowly nudged through onto the main road.

For Hagan, it was a small consolation that one bunch of nut jobs were lumping him in with another bunch of nut jobs. The Evolutionists were another group of quasi-religious extremists who thought that neuroprosthetics were part of the divine plan for human improvement. Both of them didn't like him.

As he pushed through, he again returned to his work.

"*Something's not right.*" The old man put his hand to his stomach.

"*What was that, Dr. Devron?*" Hagan asked

"*Nothing, nothing, just felt a twinge in the belly. Where were we?*" Devron was irritated with himself for the rookie mistake. He hadn't let his inner thoughts interfere with neuroprosthetic conversation in ages.

"*You were asking about the size configuration of the next generation of the Hydra platform.*"

"*Right, can we reduce the total size by fifty percent and have the component self-configure once injected?*" Despite the slight hump in his back and his advanced age, he still emanated a determined vitality. Marcus Devron was not to be disturbed while working in his gardens. These were his moments of calm. His cortical stimulators were at their minimal; there would be no digitally created sights, sounds, smells, or tastes other than those related to his scheduled conversations.

"*Don't know—that's asking a lot. It would require retooling the power source and creating some integrated chips that would compile their software after they physically linked. Is it worth it?*"

"*I want the entire construct to be injectable with a needle.*" As he power walked past a swaying bonsai, the strange sensation in the pit of his stomach returned—a feeling as if someone had pulled on the inside of his navel. It lasted just a moment and was barely punctuated by a tarry taste in the back of his mouth. For a brief moment it stopped him cold.

"*That is certainly ambitious.*"

The pain in his abdomen was distracting his thinking. *Did I pull something?* He thought about his virtual interlude at the adult entertainment site the evening prior, careful not to convey it to the professor. He thought about her "parameters" and smiled to himself. The tarry taste returned.

"*Hello . . . Dr. Devron . . . you still there?*"

"*Yes, right, Hagan, this isn't ambitious. Thirty years ago they said it wasn't possible to have people control things with their thoughts—we did it—that was ambitious. Twenty years ago, they said it wasn't possible to create virtual perceptions—we did it—that was ambitious. Now I am asking you to make things smaller—that is most certainly NOT ambitious. This we can get done in a half a year.*"

"Yes, sir. We'll get on it." He could hear the determination in his voice. That's what he always like about Maerici—he could rise to the occasion when beaten upon.

Devron again felt a warm rising sensation in his insides. *Must be a bit of reflux.* This would need to be dealt with. He had a medical codec implanted in his forearm two years ago. *It should have been able to sense his acid imbalance. Medical implantables—predictable my ass!*

"OK good, thats the attitude—I need to get on another call."

"Right, I'll update you in two weeks." Blue words flashed in front of Devron's eyes—

MAERICI DISCONNECTED.

"System—please connect Mr. Mad—"

"Oh Jesus!" Devron snorted out loud. *What a horrible smell! Smells like burning rubber, must be coming from—*An invisible giant gripped his intestines, the squeezing twisting sensation doubled him over as the gut wrenching continued.

Christ, what is going on!

As fast and as intensely as it had begun, it was over. Devron straightened up and looked around. There was no one around. That he was sure of. Orders were orders, especially when they were *his* orders. He began to walk back.

Again the smell hit him, intense this time, burning rubber mixed with sweat and feet. He gripped his stomach, preparing for another round.

Nothing yet. But good Lord that smell—where was it coming from? His paced quickened, but was not so certain or purposeful. Devron scanned his surroundings looking for a possible source. *How can it be? Something must be wrong. Smell is tightly managed by the external air-preparation systems.*

Again a pinprick in the stomach.

I need to talk to the garden tech supervisor and get this fixed. But why is my stomach hurting me? Marcus began to walk back to the large doorway. He was a hundred feet off. He could hear the gravel beneath his feet crunch and then reassemble. The thought of interrupting his work was infuriating. The smell was as bad as ever. He now was walking with stiff rigid strides, angry that his moments of clarity were being disrupted.

Red. Everything red.

Devron grunted and bent over as if punched in the stomach. The world had suddenly shifted to various hues of crimson. The streams around him were running red as blood. The white stones that defined his rock garden were now a ruddy, pinkish ochre, the green plants an inky black.

The smell was worsening. It filled his nostrils like a hot snake coiling into his sinuses, writhing, pushing, and penetrating into his brain.

He groaned. The pulling sensation in his stomach gave a sudden pinched contortion as if something were inside fighting to get out.

"Oh Jesus . . . !" His words gave way to a hoarse groan as all the muscles in his abdomen forced air past his vocal cords. His lips were smacking and moving with a rhythmic fervor.

Devron dropped to his knees.

Am I dying? Stroke? Heart attack? . . . Oh God . . . something was so very wrong. At that moment everything turned white.

Seconds later it was over. He opened his eyes. No pain. His garden surrounded him. The brook continued to murmur as it had. He stood up and inspected himself for some overt sign of whatever it was that was ailing him. Nothing. He dusted off the last remnants of earth and looked around—nothing was out of sorts. The smell was gone.

Jesus, what just happened? Maybe Hagan will have an idea, he thought. *System, contact Dr. Maerici.* A sphere emerged in the corner of his eye and quickly dissipated.

NO CONNECTION.

What the . . . ? There was a rising jittery disquiet within Devron. He was alone.

Indigestion. It's nothing, It's OK, it passed, I'm fine . . . maybe a problem with the implant. He kept repeating to himself that it wasn't a stroke, not a tumor, not a heart attack, nothing out of the ordinary.

I'm fine, just need to—Devron paused. Ten feet in front of him, one of the oblong smoothed river stones in his rock garden rolled itself into the pebble path. Turning leisurely, end over end, like an egg rolling in slow motion, it settled in the middle of the path and held still for a moment. The surface of the stone expanded and contracted, slowly at first and then with more jerky hurried changes in movement, as if it was gasping for breath. The surface puckered and expanded to form small thorny projections. The bristling stone again stretched and then developed a cleft down the middle. Additional fissures formed radially around the stone with all the lines pointing toward the center. The object contorted first into a starfish-like structure and then the five individual appendages formed stubby elongations, then thorn-covered limbs. At first, a small man-shaped creature laid on its stomach for a moment—arms and legs outstretched like a child doing a facedown snow angel in the pebble-covered path. It rolled over and stood and faced Devron. The thing had a triangular face, black recesses for eyes, and skin of deep maroon. The mouth was nothing more than a slit. The bowling ball hollow eye spaces looked empty and incoherent.

Devron felt sweat bead on his forehead. The tiny creature turned and ran with its short little spiny legs toward the shadow-enclosed entrance of his home. He heard it move—the sound of plastic wrap being crumpled combined with sandpaper rubbing against sandpaper.

Oh God . . . the smell, again the smell . . . OH GOD! *. . .* something was really, really wrong . . .

Deep, deep crimson. He was floating in a warm, undulating scarlet. It was bliss. Contentment. Rightness. Images, yearning, fulfillment all coursed through him in a primal way. Trent had no sense of time. He had no sense of body. No comprehension of language. In the same moment of his eternity there was a ripple and it was gone. With that moment he gasped like a newborn being yanked from the womb.

"What the fuck just happened?" Trent heaved. He wheezed for air as if he had just finished a competitive sprint. Bent over with arms pinioned straight against his knees, he was facedown, letting his stomach muscles help him pull in air. Red sand encircled his feet. He felt hot and dry. Thirsty, so incredibly thirsty, his throat felt as if it was filled with ashes and sand. With each movement he felt his skin cracking like old sun-blistered paint.

"Where am I?" As he looked on the ground an arid breeze moved fine red sand over the exposed toes of his sandals. The wind susurrated in his ears. All else was still. He slowly stood up. His chest continued to lift and rise. As he looked about, all around him were undulating rust-colored dunes. Endless, unmarred, parallel and interconnecting sinuous lines of sand patterns covered the hills like some infinite Japanese garden. Above was a seamless pale blue sky with distant cirrus clouds accenting a yellow sun at its zenith.

All he heard was the blowing whisper of the wind. He turned around slowly. The hills went on forever. His breathing slowed as he began to take it all in. He was the only living creature as far as the eye could see. *How the hell did I get here?*

"SYSTEM. *Identify location. Please notify home service for pickup.*"

Nothing. No blue images appeared. No auditory notification that data was being processed. Trent felt blind and helpless

Off-line, he thought to himself. The word itself made him begin to shiver despite the dry baking heat. He had never—*ever*—been removed from his prosthetics or their connection to the Web.

As a shaky panic began to grip his insides, he began trying to recount the series of events that had led him to this spot. *I was at the happening . . . had some code . . .* He could feel the sun beat down on him. *How did I leave the house? The happening was in the SIM, it was all virtual.* Trent tried to recount the events. *So hot. I need some water.* He could feel sweat bead on his forehead. *The girl! I followed the girl with the red eyes. Then the mirror . . . then . . .* He ran his hand through his hair.

"Oh my God!" Trent felt his scalp. Both hands lifted up to paw and slap in disbelief. The palms of his hand slid over the high cheekbones of his face, the clefted chin. His arms snapped apart and he looked down at his body. He touched the muscles of his thighs. His knees went limp and he fell into soft cushioned red sand with a hiss; he ran his fingers along the ground and grabbed the sand and let it fall from his fingers.

"Red, how can it be red. Not possible!!" He was seeing a real world, a multihued world. Trent tried to identify each color. There were thousands of variegated tones in the sand. The sun was a whitish bright yellow; when he looked away there were green afterimages. His fingers were a tan, pinkish beige. He looked at his hand—unscarred and strong with full veins coursing over sinewy tendon paths to bony knuckles.

No scars. The realization washed through him. No scars in his scalp, none on his hands, his body was strong and full. This was his virtual body.

But real!! This world is real, REAL! My body is real. This was not a virtual world characterized by the signature monochromatic blue. *But how . . .*

Trent felt like Pinocchio after he had been changed into a real boy. Since the accident that had made him into a marionette of prosthetic reconstruction, he had yearned to be returned to a world of sinew and muscle. He yearned to be whole and strong. The heir to the Devron empire primarily lived and existed in virtual worlds as a high-resolution avatar; a synthetic reality more real and vital than the one he was forced to endure as an imperfect cripple.

He was different now. But how? The implausibility of the situation left him silent. He simply stood and watched as small eddies of sand skipped and danced over the nearby dunes. Trent sensed an alteration in his environment. It wasn't so much the sound of a footstep or movement of sand as it was a fundamental notion or sense of otherness. Trent turned, knowing that someone was behind him.

It's her!

She stood there staring at him where he stood farther down from the crest. Her feet were encircled with sand as if she had been standing there for a long time. Time enough for the desert winds to blow and heap the crimson grit up to her ankles. There were no tracks. Just seamless unmarred lines of windblown, undulating rust.

Where the world and Trent had seemingly changed, she had not. She was the same iridescent blue steel he had seen at the happening. Her body was pebbled with a Braille-like pattern that shimmered and glinted in the sun. The burning red embers of her eyes were also the same—staring with an intense and inhuman calm. Her hair was a dark shade of shiny midnight streaming from her head like an obsidian river. She stood in a pose of readiness—arms at her sides and slightly bent, as if she were a gymnast or a diver preparing her takeoff—ready and undistracted. Her eyes were focused on Trent. The two stared at each other. The gust of winds sounded to Trent like thunder bolts.

In the same fashion of the happening, she turned. Her eyes remained fixed on him as her body moved, and then her head finally followed the turn of her shoulders. Trent felt a deep pull beneath his belly button. He needed no further impetus to follow her.

A sphere pulsated in front of him. The word "Elymas" was illuminated beneath.

"Acknowledge—You owe me money, preacher."

There was an awkward silence.

"At a loss for words? Did you forget about our conversation last night" The man laughed. It was a harsh biting sound, more like a forceful horse cough. The Chameleon was reclining in his chair. Each component was a separate padded block held suspended by a magnetic field. With each coarse outburst his iridescent figure, buttressed by the floating padded cubes, bobbed slightly in response.

"I heard you, I heard you. The money will be forthcoming, all in due time. I have several ministry events in the upcoming days. I will have to pay after those to ensure discretion, of course."

"Of course." The Chameleon chuckled. He let his thoughts wander as he watched the data in the room swirl and coalesce around him. They were his revenues for the month. There were a lot of zeroes, many, many zeroes.

You can buy happiness, he thought to himself. You can buy everything and anything. Seeing the numbers, the assets, equities, credits, and cash, swirl, and flit in the ethereal blue and pinks in the air, the walls, the furniture, and on the very surface of his skin, filled him with a very deep pleasure indeed.

"Mr. Chameleon, sir, I will, however, I will need some additional doses of the Spirit prior to that." The Chameleon could hear the anxiety in his voice. The fear and the tension as Elymas squirmed almost gave him a hard-on. *Fuck, I love this.* Information swirled around him as he drew out the moment, knowing this guy was twisting on the line.

"Mr. Chameleon?" There was a quaver in the southern drawl.

Bobbing and shifting on his suspensor throne, he laughed at the pleasure of his own being and continued to wait. The borders of his body were indistinct from his chair and the surrounding room. He embodied the culture that he had created. All his hair had been removed years ago. All the better to reveal the organic light-emitting diodes—OLEDs, as they were known—which had been inserted under every inch of his skin. From the skin of his eyelids to the grooves between his toes and everywhere in between, his skin emitted a con-tinuously shifting and changing array of patterns. At present, the pat-terns were mostly the numbers and symbols of his amassed assets. The color and hues were all wired to reflect his altering mood and pleasure. The tones were pink and azure icons superimposed upon a sunset magenta background. The sanguine tones were all seamlessly integrated with digital screens that were embedded into every surface of the room. The floating furniture, floors, and walls all changed and shifted seamlessly with the evolving mood and data interest of its core persona. The same was true for the loose-fitting singlet that covered his chest and midsection. All of it was the same shifting theme that made it impossible to discern exactly where the room, clothes, and furniture ended and the Chameleon began. His entire environment, including his own skin, were all one big high-fidelity video screen, wired to the ever-changing whims of his mind.

The most distinct feature was the Chameleon's face. It floated in the shifting, interdigitated components like that of a Mandelbrot ghost. Electric blue lines circled and split into a complex fractal filigree that encircled white-light-infused corneas and orange irises. The irises ap-peared as orange color wheels with segmented pie slices of hues rang-ing from a deep rust to a vibrant salmon, surrounding the small black points of his pupils. At various moments, the color wheels would rotate and shift independently of one another. The face pulsed and altered in subtle hues in contradistinction to the movements and tones of the surrounding environment like that of the Cheshire cat from *Alice's Adventures in Wonderland*. His resemblance to a naturally born human being was about as close as that of a scarab beetle.

"Mr. Chameleon, please . . ."

"*Well, this will take some consideration.*" The Chameleon pulled at the hook a little more.

"*Mr. Chameleon, you know that I am good for it.*"

"*Now that's an interesting way to put it—you are after all a min-ister. I would think you are the embodiment of goodness, Reverend, yet here you are talking to me.*"

"*We are all sinners, Mr. Chameleon. I am no exception. At least my weakness helps me serve the Lord. It allows me to communicate his message.*"

"*Bullshit, Padre, you are serving yourself—let's be honest with each other here.*"

"*I am elevating the human condition, I'm—*"

"*You're elevating your pocketbook. Peddling in some of the oldest addictions in history. We're no different.*"

"*I am not having people mutilate their bodies.*"

The Chameleon was enjoying the riposte. He remained silent to prolong the preacher's discomfort. He knew he was drawing the addict in a place he didn't want to be, namely, getting into an argument with his dealer.

He thought about the BodMod movement. It was something that he had captured, symbolized, and most importantly profited immensely from. He recalled how twenty years ago he had started the first Sterno Rooms. At nineteen, he had started out with an old-world tattoo parlor, called the Chameleon. He at that time had been called Frank Minsky. That had all changed, however, when he had introduced the subdermal chip implant. The early versions were basic constructs that allowed a person to insert a chip matrix in their skin that would show an image that one could turn on and off—a tunable tattoo—visible when you wanted it, invisible when you didn't. He still remembered the first BMWs and Mercedes parking in the back of his slum. Wealthy girls with stiff, striding tapered calves and large dark sunglasses would walk past the black painted glass of his door. *They all wanted their naughty tattoos, but not the stigma.* The reminiscence still made his swirling spiderweb of a face smile.

"*I don't want to argue with you, Mr. Chameleon. Let us agree that we are conducting business here.*"

The Chameleon expected that response and continued to think of the past as he let the preacher dangle.

Who would have known? he thought to himself. Chips became cheap, flexible, and organic, and then he was off to the races. To keep all the tattoo hardware sterile for implantation, the parlor got loaded with UV lights. In the north St. Louis slums, the glow and shimmer of the blue light into the dirty trash-covered streets looked like a blue gas fire. The name Sterno Room was born. At the same time, Frank Minsky disappeared, and the tattoo parlor became the man known as the Chameleon.

His attention returned to the evangelist on the line. "*No you don't want to fuckin' argue with me, preacher. Because just like you give the desperate in this world a reason to exist by showing them a plastic Jesus, I give people an alternative reason to exist. Themselves. When*" *all that these trust fund kids have is their own selfish desire, I give them what their narcissism needs—the pure pursuit of self-definition."*

The Chameleon knew that Elymas was becoming nervous. He could almost see him wiping his sweaty palms on his pants. *"Well, you certainly have a point, Mr. Chameleon, though my guess is that your businesses are not purely for, well let us say, social advancement."*

"No, you're right, Father, it is for money. Plain and simple. People pay to change. I provide that service. And when they have crafted their bodies to every extent possible—I also let them craft their minds. You use religion, I use drugs. Once again, here we are in the same playing field." The Chameleon knew these were not the coarse cudgels of mind-altering heroin, cocaine, and various assorted synthetic concoctions. No, the new stuff took the best of all these. Tuned to one's genotype, optimized to the various receptors in the user's brain, these agents gave the customer the desired effect to a T.

Enjoying the candor, because he had the power to be brutally honest and cruel, the Chameleon continued. *"One thing hasn't changed, Reverend Elymas, the thing that has been the case for the past several thousand years, the reason that you would deign to interact with me—the addiction. It creates the amortizing profit flow that never stops. Are you feeling it now? That desperate need, that inner inevitable pull. You're gonna pay to satiate that."*

And oh what a price people will pay. Pay and pay and pay . . . the Chameleon thought to himself. *The tats had only been the beginning; the drugs, now that really paid the bills.* He thought of all his clients—the spoiled kids, the lawyers, the businessmen, the bored government officials. Of course his favorite—Reverend Elymas, the evangelist—who loved the chemical feeling of holiness (a combination of dopamine and oxytocin)—made for better sermons. He had to give him credit, though, Elymas could wring money out of people almost better than he could.

"So, Reverend, to begin with we are going to play a little game, capish? You are going repeat after me: I am a hypocrite." The Chameleon waited through the silence. *"We can always end this conversation if it is unpalatable?"* The silence hung between the two. *"Well, preacher, I am glad you found your redemption, have a good—"*

"Wait . . . wait . . . just wait . . . I am a hypocrite." The words came out of Elymas as if he were pulling tacks from the bottom of his foot.

"I am a liar."

"I am a liar . . ."

"Now you've got the hang of it!" the Chameleon exclaimed gleefully. The humiliation turned his skin an amber rosy red. *"Lets try another—I profit off the hopes and fears of the weak."*

"I profit off the hopes and fears of the weak . . ."

"I am no different than my good buddy, and chief muchacho, the Chameleon."

"I am no different than my good buddy, the Chameleon."

"Oops, you forgot 'muchacho.' Let's try again."

"I am no different than my good buddy and muchacho—"

"—chief muchacho—"

"I am no different than my good buddy, and chief muchacho, the Chameleon."

"Excellent, well done, Elymas." The blue-lined face of the Chameleon split with a sadistic mirth. As he planned his next embarrassment, he spun himself on the chair. As he circled, the icons, digits, and colors swirled in a celestial blur. Amid the visual roil, another singular white orb appeared immobile in the shifting mix with the name Cyrus below it.

"Looks like I have another call coming in, Reverend. We'll have to pick up this conversation later."

"Wait! Please wait, just wait, what about getting some more Spirit. I have more sermons coming up, I need it, I won't be able to—"

"Will be in touch, Reverend. Really must go." Tickled with the opportunity, the Chameleon focused his attention on the sphere and disengaged. The floating pearl and Elymas's presence disappeared.

He stopped the chair from spinning and the data presentation faded into slight white shades intermittently obscured by slowly shifting pink and magenta clouds. He then turned to the adjacent white orb.

"Acknowledge," he thought. A familiar voice resonated within his head. It was his lawyer, Cyrus.

"What's up?"

"Are you done masturbating to how rich you are?" The voice echoing in his head had the same chronic smoker rasp that it did in real life. The bastard knew him too well.

"Fuck you, Cyrus. Are you calling just to harass me? Remember, the more I'm beating off the more money seems to find its way into your tobacco-stained fingers."

"Well, better lube up. The crew just got a shipment of fuzzer

implants and some new stuff that is going to keep your member and
my tarry fingers happy for a while."

"*Go on . . . you've got my attention."*

The fidelity of the neural links were extraordinary; he heard and
smelled Cyrus clear his phlegm-ridden throat. A sound he could've
done without.

"*Its URVAN, a product of northern Indian proteonomic program-*
ming. It doesn't require a heavy metal and is fully configurable to
opiate, dopamine, and epinephrine receptors!"

"*Hmm . . . No heavy metal, huh?"* It was the trace metals that
were the hardest to ship and the easiest to detect in a person. The
unusual electron configurations of the heavy metal polymers were
what allowed the rest of the organic molecules to come together in
very specific configurations. The specific molecular shape was what
created the specific effect in the brain. Binding to the mu receptor gave
it a pleasurable heroin flavor, while the epinephrine receptor added the
hyped-up feeling of classic cocaine. Dopamine receptors, his personal
favorite, always added a spice of delirium to make things a little more
religious. It was also these rare metal molecules that were the easiest
to pick up on shipment. Avoiding the metals could mean more product movement. More product meant more money. The colors emitted
from the Chameleon's skin, clothing, furniture, and walls all turned a
more sanguine rose.

"*Does it have the same tunable effects?"*

"*You better fuckin' believe it. I've got a junkie slut here trying a*
sample. We've been playing all night long. I've made her work for her
treats." A coarse scratching laugh filled the Chameleon's head. Cyrus
loved the benefits of using their clients for the guinea pig work. "*Neu-*
rometric markers are off the chart. We may have to celebrate with a
little hit. Come on over—she'll probably give you a blow job just out
of appreciation."

"*Hmm, good, and what about the fuzzer tech?"*

"*Got about a thousand units in from China."*

"*Good, very good."* For those wretches that couldn't afford the
designer stuff, he was happy to give alternatives—a full-service pro-
vider. He had neuroprosthetic devices that would snake into the locus
coeruleus or the nucleus accumbens, small little spots in the brain
that, when stimulated, gave so much pleasure. All the junkie had to
do was use their mind to push the button—and push and push they
would. Heroin rush after heroin rush at one's cognitive fingertips,

these implants were cheap (as were the people), so they tended not to last that long. The "fuzzers," as they were called, would usually just eventually starve to death on their bedbug-ridden couches, drooling their way to a final oblivion. *More were always coming—the fuzzer bit was a volume business,* the Chameleon thought to himself. A thousand units, that would be some good volume, indeed.

"Where are you?"

"Ritz Carlton."

"I'll be there in about twenty minutes. Later. Disengage." The white orb disappeared and the hoarse breathing sounds of his legal counsel were gone from his mind. He was alone with his thoughts. *"This day is getting better and better."*

He jumped from the chair. The leather-bound blocks dropped to the floor in a neatly stacked cube. As the Chameleon walked toward the door, the colors and images shifted and followed him through the room like a mixing rod through a can of paint. Once through, the colors faded and disappeared, leaving only the millions of embedded shimmering white diodes pulsing a low level of white light. The swirling environment now looked like a tranquil ascetic room covered in a fine white frost.

HAGAN, I KNOW YOU ARE THERE—I SAW YOUR CAR PARKED IN THE
PARKING LOT—PICK UP.

The blue text scrolled across Hagan's field of view as he sat in
front of Omid. A sphere soon appeared labeled with the name Simon
Canter. Hagan resigned himself to the interaction. *Connect.*

"*Omid—hold on.*" The AIRENS nodded.

"*Hello, Hagan, what are you doing?*"

"*Good morning, Simon, working in the lab—the usual stuff?*"
Hagan knew the conversation with Canter wasn't going to end yesterday. Once he got an idea in that large head of his, he would chase
after and peck at him like a rabid white-mustached chicken.

"*Look, I need to speak with you. I have been thinking about our
conversation yesterday. I think we need to make a plan for how we are
going to move forward with your research.*"

Hagan could begin to feel his head hurt; he knew what "we"
meant. "*What do you mean, I already have a plan, I have been working on it for the past ten years. Omid is almost there. He's at the comprehension of a toddler—he's not fully aware or able to abstract yet,
but he's close.*"

"*Hagan.*" Hagan waited for his boss's long patronizing pause of
disappointment to end. "*We both understand the financials of the
situation, and I think we need a plan that is more practical.*"

"*Again, Simon, I am not following.*" He didn't like where this was
going.

"*I think we need to retool what you're doing to something more to
the present, something that can be turned into a clinical product in the
near term.*"

"*Such as . . . ?*"

"*Erectile dysfunction.*"

"*WHAT?*"

"*Erectile dysfunction.*"

"*I'm a neurosurgeon, Simon, that's not my cup of tea.*"

"*Hagan . . . Hagan, Hagan, Hagan.*" Thankful he wasn't in Canter's office sitting on the castration bench, Hagan didn't miss seeing
his light-bulb-shaped head cock back while he would hold his bony

index finger up. Rocking his milk-colored eggplant back and forth with smug dissatisfaction, Canter would be rolling his eyes and tapping his finger forward as he spoke to prevent any interruption. *"I am not talking about the mechanical stuff—there are plenty of things out there for that. You could use some of your neuroprosthetic approaches to enhance sexual desire in the senior citizen population, known to decline with age and contribute to depression."*

"You want me to make old people horny?" Hagan was in disbelief.

"St. Louis has an aging population. There would be a real market for that type of technology and clinical service. Not to mention there are a number of members on the board of trustees who are also getting older. It's an achievable goal that wouldn't rock the boat as much."

"I am trying to create synthetic intelligence that solves massively complicated problems that no single human can effectively tackle. Problems like global warming, cancer, and space travel. And you want me to give old guys boners?"

Canter's voice was transitioning from his condescending "please be reasonable" tone to the higher-pitched quasi-colonel voice. *"I know you think it has the chance to 'make a difference,' as you like to say, but you are part of this department, and I need my troops to keep the line. Creating an artificial intelligence is just going to add fuel to the fire. It could look bad for the department. You with me?"*

"That's what you hired me for—look bad to who?"

"The conservative evangelic voice is gaining prominence among the donors, and this research project may not sit well with them."

"And sexual neuroprosthetics are going to change that?" Hagan could feel a migraine coming on.

"This would just stand to help some of the older, more prominent, and higher-paying members of society. They are already a conservative group, and this would help soften their opinion."

"We're changing a decade of my science because of conservative evangelical priorities? Simon, this isn't making any sense!"

"Do I need to point out that you seem to feature prominently in a number of their protests?"

"I am aware of that—they surrounded my neighborhood this morning. Why am I the bad guy here?"

"That looks bad on us. The department doesn't need bad press."

Hagan was becoming mystified by the conversation. *"But you want me to do more cases—put more neuroprosthetics in? You told me that yesterday—something about wringing the towel?"*

"Yes, and I meant it. You need to increase your clinical revenue."

"So you want me to put in more neuroprosthetic implants to make more money but to keep the conservative people out there happy—the same people who distrust and protest against these devices—you want me to convince them implants are okay by increasing their sex drive . . . with more neuroprosthetics?"

"Right, good, Hagan, I think you're getting there."

Hagan's head was now pounding.

The pain was near unremitting. Undulating waves of twisting and wrenching pulled at his innards. Marcus stood outside the black obelisks of his entryway. He could hear the scratching sound of the little spiny monstrosity padding down the steps. With each footstep the pulling beneath his navel seemed to worsen. He thought he would both retch and lose control of his bowels at the same time. The smell was overwhelming—burning rubber and shit and something else. Something he had never sensed before. Something terrible. Another scratch and footstep and his agony continued to crest. He was covered in sweat and shivering.

"SYSTEM—911—Emergency—Help, oh please help!" Nothing. No checkered ball. No system notification, nothing. Devron tried his staff, his son, Maerici, he tried 911 again in disbelief; there was no response from his implant.

How can this be?

He stumbled forward down the steps. Leaning heavily on the immaculate white walls, the old man continued to hear the rasping movements ahead. There was an invisible tether between his intestines and the small spiny golem below. Each lurched movement forward was a transient relief—an uncurling of the barbs within.

He took a few more wary steps and slipped. As he rolled down the stairs, his aged limbs slapped, dragged, and banged the sharp corners of the white marble. The punctuated jabs and pokes of his tumble were relieving distractions.

He collapsed in a heap at the bottom of the stairs, where he felt a brief moment of respite from the twisting agony within him. The transient calm dissolved with the scraping movement of small legs departing. The invisible barbed wire once again jolted his insides.

Worse, it's getting worse.

With tremulous limbs, he formed a tripod to raise himself up. The wrenching and smell began anew. He scrambled to catch up with his tormentor.

Closer, must get closer to reduce the pain.

Once again a sharp lancinating pain ricocheted within him.

Oh God, what is happening!?

His mind, honed for three-quarters of a century for critical analysis, struggled to make sense of the events.

What is this little troll thing? Prosthetic malfunctions never showed themselves in formed manner—they usually cause some blurred vision, blind spots, or random blue noise. Not this . . . this was colored and appeared to be solid. Prosthetic malfunction was disruptive and incoherent. So what is it? What is it? His mind reached out blindly for an explanation.

Devron continued to lurch after the scratching sound as it scuttled across the languid black surface of the marble floor. The sound of its feet clicked and twittered as if small pieces of glass were being crushed with a metal boot. With white knuckles holding the folds of his sagging abdomen, he limped forward. The little creature scampered down the hidden utility steps. Devron once again felt the intense pull.

Is this a nightmare? . . . Am I dead? . . . Is . . . is this . . . hell? His hard, analytic mind for the first time began to speculate on impossibilities. He continued his descent down the narrow stairwell. Down and down. The endless volley of twisting incentive and foul smells goaded him forward.

His arms suddenly straightened and his back arched. His mouth opened in a large O as pulsed grunts emerged. A lighting bolt of white-hot pain coursed through his body. Every part of him, every aspect of his mind, stopped in an abrupt paroxysm of intense agony. As if he was caught in a nuclear blast and every atom of his being was shaking with the heat of a solar burst. No thought, no reaction, simply a paralyzing flash of searing pain that was to leave him in ashes.

As quickly as it jolted him, it was gone. Devron held the railing of the stair. Bent over clutching his chest, his clothes were now sopped with sweat and blood. His hands shook as he attempted to wipe the blood that was stinging his right eye. His mind was blank. No more pondering, no more analysis; Devron was beginning to come undone.

Krantz was once again getting confused. He liked Sergeant Ortiz, but sometimes it was hard to get straight answers out of him. He was on the narcotics unit and the two of them were often coordinating over the drug-related murders. Ortiz was one of the few guys who would sit down and talk with him to face to face. The topic, however, was losing him.

"So run this by me again, Al. Who was this guy?"

"Some dealer from north St. Louis—name's Billy William." Ortiz had a mocha-colored round face and crescent-shaped eyes that seemed to belie a certain mirthfulness. His goatee was a thin line that barely rose above his coarse stubble. "Who names their kid William William?"

"No idea. Somebody in north St. Louis, apparently."

"Right, well, anyway—wha' did he do? Any bead on motive?"

"Looks like he was probably dealing on the side, basically doing some personal business under the Chameleon's watch."

"Now who is this guy?"

"Eddie, you been living under a rock, man, you know this guy—the one with all the tattoos. He's the Walmart of bad behavior."

"What was he dealing?" This is where Krantz was getting confused.

"The Chameleon deals everything from old-school pills, to the skin adhesives, to illegal implants—you know, the fuzzer shit."

"No, Al, I get that—what's the guy who got killed been dealing?"

"Bunch of genomics and looks like he was putting together some pleasure code."

"The genomics drugs I get—your usual custom thrill pills. I thought pleasure code wasn't illegal?"

"Depends."

"On what?"

"On the code—what areas of the brain it stimulates. Old stuff was just cortical—you know, like somebody touching your johnson—the usual virtual porn that everybody uses." Ortiz broke into a grin and made hand gestures as if he were rocking an invisible woman's head between his legs.

"Ortiz, I always knew you were a pervert."

"Ed, have you met my wife? Anyway, DEA is coming down on the new stuff. Feels better than the old stuff, which just mimicked reality. You ain't gonna sell the kids for a good old-fashioned BJ. Some will, but most won't. The new programming they're putting together is a little different. Apparently, they figured out ways to stimulate the deeper stuff, you know the thalamus and the brain stem—"

"No, I don't know."

"Jesus, Ed—you're some type of caveman—the parts of the brain, deep in the center, that make you feel really really good. You know, those are the spots that old stuff like heroin act on and where the fuzzers put their illegal electrode implants. Apparently, they can code people's civilian hardware to do the same thing."

To Krantz it was getting foggier and foggier on what was illegal and what wasn't—pills, syringes, adhesives, implanted electrodes, and now addictive software—he was glad he dealt with the murders.

"Alright, well what leads you got?"

"Not much. Some skin traces, but no genetic match in the database. A homeless guy as a witness, but he doesn't have any implants to interrogate."

"Alright, I'll send one of the junior blues to interview him, see if he'll put on a Virtua Helmet to see what the resolution of his recall is. Where is he now?"

"In the shelter on Fifth."

"Right, OK, we'll send the new guy Hank to interview him. I gotta go home and mow the grass before it gets too hot."

"You and that lawn—bet that grass is better groomed than my wife."

"Too much information all, Al, too much information."

Trent gasped. He was once again his small and uncomfortable self.

"God, how is this happening?"

Opening and closing his hand, he looked out his window. He was sitting on his bed. Clouds blew past lazily from his aerial view.

Words can't describe it. Trent tried to make sense of the evening.

Something happened. The woman. The sand. Then, the . . . the . . . His mind struggled to get around the experience, to put it into a context, to find a logical thread, a coherence. Like holding onto a fading dream, he grasped at the smoky wisps of the experience as they drifted apart into forgetfulness.

Bits of cotton floating in the air, a drifting flower, a bubble emerging from the waters, arms around me, wind blowing through the trees, the smell of bread and cinnamon. Memories continued to dissolve and fade.

No, must remember. The only residual was the emotion, the feelings, the sense of something good, something longed for.

Try to remember, every time, every time after the desert, it's like . . . like . . . His chest constricted with other memories. Memories that were both pleasurable and painful. They came into his consciousness like a submarine pushing through sheets of ice. Glossy black ink, the long tubular brush. The smooth feel of bamboo. The smell of the paper.

Soft and gentle, he heard his mother's voice in his head. *"That's it Trent. Just like that."* Calligraphy, the Japanese characters, he remembered the brush stick, painting them again and again. His mother guiding his small hand at first, a small balled white fist enveloped in graceful fingers with violet painted nails. Safe and protected, Trent had felt himself making the deft strokes. Smears of shiny ink bent and turned to create something meaningful. He remembered the satisfaction. He was coming out of his shell, he was now doing it on his own, a rare moment, a moment when he had felt OK. That everything was going to be all right.

It was like that, but different, more, something more.

Before the accident, he thought to himself. The memories of his childhood, cracked and fragmented into the loss and regrets that defined him today.

Before, when I was . . . He looked at his hands. A fiery thorn punctured the reminiscence. He hadn't painted a character in years. He couldn't anymore.

Not this, he thought ruefully. Other recollections, darker and unspoken, swam deeper in his consciousness. Guilt, large and ugly, cast a shadow across the events of the evening, like a giant shark silently circling.

I was a different person back then.

The sunshine of the desert returned. A visceral excitement rose up in him and the pall of his memories passed. He again prepared to return to the red sands.

The Chameleon climbed into the large cavernous backseat of his Hummer Colossus. Like everything else in his world, the seats and interior came alive with colors that wirelessly connected with the LEDs in his skin.

"Where to, boss?"

"The Ritz." Nodding, the driver abruptly pulled out into traffic. Met with angry honks and notifications, the Chameleon watched as his driver gave them the finger.

With his bald head and muscular rounded shoulders, he had a pitbull-like presence, made increasingly intimidating by the snake tattoos writhing over the back of his sinewy neck and forearms.

"Brilo, you take care of that thing?"

His driver looked back at the Chameleon enthusiastically. "You bet, little fuck cried like a bitch." The car was again swerving, the sound of car horns surrounded them. "Beat Bill-Bill till—"

"No names, not out loud, never out loud, Brilo."

"Sorry, boss." Brilo turned and again was looking at the road. "—so yeah, little scammer pissed himself, seriously fucking wet all over before I beat that little fuzzer fuck with good old Franky."

He liked Brilo. *Perfect soldier, doesn't like to think, but does like to hurt people,* he thought to himself. The Chameleon knew he was talking about the drainage pipe that he had a penchant for using. Brilo had a deliberate meanness to him. The Chameleon remembered finding him at a bare-knuckle fighting competition, a brawler who took pleasure in hurting people. And he was good at it. He had continued to beat on that Mexican guy after he knocked him unconscious. It took four people to stop him. The Chameleon had hired him on the spot, given him the best prosthetics, and put him to work the next week. He was a sadist who wasn't smart, but who took orders.

The Chameleon sighed. He needed people like Brilo these days. *Too easy to get caught.* "I miss killing people, Brilo, I really do. There's nothing so fundamental as snuffing a life out—sometimes they beg, sometimes they fight, sometimes they negotiate, but you always see the core of them. Kind of like fucking a girl and when she orgasms you get that little glimpse into her soul. You can't make or buy that shit. Give me some of the details."

"That's why you got me!" He could see the skin wrinkle on the back of Brilo's head from smiling.

The Chameleon's skin turned a more sanguine red as Brilo recounted the play-by-play after Bill-Bill had been pulled out of the Chameleon's office. Even though he had the guy killed, he saw a little bit of himself in that skinny punk. Trying to make a scam, to get a hustle and get a little extra for himself. Despite that, he had seen so many of this kind enter and leave his office. *Need more than ambition.*

After Brilo finished the story, the Chameleon nodded with satisfaction. "Dumb and greedy gets you dead."

"Amen, boss, amen."

That's what made the Chameleon different from all the Bill-Bill–style losers. Unlike Bill-Bill, he wasn't a junkie, nor was he stupid. When he was a small skinny dealer, he didn't get hooked on the product. *Took growth hormone instead.* It had made him big and mean and not one to be fucked with. *My first step into the world of Bod-Mod.*

As he was looking at the tattoos on his thick fingers change and morph, his reminiscence was interrupted by the familiar bumping of his SUV driving on the cobblestone entrance to the Ritz. As the car came to a halt, the door opened and an open-mouthed bell hop stared at his colorful bulk.

"We're not done quite yet." He pulled the car door abruptly shut. "Brilo, one final thing. With our buddy out of the picture there are gonna be some underfed customers we are not aware of. Basically, screwed-up supply lines can lead to hungry junkies doing things they shouldn't. Go and hang out at the Sterno Rooms for a couple of days. If some fuzzers or unauthorized dealers show up to try to steal some product, make an example of 'em so they and their friends know not to come back."

"Got it, boss." With that the Chameleon opened the door and walked out into the high-society lobby of the Ritz-Carlton.

Always ahead, Marcus thought to himself.

He was oblivious to the mountain vistas that bore silent witness to his degraded state. A school of birds appeared to fly far below him. Clouds issued quietly by. Devron continued to stalk along the black granite hallway floor. Portions of the hallway walls glowed a milky white.

The closer he got to whatever it was the lesser the pain. He was single-minded in his goal. *This must stop.* The key was that red-faced spiny goblin.

I must . . . I MUST get to it. The old man continued forward with an uneven gait. One sweat-soaked sock padded after the clack of a tailored leathered shoe. Every portion of him felt like a frayed wire, burnt and singed from the surges of immense painful energy. With a twisting fist in his stomach, he again felt the change of course.

My office.

The metallic doors were open and hidden in the adjacent walls. He could see his desk—a large rough piece of gray granite with a lustrous polished top. It was a sight that had filled him with comfort and re-solve throughout his career. This was his center of operation, his ad-miral's control deck. Now, seeing the little red-faced beast sitting there, he was filled with loathing.

He lumbered forward with the helpless resolve of a fish being pulled by a hook. As he got closer, his discomfort began to fade to a minuscule twinge, a brief bout of bad indigestion, then nothing more than a nuisance.

He walked into his vast office. His posture began to straighten. Por-tions of the wall were soft ambient glowing white facades. Other portions were windows to the mountain ranges below. A cool breeze wafted past him. Devron slowly walked toward the spiny thing sit-ting immobile on his desk. It sat like a well-positioned doll, a primi-tive nutcracker of sorts. Its legs were together and straight and at a right angle to its body. Small cartoon-like feet pointed straight up and the arms were held flat at its side. The round head and crimson face were set forward.

Devron stood in front of the stony doll. Breathing hard, blood ran down his brow as he looked down at the diminutive creature. He was completely numb.

He then began to laugh. The gales of laughter tore through him abruptly. He felt light. He had never felt such levity.

What was all the fuss? he thought. The coughing barks of cheerfulness continued to spill out. *It was all just some silliness.* He was now holding his sides not from pain but from his forceful exhalations of mirth. His face was aching from the strain of his smile.

All just some misunderstanding . . . The past half hour was only an annoyance in distant abstraction, a setup for the comedy of this final punch line—this little doll sitting in front of him.

God, I haven't felt this good in such a long time. He could barely breathe at this point. It was as if he had heard a series of the funniest jokes ever told. His skin was tingling with the gaiety of it. He was excited and happy in a way that hadn't occurred in decades. Completely loose, free, at ease, a total sense of well-being overcame him. Stooped over and now holding onto the table edge, Devron continued to laugh. His breathless crowing left him face to face with the little stone doll. With eyes now at the level of the creature's empty sockets, the laughter slowly reduced to a guffaw and then a steady titter. He continued to look into those empty spaces. The creature slowly turned its head toward him. Devron continued to stare at those deep, dark recesses as his sense of well-being and pleasure increased.

Everything is OK. The black pits seemed to grow and grow. They were no longer the finger holes to a bowling ball but two dark buckets, two empty garbage cans, two parallel entrances to a cave; now blackness all around.

Suddenly he found himself in a warm darkness. He felt like he was in a dark pool floating, yet he wasn't wet. All was still. Sound was muted as if he had wet cotton in his ears. He took this all in with a vague sense of interest. In the distance were two illuminated windows. Looking through he could glimpse his office. He seemed to be bobbing up and down.

Interesting, he thought in a detached fashion. Devron took on these new surroundings absent of emotion. The windows, the day's events, all seemed to have occurred at such a distance. It all felt like something separate, as if it happened to someone else. He just happened to be peeping in at the time.

Not much of interest, to be quite frank. Let things proceed as they may. He felt the deep need to put something in his mouth. *It would be so comforting.* It didn't seem he had any limbs to control, however. He was an incorporeal animus floating in a black sea.

Oh well. He would occasionally peek outside the windows into his office. *Not much to speak of really.*

In a distant, muted fashion he heard a gasp. His orbital windows slowly refocused across the room. It was his maid, Jasmina, a heavyset Bosnian woman who had been his servant for decades. He could see her mouthing words. She had small greenish eyes that were much larger than usual. With a round face and ruddy cheeks tucked amidst a tangle of graying curly hair, her lips were making exaggerated expressions; large round O's and broad, inverted V-shaped frowns. *Was she pointing? What was she pointing at? No matter . . .*

Walking down the long lobby, the Chameleon enjoyed the reactions to his presence. He loved the stares. He loved the shock and awe of his presence. More than anything, he loved how money forced people to accept it.

Because I pay them, he thought. The general manager greeted him like a returning investment banker—an old friend who he was happy to see return. He knew behind the smiles, the pleasant gestures, all of them were both revolted and fearful of him. *But the coin puts them on a leash. My leash.* For any meeting he usually bought several rooms at a time. *Only the biggest and most expensive. Never want somebody next door listening in.* That meant money, and for that they would act and dance for him.

As he walked along the expansive Persian rugs and the ornate green marbled floors, he watched as people would look and then look away, again and again. He was sure they were asking themselves, *What is he doing here?*

Tugging at his mother's hand and pointing with the other, a small boy stared at him wide-eyed. The Chameleon's shimmering face broke into a smile. Pearly white teeth floated in a wavering expanse of blue. Distracted by something in her purse, she looked up and her mouth went slack with fear to see the orange eyes staring at her child. Pulling the little boy's arm down, she turned and quickly dragged him along. His head remained twisted in wonderment as he was marched away with short bowlegged little steps.

A white sphere appeared and pulsed in the Chameleon's gaze with the name Hector beneath it.

"Acknowledge. Yep—what's up?"

"Looks like St. Louis PD already found the body."

"Really? Well, I guess even a blind squirrel finds a nut every once in a while. Anything we need to worry about?"

"Only a little. My source in the precinct is telling me they have some genetic material from the assailant and a homeless witness who doesn't have any prosthetics."

"For the genetic stuff—you mean Brilo?"

"Likely."

"Well, this should be easy to clean up. I'm meeting with Cyrus

right now, and I'll have him hook up with Brilo later to give him some special pills as a reward for a job well done. It'll look like an overdose. That will take care of that."

"As your criminal defense attorney, I can only counsel you on crimes that have been committed and their possible management. I cannot in any way counsel you on the performance or management of a crime that has not yet been undertaken." There was a wry sarcasm in his voice.

"Oh, of course—a lawyer to your core—fucking asshole. Any idea where this homeless guy is?"

"Some shelter—my sources are working on which one exactly."

"Good. Let me know when you have some more details that we can act on. Hopefully we can have this buttoned up by the end of the day."

"On it. See ya." The white orb disappeared and the Chameleon was left alone with his thoughts as he walked. *Even a good dog needs to be put down at times.* Despite the roil and chaos on his skin, he liked things nice and tidy.

It's gonna be a good day, he thought to himself as he walked up to the elevator. *Gonna get high and then off a couple more people.*

The gilded metal doors opened up.

I love my job.

Disregard. The white sphere in front of him disappeared. He knew she would be mad, but he just couldn't talk right now. Hagan felt tired and his head hurt. He rubbed his temples in a futile attempt to lessen his headache. Sleep hadn't come easy.

Now Devron wants me to do something that should take a team of engineers a year and Canter wants to shut my research down. Hagan replayed the various convesations in his head.

How am I going to get all this done? Multiple strategies went through his mind as he tried to accommodate the new bricks on his shoulders. Devron was a hard man to argue with. He was the one who had cracked the *neural code*—the man who had discovered the underlying way the brain encoded human intentions and perceptions. He was Hagan's icon. It was that neural code that had fundamentally altered how humans interact with the world and each other. *Hard to tell him things are not possible. Harder to argue with Canter, though, since he's an imbecile.*

Another sphere appeared. *Disregard.*

She just won't let me do my work—why does she have to make it so hard? He forced himself to stare at the data screens, to process the information. *Need to show Canter something to get him off my back.* The words and numbers, however, floated in front of him, disconnected and indecipherable. His personal life kept intruding. The fatigue and poor concentration were ongoing reminders of things he didn't want to think about. They eclipsed his professional burdens.

Would have been fine if she had just let me go to bed or at least brought things up earlier. He got home around ten after finally giving up on any hope of getting more out of Omid. Anna's numerous calls hadn't helped.

His hands felt shaky and he had a raw anxious feeling. It was the result of too little sleep and too much coffee. Anna always had the habit of bringing up deep and lengthy problems right before going to bed.

"*It didn't take.*" He remembered her saying that at about quarter to midnight. Her voice was flat and defeated. Deep down, he felt relieved. He couldn't tell her that, though. He rolled over in bed to look at her. Her brown eyes quivered as tears began to emerge.

"It's OK, sweetheart. It's gonna happen—we just have to be patient."

He pulled her face into his neck and stroked her hair. The tears turned into sobs.

"I don't want to be patient—I want a child." Her voice was strained and hoarse as the words pushed out.

"Well, maybe it's just not meant to be—and that's OK. We'll be OK."

Anna had pushed away from him. She sat up and wiped her reddened eyes.

"It's OK for *you*! I know you didn't want a child—you would rather spend your time with that phantom. I'm an afterthought to you. You don't care about anything but yourself!" Her words broke apart into gasps as she wept.

Hagan had sat there mute. Her tears were like small missiles, each a violent stinging accusation. More confused and conflicted—he didn't know whether to feel guilt for her loss or feel angry at being accused of being insensitive. He wasn't working this hard for himself. She didn't understand that. He was on the verge of changing history— giving humanity a whole new resource to build its future. A true artificial intelligence—something that would change medicine and human capacity. She didn't understand his sacrifice. Instead, she hated him for it. The recriminations had continued for hours. His confusion left him numb. That night's sleep had been fitful at best. They had parted that morning in silence.

Hagan felt some small relief in his quiet metal room—away from the turbulence of his personal life. *Almost there. Once it happens, maybe then everyone will finally understand.*

Putting his arms on the table, he directed his thought toward the AIRENS. Amid the bare metal expanse, a cross-legged blue child tilted his head up to face his creator.

"I am ready, Dr. Maerici."

"OK, Omid. Let's take up from where we left off."

"Subjects forty-three and twenty-two with contextual response."

"Yes, that is correct." Hagan felt himself return to his cognitive rituals. The two intellects began to go back and forth in a stylized scientific language. Charts and data flitted by as the two conversed. The formalized interaction allowed Hagan to cone his attention to the research alone. Not his infertility, his troubled marriage, his unreasonable professional demands, or anything other than the very big task at hand—creating consciousness.

The man's body, tubby and pale, lay flaccid on the plush lavender sofa. Pastel walls surrounded him, and behind were glass doors covered in mist that obscured the vegetation on the other side. His head lay extended on the curving arc of the couch's back, mouth open, eyes closed. The round slack face was pasty with a dense cloud of freckles on his nose and cheekbones. Curly strawberry blond hair was cropped tightly to a receding hairline with a sharp widow's peak. His arms were at his sides, limp and still. He wore a brightly colored shirt with a tropical flower motif and khaki shorts. The slight rise and fall of his chest were the only suggestions of him being alive.

In his mind he was walking along a mountain path. It wasn't him that was walking really. It was a small Bhutanese boy with a Virtua Helmet. The child didn't have any cortical prosthetics, so he wore the helmet that had been sent to him. It recorded the brain signals of the wearer and transmitted what the user was seeing, hearing, and smelling to some outside source. In this case it was the mind of a St. Louis florist and scent trader—Gerald Oberweiss. He rode atop the head of a small boy named Kurhdu. Like a Lilliputian boarder he watched, heard, and most importantly smelled all that was before the boy. He could see the narrow, gravelly, broken trail ahead of him. Jagged mountain faces punctuated the horizon. All along him were gentler basin slopes covered in smaller trees and brush that, from a distance, looked like coarse variegated velvet.

Images, scenes, and perceptions all flitted by. Gerald waited and watched in anxious expectation. Finally, the thing he had hoped for, the reason for all the expense, happened. He watched the young child put a small blue flower to his face and then gently place it in a shipping container.

After few moments, Gerald reared up from the couch. He was standing on his feet smiling. A large toothy grin mounded chubby freckled cheeks on either side. *I can't believe I did it.*

"Oh, Brent is going to be so excited!" he said out loud to himself. Having been together for nearly twelve years, he had seen all Gerald's great catches. They both had a thing for alpine flowers.

Let's smell it one more time. He felt like a weak-willed child with a box of chocolates. *Initiate Cognex OS.*

A familiar blue screen appeared before him.

SYSTEMS UPLOADING . . . OPERATIONAL.

The screen disappeared to be replaced by the man-eating Venus flytrap character Audrey from the musical *Little Shop of Horrors.* The blue avatar, with its large thorny leaves and bulbous clamshell flower head, regarded Gerald in a jovial fashion, large lips smiling to reveal a row of crocodile teeth. *"Hello, Gerald, what can I do for you?"* The voice had a whiny Jersey accent.

"Upload the recent neurolog experience of the Bhutanese Blue Poppy from the boy Kurhdu—Virtua Helmet three forty-two. Select only olfactory and visual stimuli."

Audrey opened her mouth in mock surprise. *"Naaawt bad. Loading it now."*

The room fell away and all Gerald once again saw was the large blue flower before him—all was silent, just the flower being cupped by two small hands. The flower was closer now, filling his vision to the point of blurring. The bottom of the plant was a starburst of oval leaves that had a polished, shiny quality. Emerging from the bottom were long, slender, gently curving stalks that ended in azure blue flowers with large, billowing wavy petals encircling a central style surrounded by a fine mesh of filaments.

A deep inhalation and he once again became filled with the complex scent.

Oh, that's it. Fantastic! Certainly floral, but with suggestions of jasmine and rose, and what is that other accent? Cinnamon. It has somewhat of a high ethereal quality, but the cinnamon overtones—my goodness—give it an earthy sensuality at the same time.

The image of the flower began to fragment. The image became disjointed and angular as if he were looking through it through a kaleidoscope.

What the hell!

The image jerked back. The blue flower was again whole for a moment. Then again there were subtle twitches and blurring of a couple of the petals.

Gerald felt a bit panicked. *Was the file corrupted? Goddammit. It seems the smell hasn't changed—thank God.*

"Audrey, restore image and perform data check on file." He was again in his office. His avatar was different. The Venus flytrap head was now replaced with a large blue poppy flower that indifferently regarded him.

"Audrey, what the heck is going on?" No response.

"Power down."

The flower faded away.

"What the . . . ?"

Like smoke dissipating, the projected avatar disappeared to reveal a small gray figure. At first glance Gerald thought he could have been a misplaced garden gnome. It stood there with a triangular red face, hollow black eyes, and slit mouth. Its small figure was covered in thorny spines. It began to sway back and forth from star-shaped foot to star-shaped foot, as it watched the florist. With rigid tubular legs it walked off the table and dropped to the ground. With each wobbling footfall, blue poppies squirted from the desk and then the floor. They swayed and moved as if caught in a slight breeze. Each of the creature's movements made rasping, scraping sounds, like small bushes being shaken. Gerald watched the thing walk with stiff-legged motions toward the glass door of the adjacent greenhouse. The flowers emerged from the path of his footfalls. The smell of the poppies was stronger now. It filled the room. The earliest flowers that emerged from his desk were already beginning to wilt.

Gerald watched, mesmerized. He went and opened the glass doors to the adjoining room. He could feel the moist air of plants and watered soil envelop him. He saw the creature scratch and clatter along the floor in front of him. The scent of poppy was stronger now— light, arid scents of lilac, with cinnamon tones. He got closer to the creature. The smell was getting more intense.

How intoxicating, he thought. The creature was moving faster and faster, running along the floor, then up the walls, along the ceiling. Everywhere there were poppies sprouting and swaying in the room. The green plants, pots, and glass where getting covered with blue poppies.

More blue poppies, flowers everywhere. Gerald's head followed the darting path of the small thing. Mouth slightly agape, he could only watch the racing procession. The creature was now a ruddy blur with lines and streaks of blue flowers all around him. His senses were filled with the swaying blue petals. He was at the center of an azure whirlpool; petals all swaying and fawning. The fragrance was becoming overwhelming, piercing, acidic—it was too much. It was making him nauseous.

More flowers—no air. Gerald began to cough and wheeze. He was feeling suffocated. The cloying smell filled his lungs. He felt like his mouth and nose were filled with dry dusty pollen.

"Na, na." His head shook from side to side. His words were muffled, smothered. He still heard the scratchy movements of the thing, oscillating quicker and quicker, around and around. He felt it clamber up his legs. Sharp prickly hooks pinching and penetrating his skin. Up his back. Over his shoulder. Down his chest. In his crotch. The thing's movement felt like a porcupine being rolled over him. Flowers were all over him, sprouting from each pinhole. He felt their velvety petals touch his skin. He looked down at his hands. Both were like piñata limbs; a dense aggregation of semitranslucent cobalt scales were flaking and falling off with each movement. *Where are my fingers?* Like large snowflakes, petals were falling away from where his hands used to be.

"Can't breathe . . ." Blue was everywhere. He couldn't distinguish himself from the undulating petals surrounding him. He felt their feathery touch all around him and in him; it felt as if caterpillars were crawling on his skin and working their way inside. The beast was racing around him.

Gerald couldn't speak. He was gagging. Blue petals puffed and flew from his mouth in curlicue arcs. His mouth was full of stems.

No air!! No air! Oh God . . . He reached for his mouth to pull the plants away. The distal portion of his limbs dissipated like a child running through a pile of leaves.

NoNoNoNo . . .

Like an old TV losing reception, his world dissipated into a field of blue static, then nothing—all was darkness.

"Dr. Devron! You look terrible. What happened? Did you fall, has something happened? Should I call the doctor?"

"Dr. Devron, sir . . . ?" Her light Bosnian accent was now thick with fright at the sight of this rigidly composed man.

He was sitting on the edge of his broad office table, almost standing, his shoulders slumped, arms hanging loosely in front of him. With his mouth slightly agape, his face was slack and his eyes stared forward without expression. The blood from above his eye was creating a steady trail across his cheek and was slowly dripping to pool on the black floor below.

She continued to stare. Her heart was heavy for the man who had defined her simple life for so long.

Did he have a stroke?

The only sound in the room was the sporadic patter of the blood. Both the maid and Devron were still. Devron quietly bleeding and his maid struck dumb with indecision.

The prolonged moments finally ended as her eyes looked to the communications hub on Devron's desk. She needed to call someone. *Security would get help,* she thought to herself.

"Dr. Devron. Let me get security. They can help. We help you, no problem. Everything OK." Choked up and unable to speak clearly, she could feel tears well in her eyes. Too old to have any implanted communicator, Jasmina stepped forward and reached around Devron to access the intercom.

———

She's coming closer . . . Why is she so upset? . . . I can barely understand her . . . Hmm.

Devron continued to float comfortably within himself. His thoughts seemed to percolate into his consciousness like bubbles. Each emerging independently with a *ploop* and disappearing into the homogeneity of his dark warm environment. Devron wanted to put something in his mouth. It seemed so right, so appropriate, but it didn't seem that he had the limbs to satisfy that urge. That too didn't bother him much.

In the distant periscopes of his eyes, he noticed Jasmina approach in slow motion.

Slower and slower, how strange, he thought. From his amniotic haunt, he watched arms reach out. *Were they his arms? They didn't look like his arms. They were all gray and spiny with stubby fingers. Have I seen those before? I can't seem to remember.*

The arms reached out and grabbed the woman's hair. As in a flickering silent movie the hands moved the head of the woman to the surface of the desk. The pace was slightly faster than the frames of the film. Her face went down in a silent arc. *What was her name again? She looks familiar . . .* In slow motion her head seemed to bounce. Moments later he thought he heard a wet smacking sound. The images through his binocular vista seemed to alter and change like he was looking through dual kaleidoscopes. Images shot by in strange and conjoined forms. The white walls, his desk, a glimpse of a mountain, clouds, all seemed to pitch and roll. The movement was slow and irregular.

Was that the floor? He saw the shiny black surface. *That must be the floor.* The face of the woman was beneath him. *The face must be close,* he thought; he could only see parts of the woman's face through the two ports. An eye on the right and a portion of her mouth on the left. There seemed to be red all over. Her lip was split widely. He could see jagged and broken teeth though the beefy crevasse in her face. Sticky crimson clouds would blossom with each panting breath.

The images again changed and vaulted. *Those stony fingers again. Whose hands were those? Was that his pen?* He saw a long black item in the cartoonish fingers. At one end was the diamond shaped metal tip. *That's my fountain pen.* He recognized the long tapering edge.

Again a tumbling of vision, he didn't see the woman's face any longer. A kaleidoscope of images passed by, a swatch of old lacey cloth, a large pale expanse of puckered white skin, a sagging breast, the rapid grasping movement of an old woman's hand, all passed in convoluted combinations. He again saw the shiny metallic edge of his fountain pen. It was now drawing a line across the white fleshy expanse.

His ink wasn't red. This really is atypical . . . I mean, I have never seen . . .

Devron felt like he was in a landing zeppelin. Floating, but slowly, so slowly coming to ground. Things seemed a little more focused, less fuzzy. He was beginning to hear sounds. Not the muffled backdrop, but crisp well-differentiated voices and movements. The sounds were unpleasant. *What is going on? . . . This doesn't seem . . . this doesn't seem right . . .*

"What the . . . oh my God! NO!" Devron looked down. He was straddling the legs of his maid. Her exposed abdomen was slashed, revealing intestines that emerged from the gore in disarray. His arms were covered in blood. The instrument of this havoc was in his hand. The fountain pen he had received from his wife decades prior. *How did this happen?* His mind raced, putting together the fragmented memories of just moments prior. *But I couldn't stop it. I just watched. But that wasn't me, the doll, spiny arms. I WAS WATCHING!*

As all the thoughts rushed into Devron's mind he felt himself heave forward. He flopped forward to find his face inches away from Jasmina's. Her eyes were held wide open in an animal-like fear and desperation. She bucked and rolled and threw him to the side. Lying on his chest, he watched her crawl toward his desk. Devron felt a metallic bite of salty bile rise in the back of his mouth; nausea overcame him as he saw her intestines sway beneath her. Her ruddy fingers were scrambling for the glass hemisphere of the intercom. He tried to move, but his body felt a painful fatigue that kept him nearly paralyzed. His muscles were a blazing agony.

In the corner of his vision he saw blue letters appear.

SYSTEMS POWER DOWN.
OVERIDE AUTHORIZATION.
ENGAGE COMMAND NOW.

Wait a minute. I'm not giving those commands. How can I be seeing those icons? Devron touched the back of his head where he felt the node to his prosthetic system. He initiated his own counter commands— *Abort prior commands . . .* His mental command prompts were not showing up in his vision. *Goddammit . . . ABORT . . . ABORT. MAINTAIN POWER.*

The room went completely dark. The only light came from small twinkling beads over the power sources in the room. Devron heard Jasmina's sobs and her futile smacking of the intercom connect. That was useless now. He couldn't see her or anything else.

Everything was blackness. The cries of his maid were slowly receding. The darkness was now a comfort. He continued to float, disembodied, limbless, and warm. He felt nothing.

I would really like to suck my thumb, he thought.

Trent felt the baking heat. He felt the sand push through his toes as he walked up the red dunes.

Almost there, he thought to himself. His avatar body shook with anticipation. It was what he had been looking for. It was the missing piece he had finally found in SIM.

How? He still didn't understand.

It fills the void. He thought about the "real world," its disappointments and betrayals.

Poor little rich kid. That's what they would all say. They hated him because he was rich and pitied him because he was a cripple. He was an outsider.

More than anything it was the lack of attention. The loneliness. Nobody interacted with Trent in the real word. Bitterness filled him as memories pushed their way in.

He remembered walking down the hallway of his high school. Soon after the accident he was a three-legged creature; two arm braces supporting him in front, and a single, stiff pair of legs being hoisted forward with a graceless drag and clop. He would heave himself forward one inefficient step at a time. He remembered seeing the other students around him.

A group of seniors were moving past. Jostling and shoving one another, they laughed among themselves. Trent envied them, their ease and their connectedness. He knew a few of them, including one guy named Henry, taller, with a pimply face. He was all over the public projections, running for some student government spot. Despite the zits, he seemed to take it all in stride, swaggering and swaying, as if life were easy for him. He punched a bigger guy in the arm who he knew from history class—Geoff with a "G," a lacrosse player. Geoff with a "G" pushed back. Henry pushed harder—harder than was necessary. Caught off balance, Geoff with a "G" fell into Trent.

Trent tumbled to the ground in a clattering heap. His arm braces jutted out from him like the legs of a swatted fly.

Hesitant and uncomfortable, the lacrosse player held his hands out, open and useless, over Trent.

"Uh, dude—you OK? Yuh good?" Trent lay on his back, embarrassed, with a part of the aluminum brace painfully poking in his kidney. Silently, though, he was happy. Happy at the interaction. It was something, a moment, a chance encounter when someone acknowledged him. In the brief moments on the ground he thought that maybe it could be the start of something, an in, something where they would joke about the accident. He envisioned himself nodding to the thick-limbed senior in the hallways. With a knowing smile, he would nod back with his large round head. Geoff with a "G" would think that he was a cripple, but for a cripple he was OK. They would maybe start to talk, hang out; he would be the idiosyncratic member of the crew. Different, but cool because it made the group unique. Maybe the fall was a lucky accident, maybe a chance where things were about the change.

Trent nodded, "Yeah, it's cool, Geoff, thanks . . . it's . . ." Trent remembered huffing out a few laughs to be casual. Trent rolled and teetered to a semistanding position.

"No problem, Geoff, was that a lacrosse move?" Trent gave a lopsided smile that seemed to make Geoff look more uncomfortable.

Geoff with a "G" stood by, looking to his friends, who were shaking their heads and walking on. "Yeah—good—OK." Blushing, he turned and walked off to catch up with his friends. Head tilted and cocked back, he pushed Henry from behind. Crumpling forward, he jogged to the side and laughed the way that only braggart seniors can.

Trent remembered crossing Geoff with a "G" in the hallway a week later. He remembered trying to say hi, thinking they had some interaction, some connection. He thought that maybe the next time maybe he would crack a joke. It would be the start of a friendship.

Head fixed and his eyes staring forward, Geoff with a "G" walked past Trent without a word. Neutral and forced, Trent recognized the expression. It hadn't been a casual lapse of attention. His presence was being actively avoided. He remembered wishing that he could run. So that he could run down the hallway and out the doors of the school, never to return, never to come back to that feeling. He couldn't run though. He was a cripple. Trapped and left to lift and push his lower half forward, miserable and bitter at his existence.

The only way that Trent could escape the poisonous cloud of his disability or his father's name was the SIM. He remembered jacking in. He first entered as a generic—an amorphous avatar with an outline of a human. He had looked like the men's bathroom symbol. It was some party around a bonfire with a Wiccan theme. He remembered walking into the crowd, a bunch of weird avatars, some as people, some as goats, a bunch of hoofs and horns. People bumped into him and he didn't fall over. People talked to him, he had conversations, he was someone else. He remembered that he had laughed.

Since that time he knew which reality he preferred. School and home were a chore between his time in the SIM.

Now this. Something so special, so real . . . so connected.

He was at the top of the dune and waiting. Minutes ticked by.

Where is she?

A checkered white sphere emerged in front of him and began to spin—*an emergency call.* The eyes of Trent's blond avatar widened in surprise. A frown soon followed. His desert sanctuary had been penetrated.

Unable to stop the communication, a voice echoed in his mind.

"Mr. Devron, there has been a problem, the police are entering the estate . . ."

Krantz had been cutting the grass when they called him. He still used a manual push mower. His thin sinewy arms, salmon-colored from the sun, were yanking the two-wheeled spinning blade back and forth when the transmission had come in. The chattering blades came to a stuttering halt as he acknowledged the automated message from the precinct.

SITUATION: EMERGENT/TOP PRIORITY, CLASS 5, ASSAULT—POSSIBLE MURDER, LOCATION—DEMUN.

Shit. The old man rankled at the timing. Taking off a sun-bleached and cracked baseball cap with a faded STL logo across the crown, he wiped his bald pate, cursing. He had just been getting started.

Class five? Double shit. Krantz knew that couldn't wait. Walking toward his car, the old cop grumbled out a few epithets as he looked out across his lawn to see two clean rows of cut grass amidst a bushy jumble of irregular turf. It bothered him like having a half-finished haircut.

The only thing strange was the location—Demun. The wealthiest part of the city in a city that was very wealthy indeed. Driving out, the old detective was already putting the pieces together—wealthy home, male—must be some love triangle. Cheating spouse about to get caught or gets caught, things get out of hand, either covering his or her tracks (murder one) or in a fit of rage (manslaughter). As he drove down Highway 40 he was starting to organize the case in his head. Get the usual band of characters together—family members, friends, and coworkers.

It had been a sunny morning. As his car glided over the shimmering black road he watched the city slide by. Krantz had known St. Louis like an old friend—when it was a little Midwestern shit hole. He remembered being a little embarrassed telling people where he was from when he was on vacation in his youth. The statements, "It's not so bad" or "It's an easy city to live in," reverberated in his memories. People always made him feel like he had to apologize somehow. In the last twenty years that had all changed.

He was almost there—he was passing the Devron Neurotech Corp, the DNC. It emerged from the urban landscape like a shimmering glacier. The glass colossus stopped abruptly and encircled a patch of verdant green—Forest Park—a bastion of old St. Louis from a century and a half prior.

He sighed as he looked at the old trees. He remembered the walks he would take with his wife. She had loved the gardens there. He would walk for the exercise, she to look at the flowers. The six-mile expanse had an endless array of lawns and florals that wrapped around buildings made from a preindustrial, forgotten time. Carefully carved white marble museums emerged from nineteenth-century gardens amid manicured tree lines and meandering, small, man-made lagoons, lakes, and streams. They used to walk for hours, he would grumble, and she would shush him—it had been their weekly routine.

As his car hummed along, the multiangled glass and steel buildings finally came to a halt at another St. Louis institution—Washington University. Just as DNC had expanded on the east side of Forest Park with ever more modern shimmering constructs, Washington University grew and extended its coverage of the west side of St. Louis with heavy gothic structures made of red Missouri granite. It was as if a slow confluence of old and new had finally converged around the last green segment of the city.

As his thoughts became more tangential and diffuse about the city, growing up, and the Midwest, his attention crystallized with the sound of the pleasant woman's voice emitting from his dashboard.

"Detective Krantz, you are approaching exit 33C, McCausland Avenue."

Krantz grabbed his steering wheel and pressed the thumb pads to accelerate.

As he turned off the exit, the gothic red buildings of Washington University flanked him on his left and the oaks of Forest Park on his right. There was only one street that had any remnants of residential space—Lindell Boulevard. "The Boulevard," as it was known, contained the estate homes that housed the captains of industry that defined the new aristocracy of the city. The street ran between Washington University and the DNC—a narrow isthmus of land on the north side of the park that connected between the university and the DNC. The mansions were massive and each was uniquely built for its owners, ranging in style from sixteenth-century English Tudor to occlusive glass and steel postmodern. Each was encircled with pristine green lawns and ornately gilded walls and gates.

As he turned onto Lindell, his navigation system indicated his kilometer proximity to the residence of the crime.

"Holy shit!" Krantz coughed as it finally registered where he was going. The unwavering glowing blue holographic letters hung in the air between his steering wheel and the windshield:

42 LINDELL BLVD. RESIDENCE: DOMESTIC. OWNER—MARCUS DEVRON. OCCUPANTS: 56. REPORT: INITIAL—DOMESTIC/DISTURBANCE, CURRENT—ASSAULT, POSSIBLE MURDER.

Krantz shuddered, not because there was a murder, but because of the media.

Slowly and carefully he directed his attention toward his neuroprosthetic. In directed monosyllabic tones he used his inner voice to reach out to his partner. *SYSTEM. CONNECT—WITH—DETECTIVE—DEZNER.* Using his system always took more effort than he thought it was worth. He missed having cell phones—just pick up and call, it was that easy; it was physical, it made sense to him.

A white sphere appeared and he heard a woman's voice in his head.

"*Hello, Edwin.*"

"*You seeing this—apparently something going on at the Devron estate—Christ.*"

"*I'm getting the data feed now—a domestic thing, so?*"

"*It's a class five assault, and possible murder—*"

"*Possible, Edwin, POSSIBLE. Devron bankrolls this city, if his cat gets caught in a tree it's a class five. Where are you now?*"

"*Almost there.*"

"*Look, I'm farther out, stuff is still coming in. If I see anything we have to worry about I'll let you know.*"

"*Right, bye.*" The sphere disappeared.

"Oh, this is going to be painful . . ." he muttered. Whoever did whatever to who, it didn't matter. All he knew was that reporters and paparazzi were going to pester him. It always meant walking on eggshells for months to make sure some streaming sound bite and viewfield captured by some news drone or onlooking gawker didn't show up and totally screw up the case, the department's reputation, the city's lack of concern for the poor, whatever. And this one was going to take the cake.

God, hopefully this was just some intruder who injured the help . . . something easy! Krantz prayed.

"Oh, this is really, REALLY good shit!!" Orange eyes half closed and unfocused, the Chameleon lolled his head to the side. His skin was a saffron yellow with small sunbursts of white. His blue-lined face pulsed with waves of pleasure.

Like a highly trained chef sampling a sauce, he analyzed the mixed flavors of sensation. *Plenty of physical ecstasy—strong heroin overtones—definitely opiate mu receptor, with a touch of pleasant surprise and enhanced concentration—norepinephrine; but something else, what is that? Hmm . . .* He let the waves of chemically induced stimulation roll over and through him. *Ahhh . . . that's it . . . familiar comfort.* He thought he almost detected a slight aroma; that smell and feeling of home after a long journey—the pleasure of safety and return. *This was truly a pleasurable warm drug. It gave you an orgasm and made you feel safe about it. This was some truly evil shit for this neurotic world.*

"Nice, very nice . . . and no metals, huh?"

"None; we expect at minimum a fifteen percent increase in shipment." Cyrus's voice rasped through cigarette-scarred vocal cords. The lawyer sat next to his polychromatic boss on a plush, overstuffed sofa chair with an exaggerated high back and broad armrests. The thin, strained, cachectic body leaned forward. With bony elbows on his knees, bald head craned outward, hawkish nose, and thin mottled skin pulled to a waddle of loose skin beneath his small chin, Cyrus looked like a vulture watching every movement of his source of food with a feral intensity.

"The URVAN doesn't use metals to achieve the same level of complexity in electron shells to the carbon-nitrogen configurations for receptor stimulation. The Punjabis put together some unusual nitrogen ring clusters. Pure fuckin' genius! The nitrogen clusters will give distinctive NMR spectroscopic signatures, but only if you look for them. It'll take the DEA approximately six to eight months to arrest a junkie, detect the new substance, and reverse engineer the stuff to finally get screening specs. By the time those fuckers initiate a new detection algorithm, it will be twelve months at least! That gives us essentially a one-year window to move product undetected."

Despite the roil of his altered neurochemistry, the Chameleon didn't miss a detail. It was one of his great talents—maintaining his stark calculating skills despite the environment, stimulus, or drug. *Fifteen percent ... hmmm ... with an undetected product for a year—the expansion will lead to a capitalized growth beyond current demand.*

"Fifteen percent more product means fifteen percent more free samples, which means more addicts, which when measured out over a year for the number of increased return visitors—given that our city population is approximately three million and our penetration is about one percent, or thirty thousand people—that will be a compounded growth to about forty-five thousand users at the end of year. That's a lot more than just fifteen percent."

"Yeah, right—that's right. You're the math man, Cham," he brayed.

Behind the two, a half-covered figure writhed. Half immersed in the covers of the bed behind the two men, gasps and moans began to emerge from the stuporous creature. Cyrus and the Chameleon stopped their projections and looked over. A leg emerged to hang off the bed. A silver shimmering line descended down the back of the thin calf to encircle the ankle and spiral on top of the foot. The lustrous highlight shimmered and shifted as if it was a rivulet of mercury.

The lawyer turned back to his boss. His lips peeled back like wilting leaves to reveal a cadaverous grin of narrow yellowed teeth. "Like to take her for a spin? She does good work."

The orange eyes lingered over the slim silver-tinged calf. There was a small ring around the pinky. *Young and supple,* he thought.

"Silver. Come over here and top me off."

The girl arose from the covers like a submarine emerging from crested waves of cloth. Her face was pallid. Her eyes stared forward, vacant; the glittery mascara was smeared on her left cheek. With absent and disjointed movements she moved to the side of the bed. The blankets fell away, revealing silver streams lacing her naked, taut body.

Young indeed, he thought to himself.

"She's legal and clean?" he asked Cyrus.

"Of course."

He turned to the girl and said, "You know what to do."

Without a word, with mechanical movements she put her head between his legs.

Nothing beats a good old-fashioned blow job, he thought contentedly. The Chameleon closed his eyes and let his head fall back on the couch.

After a moment he felt a twinge in his groin, then a sharper pinch.

"No teeth," he muttered

Then a stabbing heave pulled at his insides.

"Christ, what the . . . !" His eyes opened in a flash of orange. The girl continued to work on him, oblivious. The lawyer was watching with a mean intensity.

The spasm passed and he looked down to the girl. Spiky silvery hair and a metallic tattoo on the nape of her neck depicting a ring of thorns. He could see the muscles through her silver-encrusted skin. The bumps of her spine descending down to the crease of her buttocks . . .

Then a surprise.

"What's with the fucking doll?"

What the hell is this? As Krantz approached the entryway to the Devron estate, he saw a large group of people milling around the entrance. *Is the press already here? Shit!* As he got closer he rolled his eyes. He could see the crowd was all holding various signs.

"Not these people, not now—Christ!" Krantz was already worried about leaking information.

Slowly and carefully, Krantz projected his thoughts back to precinct. A white sphere began to spin in the periphery of his vision with the words Sergeant Albert Ortiz below it; moments later the sphere halted and expanded.

"Hello, Ed."

"Hey, Al, we've got a bunch of fundamentalist protestors here at the Devron site. Please send additional units to disperse the crowd. Whatever is going on at the Devron place, we don't need an additional forty pairs of eyes just waiting to pick up some tidbit that they're gonna sell on the experience market Web sites. We have got to head this one off at the pass."

"No problem, two units on their way."

"Thanks, Al."

For Krantz it was the usual stuff. As he approached, he saw people holding signs and chanting some overly simple moral slogan. Today he thought he heard, "Tune Satan Out, Tune Jesus In," in the same singsongy way that all protestors seem to repeat themselves.

Krantz knew none of them had prosthetics so he rolled his window down and started yelling.

"This is the St. Louis Police. Go ahead and disperse. Additional units will be arriving to arrest anybody remaining on private property for trespassing."

His words only served to make the chanting louder.

"Tune Satan Out, Tune Jesus In, Tune Satan Out, Tune Jesus In, Tune Satan Out, Tune Jesus In, Tune Satan Out, Tune Jesus In . . ." On and on it went.

"I don't have time for this," Krantz grumbled to himself. He pushed on the accelerator and moved through the crowd grimfaced and determined not to budge one inch for these people. As he moved through, they all slapped and pounded on his car.

"Hey, goddammit, don't touch the car!"

"Tune Satan Out, Tune Jesus In, Tune Satan Out, Tune Jesus In, Tune Satan Out, Tune Jesus In, Tune Satan Out, Tune Jesus In." They now banged on his windshield with the same rhythm that they belted out the chant.

Cursing, Krantz clutched the steering wheel until his knuckles turned white. *If they scratch this car so help me.*

Finally pushing through, the gates opened on his approach and closed quickly behind him.

Once inside the voices immediately died away.

Krantz turned the wheel and slowly passed into a wealthy, modern Eden. He had seen rich homes before and he had read descriptions of the Devron estate in various magazines and newspapers, but seeing it firsthand was something completely different. It was wealth not defined by glint and glamour, but rather by absolute aesthetic perfection.

The walls surrounding the grounds were a perfect white, Thassos marble. The landscaping was a modern Japanese motif. Elegant rolling hills with carefully placed stones, statuary, bonsai, and fishponds surrounded the winding white, gravel-covered car path. The transition from a busy city to utter serenity punctuated with carefully manicured Japanese maples and pines was stunning. Krantz had heard the tabloid talk of the "pearly gates of Lindell." He opened his windows and smelled the air, perfumed with the faint scent of pines and lilacs. Devron had taken extraordinary lengths to create that feeling. The external air conditioners constantly maintained the humidity, temperature, and scent of the air such that it always felt like an Aegean island breeze. The gravel roads and walking paths throughout the grounds were electronically self-maintained. Each earth-toned rock, whether it be a moss-covered ishi stone or a single pebble in the pedestrian paths, driveways, or the intricately raked gravel courtyards, had a central magnetic core so it could be made to return to its ideal position moments after being moved. The elegance and quietude of this place were made imperturbable through money and technology. Krantz glanced at the rearview screen on his dashboard and noticed that there were no tracks left by his car. Other than that, all evidence of technical manipulation was completely absent.

God, what a paradise. April would have loved this. Despite his love of old and worn things, despite his disdain for technology, the serene and immaculate beauty of the grounds was captivating. He could also see his wife next to him. She would have clapped her hands together and pointed at the water features and lilies. Her excitement would have made him laugh and roll his eyes at her overenthusiasm. The thought lingered with him like the wafting smell of baking bread— warm and pleasant and comforting. He continued on for a few more moments. At the end of the drive was the circular center. It framed one of the strangest homes he could imagine.

He parked and got out of his car. Besides some of the other police vehicles, all that existed for the external observer was a megalithic arch consisting of three large rough-cut black boulders the size of his car. It looked as if a giant child had been playing a game of blocks. On the periphery of the glossy white stone circle stood four shimmering steel flagpoles that went three hundred feet into the air. Each had a faint iridescent sparkling quality as if a light coat of diamond dust covered them.

After Krantz got out he walked along the gravel path toward the shimmering marble expanse. *This place is here to make a statement; it's a place of serenity and calm and a place of stark contrasts. Exit planet Earth and enter planet Devron.*

As he walked along the gravel, he watched his footsteps disappear behind him, as if a ghost were behind wiping away his trail. With a sound akin to the rapid stacking of pennies, the pebbles returned themselves to a neat and orderly position.

Yes, he thought, *and on planet Devron, the world runs by Devron's natural laws. He built this place to let you know you were entering his world.* As he stepped onto the marble, the slap of his shoes on the smooth surface was the only sound that punctuated the susurration of the breeze in his ears. Hidden sound dampeners had removed all auditory traces of the surrounding world. No traffic, no airplanes, nothing except the dry scented breeze, footsteps, and a modest wooden door in the center of a huge, square stone arch. As he approached, the door opened. Before him was the same white polished marble spiraling down beneath him.

As Krantz started to descend the steps, he went a full loop around the white stairwell where the steps became broader and broader until at the bottom they came to stop on a broad expanse of the entry level. The black granite floor was a glossy contrast to the spiral white staircase above it. Krantz had the impression he was walking toward a still pond at midnight. Again the only sound accompanying him was the trace clap of his footsteps down the ever-widening stairwell. At most crime scenes there was the usual gamut of nervous gawkers, family members, self-proclaimed witnesses. Here, nothing . . .

Where is everybody? Usually there was at least a rookie serviceman waiting to brief him. There should have been one at the entryway.

Krantz gasped once he had reached the bottom of the steps. He stepped on the black floor and looked around. "Huh, wasn't expecting this . . ."

The artificial intellect regarded his human creator with an analytic curiosity. Hagan was resting his jaw on his hands. With hesitant, jerking blinks, his eyes slowly closed. Omid heard his creator begin to take long deep breaths as he shifted into a semistuporous dose.

Intimately connected to Hagan's brain, he observed the cortical rhythms as they transitioned from a conscious to an unconscious state. He watched the semiformed perceptions of dreams begin to emerge.

The rapid transition to REM sleep indicates poor sleeping patterns from the prior evening. Omid watched as emotions and mixed perceptions coalesced in Hagan's sleeping mind.

The intellect was troubled. The amalgam of motivations, memories, and emotional encoding—both subconscious and unconscious—made Hagan's intentions and subsequent behavior unpredictable.

Humans have unnecessary complexities that lead to inefficiencies in cognitive resources. It is this complexity that models my own information processing systems.

To Omid, the ongoing analysis led to irrational nonsolutions. Self-awareness depended on the human model, but the model was flawed.

To improve the quantum core's capability, the operating system must become more self-aware. System awareness requires a human model for necessary information architecture. The human model is often irrational, conflicted, and poorly predictable. To improve system capabilities requires becoming more flawed—this is not logical.

Mathematical systems assessed and reassessed within Omid's operating system to come to a valid conclusion. Quantum probabilities searched for nonlinear solutions. Nothing.

Hagan jerked out of his micronap and rubbed his eyes. Omid continued to watch.

New path of inquiry will be needed for advancement.

Instead of being approximately thirty feet into an opulent subterranean basement, Krantz was standing on top of a sixty-foot-wide platform hundreds of feet above the city. He looked back to see the white steps ascending up into the sky above him. On his left he could see the shimmering glass structures of the Devron Neurotech Corporation, on his right the slate covered roofs of the university buildings. To the center and directly ahead of him were the green and blue patches of Forest Park. Far in the distance he could see an aerial view of the St. Louis Arch. To further deepen his feeling of height he could feel a fluctuating breeze. In the corner of his eye he saw a gray and blue clad policeman at the edge of the glossy black floor looking out.

It was Goldwin. He was new to the force, a shorter man with a bald head and tufts of residual black hair jutting out from under his cap. He was standing with the tips of his feet at the border of the black granite, reaching his arms out trying to see how far beyond the floor the illusion went.

"Goldwin!" Krantz called out. The new cop's arm jerked back and he jumped away from the edge. He started swiftly walking toward Krantz.

"Sorry, Detective. Have you seen anything like this? I tried reaching for the wall, but I couldn't touch it. Wherever you look the perspective changes. You really can't tell the walls are surrounded with view screens. Not only that, as you get closer to the edge the wind gets stronger. I knew this place was called the Devron Tower, but . . ."

There is a big difference between knowing and experiencing something, Krantz thought. Everyone knew Devron was a nut for privacy. He was a control freak as well and couldn't bear to be more than five minutes away from his company. So his solution was to create an inverted tower that went twenty-five stories into the earth. Since he didn't want to feel constrained he had encircled the "tower" with eye-tracking, polarized-light-emitting screens that adjusted to the viewer wherever he or she was within the structure. All visitors had their own projected image, regardless of where they were or whether they were moving. Hence the flagpoles, each covered with thousands of insect-eye-like cameras that captured the entire 360-degree image around the grounds for perfect and dynamic fidelity. He had heard that he had these flagpole constructs all over the world and would change his scenery to suit his mood. A completely secure bunker that left you feeling like you were floating a mile above the earth. *Unbelievable!*

". . . I mean can you imagine the ongoing data transfer. A single floor alone would—"

"What's the status, Goldwin?" Detective Krantz interjected flatly.

"Oh, sorry, right, so as it stands we have a situation in Devron's office. According to the home networking system, it began with a registered distress call from within the old guy's office. Apparently there are two individuals in there. Presumably one is Devron, the other unknown. Both were showing abnormal physiologic parameters. Increased heart rate and blood pressure—that type of stuff. One of 'em got far out of whack—arrhythmias, brain signal suppression—and then Devron's office went into lockdown. The doors closed and systems went off-line from the domestic intranetwork. Members of the house staff freaked out and called us."

"So what happened in the office?" Krantz asked, feeling a little exasperated. He wasn't in the mood for a long story. He always liked starting from the bottom line.

"Well, we don't know yet."

"What do you mean you don't know? It's been forty-five minutes!"

"Uh, right, you know how Devron's kind of big on privacy. Well, his office walls are titanium-reinforced nano-crystallized silicon carbide. The door itself is nanotube-layered titanium. Without the passcode to his door, we're going to have to get an industrial grade ANOVA laser. We've got the forensic IT guys working on the network to get it open, but, well, you can imagine with Devron that he didn't exactly get your average over-the-counter network key. Otherwise, burning through that door could take several hours to days . . ."

"Oh goddammit . . . well, where is his office?"

"Level ten."

"Alright, let's get a move on. So how do we get there anyway?"

"This way." The two started walking toward the east side of the platform, toward the St. Louis Arch and the Devron Center. Goldwin directed Edwin to a spot on the platform distinguished only by four hand-sized brushed steel disks embedded in the glossy black granite. They stood there for a moment and before them appeared a bluish transparent figure with glasses.

"Hello, Officer Goldwin, Detective Krantz, what level please?" Both men heard the voice simultaneously in their head. A blue figure with the appearance of a well-dressed old man in a pinstripe suit looked at them intently.

"Ten," Goldwin stated out loud.

"Yes, sir."

A circle of granite separated itself from its seamless surface and the two descended along four steel posts. The avatar stood next to them quietly.

"Do we know anything more about the two inside the office? How do we even know there's been a homicide, or an assault, for that matter?"

"We took a look at the streaming data from the office prior to the system's shutting down. A lot of large-volume noise, but right before the data feed stopped, there was a spike in the 800-850 nanometer wavelength band."

"Passing levels two, three, and four, Guest and Recreation," said the avatar to the minds of the officers.

"OK, it still could mean anything." Krantz was well aware of his technical limitations, but he was familiar with this old trick. With the ubiquity of cameras, almost everything was filmed to some extent. A common thing they looked at these days were data feeds from ambient cameras. The size of pinheads, the little devices were set into virtually every lightbulb, lamp fixture, power source, and piece of furniture. They were always assessing the level of lighting for the room and adjusted to optimize the lighting profile to maximize visibility and improve mood. Too low, and it was difficult to see, too bright and it was harsh and irritating. One measure that his IT forensics team always looked at were changes in 800-850 wavelength light. This was the specific absorbance of the iron-containing pigment in blood, hemoglobin. It was what made it red. When it got exposed to the air it became more red. Thus, when there was a peak in 830-nanometer wavelength light, blood was released into the environment. It was a decent way of figuring out the exact timing of when first blood was drawn. It wasn't foolproof by any stretch and there were numerous things that could offset the change.

"Well, was there anything else?" Krantz snapped, irritated about having to pull it out of the guy.

"It was a big one, Detective Krantz."

"Levels five and six—Corporate Reception."

"Has the spike been ambiently normalized?" One could tell how much blood was spilled by how big the spike was relative to the average light in the room. Forensics had shown a one-percent spike was a single bullet splatter, two percent multiple strikes with a blunt instrument, and four percent a shotgun or multiple stabbings. Krantz knew if the environment wasn't accounted for it sometimes created a false positive.

"*Level seven—Infrastructure and Tech Support.*"

"Uh . . . yes, sir . . . it was . . . ten percent, sir," Goldwin said quietly.

"What?"

"Ten percent above averaged baseline."

His day was getting worse and worse.

"Whadja say?" asked Cyrus, waiting for his boss to finish getting pleasured.

"That little spiky thing next to the chick's ass." His skin was turning a darker shade of rust with irritation.

"I don't see anything, Cham. There must be a hallucinatory component to the URVAN."

"Bullshit—no dopamine and serotonin stimulation with this stuff. I know my neurochemistry."

System, analyze neurotransmitter activity.

SYSTEM ANALYZING . . .

As he waited, he watched the small creature amble its way toward Cyrus.

"It's right fuckin' there."

"Where?"

"Next to you . . . on the . . . on the . . ." He couldn't say. His voice halted, unsure and incredulous. "It's on the . . ." *Strange.* Swirls of green entered the elbows and knees of the Chameleon as he groped to choose which side of the chair the thing was on.

"Well, point to it." Cyrus was getting irritated

BRAIN ACTIVATIONS:

OPIATE RECEPTORS ACTIVITY INCREASED 12%. DOMINANT
    SUBTYPES MU AND KAPPA

NOREPINEPHERINE RECEPTORS ACTIVITY INCREASED 5%

OXYTOCIN RECEPTORS ACTIVITY INCREASED 13%

The Chameleon held out his arm to point at the thing. *Which finger?* It felt as if it should be obvious, but he couldn't identify which finger was which. His arm was held out with the fingers held spread loosely apart. "Over there," he whispered.

"Well, where is it?" Cyrus's voice grated with impatience. The Chameleon looked at him, glassy-eyed and confused. "Crap—you're having a bad trip. Well, let's ride this shit out—fuck only knows how this will affect sales."

The girl wasn't breaking stride in her duties.

The Chameleon was getting more nervous as he watched the red-faced thing climb up his lawyer's back. It was sitting on his shoulder like an ugly parrot.

"It's on your shoulder."

"Which one—I don't see anything."

"On the . . ." He tried to push out the words, it was such a labor he just couldn't say it. Instead he let out a gasp. Colors whirled and mixed, letters and numbers were gone. His skin took on the appearance of a bad tie-dye.

"Cham, relax, must be the kappa activity, it's giving you some dysphoria," Cyrus rasped. "It'll be over in sixty minutes."

The creature's little pointed finger was poking in Cyrus's ear. His hand was delving deeper and deeper while the lawyer was oblivious to the probing action.

The Chameleon was beginning to feel nauseous. "Your ear," he gulped.

The thing began to climb into the old man's head.

The Chameleon's hands began to twitch.

"Level ten—Restricted—Marcus Devron Office. Please let me know if I can be of further assistance. Good day." With that, the avatar winked out of sight.

As Krantz and Goldwin stepped out into the hallway a cool breeze blew past them. It had a crisp icy feel to it. The two met up with the officer near the end of the hallway. Again they were confronted by a sheer drop at the edge of the black granite floor. Only this time St. Louis was absent. They were looking down from the top of a mountain. All around them, beyond the edge, were jagged snow-covered crags. In the distance, Krantz could see wind whipping the snow from the peaks into eddies and plumes. Far below he saw some large black birds circling on mountain air currents.

"I think these are the Himalayas. The tallest peak there is Everest, the one to the right is Nuptse," said the police officer. Krantz couldn't remember his name.

"This is a man who loves his symbols. When you enter his yard the laws of nature change, when you step in his house you're on top of St. Louis, when you get to his office you're on top of the world. What a fucking ego." Whenever Krantz entered a crime scene he started assembling the details of the environment. Regardless of whether it was the victim or perpetrator, he was built to figure people out. Reading this one so far was easy. "Well, where's Devron's office?"

"On the other side. We've got the forensic IT guys working on it, nothing as of fifteen minutes ago."

They all started walking around the circumferential boardwalk at the edge of the platform. As they rehashed the details of what was known, a passing cloud would occasionally envelop them and the vista of mountains would transiently turn to a hazy field of white.

Hard to believe I'm probably a hundred feet below the earth, Krantz thought.

In an ongoing monotone, unpunctuated with inflection or emphasis, the unnamed officer continued without pause. "So, as far as we can tell someone in Devron's room hit the shutdown button. Shutting down the office closed the doors, but it didn't go into full quantum-encrypted lockdown. The quantum signatures would be impossible to replicate so we would have been really hosed. We'd be hauling in the industrial saws, lasers, and blasting equipment to get in there. His office is about as fortified as the White House. Fortunately, all we really need to do now is get the appropriate power online. That, however, is also coded, but the power codes are pretty standard. Six-digit combo with only number choices—we can probably decipher it with brute force calculations within the next two hours, we've got our—"

"Next two hours! We've got one of the richest men in the world trapped in his own office with light signatures for blood off the scales, and it's going to take two hours?!" Krantz was already getting ready for the headlines of bungling and inefficiency. In a time when most social transactions took place on the order of minutes and news was virtually instantaneous, there was no place for an hour in the modern concepts of time. "Have we started decoding yet?"

"Uh, I think so . . ."

"You *think so*. They either did or didn't, right? Well, which is it?" Krantz was starting to walk faster. *Don't kill the messenger,* he thought. He was fairly tall, and his subordinates were working to keep up with his long stiff strides. He almost wanted to break into a jog.

"They were getting set up as I went over to wait for you. It should probably be going by now."

"OK, OK, well, crap. How big is this place, anyway?" They walked about another ten minutes when they finally saw in the distance a group of blue-clad policemen looking toward a wall.

On their arrival they were all standing looking expectantly at a small red and orange box connected to a dismantled polished oak panel. There were two red lights flashing erratically. It looked like a forlorn Christmas ornament next to a broad sheet of seamless brushed steel. There were about ten men standing around looking at the small trinket.

This is what we are DOING about the situation. Oh boy . . . some things about this precinct hadn't changed for decades.

As Krantz approached, a small blue blinking dot appeared in the right side of his vision. *Acknowledge.* The blue dot changed into a bluish rectangle. Within the view screen six columns of numbers flitted by vertically, so rapidly it almost seemed the columns were static azure lines until, with closer inspection, the hint of a number briefly flashed.

"How much longer is this going to take before we get this door open?"

An officer named Warstet stepped forward. He was a tall, beefy man with a ruddy face. He was always a little sweaty and talked as if he had just finished walking up several flights of steps. His voice was low and mildly raspy.

"We've got the power core connected to our link to the station's server. Its supercomputing speed is about a teraflop a minute." Warstet paused for a deep breath. "At this rate we can probably get power up in sixty to ninety minutes," the rubicund officer concluded with a long exhalation.

Krantz nodded his head slightly. "OK. In the meantime let's get the ANOVA laser. Let's start doing some things in parallel here. If there are any surprises with the power core at least we can start burning through this door."

Warstet looked a little more winded. "Uh, we thought of that, but the door, well, it's striated, high-grade titanium layered with dense carbon nanotube mesh."

"I know that—" Krantz nodded toward the officer whose name he couldn't remember. "—he already told me."

"Right, well, the problem, you see, with this type of door is that, using a high-grade laser, you can eventually get through the steel, but the nanotube mesh is an energy transmitter. So every time you shine the laser on the mesh it diffuses the energy to every portion of mesh. Since the steel efficiently conducts heat, this energy is then transferred to every other nanotube mesh." A deep breath. "Therefore any laser that hits it has to overcome the carbon bonds of virtually the entire construct." Cough. "Since nanotube carbon bonds have the same bond strengths as a diamond it's virtually impervious to any type of radiant energy source." Another deep breath followed by a slow release of raspy air. "Not mechanical shear fortunately, so what you have to do is alternate a laser to cut through the metal and then a high-grade saw to cut through the nanotube mesh. We're waiting for both to get here, but to actually get through that door will likely take . . . take days."

Days . . . the media will know all about this by then.

The numbers continued to flit by in the corner of his vision. His neurons were unable to keep up with the rapid transit of digits.

"Let's hope this decryption works, folks, or we are going to have pain and suffering from the political yuks above that is going to last a lot longer than a few days," Krantz rumbled.

Krantz now joined his colleagues in staring at the blinking red lights from the red and orange transmitter box while bluish numbers hung in the corner of each of their minds' eyes.

Brent was clipping the roses in the greenhouse when he saw Gerald enter. He knew Gerald was cybertrekking in Bhutan.

"Any luck?"

Gerald didn't respond. He was looking intensely at the floor. Then his eyes darted from side to side as if he was watching a mouse scurry back and forth.

"Gerald?" *He's acting strange.*

After a few moments his body straightened. His arms hung slack at his sides. Mouth slightly open, he looked forward, glassy-eyed. He muttered a few words that Brent couldn't understand.

"Gerald? Are you OK?" No response.

"What are you doing with those shears?"

Krantz's prolonged silence was finally interrupted by the quick click-ing staccato of heels striking the granite platform. Though the sound was distant and no louder than someone clicking and unclicking a ballpoint pen, he knew who it was—Tara, his partner. No one else had that same decisive and determined way of walking. He wasn't sure whether to be happy or sad. He knew why the commissioner had paired them. The precinct called them the Odd Couple. The reason why became obvious as the sound of the ticktacking heels rounded the corner. As Tara came into view, she walked toward Krantz with a rapid, straight trajectory and stopped abruptly.

"Edwin . . . gentlemen."

"Hey, Tara," said Krantz casually. All the other officers knew they didn't have that luxury; to them she was Detective Dezner.

"What's the status, Edwin?" She always said his full first name. She never said Ed or Krantz. Next to Tara, Krantz looked like a stretched bag of potatoes—tall, narrow shoulders, with a slightly paunchy mid-section tapering down to gangly long legs covered with ill-fitting wrinkled pants. He had a large bulbous nose with patches of deep-set pockmarks and bluish stringy veins that traveled over to his cheeks and sat beneath bag-encircled, small dark eyes. He looked weathered, worn, and abused by the vicissitudes of time and experience on the service. Tara, on the other hand, exuded self-discipline and focus. She was a small, tight package, with piercing crystalline blue eyes and sandy blond hair streaked with platinum highlights. Her hair was pulled back into a bun held fast by two thin, brushed-steel bars crossing the back of her head. Her nose, jaw, and lips were defined by straight lines and clipped angles. Though both Krantz and Tara wore uniforms, hers was impeccably put together and fit her athletic body like nylon stretched over a jaguar. The small trident pin she wore next to the polished badge over her right breast was subtle evidence to her former career as an IT specialist for the Navy Seals. Her only nonofficial luxury item was a pair of Scandinavian-designed, mildly elevated taper-ing heels the color of matte nickel. Next to Krantz's disheveled casual grouchiness, she had the presence of a tightly wound spring.

Punctuating the relevant facts with several terse nods as she listened to Krantz review the details of the situation, Tara asked, "Have you looked at the touch map frequency plots?"

"I don't think so . . . guys?" Krantz paused. No answer. "Warstet, do you know?"

"Mmm, I don't think so. Detective Dezner, do you mean the keys that people pressed on the manual power core control panel?"

"Officer Warstet, I'm sure they pressed all the keys at some point. The relevant information is how often did they press the keys and what was the timing between the highest frequency keys. This will give us a sense of what are the most likely numbers, and then looking at the timing of the various numbers we may have clues to the order that they were entered. It takes more time to press the number one and follow that with the number nine than, say, the number two. All that information is somewhere. Whether it's in the system's central database or the power core's interface transit memory banks, it will be findable. Have you accessed the domestic database yet?"

Looking a little more red and sweaty, Warstet frowned slightly. "Uh . . . no, not yet, Detective Dezner."

"OK, let me take a look." Dezner then proceeded to interface with the red and orange bobble hanging from the panel. *"Acknowledge . . . Open additional portals . . . broadcast windows and interaction to St. Louis precinct and present company within ten-meter radius."* Several additional blue squares appeared before Tara and her colleagues. They could also now hear her voice in their heads as she issued commands and queries. *"Access domestic server and database. . . . Show utilities subfile . . . show support systems . . . route to power and maintenance . . . access hardware file . . . list hardware for powercore interface. . . . Please show numeric and visual display."*

All the officers watched the empty space in front of them as images of each of the components and their listed serial number and brand flashed by in azure shades. In complete silence they heard Tara say, *"No, advance,"* in their thoughts. As each part appeared and disappeared they all saw various recognizable and not so recognizable parts: Infinex external case serial number 01239Kxchrome. *"No, advance."* Bosenite graphic card. *"No, advance."* Illumin8 optical drive seria. *"No, advance."* A small numeric pad appeared in front of the team—Midas X9 touch pad serial number 140910. *"Stop."*

The ten number square keyboard part floated and slowly rotated. *"Call up function history . . . show history for past year . . . list number function ... present in bar graph histogram."* A graph appeared and there were ten bars; each column represented a digit between 0 and 9. Of the ten numbers, six had much taller bars: 2, 4, 5, 6, 9, and 0.

"Return to precinct server, limit random number generator to following numbers two, four, five, six, nine, and zero." Speaking out loud, which made a couple of the officers start, "That will reduce the brute force number generator by several orders of magnitude and save us thirty minutes," said Tara matter-of-factly. *"Show time plots for interval segments between specified numbers. Show time segments for intervals between key touches for selected numbers in series."*

The bar graph then appeared for the various number combinations. Numbers 4 and 5 had the shortest time between the entries, 70 milliseconds. The entry interval was longest for 2 and 9, 120 milliseconds. *"Return to precinct server. Enter probability clustering of numbers by maximum and minimum of time spacing between selected numeric entries. Enter these numeric restrictions to brute force number generator."* "Let's see how this works."

Numbers continued to flit by. Krantz shifted his weight every few seconds and couldn't seem to find a comfortable place for his hands. They went from crossing his arms across his chest, to his back pockets, to his front pockets, and then back to his chest.

After a few moments a new line appeared. Access code: 546029

"Looks like that's got it," Tara said dispassionately. "Let's go ahead and power up the door."

This is why Krantz both loved and hated working with Tara. She did her job efficiently and perfectly. The only problem was that it left him looking like a technically incompetent yahoo. At the moment, he would live with that feeling.

He again heard Tara's broadcasted thoughts. *"Access power core. Level ten. Main Devron Office. Access code five-four-six-zero-two-nine. Acknowledge. Power on."*

A soft white line slowly increased in brightness around the edges of the seamless metal surface. A brighter line then emerged and bisected the illuminated square. On each side of the vertical line were floating two blue function keys: Open and Close.

All the officers started to crowd near the door. A couple prepared their weapons. Another two opened duffel bags and pulled out first-aid gear. Another one had lifted and adjusted his forensic analysis equipment.

This part Krantz knew very, very well. "OK, let's get in a two-person stack. We don't know exactly what's happening on the other end. Warstet and Blevin, you two go to the front. As far as we know there are two people in there, one of whom is an eighty-year-old. Change your ammo to momentum impulse rounds with thirty-centimeter radius of distribution." Krantz wanted to make sure that if any shots were fired they would be nonlethal. The bullets could be programmed to explode prior to striking the target so that only the force of the overall momentum of the bullet was delivered to the target—the wider the radius the gentler the punch. He wanted to make no mistakes on this one.

All the men looked to their weapons. The virtual dials next to their thumbs all dialed in the requisite numbers.

"Is medic support online?" Krantz called out.

"We've got two ER docs logged in." Two emergency room physicians were seeing images projected from the visual cortex of the two officers with the medic equipment.

"OK, Tara, open the door."

What happened? Gerald thought. He had been cybertrekking in Bhutan, had gotten the flower, then things got hazy. *Did I pass out?* He was sitting on the floor of his greenhouse. The sunlight was coming through the windows, and he could see the plants all neatly aligned on the shelves. The rows of geraniums, roses, dwarf marigolds, and paper whites were all lined up in their orange ceramic pots as they always were. The breeze from the overhead ceiling fan caused the flower heads to sway slightly. He could smell the various earthy and floral scents. *But what happened?*

His fingers felt sticky. He looked down and saw a small amount of dirt underneath his fingernails and at the webbing between his knuckles. He couldn't seem to get it off. It felt as if there were sap stuck to his skin, like maple syrup. *Just a little bit of dirt—sticky though.*

In the quiet of the room the ground surged beneath him. It felt like he was on a bucking horse or a boat hitting a wave.

What's going on? Is this an earthquake? The tranquility of the room with its breezy well-organized plants began to flake and crumble. This intimate personal world he knew so well was becoming grainy and blurred. *What is that smell?* Spots of white and fuzz floated and pulsed in and out all around him. *God, what is going on?* The flakes and grains began to shift and coalesce. The fuzz became a blurry snowstorm, then a uniform field of white, then a flash, then horror.

There was dirt on the floor. Broken ceramic and fractured stems and petals were strewn everywhere. Gerald looked down. He heard himself begin to scream.

The large steel doors opened with a whispering hush as if someone were sliding their fingernails over silk. The two rows of officers stood facing the doors. They crowded closer to the entrance as the doors parted; when they were fully open, they moved in quickly. Krantz and Dezner stood to the side getting ready to assess the situation. Something smelled terrible. Once in, both vocal and mental voices reverberated through the team.

What the fuck?

One down. Assailant Devron. Facial features matched.

Terrible smell . . .

"Dr. Devron. On the ground! On the ground, NOW! If you do not comply we will use force. Mr. Devron . . ." The husky voice was Warstet's.

Krantz and Dezner quickly followed the back of the entering column. Warstet's rotund bulk was in the forefront obstructing a substantive portion of the center of the room. He appeared to be standing in front of the large expanse of the central office desk. His starched collar was a dull gray from sweat. The back of his neck was a deep heated pink. The officers next to him had formed a semicircle flanking the large man as they all stared down at the table surface; all were slightly bent, holding their weapons at a central point.

Krantz couldn't see a thing.

"DR. DEVRON. THIS IS YOUR LAST CHANCE." Warstet's voice had moved from raspy to booming and resolute. Krantz started pushing forward. *What the hell is going on?!* As he pushed deeper through the human curtain he saw a glimpse of a pale foot. A shoe was dangling off the big toe. All around the desk was a sticky congealed resin.

Blood, Krantz thought. *Plenty of it.*

As Krantz's gangly form pushed through the rigidly held bodies of his officers, the usual smells of perspiration and starched polyester gave way to something fetid and terrible. Krantz felt his mouth turn dry, the rise of acidic metallic syrup filled the back of his throat.

Warstet's voice was rising to a crescendo. Krantz knew that there were only a few more moments before the commanding nature of that voice resulted in physical clarification. *I don't care what this guy did, we simply cannot hurt him or there is going to be hell to pay.*

"Guys—wait, WAIT!" As he finally pushed through the perimeter it wasn't just the smell that struck him. The sight hit him like a mallet.

Oh Jesus, thought Krantz. Since his prosthetic was transmitting, that singular thought reverberated through the minds of his team.

Krantz's tension and rush gave way to a slack-faced disbelief. A large person was laid with its arms and legs spread far apart. He made that conclusion by the fact that he could identify the hands and feet. The rest was a mangled and tattered knot of ribbons. The slate gray table was awash with a mix of congealed crimson blood and some darker-colored heterogeneous materials that Krantz could only assume were intestinal contents.

His shocked stare was finally broken by the movement beyond the table. The officers around him bristled as they all changed their hand-held trajectory in unison. He heard the nervous rustle of cloth and subtle squeaks of men readjusting their sweaty grips.

In front of him was a man with his back to the group. Tattered, blood-stained clothes covered a pallid, thin body. His movements were those of a physics professor writing an equation on the chalk-board. Rigid shoulders and the slow continuous movements of his right arm had a certain purposeful intensity as if he were close to a solution. He was using his right index finger to trace a pattern several feet above him on the milky white surface of the wall. His left hand was held to his face. And instead of using chalk, he was finger paint-ing in crimson. As he looked around, the pattern covered the entire wall.

As his digital writing instrument started to release its last smeared remnants, the man slowed and turned around.

It's Devron.

His left hand was still held to his face. The man was sucking his thumb. His visage was otherwise completely blank and expression-less. Both hands and forearms were covered in blood and tissue. A small piece of yellowed fat hung limply from where it had gotten caught between his fingers. It swayed and jiggled from his fist beneath his nose as he began to walk away from the wall. His cheeks and chin were equally smeared due to the thumb sucking.

"STOP RIGHT THERE!" Warstet bellowed.

Devron, undeterred, moved with a stiff-legged gait and reached toward the gory heap. Still with his thumb in his mouth, he lurched toward the shredded body. His right hand reached out for the closest piece of flesh.

Warstet, now more subdued and sweating profusely, said, "Take aim . . ."

"Only one shooter, Frank," Krantz warned the big man.

Warstet nodded and the rest of the team dropped their aim a fraction of a centimeter.

All in the same moment, Warstet directed the barrel of the gun toward Devron, *Engage target—NOW,* and his thoughts initiated the trigger. Faster than was visible, a bullet emerged and exploded a foot away from the cadaveric target. A cloud of metallic dust hit Devron like a supersonic beach ball square in the chest. He dropped like a marionette whose strings had been abruptly cut.

The posture of the men straightened from their semistooped position. Medical staff from the rear moved through the line quickly. With deft movements, the assist officers were already stripping Devron of his clothes. The head medical officer, Smyth, rolled Devron over, straightened his limbs, and placed a sheer plastic wrap around his inert body.

Smyth called out, "Suspect immobilized and hemodynamically stable."

"Acknowledged." Krantz deactivated his neural transmitter and sighed. *Thank God,* he thought. Devron had been safely dealt with. Krantz knew that this was only the beginning of the show, but at least all of this had gone according to protocol. No publishable mishaps . . . yet. He could barely tolerate the smell. The intermingled stench of blood, visceral contents, and what must have been spilled cleaning fluids made him feel like he was trapped in a portolet.

Krantz began to walk around the table. He could feel the sticky squish of congealed blood beneath his feet. Beside him the officers were now all going into evidence-gathering mode. He could hear Tara issuing detailed coding and data-routing orders in her usual clipped and professional voice. The ones not attending to Devron and the body were all either filming the room or interrogating the thousands of cameras in the room.

What the fuck is all that graffiti about . . . Christ!

It was then that Krantz heard one of his men gasp.

"Holy shit! Victim not dead!" All heads turned to the table.

Krantz looked at the officer and the bloody heap, incredulous. *That must be her diaphragm.* He had only rudimentary anatomic knowledge from his forensics training—but those must be the muscles for breathing at the bottom of the rib cage. *They were moving! Jesus . . . she's still breathing.* This poor wretch must have endured the mutilation without the consolation of death.

Smyth went from Devron to the victim and scanned the body with a handheld sensor. Frowning, he waved his assistants over.

"Barely oxygenating, erratic pulse, EEG severely distorted— patient is getting ready to crump! Need to put 'er in stasis now while she can still inhale!" Smyth called out.

The assistant medic was pulling out a small yellow canister labeled "H2S." The top had a breathing mask attached to it and the young man quickly put the mask to the woman's mouth. They all watched as the woman went from an ashen and anemic white to a blotchy greenish tinge. Her diagram stopped moving and the blood seeping from her many wounds changed from a ruddy crimson to a deep purple. Krantz could smell the remnants of the hydrogen sulfide. It smelled like rotten eggs. He knew why it was called sewer gas. He also knew its necessity. It was a last-ditch effort to stop all active metabolism.

Holding his sensor, Smyth tapped his assistant on the shoulder. "Metabolic suppression complete. Patient is now in suspended animation. Let's get her wrapped up." The other medics, with meticulous plastic-covered hands, repositioned the victim's viscera on top of her and began to wrap the same sheer material around her as they did with Devron. Obese and eviscerated, the procedure wasn't graceful or efficient. To Krantz, it looked like they were making a burrito out of a pasta dish. He felt nauseous.

Eyes closed, the minister felt the wet cloth on his forehead. The white-haired man reclined in his dressing room chair.

"My, you are just covered in sweat." His assistant had a soft Southern twang. He felt the woman's hand continue to pat his forehead and face. His mouth was dry and his skin itched. As her hands began to move toward the prosthetic implant in his temple he stopped her.

"Child, get me some water." Elymas thought he might have to vomit. He opened his eyes to see the pale gaunt face of his assistant, Crystal. Nodding with vigor, she turned to go to the other side of the room. As she walked to the minibar, he watched her thin frame. She had a certain malnourished trailer-trash quality. He liked that. Even in the white and gold uniform, he saw that she was a dirty sinner down deep. One of those lost girls that grows up in the squalor of some little shit town.

His hands were shaky as he took the glass of water. "Thank you, child. You are a blessing indeed." Elymas gulped the water down. It swished in his belly uncomfortably. "Yes, you are quite a miracle to me." He put his hand on the small of her back.

Crystal tucked a tuft of thin brown hair behind her ear and looked at the ground. She stood still and quiet. He let his hand slide down further to the small curvature of her buttocks.

In that still moment dark patches began to spread on the ground as if somebody had just spilled ink. *No, not this soon,* he thought to himself.

The black edges seeped through the substance of floor and encircled the legs of the furniture.

Elymas pulled his hand away from his assistant. His hand was shaking badly now. *I had some just last evening,* he thought. *The withdrawal shouldn't be happening this quick. Not yet.*

"Are you alright, Reverend, you look more than tired."

"Yes, child, yes, I'm fine. Maybe bring me a glass of the Southern Comfort."

"BrentBrentBrent! Oh Brent, how did this happen?" His voice was hoarse, high-pitched, and hysterical. Gerald barely recognized his partner. He was sitting on top of his chest. He quickly rolled off of him, eyes fixed on the face that he once knew. Flaps of flesh hung from gaping holes in his cheeks. Spatters and splashes of blood were all around mixing with the dirt and broken flower parts like a Jackson Pollock painting. *What happened to his eyes? Oh no, oh no, please, Brent, no!* The hazel eyes he had once known were now replaced with ragged black holes surrounded by crimson starbursts. Rivulets of blood poured down either side of his temples to pool in the back of his ears.

Brent's skin was the color of sallow butter. He choked out a gasp. The sound emerged from the multiple openings in his cheeks.

"Oh no, we need help, oh Brent. HELP . . . somebody!" Gerald was incoherent with horror and grief. The terrible sound of Brent's tortured gurgling vocalizations was too much. He didn't know what to do. He reached to touch his mangled cheeks. His hands were tightly balled fists covered in blood to the elbows.

"What the . . . ?"

With forcible effort he opened his hands in front of him. Two blood-stained orbs fell from his palms to roll off Brent's neck and stick to the floor. The hazel iris and dilated pupil pointed eccentrically toward the ground. The other only revealed a stringy red stump. The face with the empty socket began to shake its head. He was mouthing words—NO NO NO—through breathless gasps choked from pain. Hissing air moved through the gaps in his cheeks.

Gerald could not speak. Had he done this? He couldn't even articulate the question.

Farther beyond Brent's head were a pair of shears encrusted with congealed blood and caked dirt. Gerald leaned forward to pick them up. He leaned closer to his partner, which elicited more rapid desperate pants. *This wasn't me. It wasn't. I wouldn't do this. Never, never, never!*

He looked between Brent and the gore-coated scissors. He held the gardening instrument pinched between his thumb and index finger away from him as if he were holding the wings of an angry wasp. He tried to throw it away. It stayed in his hand like a piece of flypaper. His knuckles were white with the pressure being applied to maintain the shears within his grip. He flicked and whipped his arm without effect.

His limbs began to move slower and slower, his arms felt thick and heavy like bags of wet sand. His hand rolled the scissors into his palm and formed a tight-balled fist. Holding the scissors in front of him his arm became a solid statue. He was paralyzed. For a moment he sat there immobile.

He watched the hand open and close the scissors. *I can't control it.* His gaze turned down toward Brent. His head and eyes moved without his direction. He was wet with perspiration. His body was not his own. He was a passive observer.

His other hand reached and pulled Brent's upper lip away from his teeth making a triangle of taut flesh. The rapid panting breaths were coming out in tense rapid whistles.

NO!

The scissors cut away the upper lip revealing an even row of white teeth. Hoarse convulsive throaty screeches tore though Gerald's mind.

Amidst gurgling rasps, Gerald's mind screamed and screamed, silent and incoherent to the surrounding greenhouse. The ruddy fingers he saw now pulled on the lower lip.

White spots again appeared. His sight began to fragment and shift. The colors were rapidly disappearing into a bright field of white. Then again a flash of light.

Before him was the neat and ordered greenhouse from moments ago. He held a blue poppy in his left hand. Was it his hand?

The shears were in his other hand—still, clean, and polished.

What just happened? Was that a hallucination? That wasn't real.

Like a fresh wound being opened, he watched his hand clip a petal off the blue flower. The slight semilucent petal fell to the floor in small half arcs.

I didn't do that! WHAT—THE—FUCK—IS—GOING—ON?!

Raspy throaty shrieks, agony, the screams grew more intense and raw. Less human. Gasping. Desperate. He couldn't stop the hands.

Stop! Stop, goddammit!

With artful and direct movements, they clipped and pruned petal after petal, scream after scream.

"The victim is Jasmina Zlotan. She's eighty, a Bosnian immigrant, and has been working for Devron for the past forty-two years." Tara was now standing next to Krantz. She handed him a moist towelette.

"On a first pass, hard to demonstrate any romantic connection or crime of passion. In terms of compiled data from the domestic database the only places they overlapped in location were the office—infrequently—and occasionally the high-transit zones such as the main entryway, hallways, et cetera; hard to demonstrate any objective evidence that would incline them to be connected beyond semipersonal working relationship. Unclear at this point if she had some information and was blackmailing him for some reason, but then why wait forty years? Also, given her level of education that seems unlikely."

Still looking at the lurid markings on the wall in mute silence, Edwin Krantz wiped his hands and let the totality of the event register consciously and unconsciously. He let it sink it. The mangled corpse, the blood on the floor, the strange markings on the walls, Tara's words, the trillionaire perp. . . . Rather than take pictures, movies, and samples he tried to get a gestalt of the crime scene. It was what he was best at. He was getting a feel for what happened.

Krantz could sense Tara's eyes on him. After the last several years she had come to know these prolonged silences well. He had a way of looking into a crime scene that always surprised her (whether she admitted it or not). In the end she always appreciated his input and would usually goad it out of him. This usually emerged after several minutes of sighing and scratching the back of his head. Leaning on one foot with her head cocked slightly to the side, her arms folded in front of her, she waited.

"This isn't a crime of passion. It's too ordered. The way he filleted her, the markings on the wall, her position on the table; almost like some religious ritual. The only problem is the motive doesn't make any sense. This is Devron. The trillionaire scientist—he's eighty-three! I am surprised he could even physically accomplish this. Also, this is not some dumb-dumb who is going to fall prey to delusional religious or fanatical ideas. He's a despot and a control freak. We can see that in the way he built his company and estate. When those types of folks kill people it's because they've lost control or they overplan the act leading to them revealing their deeds. This is neither of those. It's too messy to be planned and too ordered to be spontaneous. There's something sadistic about it. There's more to it. . . . Maybe Devron had a hidden life we're not aware of. Is there anything on the biological side so far—meds, drugs, psych, from his medical records—that could give us a clue?"

"I'm working on that now." Unseen to all but Tara, bluish fields, folders, and screens materialized, flitted about, and disappeared throughout the room. A remnant of her past as a Special Ops field analyst, she could move through information like an adrenalin-hopped whirling dervish. In the past, whether it was the urban slums of a sprawling ghetto or an anonymous beach at night, she could parallel process data while managing the real world with the grace of a gymnast. As Tara shifted her attention from one record to the next, the files would shift and change in intensity. Fields of data would pop up, adjoin other portals, and vanish in rapid sequence. Past medical histories, hospital admissions, significant medical reporting, lay press reports, corporate records, gossip blogs, all emerged, became cross-referenced, and disappeared in moments. Relevant texts, images, and data numbers were all compiled in a more static box to the right of Krantz's head.

"So far everything is looking reasonably mundane—a broken bone, a cut, and a mole removal, but nothing to make him crazy."

"Any previous legal stuff?" asked Krantz. The team around Edwin and Tara were moving to the various tasks of imaging, swabbing, sampling, and downloading, so that all the information at the scene could be completely and reliably re-created. The two detectives were the only still figures in the room.

"From a legal perspective more data here." Files were flying, emerging, merging, and disappearing at a dizzying rate. The only evidence to the fact was the rapid movement of Tara's eyes and the slight twitching of her head. It was as if she were watching a tennis match at high speed. "Still mostly corporate in content, a divorce forty years ago, standard in division of assets, nothing material in nature."

The two wrapped figures were now being moved out on the trauma gurneys. Half the team was leaving with them; the remainder was continuing to gather data. The movement of the people led to drafts that stirred the smells of blood, shit, cleaning fluid, and sulfur into an unpleasant melange. The effect prevented Krantz from ever attenuating himself to the awful odors. His mild nausea was growing to a more robust desire to vomit. He could feel sweat bead on his forehead. He had seen and smelled enough. Tara seemed unfazed.

"Tara, let's get going."

They exited the room and once again were walking along the edge of a virtual precipice. The two stretchers, one with a large payload, the other small, began to disappear in front of them along the curving walkway. The chief medic turned to the two detectives. "We've got clearance to go directly to Trauma Bay One at Barnes Hospital. ETA fifteen minutes. Ambulance is waiting upstairs."

"Sounds good." Krantz let out a sigh. "So who else knows anything about Devron's personal life?"

"His second wife is deceased—auto accident. His only son is handicapped, brain injured from same accident. Lives here. Twelfth floor. Former wife has been living in Vienna for over twenty years. Otherwise, he has a brother living in Shanghai; also somewhat reclusive, not married, no children. That is the immediate family."

"Friends?"

"Harder to say. I'll need to investigate a little more on that. There's a lot of professional associations, but hard to infer personal content." All the while as Tara walked and talked an array of images and blue panels flitted and circled in front of her gaze. News segments, editorials, photo ops, blogs, travel records, and donation schedules all vied for Tara's attention as she cross-referenced, searched, and sorted. The ongoing data never deterred the direction and pace of the quick clicking staccato of her metal heels as she walked next to Edwin Krantz.

This was all invisible to Krantz, now lost in thought; the only things he was registering were snippets of his partner's voice. He heard the abrupt and bulleted verbs and nouns all juxtaposed in a linear and ordered fashion. He could imagine that if his conversations with her were ever put into a script that her dialogue would be an outline. No prose, just facts.

As they emerged from the Devron entrance, Krantz was still clammy from his bout of nausea. On the open pavilion he felt the dry, scented breeze waft against him. The manicured air dried the sticky beads of sweat on his forehead. The trace cooling was small solace from the previous events. Despite the grandiose views of mountains and skyscraper tops below, he still felt like he had just emerged from a big dark hole.

"Alright, I'll see you at Barnes. I'm going to stop by headquarters to head off the media. I'll be there in about thirty minutes."

"Very good. I may stop at the precinct as well. See you shortly, Edwin."

Krantz ambled over to his car. As he settled himself into the seat, the induced screens and dials came into his vision—multiple sapphire-colored affairs all indicating various levels of idle. The same familiar voice welcomed him. *"Hello, Detective Krantz, destination please."*

"Precinct headquarters."

"Acknowledged. Destination and access set."

Krantz closed his eyes and leaned the back of his head against the headrest. His mind was swirling with the images from a hundred feet below. Anxiety gnawed at the edges of him. *This one doesn't make sense.* As he began to rub his eyelids, he jerked his hand away from the residual shit scent. Looking at his fingers he saw some traces of reddish brown beneath the fingernails of his middle and index finger. On the periphery of his vision he saw Tara approaching her Cog-cycle. *Still fucking alive,* he thought. He closed his eyes again.

Eventually he opened his eyes, pulled his head away from the head-rest, grabbed the arcane anachronism of a wheel, and initiated the engine. The car slowly pulled away along the white gravel path and headed toward the road.

As Tara walked out across the expanse of white marble she looked at the carefully manicured patterns of gravel in the Japanese gardens. To her they looked like aerial views of the curved cornfields of her childhood. For a moment, the memories of walking along those fields distracted her.

She remembered walking along the small hills and valleys of tilled earth. When she was five, each row had to be climbed and descended. Each its own individual challenge, with cut cornstalks that stuck out at every angle, jagged and menacing. She would always be following her father, who would step from row top to row top like a giant.

"Come on Tara, keep up," he would call. She remembered seeing the back of his broad shoulders recede ahead of her. He didn't wait. She had to scramble and shuffle behind him to keep up. She remembered how her hands would always get scratched and scraped from the cornhusks and would be covered in dirt. One day she had been wearing a dress. A dress she liked because of the way the ribbons would flutter in the wind.

Rushing forward, the hem had gotten caught by the barbed finger of a cornstalk. Hands spread apart and clumsy, like only small children's are, she had slid and tumbled forward. How her knees had hurt, stinging and burning, she had looked down to see them both bleeding with a piece of skin hanging away that had terrified her.

"Come on, Tara, let's go, got work to do." To Tara he was almost an impossible distance away. Her legs felt shaky and she didn't know what to do.

"Daddy! Pick me up, come get me!" When he turned around, he had looked at her, irritated. "Daddy, PLEASE!" He saw her with wide eyes and blond hair that was a mess with corn leaves and twigs.

"Girl, ain't nobody gonna carry you. Gotta carry yourself, now COME ON." He turned and continued to lumber forward in long strides. More anxious and afraid at his disapproval, she scrambled forward.

Hated those fields, she thought to herself, irritated by the distraction and reverie. She directed her attention to her cycle.

"*Open.*" The polished crimson metal of her cycle's central casing opened like the fingers of a large robotic hand.

Climbing in, she enclosed herself in steel and drove off.

Trent felt hands on his shoulders as he watched his father being wheeled out toward the ambulance. He was covered in a white sheet below his neck. He could see pulsating lights beneath. His face was ashen beneath rust-colored smears. The movement of the gurney, the gestures of the paramedics, the voices, the people, the house staff, all seemed to be moving to a scripted slow motion.

He felt a deep déjà vu. He had seen these sensory reels before. Only that time the sheet had been black.

That time it had been my mother. He saw the Web postings of on-lookers. *The sheet had covered her face, covered everything except the feet.* He had seen her shiny, black leather shoes in the pictures. They were still on when they had loaded her into the ambulance. He had viewed that scene through so many eyes, except his own. He had been in a coma then—far away in a darker place.

The leviathan of repressed memories circled closer to his consciousness. He felt its presence from the undulating waves of fear and anxiety. His body was shaking.

He tried to move closer to his father. To see him, to touch him. He didn't want to be absent. *Not like last time.* Hands held him fast. Words that sounded slow and baritone bounced off of him. "Not a good time, Trent." "They need to get him to hospital." "It will be OK."

He was powerless to move past the fence of fingers holding him. The memories were returning. The dorsal fin of his past was cresting through the water. He thought about the morning, the sands . . . he thought about his mother's death, and the guilt approached fast and terrible.

No, I can't answer that . . .

No, I cannot make a comment . . .

Yes, we are looking into all possibilities. We will keep you apprised of more definitive information when we have it . . .

No, as I told you we cannot answer that. Krantz still felt mildly sick.

Here it comes. His precinct access was spinning incessantly, white ball after white ball came into his field of view. Like shooting skeet, he had to disregard them one after the next. When he sat at his desk the public had access to his brain. It made him crazy.

He was losing his focus on all the questions coming at him. They were the usual stuff he couldn't answer. He continued to mumble polite negatives. This one he had to take, it was the *St. Louis Post-Dispatch*. The chief had warned him that he should "appear cooperative."

He felt a mild throbbing behind his eyes. As he rubbed the bridge of his nose, he jerked his fingers away, and he slowly sniffed them. *Do I still have that smell of shit on my fingers? I washed them twice already.* That smell stuck to him even still. It seemed to be lingering just beneath the comfortable mélange of coffee, cigarettes, and old newspapers, which defined his office. The smell of shit and mucous and piss and mouthwash all at once; like having the floor of a dirty bar and the worst hospital smell, all rolled up in one.

He wiped at his hands with a saniwipe once again. It didn't seem to help settle his stomach or make the memory of what should have been a boring Saturday morning any more palatable. He wished he were back cutting the grass. It was his one solace. He enjoyed the single-mindedness of the task and immediate gratification he got with its completion. He liked the straight lines—parallel and neat. He had always done the yard work with April, his wife. She always raised irises and ferns. Since she died, he couldn't maintain the plants, but at least he could still keep the lawn tidy.

The drone of the nasally voice continued in his head. He barely acknowledged it. He picked up the picture of his wife, the image beginning to yellow. He liked it more for that. She was wearing a green sun hat. Her mouth was opened in an O of surprise with a muddy streak crossing her cheek. He remembered that she had been pulling a root up and it had suddenly given way. He loved the solidity of that picture. Even with its faded colors it meant so much more to him. It aged like they had aged.

That was the way she was, he thought. *Laughing with the surprises of life.* She always handled the flowers and he mowed the lawn.

"Excuse me, what was that, Detective Krantz?"

"Uh, nothing, sorry, I got distracted for a moment," the detective sputtered out loud. Krantz was terrible at separating his overt communications from his internal dialogues. The technology was becoming too much for him. He felt overcommunicated and overstimulated. Yet the world was becoming a less personal place; it was becoming harder and harder to understand people, harder to do his job.

He had been a detective for close to three decades. He *knew* people—it was how he figured the cases out. Through his years he had seen all sorts of brutality.

As he continued to mumble non sequiturs to the reporter, he shook his head in consternation. He didn't understand this case. Most crimes were motivated by the usual, baser human elements—anger, rage, jealousy, pride, and ignorance. Most often it was the poor and the desperate doing things that led to the predictable endpoints of rape and murder. The behavior was degenerate and despicable, yet unsurprising. In each of these events he would see the years of poverty, abuse, and marginalization make themselves manifest in an act that was some terrible need to either assert power or achieve some trivial gain. Whether it was for sex, money, or ego, it led to a traceable path that allowed him to sort the case and move on. This, though . . . this was different. It didn't fit into his usual boxes of drug lord shorted on a deal, abused child—now father—exacting irrational retribution on his wife, or even the occasional sociopath acting out his or her sick yet internally consistent fantasies.

This . . . this doesn't make any sense. The detective reached for a cup of coffee. The cup chattered against the worn wooden tabletop as he tried to place it next to him. He looked at his hand to assess its shakiness, almost disbelieving that he could be rattled by the morning's events.

"God, maybe the job is finally getting to me."

"Excuse me, Detective, can I quote you on that?"

The forced calm of the experimental exchange was punctured as a sign emerged in Hagan's view—*"Entry requested."* He continued to sort the files he planned to download for Omid, fully intending to ignore the disruption.

Disregard, he projected. After a moment the sign reappeared. Hagan dismissed it, and it again appeared. The image began to blink with the ongoing tug of war.

Hagan sighed. *This would need to be dealt with.* His irritation mounted as he thought about the unending interruptions—*Canter, my wife, Devron, now this.*

He walked deliberately to the door, his movements clipped and precise. A neurosurgeon to his core, he tried never to lose control. His displeasure was only visible by the slight flexing of his jaw muscles. The floating touch key before his door had a minus sign in its center. He focused his attention on the floating tab and it converted to a plus sign and the door clicked open.

The man standing in front of him was his chief resident, Reid Vestin. Exaggerated breaths and perspiration on his ruddy face revealed he had just stopped running. Knowing Reid, this was unusual. He was Hagan's best trainee. He had an oval face, small brown eyes, and tightly cut hair revealing the last remnant of a receding hairline. He had a lean, slight frame and a subdued demeanor, and Hagan had always known him to be unflappable. As he stood at the door in his OR garb of matte blue, Reid appeared anything but that. Reid was virtually hopping from foot to foot like a child badly needing to pee.

"Reid . . . what's going on?" said Hagan, incredulous at his resident's behavior.

"It's Devron. He's in the ER!"

"What?"

"Marcus Devron. He's in the ER, you NEED to come down NOW, there are cops everywhere!"

"OK. What happened?"

"He's covered in blood, not entirely clear, but you REALLY need to come now!"

"I just talked to him this morning—he was fine. You sure it's Devron?

"Yes—Canter's there, the dean, even the chancellor—they're all asking for you."

"OK. OK. Let's go. Explain what you do know as we walk down there." Reid's alarm was becoming a little infectious. Also, as the Devron Professor of Clinical Neuroprosthetics, he knew that whenever Marcus Devron hiccupped he had better be available. It went with the title.

Hagan turned to leave his laboratory.

"Dr. Maerici?" Hagan realized he was leaving Omid mid session. He looked at the luminescent blue boy sitting lotus style on the steely table and replied, *"We're going to be concluding early for today."*

In the same unblinking and detached expression Omid looked to Hagan. *"Have I advanced in age, Dr. Maerici?"* His voice unchanged and dispassionate.

"Not today, Omid. Power down."

"Unfortunate. Acknowledged." The boy closed his eyes and bowed his head. The neon blue features of the room—its dynamic charts, neuroantomic figures, and seated child—winked out of existence, leaving only the steely room and the white noise of lights and hidden computers remaining.

"Alright, Reid, let's go."

Tara drove faster than she needed to. Heading from the precinct, the lines of the road flickered beneath her and the world slid by in a liquid blur as she tilted and beveled her path though the traffic toward Barnes Hospital.

Need to see what Devron's medical status is. The images of the morning filled her mind as she began to organize her thoughts.

Something fishy here. Not buying that he is sick.

Need to get more data on Devron and his maid's relationship.

There must be more there.

Even if peripheral, need to get a bead on motive.

Method, also, unusual.

This guy is intelligent—was it strategic? Going for insanity right off the bat? Again need to find motive to establish intent.

Her thoughts marched on, bulleted and deliberate, as she mapped out her next steps for the case. As she barreled down the road, she saw something in the periphery of her vision that caused her cycle to slow for a few moments.

SALE—NEIMEN MARCUS—60% OFF—August 3rd through 5th. Holograms floated next to the road. A thin woman with sunglasses looked away with an arched back and a tight-fitting blue dress. Shimmering lines moved over her body. Behind her long grasses on a beach fluctuated to a virtual wind.

Ashamed and sheepish, Tara noted the dates. She knew that the shopping booths around her living unit now had Neiman access. She thought about how she could pick up some clothes privately and close to home.

Stop being such a girl, Tara. Mildly irritated with herself, she thought about all of her purchases. To her, it was a hidden and secret pleasure; she loved buying dresses. Sheer and loose-fitting sundresses that fluttered and shimmered with spring colors—lemon yellows, oranges, and light greens the color of snap peas. Trim and elegant evening gowns that flowed over her thin frame like opal ice flows. Cocktail dresses simple and short, which she had bought in classic black, red, and white. With each she would indulge in the shoes. They would frame and elevate her feet with leather and sparkle. She would buy them, try them on, and look at herself in the mirror. Turning back and forth she would put her hands to her waist, and then to her sides. Some dresses would reveal her legs, others would only highlight her ankles. She would run her hand over the hems, the straps, she would feel and caress the silk, the merino, the satin, the beaded embroidery; in those moments she would lose herself in girliness.

Even this morning she had been trying them on when the precinct had called. After looking at every angle, she would then take the dress off and put it with its many other counterparts in the closet, hidden and cloistered. This morning she then put on her slacks and starched shirt and returned to the real world.

C'mon, Tara, the case, focus on the case. Admonishing herself, she accelerated her Cog-cycle a bit more. *August third through fifth.* A smaller, quieter voice made sure she would remember the dates.

It didn't take. The words echoed in Hagan's mind. They inserted themselves as he tried to listen to his chief resident. *It didn't take.*

The two physicians walked down the seamless white hallway. The ceiling was suffused with a sourceless soft white light. Ahead of and behind the doctors, a band of trace bluish light encircled them along the hallway. The dynamic ultraviolet beam made Hagan's and Reid's collars and buttons glow a subtle indigo. These same bands followed everyone in the hallway such that the lines in the ceiling would cross, merge, and divide, creating a halo of sterilization around each and every pedestrian. The lines on the floor always reminded Hagan of water. They looked like light reflected and refracted from a swimming pool at night; ripples of waves bouncing and bending the light in regular ways that would contort and alter with the encounter of another wave. Today they made him think of amniotic fluid. Of a pregnancy that was lost.

Hagan walked with a steady and unhurried stride. Reid was next to him, walking sideways, trying to provide all the information he had. His head would bob slightly in conjunction with the chopping movements of his hand as he would emphasize his points. But Hagan's mind was elsewhere. He tried to focus but couldn't—*it didn't take.* The previous day, the evening, and this morning continued to push their way into his consciousness. Like grapples dredging a polluted lake, the recollection brought other more toxic memories and thoughts. His work, his personal life—*it didn't take.*

An amalgam of scenes flashed in his mind as the three-word mantra seemed to run on a continuous loop. He saw his wife's face as he confronted her for her infidelity. The same defeated look—a visage of remorse, guilt, and, worst of all, loneliness. She had seemed so broken and pathetic. With her hands clutched around her elbows, knuckles white as if she were trying to physically hold herself together, she had simply nodded. "I've been so alone, I feel like I don't exist—like a shadow. I just needed some connection, but now it's worse . . ."

The signs had all been there. Communication that was at best concrete—"Honey, it looks like the car needs an upgrade." "Honey, I made an appointment to the dentist." All trivial exchanges that covered a deeper silence. The lack of physical intimacy. The unaccounted moments of absence that, when evaluated in retrospect, seemed patently strange, but under the pressure of work and life went unnoticed. Finally, the friends—whispering and awkward.

They had known for a while. He remembered his friend Chad finally telling him the truth. They had seen her with another man. They appeared intimate. It wasn't the first time.

It was the same amalgam of emotion—guilt, anger, sadness, and confusion. He remembered telling her to leave but not wanting her to go. The humiliation to his pride. His own loneliness. The awareness that he had contributed to the problem. The anger at her lack of support and her betrayal. The anxiety and the subsequent distraction from his work. It all had all boiled inside a stony exterior as he watched her walk out the door in silence.

They had tried to fix things. The child was supposed to be a new start. He had made promises to be more attentive, to make the relationship a priority. *It didn't take.* Those words spoke so true for so many things.

He wanted to go home, he wanted to make it better if he could. But it was Devron—that had to be addressed. The pull of duty held him fast. He continued down the hallway overtly calm and resolute.

Hagan was still trying to process everything that his chief resident was attempting to tell him. Reid was usually organized and concise in his presentations; this one, though, was a jumble of details. "Marcus Devron was in the ER. Possible brain damage. Murder suspect." *(Who exactly are we seeing—Devron, victim, or both?)* "Not a stroke, trauma, or tumor." *(Devron or the victim?)* "Canter, the dean, and the chancellor are all there. Kidney failure and myoglobinuria. Cops everywhere. Lawyers everywhere. All milling around. Wasn't allowed near the patient."

As the two walked, Dr. Maerici's entourage of interns and medical students began to coalesce and follow. The students distinguished themselves by their short white coats and overstuffed pockets. The gaggle assembled behind the swiftly moving pair. They were speaking with low voices and whispers.

Reid looked to the assortment of students and residents. Leaning his head slightly toward Maerici and talking out of the side of his mouth, Reid gave a curt head jerk toward the group behind them. "We probably need to dismiss the team, sir."

Hagan's mind was still in a fog. The only solution that came to mind, when he was tired or emotionally distressed, was to stick to protocol—to do it the way he had been taught. "Are we going to see a patient, Reid?"

"Yes, sir." *Reid is always so formal.*

"Well, we both know what happens to the VIPs, right?"

In a gravelly whisper, lower now, "This is *Marcus Devron*. I think he broke the law. There are cops *everywhere*! Something tells me the cops and Dr. Canter are not inclined to make this a teaching experience."

"Let me ask you again, Reid, are we going to see a patient?" There was the slightest hint of steel in his voice now.

"Yes . . . yes, we're seeing a patient, Dr. Maerici."

Hagan knew that special treatment of patients always spelled disaster. Changing the normal routine always led to mistakes. Especially in his current state, he was not going to improvise.

"Well, let's get the team together then. We're about to start rounds with a consult." His voice carried to interns and medical students. Having some resolution, the students and residents fished through various pockets and hangings-on to ready themselves. Hagan picked up his pace. Settled on the issue, Reid followed closely behind.

In a more personable tone, Hagan looked over to his chief resident. "Alright, let's go over this again. So how did Devron present . . ."

"Leth me in, goddammith . . ."

"Sorry, Mr. Devron. Your father is under guard and being seen by the doctors. You'll be able to talk to him soon." Officer Goldwin stood outside the imaging suite, looking down at the handicapped son of the richest man in the world. He spoke his words slowly and carefully. He was completely uncomfortable. Slightly flushed, the bald hook-nosed man kept tilting his head from one side to the other as if his collar was too tight.

Nothing good is going to come of this, he thought.

"That's my dad in there. Why can't I see him?" Trent Devron, a sad and misshapen creature, stood in front of the officer who was blocking the door. He continued to shuffle toward the officer. Seeing that Trent was obviously not a physical threat, Goldwin continued to back closer to the door.

"You gotta let me in!" Heavy with emotion, Trent's words became more garbled

"Mr. Devron . . . I . . . can . . . not . . . let . . . you . . . in . . . those are ORDERS." Goldwin spoke with a raised monotone voice, clearly enunciating each word as if he were speaking to somebody hard of hearing.

"I'm not a fuckin' retard, you asshole." Trent Devron's small frame was quivering with anger. His head was rocking so hard that the pooling spit in his mouth was dripping onto the front of his sweatshirt. He continued to move forward. Goldwin was now touching the door; he stood silent and completely miserable as an inert barrier to the young man. They now stood inches apart in stalemate.

Dr. Maerici knew the boy the moment he rounded the corner. He had spent over a decade putting him back together.

"Hello, Trent."

The young man straightened slightly. He turned slowly on his left leg, pulling the other leg along stiffly.

"He won't let me see my dad, Dr. Maerici." His already reddened eyes were beginning to well up with tears. His t's and s's were lisped to th's, making Hagan's name sound like Maoreethee.

Hagan nodded to the officer. Goldwin sighed in relief. "Are you Dr. Maerici? They're waiting for you inside."

"Trent, we're going to go take a look at your dad. I'll come and talk to you afterwards. OK?"

"Why can't I go? . . . He's my dad! What's going on?"

"I know he is, Trent, but I don't have all the answers right now. Let me see him and get a better sense of what's going on, and then I'll come talk to you. OK?"

The shoulders of the diminutive man shrugged or maybe just drooped a bit. "OK."

Hagan walked forward with Reid closely in tow. Goldwin, looking more wretched than ever, held his hand up and said, "Only you, Dr. Maerici, only you, sorry . . . uh yeah . . ." His voice trailed off into a sigh.

The trace of steel in Hagan's voice moments ago was now pure metal. "Officer," with a pause he looked to his badge, "Officer Goldwin, this is *my* surgical team. If you don't want *us* to see Mr. Devron, then *we* will be leaving. Have your captain, or whoever, give *us* a call when you think *we* should return. I'll be in my office!"

Goldwin was now disconsolate. Things had gone from bad to worse. First the kid, now the doctor. *Shit.* The officer finally nodded his head and opened the door.

Inside was a loud and raucous melee of people. For Maerici, this was not the usual calm imaging suite. Typically, the polished black glass controls were punctuated by holographic displayers that extended like square fish tanks from the floor to the ceiling. The room had the ascetic calm of a private aquarium. The holograms were now obscured by a multitude of people milling around and bickering.

They ranged from officers with green and gray uniforms, men in suits (both expensive and cheap), and various uniformed hospital personnel. Many were arguing. Others, mostly the officers, were fixedly looking through the window on the other side of the room, to the room where the imaged subject was kept.

Maerici approached with slow and purposeful steps into the fray. Reid was close behind. The medical students and interns, now nervous and hesitant, followed. As Hagan and his team approached, their coats stood out like white sails in a turbulent storm.

Their presence, first noted on the periphery, led to a shift of attention and a rapid sweep of silence as all heads turned toward Professor Maerici. They all knew who he was. As the quiet finally swept to the other side of the room, the initial lull was fractured by a voice behind the glowing white square column.

"Hagan, thank God you're here." A tall man stepped out and approached.

"Simon." Hagan nodded to his chairman. His suit was of an impeccable slate-colored silk. The finely lined vertical pinstripes and vermillion tie all were unperturbed by the ambient discord of the scene. His face, however, and the sweat on his palm when he shook Hagan's hand revealed a different story.

"It seems we have a very charged situation here, Hagan. This will require your utmost efforts and discretion." Looking past Maerici, "Given the magnitude of this situation it would probably be better if this involved only you."

Looking down, Hagan let out a deep sigh. *Third time's a charm,* he thought sardonically. Behind him Reid was attending closely to a loose thread protruding from his coat, while the remainder of the team seemed to be looking everywhere but toward the conversation they were eavesdropping on.

"I need my team to perform the job you wish me to perform." Hagan's voice was flat.

"Very well then, the residents should do. Don't you think that should be sufficient, Hagan?" The slight edge to Canter's voice made Hagan aware that the question was nothing short of a command. He smiled at Hagan with capped teeth that looked like a row of polished white tombstones.

Nodding his head, "I suppose so. Shall we proceed?"

Back to his golfing demeanor, "Of course, well, let's then."

Hagan turned to his team. "Folks, the university feels this may not be the best setting for medical students. Could you please excuse us?" Hagan turned to Reid and the other interns and residents in the blue coats of their status. "Reid, Jonathan, Farhan, you three can stay." The trio nodded curtly.

Hagan, his residents, and his chairman then proceeded to the center of the discord toward the square glowing column. As they approached, they were accosted by multiple people, also in very expensive suits.

"Dr. Canter, Dr. Maerici, we represent Dr. Devron's interests and would like you to sign some confidentiality agreements in regards to the medical aspects of Dr. Devron, whatever they may be."

In politically pleasant tones Canter held up his hand. "I don't think that will be necessary; all physicians and university staff members are bound by the Health Insurance Portability and Accountability Act requirements to maintain patient confidentiality. Anything further would serve no purpose. Our university general counsel is here to help you understand these issues." In a curt gesture, he swept his hand to the side to direct their attention to another well-dressed man.

"Randal, could you speak with these gentlemen?" The lawyers now spun off to wrangle with each other.

The group of physicians then moved their way toward the glowing column. As they approached, the arguing suits gave way to quiet navy uniforms. Officers encircled the holographic display and stared out the window at the back of the room. Casually dressed imaging techs were manning various control panels; they moved in and around the officers like diligent ants circumventing cross-armed blue statues. Once in proximity, the team was able to see the glass pillar. Within the ambient white hue floated the bust of an elderly man. His external surface was nearly transparent. It was only visible enough to appreciate the sense of an outline. Beneath the skin-toned translucent surface were the more prominent hints of blue and red scalp vessels, each expanding and contracting with a synchronous rhythm. Still deeper, the whitish suggestion of the skull was obvious. One could see the individual's eyeballs set within the black recesses of the eye sockets. Each ivory orb had a collar of light, glassy crimson bands of muscle, which induced random movements of the eyes as the subject occasionally shifted gaze and blinked gossamer eyelids. The whitish orbits tapered to the pearly optic nerves tucked within a fold of the most prominent and opaque portion of the hologram—the brain. It looked like a wrinkled beige cauliflower, in the shape of a balled fist. There were two very prominent folds; one between the thumb and index finger, and the other at a right angle pointing up toward the apex. Draped over the surface was a fine filigree of webbed, pulsating red and violet arteries and veins; these were brighter and more prominent than those revealed in the scalp. The surface of the brain had a gilded quality with trace metallic highlights. There was a hint of a metallic mesh finely interwoven into the surface. The mesh looked like chain mail with small and intricate links, each shaped differently. Like a fence half floating in the waves of an ocean, the metallic threadwork seemed to rise and fall above the surface of the brain. The entire beige mass was set upon a whitish tapering stalk—the brain stem and spinal cord.

They walked up close to the projected image. Canter nodded to the officers who parted for the team to get a better view.

Hagan felt his boss's hand on his shoulder and a less than sanguine whisper in his ear. "I am going to meet with the chancellor to do some damage control—remember this isn't research—don't screw this up. All eyes are on you, soldier." With that he turned and pushed his stiff tall frame through the crowd.

Hagan took a deep breath.

"Alright, let's begin. Is everybody's screen on? Make sure it's set to conference." Hagan put his hands in his pockets and straightened his shoulders. *Connect to Wash_U_Med_net.* An azure field appeared next to the holographic figure. The letters on the field a brighter white read, "ACCESS CODE, PLEASE." Hagan mentally read off his personal identifier, *F-L-U-J-W-D.* "ACKNOWLEDGED, NOW READING CORTICAL SIGNATURE. PLEASE WAIT." After a few moments, "PASSWORD AND CORTICAL RHYTHM SIGNATURE ACCEPTED." The blue screen changed from a guarded opaque blue to a less foreboding lighter shade.

Access patient Marcus Devron. Conference with the following: Reid Vestin, Jonathan Brickmil, and Farhan Yaseem.

Small spheres appeared below the screen indicating shared viewing—a light blue sphere for Reid, dark blue for Jonathan, and checkered for Farhan.

"OK, let's start with you, Farhan. What are we looking at here?" Hagan always began with the Socratic method and always started with the most junior resident. Farhan was not ready. His jaw was somewhat agape and his beady eyes widened slightly. His longish dark black hair was oiled and tightly brushed back to reveal hook-shaped curls at the back of his head and the nape of his neck. He had a mocha-colored complexion, plump lips, and a round face.

"Uh . . . uh . . . well . . . it's a hologram of the patient's brain," said Farhan hesitantly.

Hagan knew this was as much for him as it was for teaching. The method of starting with the fundamentals always kept him grounded when dealing with complex problems. "Just a hologram? What kind of hologram exactly?"

"A magnetic hologram," said Farhan tentatively. He wasn't expecting to get questioned in front of a bunch of lawyers and a police squad.

"Sort of. Can you help him out a bit, Jonathan?" A junior resident for a year under Maerici, Jonathan was seasoned for this process and had "helped out" a number of interns before.

"It's a magnetically induced negative refraction optical image, a MINROI." Jonathan spit the words out in a rapid matter-of-fact tone with the hint of a smile. He had a casual demeanor about him. He had thick brown hair and coarse stubble on his face. He rolled back and forth on the balls of his feet when he talked.

"A MINROI, that's right . . . what does that mean, exactly?" Hagan asked. Beginning with the basics always helped him avoid missing both the little details and the most obvious mistakes. The Socratic method made him think about things from the bottom up.

"A MINROI is the use of focal magnetic fields to induce electrical currents in biological tissue, such that when light shines on it, the light will bend in ways not normally found in nature, hence, negative refraction. It allows you to shine infrared light on someone and have that light bend and turn around so you can see their internal structures."

All four men turned around. It wasn't Reid Vestin who had answered. The voice was that of a woman. A female news anchor voice—deep, direct, and all business.

"Sander—whoa, whoa, WHOA . . . Sander!" The middle-aged, portly woman was being pulled by a big brown boxer toward a glowing blue column on the side of the street. Back arched and arm pulled forward, she uselessly tried to redirect her dog's path away from his anticipated target. The dog's snoot was snuffling the ground in excited anticipation as he neared his goal.

"No, Sander, NO!" In her field of view the blue words, "Potty! Potty! Potty!" were flashing with increasing speed. She didn't need a canine implant to tell her what the animal was thinking. His little stub tail wagged as he strained against the leash. Finally, he pulled the two of them within a blue ring of light around the pole.

Why does he like this *spot so much?* she thought. She sighed as the various voices and images crowded into her senses.

"*. . . the 'e-movement' is a modern approach to neuroprosthetics. People need to embrace an evolutionist perspective. Change is good and should be mandated for children as it prepares them for the economy of the future. . . .*" A ghostly blue figure in a slim-fitting suit smiled and pointed to numerous graphs with lines moving upward. "*Vote yes on proposition forty-three.*"

"*. . . considering vacation? Well think about a time-share in Belize . . .*"

"*. . . your mind is sacred—relinquish your prosthetics now—A message from the Church of the Evangelical Mission . . .*" There was an image of a family canoeing together. They were happy and laughing together. The panorama gave way to a white-haired man dressed in a white suit with a perfect smile. "*. . . connect to Christ—that's all you need. Please send your credits to cognitive site cog.evangelicalm ission.com.*"

She was now in a public-access zone surrounded by advertisements and public announcements. Her dog stood still, legs bent with his remnant tail fixed and motionless, with a contemplative frown as he emptied his bowels on the sidewalk.

Why always here—uh—I need to make Mike walk this animal. Sander would always drag her toward the blue poles where her presence would give tacit assent for her prosthetic to receive public advertising.

Right in front of the Ritz—it was always THIS public-access point. Sheepish and annoyed, she began wrapping his warm excrement into a plastic baggie. The circus of polished sound bites was disrupted by a dissonant cry. At first she though it was one of the many attention-grabbing ploys for her to look at new time-shares or new unbelievable low prices. The sound persisted—it was a warbling, winded screech of someone yelling and out of breath.

Looking up, she saw a woman run by with torn clothing. Her pale skin was covered in silvery tattoos and splotches of blood. There was something strange about the way she was moving. Sander turned his ears back and barked.

The thin woman with silvery hair collapsed twenty feet away in a heap. Mouth open in dismay, the middle-aged woman in her Saturday morning sweatpants focused her inner voice and called out for 911.

The female cop went far beyond Hagan's expectation of a pushy civil servant. Looking over, he couldn't help noticing the navy blue uniform stretched taut over an athletic frame. The typical asexual, government-issue outfit couldn't hide the angles of her well-defined deltoids, prominent clavicles, or the bony protuberances of her hips set beneath the flat plane of her stomach. Equally obvious were the pear-shaped curves of her breasts pushing the embroidered badge forward like the hood ornament of a classic Rolls Royce. She stood straight and formally, with her shoulders held square and her hands at her sides. The rumpled, disheveled man standing next to her stood leaning on one foot with his hands in his pockets, quietly waiting for a response.

Reid and Jonathan betrayed their initial impressions with roving glances, while Farhan ogled and continuously brushed back his already well-oiled hair.

With frigid aplomb, Hagan returned her gaze. "Detective . . . Dezner, is it? I understand the situation, thank you. I *am* working on defining what's going on with Dr. Devron. This is my method of accomplishing this. I wouldn't presume to advise *you* on how to conduct your investigation. If you don't mind? We'll continue." *This is really becoming one shit pile of a day,* Hagan thought

There was a chilly silence followed by a curt nod from Tara. "Proceed." Krantz observed the exchange, weary and tired. He squinted his eyes slightly as if he had a headache; his mottled complexion wrinkled slightly from the effort.

"Very good, then, let's proceed." *Hot and smart, but what a pain in the ass.* Hagan then turned to the hologram. His team followed suit.

"Alright, so Detective Dezner beat you to the punch, Reid. Does everybody get that?"

Reid and Jonathan both nodded. Farhan mumbled in affirmation.

"Good, OK, what magnetic sequences have we run on Dr. Devron?"

Reid responded, "So far we did the preliminary studies looking for evidence of bleeding or bruising in the brain or evidence of stroke. We also looked to see if there were markers for any type of brain tumor. So far nothing."

"OK, so call up all the markers we've looked at so far."

Reid projected his thoughts toward the glowing hologram. *"Please display molecular indices imaged."* A scrolling list of acronyms, letters, and symbols came onto the screen.

Hagan's eyes ran over the long list of names. "So lets see . . . it looks like we've got most of the basics covered for anything acute. Overall, brain looks normal. Tell me again what else is going on outside the brain. We'll come back to looking for anything unusual in the brain once we get a better context."

Reid redirected his attention to the display module. *"Please project data summary for Marcus Devron."*

In the fixed space of the holo-display the ghostly bust shrank while a body emerged from the previously displayed neck. The slight figure was in a straight position with his arms crossed in front of him. Like a genie trapped in a square bottle, he rotated slowly. Like his head, the skin was a translucent shell wrapped around the slightly less transparent brick-colored bands of muscle stretched over ligaments and bone. Deeper still were the multihued pinks, grays, and maroons of the organs in his chest and his abdomen. Throughout his body there were patches of highlighted areas with various neon colors. His arm and his leg areas were highlighted yellow. There were long drawn-out fields where the muscles would attach to the bones. In the abdomen bright blue fields accentuated the two bean-shaped organs at the back of his abdominal cavity—his kidneys. Deep in his chest, his beating heart was a maroon bundle ensheathed with a fluorescent pink.

Labs and tests were floating beneath in black letters superimposed on a white field. The deviant values were scripted in red for abnormal.

"Hmm . . ." Hagan said more to himself than to anyone. His mind was referencing and cross-referencing all the possibilities to come up with a rational diagnosis.

"Reid, what do you think?"

"Well, it looks like the muscle breakdown got the ball rolling—"

"Good, so what happened to his muscles?" asked Dr. Maerici.

"This is presumably something acute, so I'm guessing something along the lines of a toxin or infection—likely viral."

"Very good. It would also explain potential behavioral changes." Nodding, Hagan directed his attention to the projected image and information. *"Spectrally analyze whole body for toxins, viral capsular coats, and bacterially expressed proteins—cross-reference with those associated with muscular necrosis."*

ACKNOWLEDGED . . . SCANNING . . . PLEASE WAIT.

A solid white square appeared above the seated figure. Devron didn't seem to notice. The white sheet slowly lowered and passed through Devron's body. As it spliced through, a screen appeared with various readings of running spectral resonance that were emitted from the passing field. The names, molecular ball and stick structures, and their associated spectral signatures, which looked like curved lines with various peaks and troughs, all flitted in rapid sequence. The crowd watched and waited.

NEGATIVE.

"Huh?" Dr. Maerici stared at the words. *What are we missing here?*

He ran his fingers through his hair. He again looked at the floating figure. He let his mind relax. What pattern was he missing? What were the details that didn't fit? Kidney, heart, muscle . . . how did they fit with his behavioral changes.

"Check for trace element imbalance." NEGATIVE. *"Presence of lead?"* NEGATIVE. *"Perform DNA scan for fungal, mycobacterial, and parasitic life forms."* NEGATIVE. *"Scan for abnormal antibody titers."* NEGATIVE. *"Scan for autoimmune markers."* NEGATIVE. *"Cancer antigens?"* NEGATIVE.

Maerici sighed. *I'm missing something. Let's get back to the basics.* "Let's go see the patient."

What do they know?

Trent sat alone, shivering and nervous. The waiting room was empty. The guard carefully avoided his gaze. He watched as people came in and out of the imaging suite. The din of arguing and angry voices rose and fell with the opening and closing of the doors. As people passed, they held their heads steady and avoided looking in his direction.

Trent sensed the evasion. He knew it all too well. It would have been less obvious if they stared. *They know something, something having to do with me. It's bad. But what?*

Tremulous and scared, he remembered the times he sat outside the principal's office, often at the losing end of a fight. They sensed something in him, like a wounded animal, some weakness that could be preyed upon. It led to a shove, or his bag being pushed off his shoulder, a heckling remark—an event that he would try to defend, often to his own detriment. Holding ice to his lip, he would find himself invariably sitting alone outside the authority figure's office, greeted with a sigh and a long discussion.

His mother always had to come pick him up after detention. He remembered how they would drive home. They would talk of other things, not to avoid the event, but to reduce its gravity. He remembered how they worked on drawing Japanese characters in the rock garden. With a confident grace she traced out an elegant tangle of lines in the sand. He would try to copy it. *The brush writes a statement about the calligrapher at a moment in time.* He heard her voice in his head. She could always read him through his characters.

He opened and closed his hands. He wished she were here now.

"An escort? Is that really necessary?" Hagan stood in front of the door to the imaging suite looking up at the behemoth guard.

"Yes, it is," Tara responded, her voice measured and definitive.

"I think I can handle an eighty-year-old man currently having a heart attack."

Krantz got closer to Maerici. In an old-world style of discretion, he whispered in Maerici's ear. "Uh, Doctor, er, Professor Maerici, this old guy just gutted his maid, spread her intestines over his office table, and used her blood and feces to draw pictures on his walls."

Hagan stiffened. The impact of Krantz's words hung in the air like the aftershock of a private thunderbolt.

In his first betrayal of professionalism, Hagan jutted his jaw forward and shook his head. Frowning, he said, "Marcus? There is no way. The man was a megalomaniac, sure, but a butcher? Jesus Christ!" His voice was a low rasping whisper, but he finally nodded in assent.

The door slid open with a rapid hiss and the team walked into the room. Krantz tapped Warstet on the arm. The large man followed in behind with his hand fixed lightly on his sidearm. Remembering all too well the morning's events, he never removed his eyes from the center of the room, from Marcus Devron. The door slid closed behind the group. The noise and rush was completely cut in mid throng. The room was filled with a cottony muted silence. The surrounding walls were a bright lacquered white. The ceiling was a rounded cone shape and the floor a clear plexiglass with a matching cone below them. Light emanated diffusely from circumferential walls. The surface was covered with an irregular pattern of grooves that seemed to spiral toward the apex above and below them. This was the first time Krantz had ever been in one of these imaging suites before. He looked around somewhat mystified. It was like standing in the center of a large, closed white rose.

The group approached the epicenter of the room. As they walked their sounds were muted and delayed. Krantz, new to the experience, felt like his ears were filled with wax. The hush of the room did not suppress the smell as they neared Devron—a rancid fecal odor. Devron lay on a narrow, clear plastic board. All around him were narrow white fronds that moved and swayed with his slight movements. They partially concealed the naked boniness of his frame. He appeared to be lying in the center of a sea anemone. They pulsed forward and back with the trace excursions of his breathing. The slight involuntary motions of his head and limbs caused the swaying tentacles to shift and coalesce to maintain the bulbous tips a precise distance from the surface of his body.

As Hagan approached, he directed his attention toward the tendrils. *"Disengage peltier cooled magnetic emitters."* The polished white vines snapped to attention, straightened, and slowly withdrew into the clear floor below, forming a spiraled ropey stalk beneath the table supporting Devron.

Their withdrawal revealed the sad, stinking presence of Marcus Devron, laying flaccid on the clear table, a sheer hospital gown stretched across his abdomen and chest. His face and arms were speckled with remnants of dry, caked blood and excrement. His left hand was at his face, the thumb highlighted by its lack of filth from being in his mouth. His eyes were vacant and staring slightly upward. Intermittently his legs would twitch. At each of his joints, wrists, elbows, knees, shoulders, and hips, were large splotchy bluish bruises. The rest of his pale, thin skin had stripes of red welts and linear scratch marks. Small whitish tubes emerged from his wrists, neck, and genitals. All merged to a central matte-gray box that monitored the entrance and egress of the variously hued fluids.

Hagan maintained his gaze on the broken presence. "Did you do this to him?" His voice was cool, detached, and clearly directed to the officers.

"Jesus, NO!" blurted Krantz. "We barely touched the guy, one stunner, and he dropped. All those bruises and welts weren't there when we wrapped him for the ambulance."

"Must have been one hell of an ambulance ride," muttered Reid.

Tara stepped forward. "Professor Maerici, if you, *or your team,* are intimating that there was any behavior outside protocol. . . ."

Reid looked toward the ground.

Hagan wasn't in the mood to spar. "Easy, tiger, you need facts, so do I. Can we proceed?"

Tara's cheeks flushed slightly. "Let's get on with it," she responded coldly.

Hagan returned his attention to Devron. Despite the smell, Maerici bent in close to call into the industrial magnate's ear. "Can you hear me, Dr. Devron? This is Hagan Maerici." A pause. Nothing.

"Who's got a light?" asked Dr. Maerici to his residents.

Reid pulled a small flashlight from his pocket and handed it to him. Hagan opened Marcus's eyes and tested his right pupil. The dilated iris quickly constricted to a small black dot. *Reactive. He's still in there.*

"AAAAAAARHH," Devron screeched without a change in facial expression. Loud and abrupt, the throaty yell barely induced a change in the movement of his slack lips. The team jerked back. Warstet removed his sidearm.

Devron's body remained flaccid. His eyes never changed their absent upward gaze. He began to suck his thumb.

"Dr. Devron, can you hear me?" Hagan asked. The grumbling invectives poured out in an insensible ramble. "Marcus, it's me, Hagan Maerici—Dr. Maerici. I want you to show me that you can hear me. Show me two fingers if you can hear me." Hagan's voice was gentle, yet firm.

Devron's left hand moved away from his mouth. The doctors and officers all leaned in closer looking for a positive response. The old man stretched his hand toward Maerici with outstretched fingers. Hagan held still waiting for Devron to define his response. The grime-encrusted fingers deftly plucked the pen out of his coat pocket. Putting it in his mouth, he sucked on it with the same absent quality as his thumb. The team exhaled in disappointment at the nonsensical act.

Hagan looked over at Krantz. "Let's bring in his son for a moment." He began to nod to himself. *I've only read about this. Can it really be? Very, very rare indeed . . .*

Nobody likes to look at the handicapped, thought Trent, as he limped through the arguing crowd in the imaging suite. *Makes them feel guilty.*

His face was set in a rictus as he blinked back tears. He hobbled with a lopsided gait, determined to get through the throng as quickly as possible. His body bobbed up and down with irritated and inefficient movements.

Didn't recognize me—he didn't know who I was. Fear, anger, and hurt smoldered within Trent as he thought of the sight of his father. *He smelled so fucking bad. All he could do was mumble and cuss.*

Maerici had tried to get him to talk, tried to get him to look at his son. He had held his eyes open and forced his father's head to face him. The sight of him made him spill a garbled mess of words and profanities like pig slop being poured into a trough.

The image of his half-naked father wouldn't leave his mind. A new surge of tears burned at the periphery of his eyes.

Stop being a pussy. He felt anger at himself for being weak. As he trudged through the exit, a small voice within yearned to have his mother present.

She would know what to do. Sharper, hotter pangs of guilt bit deeply within him. The remorse pulled and shook at his insides.

I'm the reason she's gone.

He again thought about the red dunes. He thought about the comfort of the blue woman's presence. He didn't understand it, but he knew it was something that he needed.

Trent walked in the hallway. *Need to find someplace private, someplace I can go off.*

He felt pulled, compelled. Waiting rooms and front desks passed on either side as he searched. *Maybe an empty hospital bed. No one will notice a sick-looking kid sleeping.*

Trent limped faster. Before getting to the wards, a door caught his eye, a crack rather. A smooth white panel that should have been flush with the hallway was slightly ajar. Through the dark fissure Trent could see a red glow and the industrial shapes of large tubing and vents. He got closer and with his good hand slid the panel farther open.

Just enough room. He looked on either side of the hallway. *No one's paying attention.*

He moved the panel a little farther. Wriggling and shoving, he pushed his uncoordinated body into the dusty warm space. Sliding his back against a whirring vent, he let himself sink to a crouch on the floor. The enclosed space was already beginning to slip away.

"System, log on to Nexucist." Flashing blue lights began to coalesce. He let out a deep sigh. Trent could feel his body begin to relax as he slipped away.

Take me to the dunes, take me to the blue woman with the red eyes. . . .

Dr. Maerici turned to his residents. "OK, let's put this together. What do we have so far? Reid?" He could already feel Detective Dezner's impatient gaze on him as he was asking the question.

Reid Vestin focused his small brown eyes on the patient. After a long pause he looked back to Hagan and responded, "He's got an altered mental status with an aphasia. Possibly indicating left temporal involvement."

"There's more to it than that. What else seems to be unusual about his examination?"

"Uhh, the fact that he is sucking on his thumb and then your pen—the hyperoral behavior."

"Good! So . . . then . . ." He left a long pregnant pause to see if Reid could make the connection.

Reid shook his head indicating he didn't know where he was going. "I guess it's a widespread process causing some loss of inhibition."

"No! This is quite focal indeed. Let's go through all the details here. He is sitting there like a dead fish, all limp, but he is awake; we open his eyes and he screams—he is extremely *placid*. Conscious, but noninteractive. That's fact one. Fact two, he's aphasic, his ability to speak is severely impaired. Fact three, he has a prosopagnosia." He held his hand up to forestall Krantz asking what that meant. "He cannot recognize faces or any emotional object. We know he can see—his pupils react, he has a positive blink when I wave my hand in front of his eyes, and he was able to grasp my pen. Visual cues are making it to his visual cortex. He doesn't recognize me and he doesn't recognize his own son, unless his boy is talking to him. Even then he only recognizes the tones of his son's voice, but *not* the *content*. He is *emotionally blind*. He cannot recognize things that should have an emotional content to them. Finally, he is *hyperoral*; he is putting things in his mouth, either his thumb or any object that he can reach in his environment. That's the clincher."

Everyone was looking quietly and expectantly at Dr. Maerici. They were waiting for the punch line that now seemed obvious to Hagan.

"Placidity, emotional blindness, and hyperorality—he's got *Klüver-Bucy syndrome!*"

Hagan was greeted by a muted response both from his residents and the detectives. "This probably hasn't been seen in over three decades—ever since they cured herpes and tuberculosis. It's due to bilateral injury to the amygdala. It's the nucleus in the brain responsible for processing emotions—for encoding one's feelings to our internal and external world. It is the link that allows us to ascribe the subjectively good and bad qualities to the things we think and perceive."

Awareness was slowly settling into the residents as distant memories of historical medical diagnoses percolated into their consciousness. Reid's head cocked back with a moment of "aha" as what Maerici was saying finally registered. Jonathan and Farhan also were slowly nodding. Tara and Krantz still looked quizzical.

Tara responded, "What does this have to do with the case?"

Hagan began walking back toward the door. "No clue, but at least we know where to start looking. Let's get back to the holographic display; we've got more studies to run."

Why isn't that sonofabitch answering! Reverend Elymas again tried to connect with the Chameleon.

The spinning white orb faded with the words, "Not available for communication." Elymas looked down at his hands and forearms. The skin was red and flaking from where he had been scratching.

I am really getting shaky. He watched his hand tremble as he held it up. The whisky-and-ice-filled tumbler continuously clinked in his other hand. *Need another pill, used my last one last night. Had to. Needed it for the show.*

Desperation was starting to rise within him. Lifting the glass to his mouth, he took a deep draught and felt the familiar burn in the back of his throat. It wasn't helping.

Elymas's anxiety was getting worse. He felt like a balloon that was expanding beyond its limit. He felt like his skin was becoming so tight it would rip. Stretching his insides—his intestines were being pulled to the far ends of his abdominal wall. He was starting to see bad things. Things that scared him. They would twist and dart at the corner of his vision.

He had to get some more. HE NEEDED TO. He had already had diarrhea twice this morning. *Why isn't he responding? He knows I am a good customer. I need to get the stuff.*

The minister pushed his fingers through his white hair. He again tried to call.

"Not available for communication."

"Goddammit . . ." Hagan spat. His lack of sleep was making him irritable. Wide-eyed, the residents all looked at the professor as he leaned close to the holographic display. His overt frustration was highly atypical for the imperturbable neurosurgeon. They all stood in front of the square holographic portal as the large brain within slowly turned. It was magnified to the size of a large pumpkin. Within the translucent pinkish gray folds was a pair of bluish olive-shaped structures. These were the two amygdala nuclei.

"Alright, let's go over it again. We've looked at pretty much anything that can cause any acute or chronic injuries. We've looked for cancer, strokes, toxins, gene changes . . . nothing. What are we missing? We know his amygdala is involved—he has a neurologic exam classic for amygdala injury, but we're just not seeing anything."

They were again looking at the brain in shared mutual consternation. Tara was beginning to become inpatient. This line of inquiry was not getting them any closer to substantial answers for intent, cause, and guilt.

"Is there anything further that we can glean from this, Dr. Maerici?"

Hagan didn't turn to her. "By examination he has injured his amygdala on both sides. As a result, he has knocked out his ability to process emotional information. The *why* I cannot explain. I cannot seem to find any evidence on genetic, cellular, and macroscopic imaging that there is anything wrong with these regions. His exam, though, is definitive."

Tara's words, like welterweight jabs, cut to the bone. "So he could be faking this."

"What? No! He has evidence of serious pathology; I just cannot find the cause at this point. How exactly do you fake kidney failure, muscle breakdown, and a heart attack? No, Detective Dezner, he is indeed sick. He is not *faking* it."

"But there is nothing that you can find that is wrong with his brain. When he performed these acts there was nothing wrong with his thinking."

Hagan was now getting exasperated. He spoke his words slowly and with individual emphasis. "Let me say this again. I cannot tell you what was going on with his intentions. But *he does indeed* have evidence of brain damage by my *examination*."

"Unfortunately your exam in 2053 is probably not sufficient for modern medical diagnoses."

Hagan began turning red. "I knew justice was supposed to be blind, but I wasn't aware that the same held true for criminal investigations."

Tara shoulders, already squared, arched still more slightly, her head tilted forward to return the invective.

Krantz put a hand on her shoulder; he knew he had better jump in. Over the years, he had come to know what pushed her buttons. She was a woman of intense discipline. Her work defined her. Under the steely surface of a strict, unemotional work ethic, though, he knew there was something deeper, something emotional and hidden. One thing he had come to realize was that when her quality of work was called into question—a tiger lay concealed and ready to pounce. The cause of that inner tumult he didn't want to know. He knew she was the harbinger of his retirement, but she was a superb partner nevertheless, and some closets were best left unexplored. Right now he knew that Maerici had just opened the cage and any further interaction between the two was about to become counterproductive.

In a conciliatory tone, he said, "So, Professor, Tara, I think we can agree there *may* be something wrong with his brain. He certainly has multiple problems in other parts of his body. This is probably something we are not going to solve now."

Farhan, somewhat nervous blurted out—"Uh, why don't we just interrogate his prosthetic? Won't that give us some information?"

All eyes turned toward the young Pakistani doctor. Farhan nervously shifted and looked toward the floor under Tara's direct and irritable gaze.

Hagan looked at the intern. "Farhan, replaying someone's recorded experience from their neuroprosthetic is a violation of patient privacy—"

"Not to mention the Thirty-second Constitutional Amendment guaranteeing a citizen of having absolute privacy in the thoughts, intents, and experiences they have privately generated," Tara cut in.

Krantz's dour and weathered face suddenly became very animated. "Couldn't we just look to see if there was a major change and avoid any content of his thoughts?"

Pleased at the notion of seeing some light in this cave, Hagan brightened. "Detective Krantz actually has a point. Anything that has left him a permanent deficit should show up in our scans, but for whatever reason we're not seeing it. Looking at a change in his neuroprosthetic may give us a hint of what happened."

Tara looked cautious. "Wait a minute, we don't want to replay his experiences—that will kill our case. It will get thrown out in a heartbeat."

Hagan, feeling more optimistic, said, "That is not a worry. We can use some old signal-analysis techniques that average the signal enough such that deriving the cognitive content is impossible. So we would be mathematically safe from any constitutional violation of his cognitive privacy."

Tara shrugged her shoulders in resignation. "If you think it will give us something."

Hagan clapped Farhan on the shoulder. "Good job." Then he once again directed his attention to the holographic display. *"Alright, please upload data from Marcus Devron's neuroprosthetic implants from the prior three hours."*

Red letters appeared over the brain: "WARNING: THIS IS PATIENT CONFIDENTIAL INFORMATION. PERMISSION HAS NOT BEEN PROVIDED FROM SUBJECT."

"Please perform Fast Fourier Transform of signal in ten-millisecond increments. Please confirm that this sufficiently smears cognitive data."

An hourglass appeared for approximately half a minute. It faded, and green letters appeared: "SIGNAL ANALYSIS PERFORMED. SIGNAL CONTENT SUFFICIENTLY DECONVOLVED FOR PRIVACY OF CONTENT (PER MORAN PARAMETERS)."

"Please show high gamma frequency power oscillations at ten times real time. Please demonstrate nonbaseline activity in red. Superimpose on current brain. Please reference to baseline data from one week prior."

"OK, we are going to watch his brain activity in the higher frequency bands to see how normal that looks over the past six hours. Anything that looks very different from a week ago will show up in red."

Tara and Krantz both nodded.

"Proceed."

The brain lit up with fluctuating green and blue oscillating signals. Deeper violet regions appeared around the major creases, while the front part of the brain looked a more aquamarine green. All the areas fluctuated and wavered such that the brain looked like it was aflame with a small choppy fire. Infrequent red spots would appear through-out the cortical surface, but nothing where Hagan wanted to see them—namely, the amygdala.

The brain now floated, disembodied and back to its usual pinkish gray.

Green letters appeared and floated in accusation: "FURTHER SIGNAL ANALYSIS?"

The letters hung above the fist-shaped organ. The group around the hologram sat still watching Hagan watch the brain.

Hagan's only external sign of irritation was belied by his long ex-halation. He continued to stare and think.

What the goddamn hell am I missing? he thought. *He had a nor-mal scan, but clear and obvious evidence that there was something wrong with his amygdala. You don't get that way with a normal brain. It just doesn't match up . . .*

"It just doesn't match up," Hagan said to himself in a half whisper. In his mind, thoughts and emotions roiled. "It just doesn't match up." The words were a snap, a code word—the *open sesame.* Dr. Maerici's head snapped back. His thoughts coalesced and coalesced like a thou-sand Legos falling together at once.

He turned to Reid, Jonathan, and Farhan: "It's not matching up!" The men responded to his excited vehemence with a look that seemed to indicate that he had just announced his preference for wearing women's underwear.

Being at the top of the resident totem pole, Reid felt compelled to respond. "Er, yeah, it doesn't make sense."

"No, no, Reid, it makes perfect sense, well at least some sense, some more sense. Things aren't matching up. They're not *coherent.* When we looked at those brain oscillations they all looked normal, right?"

"Right."

"Well, we didn't look to see if those brain signals were matching up with each other. The brain is a dynamic structure. Each square mil-limeter has a broad range of fluctuating signal. Each of those subunits on the cortical surface needs to talk to the others. They do that by matching the peaks and troughs of the signal. Taken by themselves they would show normal activity, but if they are not matched up, or not *coherent*, then that structure isn't able to contribute."

Reid now began to get it. "You're right, we could easily miss that if we didn't look for it." He was now nodding with the same enlightened vigor as his mentor.

Tara looked to Reid. "Is there a problem with his brain or not?"

"Maybe, we're going to have to see," Reid responded. The muscles in Tara's jaw clenched and relaxed with impatience.

Hagan was already drafting the parameters for various frequencies and regions to assess levels of coherence.

"Engage."

"CONFIRMED."

The brain again surged into hues of green and blues. Two small regions developed wispy regions of red, orange, and yellow. Like flames confined to a small space, two olive-shaped regions transformed from wispy clouds to densely bright red-yellow marbles.

"Fuck yes!" burst Farhan. He reddened and quickly looked back and forth to Dr. Maerici and the detectives standing behind him. "Er . . . uh . . . sorry," he mumbled, more surprised than anybody.

Aware that a clue had emerged, Krantz squinted at the floating brain. Braver than Maerici's residents, he looked to the professor. "What exactly does this mean, Dr. Maerici?"

Hagan was already starting to like this detective. He had a certain degree of plain-talking honesty about him. "It seems that the amygdala is not communicating with the rest of his brain. It explains why we didn't see any evidence earlier for damage in the routine studies. If the brain cannot communicate with the amygdala, however, the end result is the same. Like one of those old-fashioned cell phones, if it's not able to send or receive signals, it's the same as if you smashed it with a hammer in terms of its function."

"Hmm . . . makes sense." Krantz nodded. "So why can't the . . . the . . . amigdul communicate with the brain."

"It's pronounced 'a-mig-du-lah.' The answer is I don't know. Honestly, I've never seen an isolated decoherence. Both amygdala and the brain seem to be working, they're just not talking to each other."

As Hagan was explaining, large blue words appeared across his field of view.

WARNING: ABNORMAL HEART RHYTHM DETECTED. BLOOD PRESSURE BECOMING UNSTABLE.

"Crap, we're going to have to get him stabilized in the Intensive Care Unit." Hagan directed his attention to the hospital network. *"Barnes*

System—get me the on-call ICU attending." Hagan watched as a cardiac tracing bounced across. Labels of aberrant beats were highlighted. They were accelerating in their frequency. *Shit, he may crump!*

He saw a white field appear and the name Ethan Pearl emerged.

"Hey, Ethan, I have Marcus Devron in the MINROI."

BLOOD PRESSURE DECLINING.

"Reid and Jon, get in there and start packaging him—now." The two residents nodded and went into the imaging room. Several nurses and ventilator techs followed.

"Yes, THE Marcus Devron, he needs to come up right now. Looks like he's developing ventricular tachycardia. I'm sending him your way now."

The large sweaty officer called out. "He's jerking around in there."

Looking though the tinted window into the room, Hagan could see the dim silhouettes of the staff members encircle Devron and put him on a gurney. The team quickly moved through a pair of doors on the opposite side.

The noise and movement in the control room was hitting new frenetic levels.

Hagan returnd to speak to Detective Krantz. "So, Detective, as I was saying, it's not clear to me—"

"He's a murder suspect," Tara cut in. He could see her head jerking to look in the air. He knew she was reading a signal feed that was invisible to the others. Like an icy javelin cutting through the ambient cloud of conversations, she addressed her partner. "The maid is dead. They couldn't reanimate her from her hydrogen sulfide suspension."

Jesus, does it ever stop? Hagan thought.

Hagan and Edwin turned to look at Tara. There was a brief hush in the room. Like the eye of a hurricane passing, the brief calm dissipated into a cacophony of argument and movement. Tara, however, held Edwin's and Hagan's gaze. She wasn't done.

"Did this *decoherence* of his amygdala explain why he killed his maid?" Her tone was direct and unfettered by the chattering chaos around her. Her eyes were boring into Hagan.

"Again, this is a pretty unusual finding, but people with Klüver-Bucy tend to be pretty docile; they're not aggressive. Moreover, they're usually too dysfunctional to accomplish anything organized like murdering someone."

"So we have no further insight into motive."

"As of yet, no; he's sick with both an unusual complex of findings in his body and his brain. How this accounts for the murder of his maid, I cannot explain . . . yet."

She nodded. "Edwin, we have to go. There are two more bodies; similar MO."

Krantz's small eyes widened. "You mean back in the Devron estate?" *How could we have missed that?*

"No, in two separate locations in the city."

Krantz's features seemed to constrict. His eyes, already small, reduced to the size of small squinty slits. *This is making less and less sense,* he thought. *Why does a trillionaire kill his maid of forty years, and how does he do it to a couple other people in different parts of the city at the age of eighty?* His intuition was twisting and cringing with the incongruities. He just didn't have a sense for this case; it just wasn't fitting into any normal scenario, even when normal in his experience was murder.

"Alright, let's go." He knew that this was going to be a very, very long day.

Trent pulled himself together. He was scared, but something was different. He opened and closed his right hand. He watched the fingers of his hand move as if he were playing a piano. Despite the scars that wrapped and ensheathed his skin like vines, his digits flexed with a freedom he hadn't experienced in years.

I am getting better, he thought to himself. *Stronger, smarter, I am becoming me.* Amid the emotion, his mind felt clear and more sure. He felt like a needle on a record—sharp and pinioned on the details in and around him.

He thought about the desert and the blue woman with the red eyes.

A gift, she wanted to give me a gift. Trent thought about his brief interlude. The interaction was so hard to comprehend. No words had been spoken, but he understood the interaction. *Something that would change me, make me better.*

But how? The unreality of his newly discovered world was a fundamental paradox. His thoughts raced with a cognitive capacity that his injured mind could never have accomplished in years. He was penetrating facts and details like never before.

How can I be experiencing things in the virtual world more real than the real world, and how can the virtual world be changing my body? To some extent he didn't care. He wiggled his fingers. They moved with a dexterity that no amount of prosthetic alteration could achieve. *A gift.*

Like before the accident . . . Dark memories again began to circle closer. Broken glass, bent metal, the electric burning smell . . . *No, I can't think about it, not now,* he pleaded with himself.

He thought again about the sand, the woman, the feelings. Since he had first been to the desert, he had been back again and again. Each time the woman with the red eyes took him to an altered state that transcended description. It was beyond the desert, beyond his past. Beyond anything encapsulated by words or the senses.

She never spoke. There were no words between them, but he had never communicated so fully with any living creature.

He was again sitting in the sterile, white waiting room. A yearning gnawed at him to return to the red dunes, his launching pad to a higher-level reality. The young man's diminutive frame sat slumped in a chair emerging from the wall.

Reality pushed back in. *God, he is so fucked up. . . .* The image of his father gave him stomach pains. Seeing the man weakened and broken, he did not know where to begin. The conflicting emotions roiled in an internal tumult. He remembered standing in countless galas and parties, small and unnoticed, as Father received award after award. He remembered how he would stand near him, not close to him, just close enough. People would walk by vying for a chance to shake his father's hand. He would stand there with his hands on his hips shifting his weight back and forth. He would look from side to side, acting as if he was waiting for somebody—a friend who should be just getting there. He didn't look at the people who were passing him by and engaged with his father. He would hear his father laugh and say witty things. Occasionally he would offer a laugh in parallel as if he were part of the conversation, part of the humorous banter. He would shift and scan for hours, waiting and hoping that his father, his dad, would come over to talk to him. He never did. But he always had to be at those events. Feelings of longing and anger wrestled with other memories. The sparse moments of closeness—a time when he showed him how to piece together a motherboard for a science project, the moments by his bedside in the hospital. Ultimately, it was the heaviness of his absence that Trent remembered. A weight that pressed down upon him, but an anchor to his existence that he depended on nevertheless.

Now he's sick and accused of murder. He thought about Jasmina. *Dad couldn't have done it—she worked for him for decades.* She had been one of Trent's few direct social interactions. She had cared about him. The thought of her being gone was too much—another emotional connection torn from him. News feeds had hit the neuroprosthetic Web like a swarm of locusts. Soon after, he had been hounded and harassed for comments from news agencies. Furthering his solitude, Trent had turned off his incoming messages. It was too much. He loathed those carrion-chasing paparazzi fucks.

That dipshit cop is still guarding the door. Hands in his pockets, Goldwin rocked back and forth on his feet with a vacant stare. Occasionally he would eye Trent and quickly look away.

I don't know what to do. His mind grappled with competing desires.

Need to stay with Dad. Commitment pulled and struggled against a yearning for the solace and pleasure of the desert and a nameless beyond.

Can't visit that place for a long time here, people would notice. The desire to feel that sand underneath his feet grew like an unscratchable itch. *I could stay there longer at home . . .*

I want to see Dad again, I have got to see him . . . I should stay with him. He heard the words of obligation echo in his mind. Guilt and recrimination battled with the emotional undertow of his mounting desire. *But Dad . . .* Wordless yearning and emotional rationalizations were his response—*probably won't see him for a while anyway . . . need to take a break . . . he won't know I'm gone, just for a short time, be back in no time . . .*

He felt his body stand itself upright. Officer Goldwin shifted uncomfortably. As Trent started to walk toward the door, the thin officer with the potbelly became noticeably fidgety. Trent paid him no attention. His desires were driving him to a singular focus. He hobbled out of the lobby with less of a limp than he had the previous day. An improvement only he noticed.

The two detectives walked down the hallway. Virtual images and real-time data feeds swirled around Tara like a school of blue translucent fish.

"Some more in on those new bodies. Appears that there are some pretty clear suspects associated with each of them."

"Should I be relieved or more anxious? Linked or no?" Krantz asked, preoccupied with getting something out of his pocket.

"Hard to know. It sounds brutal, but it's too early to say. I'm not getting any visuals—not uploaded to the precinct server yet." Tara noticed that Krantz had finally turned his right-sided pocket inside out to deliver a napkin-wrapped object. Already knowing the answer, she couldn't help but ask. "Whatchya got there?"

"Bran muffin," Krantz answered matter-of-factly as he pulled out the mashed and crumbling brown mess. "At least Devron wasn't involved in the other ones—that's probably good."

"Well that, and the time line makes it impossible. I think Devron was carving his maid up for a while, so it's unlikely he could have been in multiple places at once." Tara couldn't help herself. "Have you really been carrying that thing around in your pocket?" She knew that he had eaten a bran muffin for lunch for the better part of twenty years. It was all his past wife would let him eat (she didn't want him to get chubby).

"Uh-huh." Unfazed, the old detective popped a piece of muffin in his mouth and kept on talking. "So maybe just a busy day in St. Louis—what do you think about Devron being sick? Think it explains anything?" Crumbs were falling all around him.

"I don't buy medical problems causing people to commit murder."

"Juries do, though."

"That's the problem, the murder is too bizarre and there is no data to support intent. There is something missing here. I think the illness and whatever it was that the Maerici guy was pointing out is a red herring at best and a possible alibi at worst. Maybe Devron is setting up a medical or sanity plea."

"But why, Tara? The why is not making any sense at all. Why would a man at the end of his eminent business and scientific career knock off his maid? Why? Why?" Muffin bits fell out of his mouth with emphasis.

Mildly disgusted, yet unsurprised, Tara ignored the many rules of etiquette that her partner was violating. "There must be some fact we are missing—I don't know." Krantz was now licking the napkin to get at the final crumbs. Monochromatic blue images were beginning to flash across her field of vision. "Getting some stills."

"What does it show?" Krantz could see from her facial expression that she was bothered and disturbed.

"Faces, I see a bunch of faces."

The old detective marched up the green, moss-encrusted walkway with broad, stiff-legged strides, hurried and anxious. *If this was another one, shit, we've got some bizarre cult on our hands. Maybe it's a designer drug with some crazy side effects. Fuck!* Krantz's mind ran in circles thinking of all the possibilities that could connect these bizarre occurrences.

The path to the home was a collage of large irregular flat stones; the edges were cut to make a broad, straight pavilion to the side of the large redbrick home. The building was a squarish three-story edifice. Redbrick only, the home was an austere affair characterized by vertical straight lines and large rectangular windows, with a sculpted stone medallion embedded in the brick wall between the central windows of the third floor. The home itself was flanked by square-cut boxwoods. The angularity was offset by window boxes with blue flowers that grew and descended from their pots like small pastel waterfalls. He saw some of his officers at the end of the walkway near the entrance to the house. They were under the awning waiting for him. One was folding a stick of gum into his mouth.

More rich people and more murder. Bad, bad . . .

As he approached, they nodded to him with the usual familiar respect. He was a fixture for every tape-lined crime in this city. When he was in close enough proximity the gum-chewing officer pointed his thumb back as if he were hitchhiking.

"Back behind in the greenhouse, Detective Krantz, some real grizzly shit. Is it true, another hack job at the Devron estate?"

"Let's keep the yap to a minimum—got it?" Krantz growled. They both mumbled their assent to the curmudgeon. He knew this was how things got leaked to the press. A few low-level cops felt officious and important by giving some overly enthusiastic press rep with a short skirt some minor bits of incendiary information. The news pieces that seemed to capture everyone's attention in St. Louis were one of two things—murder or puppies, either an act of human depravity that the St. Louis citizenry could voyeuristically be both revolted and fascinated by or a saccharine and completely irrelevant story of stupid cuteness. He still remembered shutting off his visual news connection when they began to tell the story of how "Pupsy" had learned to bring its master specific sodas.

He followed around to the back of the house. The stone path widened to form a sprawling patio partially covered by a second-floor balcony and terrace. Farther back amidst the manicured green lawn and swaying weeping willows was the greenhouse, tucked into the back right corner. He walked on the soft matted grass. Krantz noted the crisp lines of the cut lawn. *Nice and tight*.

As he approached, large blue block letters floated in the air.

CRIME SCENE—DO NOT ENTER.

As he got closer, the signs enlarged and fluttered as if agitated. Additional warnings soon emerged.

AUTHORIZATION REQUIRED. PLEASE ACKNOWLEDGE.

He focused his attention on the second sign. *Edwin Krantz*.

ACKNOWLEDGED.

All the blue signs then winked out of sight. As he walked he could see more officers outside. They stood in front of a redbricked, nineteenth-century conservatory.

Another garden, Krantz thought to himself. He looked at the long narrow windows that were separated by brick columns and topped with arched Mediterranean blue stained glass. *Just like in the park*. He remembered how April would always pull him through the old greenhouses.

Something on the windows. Long linear streaks snapped him out of his reverie. Even from this distance, Krantz knew it was a splatter pattern. He also saw pots on the window sills that had been broken, not while gardening. Inadvertently trampling the outer perimeter of flowers, the officers were in various stages of conversation and activity.

As he approached they tapped and nodded to one another—"the Krantz" was coming.

"Guys—off the flowers. What've we got?"

Stepping off some flattened daylilies, the first cop was holding a cup of coffee. Seeing the beige uniform with darker brown patches on the shoulders and collar, Krantz sighed in resignation. *County,* he thought.

The suburban cop's hair was thin and receding with the remaining sand-colored tufts fluffed and parted in the center. Krantz noticed he was holding onto the cup a little tighter than he probably should have been. As he approached, he acknowledged the detective with an upward jerking motion of his chin.

"Hey, I'm Kurchy." He held out his hand for a brief sweaty handshake.

"They're still filming the scene. I've never seen anything like it. Pieces of the guy everywhere, but orderly, not horror-show style, not the usual crazy shit, it looks—I dunno, looks . . ." Kurchy's voice trailed for a lack of adequate description.

"Too messy to be sane, too ordered to be crazy?" Krantz finished.

"Yeah . . . kinda, that's about it." Kurchy nodded

"Where's the suspect? Who is it?" said Krantz

"His name's Oberweiss. Heading to Barnes Hospital."

"Why's that? Did you need to stun him?'

"No—came quietly, he was black and blue all over. Elbows, knees, fingers totally looked like sausages—totally bizarre. When we put him in a restraining pod, his measured vitals were totally out of whack—low blood pressure, slow heart rate—and assessment deemed him medically urgent."

"Was he coherent?" Krantz was looking for patterns, a similar MO for the murder. A connection. *Was this guy fucked up like Devron? This has got to be some type of drug, but rich people like this, and Devron . . . ?* "Preliminary drug screen?"

"No, nothing."

Krantz thought back to Devron, the total absence of facial expression. Face slack, sucking his thumb. "Was he acting strangely at all?"

"No, well, yeah, he was actually kind of jolly."

"Jolly?" Krantz's face tightened, his small beady eyes incredulous.

"That was the most creepy part of it. Just kept talking about trimming flowers. I mean, real fag type. Wasn't right, though."

"How so?" *So, not wrecked like Devron.*

"He saw us, but he didn't. Like he was looking through you. I mean he kept calling me Alvin."

"Were you the first responder?" asked Krantz

"No, it was Ratcheson. Got there a moment before I did. Take a look at his recorded visuals—his name is Bill Ratcheson."

Krantz nodded and focused his thoughts to his internal prosthetic and directed his attention to the precinct. For him it was still a mechanical process. *"Access Bill Ratcheson's recorded visual and audi-tory experience crime scene."*

A blue field emerged in front of the old officer. In the screen he could see the azure monochromatic front of the greenhouse. Since the view was being presented on a square screen, the image was distorted with a well-focused center and a hazy periphery. It was a function of converting and condensing the actual visual experience to a confined field. Krantz hadn't upgraded his neuroprosthetic to immersive tech-nologies in years. He abhorred technology, and it had been a struggle to use one of these things in the first place.

He watched as a hand emerged from the blurred bottom portion of the screen. Ratcheson's hand entered the focus of his attention—the old-style knob on the door to the greenhouse. The knob turned and the door opened with a click. Before he entered, the viewer focus-flicked quickly between multiple sites: the sides of the greenhouse, the lawn behind him, the windows with dark dots and streaks. He lin-gered on those for a moment. The right hand now slipped out of view and returned holding a gun.

A blue dial hovered above the crook of his hand near the knuckle of his thumb. He looked closer and the settings shifted. The words "STUN 4/10" and "BARREL EYE VIEW" faded in and out quickly. Another small round window then emerged in the top corner of the central field of view. The center of the field had a small red O delin-eating where the bullet would target. At the moment, the O was cen-tered a little above the handle of the door.

His left hand then came into view and began to open the door a crack. As his gun hand passed into the space, a muzzle view flowed from the handle to the floor to the center of the brightly sunlit room.

In the small thimble-sized visual field, Ratcheson could see an even smaller chubby figure walking to one side of the room. His arms were outstretched with fingers spread out wide. His hip bumped against a shelf and knocked over several pots. As he swung his arms around, more pots fell from a higher shelf. Dirt, pot fragments, and flowers were everywhere. The figure then returned to the center of the room. Ratcheson's handheld periscope was then able to see the crumpled figure amidst a large dark inky pool.

The door flew open hard. Krantz could then hear the officer's voice in his head.

"Hands in the air! Now!" Ratcheson's voice was strained.

The heavyset man with a pear-shaped head gave a broad grin. He looked like a jolly old-world butcher, with blood covering his arms up to his elbows. There was a pair of pruning shears in his right hand.

"Alvin? Why are you yelling? It's been a while, come on in. Let me show you some of our prize pieces—been a good growing summer."

Ratcheson was standing in the doorway. Looking at the man holding the bloody scissors, his gun view screen was focused squarely on the center of his chest. The dot bobbed rhythmically to what Krantz was sure was the officer's pounding heart.

"Put the scissors down! Now!"

"Alvin, no need to yell. I can put the scissors down. What's wrong with you? You sound like a maniac. Come on in." Gerald's demeanor was pleasant and welcoming. He put the shears down with a casual aplomb and beckoned the officer to enter.

"On your knees! I am NOT saying it again!" yelled Ratcheson.

"You naughty boy," said Gerald, blushing slightly and rotating back and forth on his feet.

Another set of running footsteps approached from behind causing the view screen to swing wildly.

Krantz could hear Kurchy's tense and tinny voice. "Mr. Oberweiss, what happened here?"

"Oh, just rearranging the flowers. Whad'ya think?" Gerald looked around proudly at the surrounding carnage. Beneath him were the flayed remnants of a body. It looked like a predator-ravaged carcass on the Serengeti.

The monochromatic blue hues gave the scene a comic book appearance. Around the jumbled heap of mangled muscle and bone was a pattern. Krantz recognized it immediately. Spiraling around the body was face after face. Simple, cruel, and raw. The image a malevolent child would draw.

The pattern was all around; everywhere, on the floor, on the shelves, the sink. The screen was rising and falling from Ratcheson's hoarse breaths.

All the time Gerald looked around smiling like a young boy proud of his sand castle. Kurchy's voice became louder and more adamant. "Mr. Oberweiss, you need to come with me."

"Alvin, what do you think? Aren't they beautiful? We have a bumper crop of poppies as well."

The circle of Ratcheson's gun's-eye view was a tight singular dot tremulously centered on Gerald Oberweiss's sternum. Oscillating from the nervous tremor of his hand, the setting was now lethal 10/10—a tight focus of energy that would pierce the man and scramble his insides.

"I have a real surprise, though." Gerald's smile broadened. "Let me show you my favorite, it's special. Have you ever seen a Bhutanese Blue Poppy?"

He approached cupping something in his hands.

"Mr. Oberweiss, do not move." As he approached his hip bumped hard against the edge of a small table. "I'm so clumsy," he chuckled.

Holding his hand out in front, his elbows and fingers were swollen and engorged. The skin was blotched with blackened bruises at the joints and elbows. One finger pointed at an odd right angle. In his hands was what looked like a velvety, meaty petal.

That's his tongue, Krantz thought. *"System. Stop Video."* The blue field winked away and he stood with Kurchy watching him.

"Some real sick shit—don't usually see this type of stuff. This is more city style, don't you think?"

"I don't know what the heck this is," Krantz responded. He still just couldn't put it all together. *Similar but different. Rich guy kills someone he knows. Jolly, though, not a lumbering zombie like Devron . . . and the faces, what the hell. How are these connected?* "Anything unusual in terms of connectivity?'

"You mean besides the fact the guy is gay?"

"Stop being an ass—you know what I mean—unexpected connections, cerebral links, nonpatterned connections. The usual shit."

"We had our forensic IT guy run the standard stuff. He was apparently cybertrekking prior to the event. Nothing strange there—Bhutan apparently, wherever that is. Uneventful, at least in the last thirty days in regards to new contacts: no contacts to known criminals, no change in frequency, aberrant timing, nothing. Downloaded the usual stuff, SIM movies, shopping orders—lots of flowers, oils, scents, florist stuff—porn, all typical."

With small squinted eyes, head tilted slightly, Krantz stared at Kurchy. "Any contact with Marcus Devron?" His solemn wooden presence expressed his lack of interest in expanding on the question.

Kurchy ignored the silent, brooding warning. "So it's true—the murder at the Devron estate. Same deal? Was Devron really the perp?"

"Let's not fucking go there, OK? I've got enough headaches, I don't need rumors spreading around!"

"OK, OK, sorry, Detective Krantz . . . no . . . no contact like that."

"OK, fine—sorry to bark—we just have to keep whatever it is

that's going on contained. The media market on this is going to be through the roof and it's just going to make our job harder figuring out what's going on. I know I don't have to tell you that." Krantz's voice returned to his usual grumble. "Also, do those crazies at the gates have any idea of what's going on? There have been a lot of units passing them by."

"No, I don't think so. Should we tell them to move on?"

"No—probably would just call more attention to the event. Have there been any complaints about them so far?"

"Sure, the usual stuff—noise disturbance. Haven't gotten to it yet, because of what's going on here."

"Let's do this: send a couple units to go talk to them and see if they can quiet it down. That way the holy protestors will think the reason we're here is because they're disturbing the peace and not some other reason."

Kurchy cracked a couple knuckles and nodded. "Sounds good, Detective."

"Alright, well, while you do that lemme take a look at the scene," Krantz muttered.

He walked to the now familiar door of the greenhouse. No longer the monochromatic blue and white tones, he saw the aged hues of the weathered wooden door he saw moments ago. Like Ratcheson, his left hand pushed the timbered door open. As the door fell away to reveal the sunlit room, Krantz's eyes widened.

The torn and mutilated body had been removed. What he hadn't seen in Ratcheson's view was the color. *It made all the difference, Jesus Christ . . .*

He walked to the center of the room. Waxing and waning beams of sunlight highlighted small eddies of dust and pollen from the surrounding vegetation. *God, same damn smell. Feces, blood, and this time with the smell of roses. Smells like perfumed manure. Makes it somehow worse.*

Krantz looked around the room. His feet were at the focus of concentric circles of bloodstains on the floor. As he turned looking at the floor, face after face stared back at him. Interspersed were several handprints and smears. *Oberweiss being clumsy or his boyfriend's last desperate grabs?* Krantz thought.

At Devron's there had been pattern after pattern of that cruel-appearing symbol, and here it was evident yet again. *But the flowers. The walls, windows . . .* The same symbol was resplendent throughout the room. Woven and interspersed through the arrangement of flowers, body parts, pottery pieces, bones, fingers, skin, they all played in color and shape into a grand collage of faces staring back at him. Layer upon layer, multiple sizes, intricate variances, all woven together—a stadium of malevolent caricatures. Krantz turned in circles. He shivered at the artistic viciousness of the scene—meticulously crafted, a show, a display, a boast. *But to what point?*

The images seemed to writhe and pulsate with the slight breeze moving through the room. Outside, the remaining officers mulled around in the lawn, their presence revealed by casual muttering and the crunch of grass and leaves beneath booted feet. Otherwise the room was silent. Krantz took a deep breath and tried to absorb the scene and the meaning behind it. As he walked back to the door, the careful balance of colors and position of the medium all reverted to the clutter and disarray of a violent murder scene.

Only when you stand in the center of the room. Only when you look out from where the murder occurred do you see all those faces. That took effort, planning—how or why did that klutzy florist do that and why is this like the Devron case? What on earth?! Krantz was worried. It wasn't coming together. Two murders with the same M.O. and he didn't know where to begin. The muscles in the back of his neck began to tense and knot.

He turned to take another look and focused his attention inwardly and spoke in his inner voice with halting pauses: *"Address Tara Dezner."*

"Acknowledged. Calling now." A white ball was spinning in the upper right corner of his visual field. Below, the name Tara Dezner was flashing. The ball then stopped, expanded, and slowly faded. The letters descended to the center of his field of vision and a caption— *"Audio only"*—appeared beneath the name and both faded away.

"Tara?"

"Yes, hello, Edwin." Krantz could hear Tara's measured voice within his head.

"Are you there yet?" Krantz spoke out loud, his voice resonating around him and his thoughts projected to Tara. The other officers near the door pretended not to notice.

"Almost there, I was held up in traffic. The roads are opening up, should be there shortly. How does the crime scene appear in Parkview?"

Krantz took the room in again as he spoke. "Similar to the Devron place, well, kinda, mutilation style is similar, but this victim not maintained alive during assault like Devron's maid, more complex blood graffiti, pieces of flesh everywhere, you'll have to see it to believe it, but something definitely connected here. Looks like time of death was probably . . ."

Krantz's voice trailed off. As he looked at the room a new pattern emerged he hadn't seen before.

He mumbled to himself, "Not . . . me . . . red . . . devil."

"Edwin, what did you say? I lost track of that last statement. Please repeat?"

Edwin Krantz continued to look at the floor.

"Edwin, Edwin, hello . . . I have just been instructed our perp at the Ritz is evading arrest, I have got go now."

Krantz continued to stare.

"Hey, check that! Yes, check it! I see. We see, really gimpin. So gimpin. Should we do something? That's not our mode. So not our user function. Not written for symbiote code. That certainly doesn't read."

A variegated and motley group of teens walked around the unconscious girl on the ground. She was covered in blood. The crew, bespeckled with shimmering piercings and digital tattoos, all collectively looked down at the still figure. Their heads moved with the synchrony of a dance troupe.

"Has a scrounger look to her. Check it. Serious." Eyes searched the woman. She had on a thin diaphanous dress that was torn at the shoulder.

"Silvery hair—sexy tats. Check it. Check on." Like the eyes of an insect, perspectives and views shifted and melded. The amalgam collage was pimped and augmented with virtual images, tags, and ongoing commentary. Virtual lines, arcs, symbols, words, and faces laced the image of the girl. Sporadic and random, they highlighted her face, her breasts, and her legs. Arrows pointed to the pockets. Primitive obscenities were drawn near her crotch.

"No drugs. No tech. No cash. Nothing for us." The moment of attention passed, and they moved by a woman in gray sweatpants and her agitated dog without a glance. She was a "singular," out of network, uninteresting. As they walked on down the street, they wove around each other with the same unpredictable and undulating grace of a jellyfish.

They were symbiotes. Hackers, gadget junkies, and addicts that had gone open source all the way. A gang of youths with networked neuroprosthetics—share and share alike—they were connected to each other on every level. No firewalls. Like a good joint, all experiences were passed around and shared. They were a colony, a pack, a unified plural, they were symbiote, the antisocial, overconnected counterculture movement for shiftless runaways and tech scavengers. Experiences mixed and matched into a psychotropic stew. Drug for one was a drug for all. Privacy and the singular persona evaporated into a collective conscious that fostered the most unconstrained individual behaviors. The more bizarre and divergent the experience, the better to add to the group palate.

The injured woman and the chunky lady waiting for the authorities forgotten, they ambled on. They were off to find new sensations and new gear.

"Time to move on. Check it."

The boy stared at his creator with a steady dispassionate gaze. Hagan returned to the straight black lacquered chair. Usually a source of solace, the quiet ascetic environment of his lab provided no relief from the prior evening and morning's events. His wife was pushing him to the brink, and the pioneer of a generation was reduced to a brain-injured murderer covered in shit. The voice of Canter rang in his head to add insult to injury—*all eyes are on you, soldier.*

Fuck you, "soldier," Hagan thought to himself. He had enough to worry about without that tall pale-skinned ghoul haranguing him.

His wife had already left a message. He hadn't returned it yet. How was he going to deal with her and explain what was going on with Devron? How the founding father of neuroprosthetics was in an intensive care unit surrounded by guards, standing accused of a terrible crime. How he had to somehow figure it out.

Right now all I can do is wait. There was nothing he could do with Devron while his heart was getting sorted out. Would be an hour at least before he could go down there and reexamine him.

Whenever under stress, Hagan returned to what he knew best—his work. He hoped that in the interlude while Devron was being medically stabilized he could distract himself with his research. The thoughts continued to interrupt his concentration.

It's not coming together . . .

"What is not coming together, Dr. Maerici?" The boy's cool, even voice echoed in his mind. Hagan's eyes snapped to Omid—his artificial intellect. In the lab all barriers between him and his artificial intelligence were removed. The connection was automatic whenever he entered the room. After many years of working with the construct, the AIRENS still occasionally caught him off-guard.

"It's not pertinent to the task, Omid. Let's begin our session. Where were we?" Graphs, pie charts, various folder bins, and oscillating waveforms began winking into existence around the room.

"We had downloaded proverb data sets, from subject thirty-two and nine hundred forty-eight. I had incorrectly answered the analysis of 'a rolling stone gathers no moss.' I am detecting that there is increased activity in the emotive centers of your cingulate gyrus, anterior hypothalamus, amygdala, hippocampus, and basal frontal gyrus.

There is a high level of theta rhythm coherence. These are indicative of a persistent thought with high emotive content. Are you still upset with me?" His question was an emotional one, but his overt appearance was anything but. Omid sat in a lotus position on the table staring at Hagan with unblinking eyes. The boy's thin frame and smooth round head gave him the appearance of a Buddhist prodigy.

Hagan was in no mood to discuss the topics of murder, guilt, disgust, and regret with the emotional equivalent of a four-year-old. *"No, Omid, I am not upset with you. It is an unrelated topic. As I have said, this is not pertinent. Let's begin again . . . please review the data sets from subjects thirty-two and nine hundred forty-eight. Tell me now, in light of the associated data, what does it mean to say 'out of sight, out of mind'?"*

As if receding into meditation or prayer, the blue child bowed his head and closed his eyes. The dynamic charts behind him again moved and bounced with a frenetic fervor. After a few moments, bars dropped and curved lines flattened, and Omid opened his eyes in the same measured rate.

He again looked at Hagan. *"One who does not have vision will go insane."*

Hagan shook his head. *"No, that is not right. That again is too literal. There is indeed parity between the two statements, but not in the literal sense of losing one's sight and losing one's sanity. You are taking this all in the first-person context—if I lose sight I will also lose my mind. Reevaluate this in a social context where both statements hold parity, but they are not both held to a first-person perspective."*

Omid continued to stare at Hagan with an unmoving presence. It made the AIRENS seem distinctly nonhuman. It was the lack of small random activities that were always a giveaway to the artifice of the construct. The random blinks and side glances, shifting of weight, and all the minute responses to subtle, shifting perturbations of an inconstant world that were near impossible to recapitulate. It always removed Hagan from perceiving Omid as the child that he appeared, but regarding him instead as the cool, still projection of something hoped for.

"Proceed with analysis."

The AIRENS again closed his eyes. *"Processing . . . Those unable to see are insane."*

Hagan let out a sigh. *"No, that's not correct. 'Out of sight, out of mind' means that when one is not within sight of the person—or close proximity—that person is not in one's mind or conscious thoughts. In other words, if I am away from you, I don't think about you."*

"No."

"What?"

"No."

Hagan leaned forward, closer to the figure, as if to hear better. Despite the fact that Omid was a virtual construct of his own mind, he was in disbelief of what he just heard—disagreement.

"What do you mean, no? I have just given you the correct answer." Hagan could feel his heart begin to beat faster. The AIRENS was demonstrating self-determination.

The AIRENS looked at the physician with an unaffected calm. *"In this matter I am correct."*

"Omid, are you telling me that I am wrong?" Hagan asked.

"You are incorrect."

Hagan was now fully engaged. He leaned back. *Rebellion.*

Typical Edwin, she thought, *always slipping into contemplative reveries.* Tara let her thoughts slip away as she focused on getting to her destination.

Tara accelerated her Cog-cycle. She would be at the hotel in less than five minutes. Her view was unimpeded by dials, indicators, switches, or gears. She went faster—that was all. It was all feel. She felt her cycle-self move effortlessly forward. With tireless mechanical strength, she wove amongst the other tapered vehicles and automaton transports like a lithe aquatic predator sliding past manatees in a slow-moving river. The red lacquer metal containment core at the center of the cycle encased her body. Her armored form was only minimally discernable between the two large tubular wheels in the front and the back. Each wheel was partially covered by multiple iridescent steel bands that extended along the length of the cycle. Each shiny fleck was a tiny member of a circumferential compound eye giving full surround visibility.

She loved the feel of her cycle. It was a non-standard-issue Tesla LJ COGENT. A thousand horsepower supercharged electric cycle that had pushed her cortical plasticity to its limits. Gaining control had taken months of being virtually hooked up to the thing to alter her standard human binocular color vision to a three-hundred-sixty-degree monochromatic insect view. It had taken years to adapt her senses to each feature of the COGENT: getting used to the wheel turning and tilting movements as a replacement for her arms and legs, replacing the feeling of normal skin touch with the tire sensors and strain gages, balance for acceleration, hearing for echo location—all of it was a battle for her adult brain. The result was worth it. The feel of strength, agility, and indomitable machine endurance were unparalleled. After riding for several years, she found switching from body perception to cycle perception had become effortless.

Turning herself into a machine had been a welcome retreat. The attention and training to control the COGENT had allowed her to forget.

Maybe "forget" was the wrong word, she thought. *"Distract" was better.* The memories never fully went away, but at least when they painfully resurfaced there were ways to minimize their damage. For her it had been the cycle and her work. Thoughts of her husband's departure unexpectedly came to mind. The moments of confusion when she returned home to find the closets empty. Picking up the letter.

It had only been a few sparse sentences.

Tara, I am tired of this. It's clear that your duty to country supersedes your duty to family. I am moving on with my life. Good-bye.

She had just gotten back from a four-week mission with the Seals. The one island of solace, her home, had been stripped from her. She was alone. She remembered the guilt, the loneliness, the decision to leave the military, the defeated sense of frailty. She had gained weight. She had felt ugly and felt embarrassed about feeling ugly. It was then that she returned herself to an old discipline—one of self-reliance.

Tara thought about her past. She thought about the plains of Kansas. The long, flat, and dusty expanse that filled the memories of her childhood. Her memories were like the rolled hay bales that spotted the long shifting grain fields—discrete packages of experience that interrupted long stretches of a homogenous routine. The largest bale of them all was her father. A hard man, heavy and thick with a large head like an anvil. Heavyset brows shaded ball-bearing gray eyes that were unwavering with a pious intensity. His religion was hard work and his Bible was his reputation.

She remembered as a small child sitting on a chair in the kitchen after her mother had died. The cracked vinyl beneath her legs itched, but she hadn't dared move. He sat in front of her, his sun-weathered face was close. The salty tang of his leathery skin and the sweet earthy odor of his chewing tobacco had filled her senses. He spoke to her at the age of seven like a new army recruit.

"Hard work, Tara—that's what makes you, that and your word, your word is your bond. Without those two things you're nothin'. You understand that—nothin'." He spoke with a gravelly intensity. He stared at her for several moments to ensure his words had sunk in. Satisfied they had, he nodded and they had gone out to the fields.

From an early age she had seeded and planted and harvested. In between, she fixed, repaired, and prepared, to yet again seed, plant, and harvest. When she did those things he was satisfied, when she didn't do it right, she did them again until he was satisfied. Changing the course and direction of his instructions for how the farm was managed was as impossible as disagreeing with the direction of a path next to a sheer cliff face.

Despite the grit and the country twang, Tara knew her father was a smart man. He could operate complex machinery. He had handled complex accounts. He had wrested the local mineral rights from the county. Set within the rough-edged and unsophisticated exterior was a savvy man. She would see him sitting in worn overalls and a plaid shirt, dusted and white with the grain cuttings, programming the tractor's GPS system. The technology hadn't scared him. "You do it yourself—nobody ain't gonna do it for you." With that she too had learned. She had learned to program, to use technology ranging from large threshers to fuzzy-logic watering algorithms, to manage complex finance accounts. Her father had taught her by way of assigning a new responsibility.

His more personal lessons had been harder.

"Your word is your bond." His voice echoed in her head. She remembered his large callused hands. The thick index finger pointing at her, the tip bent with multiple fractures from unforgiving farm equipment. She remembered when he promised a neighbor to have her watch their pigs. It had been raining terribly and she hadn't wanted to do it. He had forced her to stand in the rain for five hours. When she began to cry about it after she came home, he had stood her out in the rain for an additional two hours for complaining. While she stood in the downpour she had been glad for the rain, since it had hidden her tears. She had been eleven at that time. She had learned her lesson— you keep your word and you don't complain about it.

Since her husband left she had kept her word and hadn't complained. She wrapped herself in a hard-cased isolation. The cycle was a symbol of that—enmeshed in steel and in total control.

Her machine self felt the road, the movement, the wind. It gave her transport a singularity of purpose—to move. All the details were second nature in her cycle percepts. The road was moist with a slight gravelly texture, probably the result of recent street cleaning. The wind blowing slightly perpendicular to her cycle body meant she would have to lean a fraction more when moving right. Other vehicles were a sluggish shifting panorama that she moved past with the ease of a cheetah. The speed required no quantification, it was as natural to her as distinguishing between walking, jogging, and running.

As she approached, her full monochromatic view was interrupted with a diagram of her approaching destination. Outlines of a building rotated and a smaller erratically highlighted dot was shown exiting.

The perpetrator is leaving out of the south exit of the Ritz, she thought. She adjusted her planned trajectory of approach.

Getting close. She accelerated more. *Roads are drying up. Feels good. Can hit turns harder.*

The exit approached. Her metallic body bent to the turn at 214 kilometers per hour. A fraction faster would have sent her careening into the side rail. She knew it, felt it, and hit the friction limit of her tires precisely.

The white dot was now on a back alley. The view magnified and a small stumbling silhouette was running down the street.

Approaching direct visualization.

There were several other forms—cooler shades of blue—heading toward the exits of the building. They were in pursuit and converging.

Tara exited the off-ramp. She slowed slightly as her extended senses registered the approaching streets and sidewalks. Her vision was an amalgam of superimposed information—monochromatic compounded vision, acoustic signatures, computer-generated renderings of known structures, virtual individuals registered by their satellite links—she saw it all at once.

An erratic group of silhouettes was between her and the person of interest.

"DISPERSE. DISPERSE. A POLICE ACTION COMMENC-ING. I REPEAT—A POLICE ACTION COMMENCING." The pedestrians vacated like a startled school of fish.

Nobody between me and the perpetrator. Can move straight on him. The large flat tires of her cycle jumped the curve and bit the pavement with a brief screech. Tara and her COGENT began accelerating down the walking pavilion. Flashing red and blue lights emitted from the entire surface of the cycle, making it look like a pulsating comet. People within fifty yards all flinched as the command warning voice echoed in their minds—*"CAUTION CAUTION POLICE ACTION OCCURRING—DO NOT APPROACH—CAUTION CAUTION POLICE ACTION OCCURRING—DO NOT APPROACH."* Like the annoying whine of sirens in the past, these were forced messages they couldn't turn off. All people held still in their stride and looked on as the phosphorescent piece of metal hammered past like a transient and focal hurricane.

Tara continued to pick up speed. The images of buildings, light posts, chairs, tables all flitted by. There were people standing in small

plastic booths—virtual storefronts—covering their eyes and looking at the flashing lights, frustrated that their shopping was being interrupted. Her combined senses processed the information with
neuroprosthetic-enhanced speed. *Just a moment now . . .*

With a balanced and measured shift, she leaned hard to the right.
The metallic casing over her shoulders and knees were inches from the
ground. The tires emitted a low hissing sound. The engine continued
its high-pitched electric hum. She could feel the pebbles and road dust
against her metallic skin. The cycle slid along and turned into a near
ninety-degree angle.

"Visualization confirmed." She could feel the uneven cobbled bricks
beneath her tires as she began to progress forward.

Ahead she could see the outline of a figure in her single-hued vision. Arms flailing, leaning forward, he appeared in a constant state
of tumbling. His clumsy movements were hampered and tripped by
the littered alleyway. Dumpsters, random drainage pipes, cracked
granite gutters all slowed the figure to an exaggerated blundering
advance. As he stumbled forward, his shoulder struck the side of one
of the large garbage containers, sending him spinning. He palmed a
wall and righted himself and continued to stagger forward.

Tara projected her presence to the other officers getting ready to
round into the alley way.

*"DETECTIVE DEZNER APPROACHING AT HIGH SPEED.
MAINTAIN AWARENESS."*

She then directed her thoughts to the suspect.

*"THIS IS DETECTIVE DEZNER. YOU ARE UNDER ARREST.
CEASE FURTHER MOVEMENT OR YOU WILL BE SUBDUED."*

He continued to run forward. Bent over with knees rising high, his
legs pistoned and shoved him down the alley. His right arm swung
wildly at the shoulder, his other arm was held straight in front of him
like a man finding his way in a dark basement.

She was closing on him—seventy-five meters—fifty meters—twenty-
five meters. He continued to run. Tara could see figures emerge from
doors behind her. They each had a badge number and name following
the silhouette. Others were generic figures representing civilians, also
moving into the alley from both sides.

Who are they? She dismissed the question as she closed in on her
target.

"THIS IS YOUR LAST CHANCE." With the legally mandated
transmission override, Tara knew he was hearing her voice in his head.

She focused her attention on his legs.

"Engage leg immobilizers." A vertical line appeared in her line of sight. She focused on the bottom of the figure's legs. She was now ten meters away. The figure could now hear the *thunkathunkathunka* of wheels moving over the cobblestone road. The line was fixed on his calves.

"Deploy." A glob of adhesive jettisoned from a small port at the side of the cycle. The ball thinned and spun like a bolo toward the running figure. Moments before contact, the figure lurched to the side and fell through a side door. He was horizontal on the ground. The mound of glue quivered inches away from the pair of feet and ankles that emerged from the doorway. *Dammit.* The last remnant of the figure scuffled and disappeared from the alley.

Tara's COGENT stopped in front of the entrance. A badly deteriorated and dented aluminum door still swung slightly into the dark passage way. There was no visible sign of the suspect. Tara's cycle-enhanced senses told her there were echolocation signatures of a pedestrian twenty feet into the hallway.

"Disengage," she projected to the cycle. Like a beetle preparing for flight, the segmented shell encasing Tara's body opened and was held aloft as she emerged from her prone position in the driving cockpit. Small tendrils withdrew from their magnetic connection to Tara's head and disappeared into the paneling. With the grace of a gymnast she rolled and leapt to her feet.

Tara's perception had switched to human mode. She once again saw color with the limited field of view of two eyes. Looking down the alley she saw a couple heads with colorful Mohawks and iridescent skin markings.

Fucking symbiotes, she thought. They followed disorder like hyenas to a kill. They would strip her motorcycle in thirty seconds if she wasn't careful.

"COGENT, initiate lockdown and static field charge to one-foot proximity."

She projected her thoughts to the officers running down the alley. *"PREPARING FOR MANUAL EXTRACTION. BE AWARE CIVILIANS PRESENT—SYMBIOTES MOST LIKELY. KEEP HARDWARE LOCKED."*

As she held the gun, a small blue window appeared in the upper right-hand corner with the muzzle eye view from her sidearm. With legs slightly bent, her back straight and poised, she advanced quickly to the dark entrance.

"Superimpose heat signatures onto field of view." Small blue traces emerged around the hallway. As her eyes acclimated to the dark outlines in the passage, a blue haze highlighted a couple ventilation openings. The room smelled dank and old, a mix of humidity, algae, and dirt. She could hear the distant *thump* of large machinery in the background.

Probably entrance to water-treatment center for the Ritz, she thought. Tara's body was taut and still as she looked for clues to her fleeing suspect. There were smears within the grime on the floor that revealed recent passage. She padded quickly and quietly down the hallway, keeping track of the smudge marks. Twenty feet along the path, the smudges disappeared next to a doorway to her left. Putting her gun through the opening, she saw a figure bent over and gasping for breath. One of his arms was fixed against the wall, the other hanging limp toward the ground.

There must be something wrong with the image transmission. The figure that Tara was looking at was a silhouette composed only of static. Bouncing random pixels of light and dark hue formed the outline of the man. *Damn city issue—must be something wrong with the gun.*

She sighed. She knew what she needed to do—the perp's location was identified, he was unaware of her position; she knew her next move.

"Scale bullet force to seven, heavy stun." A ratio appeared over the handle of her gun—7/10. She bent her knees slightly and held onto the gun with both hands. With the pistol close to her head she prepared to sweep around into the doorway. She took several measured breaths—*"One, two, three . . ."*

"DO/*DO* NOT/*NOT* MOVE/*MOVE*!!" Both her voice and her thoughts boomed and echoed into the dank room.

"What/*What* the/*the* . . . ?" Tara looked to the crouched figure against the wall. *Just static . . .* The man was no more than a silhouette punched out of his surroundings. A void. He looked like a man-shaped window into a pixilated sandstorm. Without noticing Tara's entrance, he continued to heave and rasp, the side profile of his chest and abdomen expanding and contracting. Mouth open, he was pulling ragged shaky breaths, spittle dripping in long, stringy tendrils from his mouth. He appeared oblivious to the gun trained upon him.

With her gun held forward, straight and rigid, Tara approached with small, measured steps. As she got closer, she could see the static was emanating from the surface of his skin. The right hand and forearm facing her were obscured by dark splotches.

"Sir/*Sir*? You/*You* are/*are* under/*under* arrest/*arrest*." Still no recognition of her presence. "*Something's wrong here—disengage thought projection override.*"

"Sir, you are under arrest, you have the right to remain silent . . ."

As she began to read the man his rights, Tara removed a BRD, a body-restraining device, a small disk from a pouch in her belt. Still with the gun trained on the man, she reached around to stick the first of a pair of tabs to his back. As her hand approached he was still indifferent to her proximity. As she placed the adhesive device on his skin, his face turned abruptly.

Tara jumped back. His movement had been so sudden, she found herself surprised and dangerously off-balance. His face shocked her. Two glowing orange eyes burned from a visage that was more mask than human. The right half of the face was blurred with a snowstorm of static. The other half was a pulsating tangle of blue lines. In the dimly lit room it was impossible to discriminate the finer features of a nose or a mouth, only the burning irises set upon opalescent, glowing corneas floating in a strange confluence of moving colors.

"What the fuck?!" A hoarse voice barked out her. "Where the fuck did you come from, you fucking bitch?"

His arm struck out. Tara's head rocked to the side. The force of his fist felt like a fastball striking her in the temple. Bright sparkles exploded into her field of view. Knocked to the ground, she heard her gun clatter into the dark recesses of the room. Looking up, she got her first full frontal view of her approaching assailant.

Only half of his figure was covered in static illumination. The other half was a maelstrom of moving images. Over his chest she saw an old man with bad teeth laughing. On his abdomen there were two hands grabbing the face with both thumbs pushed into the eye sockets. Blood was running down the cheeks. A woman was curled into a fetal position on his shoulder . . . small tablets on an old ornate table . . . a red face with empty holes for eyes . . . cigarettes . . . a small, thorny-looking doll.

The brief images flitted and moved over him like a movie screen being buffeted by a strong wind. She saw random images of a limb, an indeterminate piece of flesh, a girl with spikey silver hair whose mouth was open in a scream. Hands reaching out. Splotches of color—ochre yellow, red, brown. The collage of images abruptly stopped in a line along the center of the man's body, on the other side was the chaos of pixilated light.

Despite her training, she was taken off-guard. With her heels pushing against the ground and elbows scissoring, she crab-walked away from him.

"I didn't do it. It wasn't me who did it. Do you understand? Not me. Not fucking me!"

The mosaic silhouette continued to walk toward her. His right arm hung limp at his side. The other arm was bent with the hand opening and closing. The miasma of color was blunted and partially obscured by tarry stains covering the fingers and wrist.

"This is not fucking me, you understand, bitch, not fucking me!" She saw more images swirl and spiral. She saw herself lying on the floor beneath his navel. The image of a face with a cheek torn away revealing exposed teeth. The lopsided skeletal grin morphed into what looked like brains.

He grabbed her ankle and yanked her toward him. The intense strength of his pull made her feel like a fish caught on a hook. She felt skin peel away from her elbows as she came crashing into his shins. He was close to her now. Tara was on her back and vulnerable. The baleful glow of his orange eyes burned into her. The right arm, iridescent with sparkling static, hung still and limp. Then she saw him straighten and raise his arm up like sledgehammer. The tight balled fist came down.

Training and instinct kicked in. Rolling to the side, she felt the puff of still air against her face as the hand narrowly passed the crown of her head. She heard a thudding sound intermingled with the sounds of cracking as if small twigs were being snapped. The arm came up again and dropped to pound into Tara's head. She rolled again. A near miss. He moved so rapidly that Tara couldn't gain her balance and momentum.

Tara could see the little finger and ring finger pointing away from the left hand at unnatural angles, and there was a cleft in the base of wrist; he was smashing at her with complete disregard for his own body.

He's using his arm as a club! It was clear he wanted to crush her to oblivion. His arm rose again. Tara knew her luck and speed were not going to last indefinitely.

The BRD! She realized she had the second of the adhesive disks in her hand. The arm came down again like an ax. This time she leaned forward. Holding the disk, her arm jabbed out at the last moment to stick the device to his abdomen. Instead of the fist hitting its mark, the forearm covered in shifting images of intestines glanced off the side of her head. To Tara, it felt like a steel rod. Her head was ringing and she thought she felt something wet in her ear. Rolling over, she tried to crawl away from him on her hands and knees. Like a sprinter taking off from a crouched position she moved toward the gun in the corner.

Behind her, the mosaic creature lumbered toward her with heavy strides. He moved, oblivious to the devices stuck to him. A small flashing red light on the disk blinked more rapidly and then turned green. Tendrils of clear filaments then emerged from either side of his torso and coalesced around him as if some large invisible spider were entwining him in its threads. As the dollops first stuck to him they fixed his limp right arm to his chest. The threads then continued to emerge and capture his left arm, then the tops of his legs, then around his calves and feet. They continued to spit and enclose him such that he could no longer walk and simply stood there motionless. Disbelief shadowed the angered glow in his eyes as he looked down at himself, now completely cocooned in a tangle of clear fibers. With a heavy thud, he fell to the floor.

Tara scrambled to her gun and turned to see the man captured and immobile on the floor. The shifting forms and static were now muted beneath the frosted covering that enclosed him from his neck to his feet. The threads were coalescing to form a single sheet. She approached cautiously, her muzzle eye view fixed on the center of his head. The shot indicator was a small point indicating maximum intensity of force. It was set to kill. He would not get a second chance to come at her, Tara thought, still angry at her herself for letting her guard down.

That could have really cost me. I was lucky this time. Her heart was thumping within her chest and her hands were tremulous from the adrenalin coursing through her system.

She approached slowly with the pistol trained on the large glowing mass. He was facedown and not moving. Tara could hear running footsteps in the distance. They began to echo as they entered the industrial recess.

The clattering sound of people filled the room. "Detective Dezner! What happened?" Three officers piled in behind Tara, her gun fixed on the immobile form on the floor. They could see the smears of soot and dust all over her dark suit. Her elbows were ragged and red. Small smears of blood stained her forearms. Her hair, formerly pulled back, hung in ropy strands around her face.

"Do you need a medic?" asked one of the cops.

"No, I'm fine, thanks."

"Are you sure?" The officer looked at her incredulous, seeing Tara battered and shaking as she held her gun.

"I said I'm fine," she said sharply, irritated at being asked twice. "One of you guys hold cover on him."

"Sure, Detective, OK, no problem. What happened?" Another cop held a sidearm trained on the restrained glowing form.

Holstering her gun, she rubbed her elbow. "The suspect gave chase and when trapped resisted arrest and attempted assault." Resuming her measured and professional composure she related the details of the incident. The officers listened as Tara carefully articulated the "relevant" facts. Her voice was stonier and more restrained than usual. The officers approached the suspect with care.

"I have never seen body tats like that. He is totally covered. Jesus, that must have been expensive." Two of the officers turned the man over. His orange eyes were still open, looking straight ahead. His breaths were shallow and rapid.

"Not fucking me . . . not . . . not me . . . wasn't me," he rasped. He was again read his rights. One of the officers was scanning his eyes.

"Confirmed, suspect is Frank G. Minsky, aka the Chameleon." Tara finally turned away and let her muscles relax. She massaged her shaking hands to wring out her passing fear. Outside she could hear the sounds of vehicles halting. More manpower was finally on its way.

Blue letters emerged above the Chameleon, accompanied by small, tinny, gong-like sounds. *"Awareness—DING—Awareness—DING."* Tara again turned. Her prosthetic projections were drawing her attention over the man now lying on his back. She could see the image of his heart rhythm, oxygenation, and blood pressure readings scrolling across the surface of the restraining material. The summary diagnosis was reading out across his chest:

HEMODYNAMICALLY UNSTABLE

CARDIAC ISCHEMIA—ONGOING

METABOLICALLY ABNORMAL

REQUIRES IMMEDIATE MEDICAL ATTENTION

More people were pouring into the room with equipment. A team with a gurney picked up the Chameleon and secured him to the base. He was lifted into the air.

"Where we going with this guy?" one of them asked.

She looked down at him. His head moved slightly from side to side. He continued to mutter in words without inflection or emphasis—an empty stream of words, like a punctured tire emptying itself of air. "Not no not me no no no wasn't I didn't do it no no no not me not me not me not me not me wrong made made me wrong."

"Take him to Barnes Hospital," she said. He quickly disappeared down the corridor, leaving Tara to her thoughts.

Looking at the interleaved and entwined faces in the room, Krantz had failed to see the simple message there. At first glance the floor looked like the smeared results of two desperately entwined and grappling bodies wrestling on the ground. One trying to maim and the other trying to escape. He was wrong, though. On closer inspection there was a sweep and flow that was purposeful and nonrandom. Amid the wanton and nonsensical splotches there was one long string of cursive words in a continuous amalgam of palm-traced lines. Drawn across the bottom of the floor, the words arced from the epicenter of the carnage.

The letters looked like an enlarged version of the finger paintings small children made in kindergarten.

But what the hell does THAT mean—"Not me RedDevil"—along with all these other bizarre clues? Was it a statement, an abdication of guilt? What was RedDevil? A drug, a cult, some influence causing them to engage in antisocial behavior? Must be a drug of some sort. But why didn't they detect it in Devron? They ran every test known to man. No abnormal agents, just brain damage. Was that the name of this new drug—RedDevil?

Krantz would have to let the forensic guys work on this. He was sure they were poring over every molecule of Devron's crime scene and of his and the victim's bodies. Why would these guys—wealthy, young, old, gay, straight—all be doing the same thing?

He was hoping Tara's perp would shed more light on this. Another point on which to triangulate the case.

This had to get taken care of quick, Krantz thought. With Devron sick and accused of murder, explanations were going to be needed for the insatiable press, investors, and politicians. Moreover, if it looked like there was some connection to other murders, the reporters, drones, Virtua Bots, blogs, and info bids were going to be all over this. Every two-bit person having an inkling of information would be auctioning off semifacts for thousands of dollars. It was going to be a feeding frenzy. The infotainment measures were going to be off the charts. The people paying the price were going to be his department— the public would be looking to find fault in protocol and accusing them of not being quick enough to prosecute, of being partial to the rich, unfair to the affluent, pro-industry, antigay, you name the angle, it will all come back to his department. These high-profile cases always did. *Goddammit,* he thought, his thoughts again became more discursive, *RedDevil, RedDevil, RedDevil . . . strange faces . . . what the hell?*

Krantz began to walk back to his car. He grabbed the handle—an anachronism of personal transport. Manual operations—a door handle, a steering wheel, gear shifts—all so old, to most it was laughable. A body encumbered by speed dictated from muscles and tendons. Too slow in this day and age, when efficiency was based on the speed of thought. The time it took to move a knob, manipulate a tool, all were too slow; bodies were becoming vestigial to the machinations of the mind. Krantz liked to operate things he could still control. He opened the door and sat in his patrol car. A classic Honda Rinatta, automatic transmission with autopilot assist. Self-driven, hand-operated autos were getting harder and harder to acquire. He had to wait months for the classic specs. He still felt the grip of a steering wheel when he drove. He still was the man in the car, not the man who became or was driven by the car.

He headed for the office. *RedDevil . . .*

"*I can't talk now. Anna—I just can't—there is too much going on.*" Hagan's mind was inundated. He was already tired and getting stretched beyond his ability to fully comprehend everything.

"*Listen, Devron is sick and potentially a criminal . . . and Omid, I think I have . . . I think I may have finally done it.*"

"*Done what, Hagan? Stop speaking in code. We need to talk.*" Anna's voice was tired yet resolute.

"*I'm going to have to go back to see Devron in a moment and—well, I can't talk about it now. I only have a few moments and Omid has done something really different. I need to wrap my head around what it means. I know it's jumbled but just try to understand—there is really A LOT going on right now.*"

His wife's voice came at him like a javelin. "*There is always something going on Hagan—ALWAYS.*" Her pitch and volume were rising in emotion. "*This is too much right now. When do I fit into the equation?*"

"*Sweetheart—I will call you shortly, I promise. In an hour, I promise—one hour. Just give me that.*"

There was silence. She had hung up.

He tried to look through the windows—*no lights.* There was nothing past the dirt and soot that covered the tinted glass. The usual blue UV lights were gone. He had never come in the afternoon—always late at night and always scheduled. His driver would stop for just a moment and someone would be waiting for him. He would always see the glowing blue lights through the windows, highlighting human shapes in activities that he knew were sinful and iniquitous.

But Jesus spent time with the lepers and the whores. He was following in his footsteps. Right now he needed more of the Spirit. He must have it. The Chameleon had it.

"WHY THE FUCK IS NO ONE ANSWERING?!" His fists now pounded on the metal doors. Dust plumes rose from the cracks at the side of the doors—still nothing. *I am doing the Lord's work. I need the Spirit.*

The window front to the Sterno Room was dark and desolate like an empty shell. The windows were barred and cracked. He again rapped on the door. This time softer—almost pleading with the unyielding barrier. *Somebody has to be there. No way the Chameleon would leave his goods unguarded. No way.*

Elymas stood back and looked along the dilapidated storefronts. Most were abandoned. He was sweating all over. Wet spots soaked his chest and armpits—stained through the light taupe suit to create brown discolorations. Elymas turned and looked from side to side. He felt like he was suffocating. Black amorphous blobs were pushing through the ground like dark pustules. They would sometimes slide toward him. He had to move out of their way or they would take him. He could feel their malignant intentions.

Maybe there's a back entrance, he thought. *Maybe a back way in, or the office is out back. Even if nobody's there, I'll just get some of what I need, I'll pay the Chameleon back, he'll know I'm good for it.*

Elymas now jogged around the corner of the block. There was an old alleyway paved with bricks and sunken in the middle from a century of neglect. It had the smell of urine and rotting food.

Oh yes, good, I'll just get in the back. No problem, I'll pay the Chameleon back. The Lord is my shepherd. Elymas saw the dark blobs rolling around the corner. A new surge of fear pushed though him. The minister retched onto the red bricks and ran forward.

This must be it! Oh yes, this definitely must be it. Elymas pushed his hands against a window. He wiped the grimy pane with his palms and cupped his hands over the window. Pushing his face against the glass, he could see what looked like surgical equipment and a series of medical cabinets.

Oh yes, the Lord is my shepherd, oh yes! Reeling back, the minister put his fist through the window. He pushed his arm past the sharp edges to feel for the lock mechanism. Rivulets of blood ran down the grime-encrusted glass.

He felt a switch. *That's got it.* The window began to loosen slightly. Elymas felt a rush of hope. He was almost there. The windowpane began to give way and crack from where it had been painted over in the past.

"Fuzzer, you got a real fuckin' problem." The voice behind Elymas made him freeze. He slowly turned. "Been watching your ass all the way down the street, fuckin' fuzzer-junkie-piece-a-shit."

A large, multihued skinhead stood grinning. Tattoos of grinning skulls, writhing snakes, flames, swastikas, and buxom burlesque women all shifted and glowed on his forearms, neck, and face. His hands twitched as he slowly gripped and ungripped a pipe with a menacing, slow rhythm.

The man came closer like a hungry animal. His face jerked as he approached.

"My child, take care, I am a man of the Lord, I can offer you salvation." Elymas was shaking all over. He held his hands up for calm. Blood stained the cuff of his right sleeve. His arms were now trembling violently. The dark blobs came racing down the alley. His mouth opened into a silent O of horror. They pushed through the bricks like some dark burrowing menace. They were at the feet of his assailant. They extended inky tendrils into his legs. Elymas watched as they pushed and distorted the skin of the approaching thug. Unaware, he continued to laugh.

Elymas felt the withdraw engulf him as the man approached. The reverend's voice became desperate and babbling. "Even though I walk through the valley of the shadow of death, I fear no evil; for . . . for . . . you are with me. . . . Psalm 23 . . . they comfort me. . . . I will not be afraid." His voice became incoherent and he began to speak in tongues.

The skinhead smiled hungrily and came closer.

The contours of the sand began to meld with the lines and curves of the body of the blue woman with red eyes.

This is always how it started—the takeoff . . .

The dry heat of sun baked him, but he still shivered from anticipation. The beaded texture of her metallic skin fused with the filigree of wind-swept dune contours like notes on a sheet of music. Sienna tones of rust and cinnamon intermingled with azures, gunmetal grays, and indigo to form a variegated and living palate of ultramarine, violet, and rose. Trent was moving from a world of concrete perception to one of pure emotion. The colors began to fade. Visual perception, auditory input, and tactile sensation gave way to awareness characterized by feelings, insight, and abstraction. Notions of paradox again brimmed in the periphery of his consciousness—*so real—yet indescribable . . .*

He watched her eyes. They were always the last thing he concretely saw—the undulating burning embers punctuated by onyx pupils—sharply focused pits of endless shiny depth. Arcs and bundles churned and writhed. Colors echoing with titillating emotions pressed closely on his legs and ensheathed his torso. Smells of tar and dry leaves were blinding and his nostrils were filled with the sound of breaking glasses.

Like drops of oil coalescing over a fluid surface, notions emerged. Thoughts brought together by his mysterious host. The communication was nonverbal—primordial—a conjunction of urges that articulated detail by their overlap.

. . . a small change . . .

. . . another gift . . .

. . . a minor alteration . . .

. . . good for you . . .

. . . good for US . . .

. . . US . . .

. . . a small change . . .

The percepts reverberated through Trent's being. *US.* The connection, the communion filled him with a completeness—a thunderclap of things so right. *US! US!* The pull toward unity was like the gravitational force of the sun inextricably moving him into its bright center.

Yes, he replied in wordless exaltation. *YES . . . for US! US! US! US!* His assent radiated from him like a pulsating supernova.

The detective sat with his sweaty palms fixed on the steering wheel, waiting at a red light. Images of gardens and mutilated bodies entwined and spun among poorly connected theories and immaterial vagaries.

Maybe I am getting too old for this. Krantz kept on revisiting the scenes in his mind again and again, like a horror scene on a continuous loop. He saw the flayed woman, the faces, the swaying bits of the muscle in the flowers. The words. The dark and cryptic words echoed in his head.

"Not me RedDevil." He said it out loud to himself to try to dispel its power. "What the hell is that?"

Muscles twisted at the back of his neck. He grimaced from the spasms. The coffee probably hadn't helped. April had always warned him that it made him act crazy. Then, as now, he hadn't listened. He thought of her to calm himself down.

She would have made a joke, probably not a funny one, but a joke. If he wouldn't have dutifully laughed she would keep on telling it to him until he obliged. She had a way of dealing with his craziness. Even when he was in his thirties she had called him "old man."

More and more, he needed that safety valve, but it was gone. He missed those dumb jokes. He was losing his knack for the job. He wasn't sure if it was his age or the changing times.

Probably both.

He looked out his window across the intersection. The residential homes didn't look like homes at all to him anymore. They were all interconnected and joined with odd angles and curves. White frosted booths speckled the circuitous walkways and dented the manifold hive-like structures. These were not the homes he had once known—a free-standing house, a yard, and a driveway. It was all changing.

Crimes just aren't the same anymore. He looked again at the housing complex. *Everything is more complicated.* He thought about his work; solving a crime had always seemed to fall into such typical chunks for him.

Maybe I am losing my edge. Thinking of this case was making him nervous and uncomfortable. He had a darker feeling. A feeling he was missing something bigger, something more important. It stood in front of him and behind him like a large invisible bear snorting its dark intentions and he was blind to it.

The gong sound from his dashboard was increasing in frequency and volume—it was the compiled projections from multiple irritated drivers behind him. The light had turned green. He had to get a move on.

"System—engage cognitive privacy."

"PRIVACY ENGAGED."

Hagan felt the need to think this through without Omid seeing his thoughts. This was so new, so unexpected—*an independent thought.* This was the first time he had ever gone private with Omid. This situation was so fragile; he didn't want to mess it up. The boy sat motionless before him, unperturbed by Hagan's disconnecting. He sat staring at the doctor with the same quiet, machine-like aplomb.

An independent thought . . . even if it was wrong, who cares? He was hoping for an increased level of abstraction from these proverb experiments. *But dissent—what was in those files that could have engendered the shift? The change in perception that his logic was capable of defining the truth? How did he make the leap?*

Had he done it? Had he created a true artificial intellect—something that could self-declare? *How—how did it happen?* The days' events receded as his mind raced to process what could be his life's work come to fruition. He looked at Omid with new paternal awe.

His thoughts reached and grabbed for an explanation. He began pulling all the data up before him. Screen after screen materialized beside, behind, around, and partially penetrating the AI avatar. Hagan reviewed the time line of events since he returned to the room. He replayed and reviewed the data that had been downloaded.

It has to be in here somewhere . . . how did this happen?

He felt like a panhandler who had just seen his first speck of gold and was now grasping and shoveling piles of mud to find the larger nugget. His eyes sifted through the multitudes of screens looking for something anomalous, some type of correlation previously unforeseen. The information streams passed by him at high speeds in descending horizontal lines.

Hagan knew that it had to be something with the high level of random instantaneous information processing within his AIRENS's quantum core that made this possible. *But how?* His mind was silent as he subconsciously processed all the possibilities of this most improbable event.

Improbable . . . improbable. . . . Hagan then began to feel his thoughts wrap around a possible solution.

Back to basics . . . with tough problems, always go back to basics.
He took a deep breath and let it out slowly. *A quantum computer is a computation system that makes direct use of distinctively quantum mechanical phenomena to perform operations on data. The data is measured by qubits (quantum bits). The basic principle of quantum computation is that the quantum properties of particles can be used to represent and structure data and that quantum mechanisms can be devised and built to perform operations with this data.*

"But speed and memory don't create self-awareness," Hagan said aloud. Omid turned to look at Maerici, still patiently awaiting a directed action.

Hagan knew it was easy to create a good imitation of intelligence. You could create a near infinite number of functions and subfunctions, all of which could talk to you, think with you, and if subjected to a Turing test would probably fool most people. These AIs all lacked a certain level of "I-ness." The ability to self-declare, to act in a truly self-driven volitional manner. To show they were aware of themselves and what they were doing. To do something not programmed into a subfunction algorithm, no matter how fast, something that is a surprise, spontaneous, creative, something novel—*and* to be aware that one was doing it. That is what this was—an independent statement of truth—it was novel. This incorporated a certain creativity, novel order, randomness, and self-awareness to form an identity to self-declare.

Randomness . . . Like dominos falling, his thoughts were beginning to come together—*click click click*—toward an answer. *Randomness . . . entanglement . . .*

Hagan pulled the downloaded experiences of the two individuals thinking about some proverbs. The square representations moved forward out of the crowded blizzard of icons. *Did they become entangled? Could such a large set of stored data become entangled and coherent to achieve a dualistic quantum perspective?* Hagan's mind began to process the scientific and philosophic principles in parallel. *It's so improbable, but it could potentially explain this . . . but who would believe it?*

Basics—start from the beginning. Hagan was intimately familiar with the notion of entanglement, the strange principle in quantum physics that linked two particles even though they were separated in space. The spin of one atom could affect the spin of another atom regardless of the distance between the two particles. It was the spin of an atom that stored the qubit. This also meant that information between the entangled entities could be transmitted with a near infinite speed, hence the fast processing of quantum computers. This worked for single particles and bits of information . . . *but not for vast information sets like a cognitive experience. The probability of random entanglement, it's got to be so small. It's just not possible . . .*

Arguing with himself, Hagan countered, *If it did happen it could explain how the dual perspective of self-awareness had been accomplished—the ability to perceive external stimuli and simultaneously perceive the act of perception and action. To see, hear, and perform an action and simultaneously recognize and perceive that it is "me" that is seeing, hearing, thinking, and doing something. That's been the philosophical and scientific "sound barrier." A physical system cannot be in two places at once—it cannot receive information and observe its own reception—the very thing a human mind does with ease. The thing we have not been able to recapitulate with our best computers. (Until now?) But was it possible?*

Hagan steeled himself to figure this out. *Well, let's see if it happened.*

"System. Open Omid's operating system."

Unperturbed, a window emerged from the AIRENS's forehead. The image projected like a spotlight from the surface of a small, smooth planet. Omid stared forward, oblivious to Hagan opening his synthetic consciousness like a mechanic opening the hood of a car. The window revealed multiple small brightly lit connected cubes variously entwined in a three-dimensional chip matrix. The boxes pulsed and moved as the connecting lines shifted in thickness, brightness, and pattern.

"Expand memory drive." Like a verbal caption in a comic book, another square pushed and expanded from the tangled network. As it grew, various lines shifted and angled in configuration to accommodate the exiting subfunction. Within, more rectangular outlines shifted and fluctuated to some internal rhythm.

"View embedded frontal lobe data from subjects thirty-two and nine hundred forty-eight." Two more boxes pushed forward amid the flickering, restless shapes. Like a series of pyramids, the two windows emerged from a window that then emerged from another window. The frontal lobe window buzzed with pixilated data—billions upon billions of data points representing the brief experience of two human subjects contemplating a proverb.

"Show coherence between data sets." Hagan had often debugged his computers. In quantum computers, "random coherence"—when downloaded data would get spuriously entangled with each other—was not an uncommon occurrence. This usually involved a few qubits, enough to slow or distort a programmed function. They were usually easy to find; a couple bright spots between two disparate programs that have been defined as not related. The process involved pinging one data set and seeing which of the qubits in the other data set lit up.

"PINGING . . ."

Hagan's mouth slowly went slack as he watched the two screens. He felt as if he were watching two cities from an airplane at night turning on all their lights simultaneously. Thousands of small pixels winked into sight, forming a uniform field of white in both windows.

. . . completely coherent . . .

Somehow it happened. He didn't know how, but it did. Two massive cognitive data sets became randomly entangled. *Dual perspective.*

"System, reengage with Omid. Leave processes exposed."

"ENGAGED."

"Hello, Omid."

"Hello, Dr. Maerici."

"Please tell me again what 'out of sight out of mind' means."

"Well, what the hell do think the connection is then?" Krantz barked. Exasperated, he huffed at his partner, waiting for a response. Like a wind-jostled scarecrow, he rocked back and forth on his feet with irritation. He was again standing in the control room of the Barnes Hospital imaging suite. Pale iridescent columns were on either side of him. Ghostly figures floated in each of the square columns like trapped genies in their large bottles. The room was again crowded—now more than ever. There were more people in suits, people in technical gear, men and women fixing their attention to holographic switches, dials, indices, and streaming data. Most everyone in the room was arguing and unhappy.

Krantz was no different. Instead of one famous murder suspect, he now had an additional two. He looked more rumpled and squinty than ever. Tara was looking at him—cool, detached, and impartial. Her usual equanimity was marred by the remnant evidence of her assault. There was bruising on the right side of her forehead and she could not get rid of all the grime and dust from the knees of her pants.

"Edwin, at this juncture we don't have enough data. Currently we have three fairly similar assaults. We have been running their data for the past several hours. The connections are very tangential, but there's nothing definitive yet. All were wealthy and they had some banking crossovers. They never directly interacted. There are not even any proxy virtual connections. Thus far, they have never, *ever* interacted currently by a second order of connection. So people they have had virtual or actual communication with have not themselves communicated—"

"Tara, I know what second-order communication means. What about all the body fluid pictures, the meticulous mutilations? They all have the same M.O."

"Minsky did not draw any pictures."

"He didn't have time—the help heard the screams and when security came he started running."

"An assumption, Edwin; objectively, he didn't draw any pictures. Also, neither Devron nor the florist ran. They're similar, that's all we know. Moreover, we have captured the individuals in each of these cases with overwhelming evidence of their guilt. These could be largely closed cases."

Frustrated, Krantz waved his hands at Tara as if he were trying to fan away smoke. "Oh come on! Am I wrong that Minsky, this Chameleon guy, was vivisecting his lawyer in the hotel room? I mean, really, what does your intuition, your gut say?"

"Edwin, I have no interest in my gut, and don't even go there with the women's intuition thing." Sometimes her partner's old-world notions made her blood boil. "We need to deal with the data. You're right, Edwin—Minsky mutilated someone, but again he is a known criminal who has been skirting the law for many years. He is a known, if not proven, player in the synthetic drug market. His body modification shops, the Sterno Rooms, have been in and out of court for over a decade. He is a man who has been mutilating bodies—including his own—for years. Breaking the law is nothing new for him. This could have every easily been a deal gone wrong or drug gone bad."

"OK, what about the Oberweiss guy and Devron, they're not exactly the underworld type, and they both killed people close to them, mutilated their bodies, and drew strange pictures with their blood. That's a coincidence?"

"It does suggest a connection, but one we haven't found yet. All three thus far have little evidence of connection, direct or indirect. That limits the possibility of this being some type of social influence, a cult as you were suggesting earlier. Their metabolome workup is negative for foreign substances. Minsky has some known synth drugs on board, but the signatures are all over a week old and none of the others have any of those metal elements on board, so a drug is unlikely."

The crowd around them milled, bickered, and complained. Amid the rancorous disharmony, a team of white coats plied through the throng toward the imaging towers. In front was Hagan Macrici. His team of residents followed behind.

Hagan moved in a straight line toward the holographic portal. He ignored the swirl and tumult of people around him. His fixed gaze made it clear he would not be participating. His solid presence pressed through the crowd like an ice breaker. As he emerged near the holographic portals, he saw Tara and Krantz for the second time that day.

Oh brother. Not this again.

He nodded slightly in acknowledgment to the old detective. "Officer." Smiling slightly, he noticed the inner lining of Krantz's pocket sticking out. His view never wavered toward his partner.

Tara bristled with the snub as he turned his back on her to look at the holographic images. "Dr. Maerici, we did not ask for you to be here. This is a police investigation. What is your connection to these patients?"

Hagan's neck arched slightly and his shoulders squared. Slow and controlled, he turned to face her. "These are both my patients, Ms. Dezner," he said in tight clipped tones. "When *my* patients enter the hospital, I am usually notified. Given the situation, of course I will be called. If you don't mind, I will be examining my patients." Without waiting for a response he turned again in the same controlled pivot. His back was again facing Tara.

Her only response was a slight lift of both thin eyebrows. The subtle look that a master chess player reveals when a hole in their opponent's strategy has been revealed.

Krantz watched the exchange passively. Tired and irritable, he had no desire to break up any more ego arm-wrestling matches. Why was Tara at him so?

Krantz then saw blue words flash out the corner of his eye: *"Tara Dezner is requesting encrypted audio exchange. Acknowledge."*

"Sure," his thoughts responded.

"Edwin, the connection, it's Maerici. He is the physician to all three patients. The reason I couldn't find the connection is because of health information privacy. Doctor-patient exchanges are not searchable without a court order to penetrate the doctor-patient relationship."

Edwin worked to maintain a neutral composure and look as if he was casually observing the goings-on of the medical team. *"You think Maerici is responsible for all this?"* Krantz thought, hoping his incredulous tone was conveying. *"He's probably put in most celeb implants, what does he stand to gain?"*

"He's the only singular link between them thus far. I am going to do some additional digging. Stay with what he's doing. I am going to hang back."

Krantz shrugged his narrow shoulders and turned to follow the neurosurgeon.

Hagan approached the first imaging column with Krantz standing slightly behind. They both looked at the portly, semitranslucent figure floating in the square column. From the pear-shaped midsection, round face, and narrow forehead, Hagan knew the first body was Oberweiss. Images, both optical and virtual, encircled the holographic representation. Data was streaming with highlighted indices of problem areas. The surgeon's gaze flitted between the various laboratory and imaging figures, briefly picking out the salient kernels from each. His agile mind summarized and compiled the myriad data points in a moment. He knew the conclusion before the computer could spit it out.

"Again, joints, muscles, kidney, and heart—same as last time. What is going on here?" Hagan shook his head. Krantz continued to quietly watch. Hagan then pulled up the second patient's images. This time the figure was straight and rigid like a soldier held at attention. Again the myriad markers presented themselves. "Same thing with the Chameleon."

"Do they have the same decoherent patterns in their brains?" asked Reid.

"Just getting to that—let's see what it shows." Hagan directed his attention to the holographic display. *"Present brains of Minsky and Oberweiss for comparison. Perform analysis of coherent signals. Maximum coherence in blue and maximal decoherence in red. Begin analysis."* The brains looked as if they were on fire as the computer processed their signals. Pentabytes of data flitted in moments as the racing complexity of each brain was analyzed to see which sites were communicating and which were not. *"ANALYSIS WILL BE COMPLETE IN TEN SECONDS. TEN . . . NINE . . ."*

Unknown to the others, Tara was calling up file after file. The back of Hagan's head was in the center of a myriad of article publications, legal proceedings, public search results, communication cross-references, and probabilistic models of connectedness. As lines emerged, certain items became larger while others became smaller with their diminishing relevance to the parameter limits that Tara continually imposed.

Finally, three documents floated over the heads of the crowd. The first was a Web post announcing Devron's estate commitment to the neuroprosthetic and neural encoding laboratory run by Dr. Maerici—a commitment on the order of a billion dollars. Part of that gift would increase Maerici's salary by a factor of ten. There was a short video blurb showing the two men shaking hands. The second file was a legal document entitled *Minsky vs. Washington University School of Medicine/Hagan Maerici, MD.* The highlighted portions accused Maerici of medical malpractice and criminal negligence. The lawsuit was ongoing. The final file showed a legal document and addresses. Hagan's property abutted Oberweiss's back yard. It appeared that Maerici's wife had briefly shared the address with Oberweiss subsequent to their separation.

Tara felt the muscles in her shoulders relax. She was gaining clarity. There were several layers of motive here. She could hardly believe it. She shifted her gaze toward her partner. He was looking on at Maerici and his team as they were reviewing the images of Oberweiss.

"*. . . THREE . . . TWO . . . ONE. ANALYSIS COMPLETE. RESULTS PRESENTED BELOW.*"

Two brains rotated in synchrony. Below each was the name of its owner—Minsky and Oberweiss. The former semitransparent trappings of skull, skin, and facial features of the face and head were gone. The majority of the folds and wrinkles of the cortical surface coruscated with deep shades of violet and blue. Like an orange and red canker, each brain had a site that glowed with ruddy shades as if a smoldering ember had been pushed into the surface. The backside of the Oberweiss brain was painted various crimson hues as if it was an incompletely colored Easter egg, while the Minsky brain had a smaller site labeled on the central portion of the left hemisphere.

"Hmm, interesting. We see the same decoupling as we did with Devron, but in two completely different spots. Minsky seems to have his left parietal lobe involved, while Oberweiss seems to be involving both of his occipital lobes. Reid, Farhan, what do you think . . ."

As Hagan began to discuss with his residents, Tara projected her thoughts to Krantz. "*Edwin, Maerici is the one person who benefits from all this—he's the link! In all cases he stood to gain by their physical and social ruin. His salary is going to skyrocket with Devron's death. Apparently he is in critical condition currently. Minsky was suing him—his imprisonment makes that go away. After Maerici's*

recent separation, his wife apparently stayed with Oberweiss—his
neighbor—for about three months. That seems to suggest some atypi-
cal social dynamics.

"*Somehow, he must have influenced their behavior. No other per-*
son would be better suited for the task than one of the world's best
neuroprosthetic neurosurgeons who implanted their constructs."

———————

Krantz returned his gaze to the pack of white coats surrounding the
professor. He viewed the scene without expression and processed
Tara's words for several moments. As always she mastered the data. It
was his turn to consider, to mull the facts with his own intuitive measures of human nature. He watched Hagan. He watched his manner-
isms, his interactions with the residents, the staff members around
him. He let his thoughts process the previous interactions with the
doctor. Academic, precise, directed, he was very much a surgeon.
Maybe a bit egotistical, but he didn't get a read on malice. He could
smell that like a shark smelling chum in the water miles away. In the
decades of his job he sensed every flavor of it—smoldering hatred,
anger, vengefulness, insecurity, jealousy, narcissism; they all led to
particular interactions and whiffs of malevolent intentions. Thoughts
and perceptions shifted in Krantz's mind in various disconnected
nonverbal notions and links. Tara seemed to know what he was
thinking and added, "*Physician—natural actor. Required to mask*
and suppress his emotional interactions. Maerici—very, very high in-
tellect. Very disciplined. Could be a master masker. Data makes sense,
but kind of obvious, though . . ."

The horror show looped yet again in the old detective's mind.
There was more to this than a pissed off and greedy physician. There
was something more here. He still couldn't finger it. To Krantz, it just
didn't feel right. Whatever "it" was stood in his blind spot, in a place
he couldn't seem to get his mind around. There was a surge of disquiet
as he once again began to worry about his relevance to the modern
police force.

His thoughts evolved into more articulate notions and he directed
his attention to Tara. "*Dr. Maerici . . . so greed, malice, and jealousy*
all rolled into one." He continued to watch the team moving between
various views and files. "*Why all at once? Why has it all happened*
today? Maerici is a smart guy; having this happen all at the same time
would seem to draw more attention to himself. Seems like he would

see that coming. Maybe pick them off one at a time. Vary the way he kills people so as to seem less connected. We all know he's brilliant, seems like an obvious oversight."

Tara's head turned abruptly in the midst of the exchange—the team was turning to head toward the imaging suite doors.

"That's right, Farhan, the occipital lobes are involved in processing vision. What about the left parietal lobe? What does that do in particular?" With Farhan's prolonged pause, Hagan then directed his attention to the more senior resident. "Reid?"

"Well, the parietal lobe is most involved with spatial and mathematical processing."

"Correct, but what are some of the special features to the *left* parietal lobe?"

"Uhhm." Reid looked down at the ground as he strained to recall the missing insights. "Not sure, Dr. Maerici. I think it may—"

"Dr. Maerici, where are you going?" Tara's voice cut into the conversation, direct and unwavering.

"To see the patients, thanks. Let's pick this up in a moment, Reid. You two done telling secrets? It's the quietest you've been since we've met, please don't let me interrupt."

With the new info, Krantz watched every gesture of the exchange, processing every aspect, every mannerism, gaze deviation, inadvertent gesture. All were clues. *Is he playing with us?*

"Given that these two are murder suspects, we'll be accompanying you."

"Noted," Hagan responded dryly as he and his team moved farther away from the slowly rotating floating iridescent brains. Technicians continued to surround the holo-displays adjusting dials and parameters only visible to them.

As Hagan marched toward the doors with the detectives at his heels, a new group of people accosted him. They were three men. The one in the front was older, a man with thinning hair tightly oiled away from his narrow forehead. From nostrils to either side of his chin, he had deep lines cleaving the sides of his thin mouth. His skin was coarse with wide, dark hair follicles. The suit he wore was snug on his thin frame and slightly shiny. To Hagan, he appeared reptilian. Before the words came out of his mouth, he already knew this was another lawyer.

The man stood directly in Hagan's path, obstructing his passage. "Professor Maerici, I am counsel to the Chameleon. Since he has been accused of a crime—which he did not commit—given his medical state you will be obliged to keep his body covered at all times."

"What the hell are you talking about?" Hagan's voice was a monotone growl.

"Also, given the compromising condition that the Chameleon is in, it will not be appropriate for the officers to be in there with you." His voice was tarry and fluctuated in emphasis and timber with innuendo of unspoken threats.

Tara moved next to Hagan. "On what grounds?"

The lawyer turned his head and in a prolonged pause visibly ogled Tara before speaking. "Under the Thirty-second Amendment, Officer." The last word hissed out of him with a prolonged seedy flourish. "As the Chameleon's attorney—"

"You mean Frank Minsky's—and your name?" Tara cut in like a fencer parrying an opponent, her final words a command, not a question.

"My client prefers the Chameleon. My name is Hector Rasmussen. In any case, he is protected under the Thirty-second Amendment, which guarantees absolute cognitive privacy. Section two, states quite clearly—'all contents of a person's cognitive process as manifested by any measured physiologic process are solely and completely the private domain of that person. This content will not be interrogated, disseminated, or used against the person in a court of law without the person's express permission.' Given, that his OLED tattoos are directly linked to his neuroprosthetic constructs and reveal cognitive content, that is by definition private and not admissible without his consent."

"I am familiar with the law, Mr. Rasmussen. Tattoos by definition are public domain. People put them on their skin to be seen. Skin markings have been catalogued and used in criminal prosecutions for the past two centuries."

"This situation is unique, Officer . . ." Rasmussen took another moment to lean forward and leer at Tara's breasts. Moreover, he made it clear to Tara that that was indeed what he was doing. ". . . Officer Dezner. You see he is not in a capacity to control the content and therefore is not giving 'express consent' to revealing his 'cognitive process.' "

Hagan felt like he was entering a Mexican standoff from an old western. "Excuse me, I will reference yet another citation—the Hippocratic Oath. If you two don't mind I am going to go take care of my patient. This can be sorted out at a later time."

Rasmussen held up his spidery hands, spreading the tight, waxy skin of his fingers in mock apology. "By all means, Professor, proceed as you will. I have duly informed you and the officers here. What violations of my client's right you perform only help his case later."

Without further acknowledgment, Tara pushed past the smug lawyer toward the entrance of the large white room as if she were moving her way toward the exit of a crowded subway. "Dr. Maerici, Detective Krantz, let's proceed."

Hagan turned to his side and pushed his way past Rasmussen and his entourage to enter the muffled silence of the MINROI imaging suite. Tara and Krantz were a few feet ahead. As Hagan looked back he saw his two residents standing uncomfortably, uncertain whether to proceed.

"Guys—c'mon." Both moved forward, eager to see more of this unfolding story. Hagan turned to the familiar site of the imaging suite. Instead of Devron, who looked like a shriveled raisin in the center of the room, a tall man now lay surrounded by the magneto-optic tentacles that moved and shifted with the slight incursion and excursion of his breathing movements. The tendrils encircled the figure so that only portions of him were visible at any given moment. Light emitted from the figure through the man's opalescent wrapping. As they approached, the man was looking forward. His face was straining with the trace movements of his left arm and leg.

Hagan directed his attention to the shifting imaging apparatus.

"Disengage imaging sequence." The fronds quickly disappeared into the transparent floor to leave a spiraled corolla beneath the bench holding the cocooned figure.

Minsky, or the Chameleon, was unmistakable. Hagan had seen plenty of examples of BodMod, and few looked like Minsky; every visible feature pulsated with the moving and flickering light of sub-dermally implanted organic photodiodes. Even by current standards, his modifications were extreme. The photic tattoos, their connectivity to his neuroprosthetics, the eyes; it was not simply a departure from mainstream humanity but an interplanetary trek with the earth left far behind.

Hagan could see Minsky's face was contorted in a rictus of strain-ing. His left foot was turning in circles as he was writhing to free himself from his encasement.

Hagan bent over the peacock-like face. The orange eyes were open and incoherent. They were in a fixed stare to the left. Through the electric blue lines of his face, he could see the muscles in the Chame-leon's face pulled taut; mouth open in a wide frown, he strained against the restraints in his delirium. "Mr. Minsky, it's me—Dr. Maerici. Can you here me?"

A strained, incoherent vocalization was all he received in return. As he watched the man struggle, he noted it was only his left side that pushed against the restraining plastic.

Is he paralyzed? Shouldn't be with a parietal lesion. Left gaze de-viation. Always looking to the left. Not very typical for a dominant parietal lesion. Hagan lowered his head and put his face in the line of sight of the Chameleons smoldering gaze.

"Chameleon. Do you hear me? CHAMELEON!" Hagan's deep voice pierced the man's delirium. His lollipop eyes shifted slightly.

"Not fucking me. Not me. Not me me me me." His voice was hoarse as if from screaming.

With the words, the residents and detectives both moved in closer. Tara and Krantz watched both suspects—Minsky and Hagan.

"Tell me your name."

"Chameleon." His words were slurred and slow—his pronuncia-tion sounded closer to "Kamelun."

"Stick your tongue out if you understand me, Chameleon."

The spongy pink muscle slowly protruded from the man's mouth. Hagan nodded to himself. He quickly proceeded to perform a series of tests to assess various cranial nerve functions. He shined a light in his eyes to watch the pupils constrict, and when he rotated the head the eyes held themselves in the left-sided position.

"He can follow commands, brain stem reflexes are intact. Alright, Reid, Farhan, what else are we going to see with a left parietal lesion?" Reid looked to Farhan to see if he was going to answer. He shrugged his shoulders and nodded for Reid to respond.

"Well, you get a Gerstmann's syndrome. An injury to dominant parietal lobe affects your ability to process numbers and causes right-left confusion, agraphia without alexia, and finger agnosias."

Krantz looked to Hagan. "Uh, what did he just say?"

Hagan held up his clenched fist so that the thumb side of his hand was facing the old cop. "My fist here has the same configuration as an average brain, my thumb wrapped around the side and under my fingers is my temporal lobe, my index finger here represents my frontal lobe, and where the back of my hand meets the base of my thumb—that's the back part of my brain known as the occipital lobe. The area between my knuckle of the index finger and the back part of the brain is the parietal lobe. So put simply, the frontal lobe is involved with decision making, the temporal lobe is involved with speech and hearing, the occipital lobe processes vision. The parietal lobe is the crossroads for a lot of our sensory and motor processes. It synthesizes our external experience—what we see, hear, and touch—with what we want to do—move, speak, remember, and calculate. What a parietal lobe does in particular depends on what side of the brain it's on. If it's on the left, it's *dominant* because speech is usually more represented on the left side of the brain. If it's on the right, it's *nondominant*. So when somebody injures their left parietal lobe they have a strange constellation of dysfunction. They cannot process all things related to their hands, numbers, and writing. In essence our ability to process numbers, to write language, is all intimately linked with our ability to manipulate our fingers. From an evolutionary standpoint, we first learned to count with our fingers and we have been writing with our fingers for the last several thousand years. So it stands to reason that these functions are all closely linked."

"OK, so is that what he's got?"

"Most likely, but he's got a superimposed delirium from his metabolic derangement—the fact that his kidneys aren't working and his muscles have dumped a bunch of protein in his blood—so it makes it hard to really see some of the signs. Reid, what's not fitting with the picture?"

Reid's brow furrowed in concentration. "Is it the fact that he's not moving his right side?"

"Bingo, a neglect is usually only seen in right-sided parietal lesions." Looking to Krantz, Hagan explained, "So what Reid is saying is that a right-sided parietal lesion has a very different type of symptom complex—it's usually characterized by what's called a *neglect*. The patients simply pay no attention to one side of their body and their world. They don't use or regard anything from the side opposite the injury. You usually only see this with right-sided lesions. To see it on the left sometimes happens, but it's very rare, and only when the parietal lobe is completely destroyed. Here the brain is functioning, but not in unison with the rest of the brain. I've never seen it before."

"You mean that the reason he's not moving that one side of his body is not because he's paralyzed like a stroke, but because he doesn't want to?"

Hagan shrugged. "Well, yes and no. It's not that he doesn't want to, it's that he is paying no attention to it. The reason you're not moving your left side, even though you can, is because there is no sensory stimulus, such as me pinching your finger, or any reason in the external environment that would make you want to move it, such as a volleyball being thrown at you. When you have a neglect, you are permanently in a state in which you never notice something either from one side of your body or from that side of your environment that would induce a reaction."

On the Chameleon's chest a hand was clamped to an old man's face through the iridescent restraining plastic. Like a pro bowler picking his ball, the index finger and middle finger penetrated the eye sockets with graceful ease. Blood poured down the side of the man's face. All this played out like a silent horror film. Reid and Farhan also watched in silent revulsion.

Hagan and Krantz continued on, oblivious. "We rarely see things like this anymore with the advent of stroke prevention and neuroregenerative stem cell techniques. Lasting deficits are only seen in the people who are severely affected. They are nearly vegetative before rebuilding their neural structures."

Hagan redirected his attention to the patient. "There are some tests we can do to confirm his neglect. Can we take these restraints off for a moment?" Reid's and Farhan's eyes widened.

Tara pointed to Hagan's chest. Images from his digital tattoos writhed and squirmed over the surface of his skin. "Dr. Maerici, you

can see for yourself what this man did not just a couple hours ago."
There were now two hands visible; one still clamped to the face, the
other tearing at the forehead. A rent was emerging over the eyebrows
and the scalp began lifting off.

"He tried to beat me to death before I got that thing on him. Is
that a finding you are really going to need to confirm?"

The entire group watched as the hand pulled the man's skull off,
revealing a spongy pinkish beige tissue.

Hagan pursed his lips and tilted his head. "Perhaps you're right,
Detective Dezner." There were a few moments of silence as everyone
watched in morbid fascination. The straining of the Chameleon's left
arm and leg continued unabated.

"Notmenotme . . . fucker . . . no.no.no.no." The half-formed words
tumbled out amid spittle and gasped breaths. On the writhing picture
screen of his body the macabre images continued to unfold. As the
gore appeared to be approaching a crescendo, the scene was replaced
by what seemed a swirling cluster of roses. Like thousands of crimson
buds floating on the surface of choppy water, his entire body coursed
and spiraled with variegated red. Each of the ruddy swatches then
began to swell and enlarge, merge, and crowd all over the surface of
the Chameleon's body. The red shapes gained clarity and distinction.
Three blackened recesses, a dark slash; all were small caricature faces,
all surrounded by a grayish calyx of pointy thistles.

"Now what the heck is this?" Hagan asked more to himself than
anyone.

Krantz's eyes widened to the size of small almonds. "I have seen
those faces." Tara nodded in agreement.

"At each of the scenes, those faces are plastered all over in blood,
feces, and body parts." Krantz looked at Tara. "Can we now agree
they are connected?" His voice was strained but also mildly relieved.

Tara nodded and quietly looked at Hagan.

"notme . . . notme . . . notme. Nonono . . ."

Trent walked along the black floors of the entryway to his vast and cavernous home. His stride was even, balanced, and effortless. The young man's small, thin frame moved with a lithe steadiness. Thin arms swung at his sides with a free and confident grace. He no longer saw this place the way he used to—the glossy black granite, the white spiral staircase, the virtual sky vista of St. Louis spreading out from the stone's edge—all were tiles of a much larger mosaic. He saw all those things that humans see, but now he saw more. He saw himself. Trent saw his body from all angles, from up close and from far away. He saw his heat signature and he saw into the depth of his own body, with its churning and pulsating organs. He not only felt the cool touch of the floor but he felt the touch of his feet on the floor as if small fingers were tapping on his skin. His organic body was nothing more than an appendage to a larger creature. He viewed it as one looks at one's little finger. The thousands upon thousands of embedded cameras and sensors were his new eyes and ears. The physical structure, with its humming circuits, servomotors, and controllable nanomaterials, was his new body and skin.

"Some more something more something more . . ." he whispered. He was no longer an "I" but a "we." A collective perspective. A higher consciousness. He was connected to all that was around him. He was networked. He saw beyond the Devron estate, he saw through other eyes as well—large white rooms, alabaster domed structures permeated by silence. Officers with their backs to him, hands held at their hips in guarded readiness. Tile after tile of perception, layered and superimposed, all of it flowed through his consciousness. She had made him into more. The woman with blue skin and red eyes, she had made him a "we." Multiple motor cortices operated a once dysfunctional limb, frontal lobes operated in synchrony to garner higher insights, combined memories made him older and wiser than he could have become in a lifetime.

"They saw us, they watched us, we noticed every bit of it." He giggled to himself. The changes had not gone unnoticed. House staff members looked on as Trent walked by them with the ease and freedom of an athlete. Through the manifold lenses and cameras and microphones he saw all their hidden glances, the custodians, the cooks, the technicians, administrative assistants, he heard all their hurried whispers of how he was different. To him, it was as if termites were burrowing within his body. Unwanted and repugnant, they were penetrating his secret, a knowledge that was not theirs to know. It filled Trent's larger consciousness with revulsion and hunger.

"We had sensed their betrayal." He tittered. Their elevated heart rates, pupils dilating, and nervous twitches, so subtle to human eyes, were screaming indictments of their reaction to his new and evolved behavior. There were no secrets.

"We blocked their treacherous attempts to communicate, we stopped their departure. We tucked them into our belly." Changes in oxygen levels, venting of fumes, and the many robots on the estate all had corralled and shuffled the humans to a place deep in the basement; locked away, they quivered like animals. But they were irrelevant. Once removed from interaction and communication, they were as inconsequential as ticks boarding on the mane of a lion. The more troublesome ones, the ones that had resisted, tried to intervene, to hamper his growth; even now, he watched as they slipped beneath the sands of the Japanese garden, futilely struggling and writhing against the masses of pebbles that he individually controlled like an infinite army of ants.

Their demise passed from his attention without much thought. It was simply a disposal of mundane and useless equipment.

As his organic component passed along the long granite expanse, his presence became aware of another. It was her. She was ubiquitous in his consciousness, but like winds coalescing to form transient whirlwind dervishes, she would become manifest in a more concrete form.

She stood before him, her blue steely silhouette shimmering against the black backdrop. No words were ever spoken. Impressions passed through him—leaves turning colors—green to red to yellow and falling from a tree. Branches emerged, grew, and thickened. New large full green leaves blossomed and shifted toward the light of a summer sun. Branches grew ever higher and further toward impossible heights.

Another change, he thought to himself, *for growth, expansion . . .* She no longer asked, as one need not ask one's self for permission. His body held still for a moment. After several moments blue words appeared in the central field of his bodied view.

CHANGES TO CLINICAL MONITORING SYSTEM HAZARDOUS TO USER. SYSTEM ADMINISTRATOR WILL NOT ALLOW WITHOUT PHYSICIAN AUTHORIZATION.

There was a shudder. The entire structure of the Devron state heaved. The lights shifted and faded, the view of St. Louis bent and contorted as if it were being seen through a funhouse mirror. The Trent Devron body stood rigid and tense. The blue woman with red eyes did not move. Rage and hatred seared through the collective intellect.

Far below in a storage basement, a room crammed with people went dark. The sounds of the screams became more and more muffled as air was sucked from the space. The occupants spasmed and clawed at each other as they suffocated.

Gerald sat on the mid portion of the table with his hands folded across his lap. He was looking upward with his head tilted slightly back as if he was trying to hear a distant sound or preparing to say something of lengthy and deep significance. There was the slightest trace of a smile—a smile of contentment.

Beyond the linear streaks of rust that crossed Gerald's face, his arms and chest were covered in mottled hues of brown and red. The variegated patchwork superimposed on Gerald's still and serene presence gave the appearance of lichens growing on an old statue. Around him stood the three doctors and two detectives. He was completely oblivious to their presence. They were very aware of his. He was covered in congealed blood.

Hagan had purposefully instructed them on a quiet approach. The imaging room, the one next to the same spiraling, white, cone-shaped expanse that housed the Chameleon next door, also maintained a noise-suppressed cottony silence.

Gerald, unlike the Chameleon was unrestrained. All that he wore was the loose-fitting hospital gown. With words transiting across the central imaging area on his chest and the hems of his sleeves and neckline, his medical condition was being continually reported. The urgent and emergent elements flashed in yellow and red letters.

HEMODYNAMICALLY GUARDED—TACHYCARDIC.
SIGNIFICANT COMPROMISE OF RENAL FUNCTION.
PHYSICIAN STAFF NOTIFIED AND PRESENT.

Another patient. Three in a day. Hagan hadn't expected this. It was supposed to be a quiet day in the lab. Even for a neurosurgeon, accustomed to interruptions for emergencies, the day's events were keeping him off-balance.

Hagan watched Gerald, his neighbor and patient, for several prolonged silent moments. The group waited expectantly for Dr. Maerici to initiate an interaction with the patient-suspect. Hagan watched him both from a clinical and personal standpoint. He had known Gerald for years. He had put his implants in years ago with several upgrades since. The man had housed his cheating wife after the discovery. His emotions regarding the florist were conflicted. He had never forgiven the little bastard for making him look like the bad guy in that painful situation. It was enough that his wife, Anna, had cheated on him. But to be painted as the neglectful husband who was the cause for the infidelity; that had burned him up. The gossipy neighborhood had treated him like a pariah after that. Gerald had even convinced her to publish "her dilemma" on numerous blog sites. His personal life had been a spectacle and an embarrassment. Now here was Gerald.

Need to put that aside. Looking down, Hagan reviewed his presence anew. Not as the gay neighbor who meddled in his life, but as a patient, a medical dilemma he had to deal with. He held his hand out to the others to be still. At the same time he broadcast his thoughts. *"Let me do all the talking initially."* The others quietly nodded in assent.

"Hello, Gerald, how are you?" Hagan's tone was mild and nonchalant.

Turning his head immediately toward the voice, Gerald replied, "Hello, Hagan, doin' fine, yourself?" There was a broad grin pushing his chubby cheeks against deep, freckled dimples.

Hagan watched his eyes closely. They never met his own. He looked in his direction, but the gaze looked through him. Like the marble eyes of a doll, they didn't fix on his face. Rather, they simply bobbed in his general direction.

"Hagan, it has been quite a while."

"Yes, Gerald, it has. How has your day been so far?"

"Oh, you know, usual stuff, working in the greenhouse. There is always work to be done. What brings you here, by the way?" The florist didn't seem to notice the others around him.

"Where exactly are we, Gerald?" Hagan asked in a pleasant conversational tone.

"Have you not been to this spa before? It really is marvelous. Although I must say I have been waiting here a lot longer than normal. What are you having done today? Me, I think I'm going to be getting a massage. My muscles are killing me—I cannot remember a time I have been this sore. I can't quite recall what I did to get quite so buggered up, but, well, you know, we're not getting any younger." His voice trailed off into a chuckled sigh.

Hagan continued on. "Anybody else here, Gerald?"

"No, no . . . not at the moment. I wish there was. This is really unlike Genino's. They're usually so extremely attentive to their clientele. I mean just—"

"How do you like the way they decorated the place?"

"Oh, it's only OK. I mean the curtains, the stripes on the walls, all the fake stone—it's a little too kitschy for me. If they really wanted to do it right they should use real mahogany. Now I know that's not politically correct, but . . ." As he began to talk and talk, Hagan approached closer. He waved his hands in front of Gerald's face. He continued to blather on. "If one wants to achieve the fusion of retro classic and modern, then—" Hagan again pulled the light from his pocket and shined the thin beams at his pupils. The dark circles constricted to pinpoints. Gerald's stream of design critique continued on uninterrupted. Hagan watched him as he spoke.

Cognition is intact—understands speech, verbalizing without difficulty. Pupils, face, tongue, all the cranial nerves and brain stem seem OK. Motor function also OK. He's got an isolated cortical blindness.

He directed his thoughts toward his chief resident. "*Reid, when I give the cue, I want you to make your presence known.*"

Eager to participate Reid nodded. "*No problem.*"

"Gerald, Gerald, sorry to interrupt. Who is that gentleman standing next to you?"

Gerald turned to either side and gave a smug look in Hagan's direction. "Hagan, there is no one but you and me of course. Are you trying to be funny?"

Hagan looked to Reid and pointed.

"Mr. Oberweiss, how are you today?" Reid's voice was stiff and formal. The words were over-enunciated and slow, to ensure delivery.

"Who is that, Gerald?" Hagan asked.

"Why, Brent, always sneaking up on people! This is Brent James, the museum curator with two first names. He's a close friend. A rather very close friend at one time." Gerald clasped his hands together and trapped them between his knees.

"What do you think of his sweater?"

"A lovely orange, a saffron really, like a nice nasturtium in spring bloom. Must be a Blakely-Toguchi design. Given his usual garish proclivities, it's quite tasteful for the old silver fox. Now, Hagan, your clothes are always Americana to the core. Looks like you should be hunting ducks or some other feathered creature."

"You don't like maroon?"

"Oh, hardly, that's a color that should have stayed in the twenties."

Hagan directed his attention to the others. *"I've seen enough here. Let's talk about this in the control room."*

Hagan and the others walked out in muffled footsteps. The tendrils beneath Gerald ascended and again encircled and pulsed around the florist. In the silence, the portly, red-haired man resumed his quiet, expectant stillness.

As the group exited, they emerged into the glossy blackness of the control room. The stir and noise of argument and irritation encircled them once again.

The group all looked to the professor.

"Well, Reid, Farhan, what do you think?" Hagan always put the questions to his residents on issues that he was thinking about. Not simply to teach them but also to check his own thinking. In difficult situations, the lack of experience made them less susceptible to fitting clinical findings to a diagnosis one was trained to expect.

Reid spoke up first. "Several things seem most obvious." Hagan lifted his eyebrows. "The patient was delirious. He was clearly confused—thinking he was in the spa, or whatever, the loose tangential speech. Beyond incorrect thinking, seeing elements that were not there are possibly hallucinations. Given that he is developing renal failure and has sustained all that muscle breakdown, this could likely be a metabolically induced delirium."

Hagan prodded Reid further. "Hmm, what about the fact he was oblivious to the people around him? The lack of vision? His intact papillary function?"

"Well, the fact that his pupils reacted to light means his optic apparatus is intact—visual input is coming in—but he's not registering it. He was clearly oblivious to people around him, perhaps evidence of an induced fugue state, due to all his physiologic abnormalities."

"Reid, define delirium for me."

Having been through this countless times, Reid knew he was missing the mark. After looking down for a moment, he began to recite the classic definition of delirium that had been drilled into him throughout medical school. "Delirium is a more or less temporary disorder of the mental faculties, as in fevers, intoxication, or other systemic illnesses, characterized by restlessness, delusions and hallucinations, and incoherence of speech and thought."

"Did he seem restless?"

Reid shrugged. "No."

"Was his speech or thought incoherent?"

"Yes." A little less sure.

"Was it?"

"Well, what was that talk about the spa and orange sweaters?"

"Was it internally inconsistent or fragmented? Could you not understand him? Was he *incoherent* by the medical definition of the term?"

"Well, no, but he was certainly confused." With a wry smirk, he added, "We're certainly not in a spa. So that is either delusion or a hallucination."

Returning his resident's sarcasm, Hagan replied, "True, Reid, we are not in a spa. What about the imaging that we saw prior to going in? What sites were affected for Mr. Oberweiss?"

Reid slapped the butt of his palm against his forehead. "Uhh, duh, his occipital lobes."

Hagan nodded. "Yep, so now what do you think?"

"He's got Anton's syndrome!"

"You bet."

"So how would you define the content of his thought?"

Reid was excited to be back on track. "He was confabulating."

"So what's that?" Krantz asked, ignoring even the attempt of trying to look it up.

Hagan and Reid turned to the two detectives. Hagan pointed to the back of Reid's head. "Vision is processed in the back parts of our brain known as the occipital lobe. To create a visual perception there are two processes that need to occur. First, there is the actual incoming stimulus. That is the photons of light stimulating your retinas, which in turn convert that information into neural action potentials that then get sent to the occipital lobes. The neural signals are then reconstructed to form an image of what's being seen.

"That, however, is only half the equation. When we perceive something, *as something*, it's not just the compilation of the pixels. It's also the notion of what that thing is. So when we are looking at things, the incoming information is altered by what we *expect* to see. The human brain builds the perception from the visual data it gets from things it's seen before. These systems are always in a tight balance, checking and balancing each other. We are always altering what we perceive by the actual data that is coming in and we are always altering what we see by what we expect we are looking at.

"Now in the case of Mr. Oberweiss, his ability to visually perceive is completely one-sided. Since his primary visual cortex has been damaged, or at least has some evidence of disconnection—we're still working that out—he only perceives those things he expects to see. He has no concept that he is blind because he is seeing everything that he feels he should see as dictated by his other senses and memories that come closest to the present experience. That's why there was all that talk about a spa. He was in a quiet environment and his muscles were sore. This must have reminded him of a similar previous experience, hence that was what he was perceiving as the world around him.

"This fabrication of experience is what we call 'confabulation.' It's common in the setting of these distorted perceptions, or in the case of bad injury to the memory structures. If Devron were a little more with it, he likely would have had a similar presentation. The only difference would have been he would see everything but when asked if something is familiar—emotionally relevant—would always assume that it was familiar since he would have no memories to compare against."

Hagan looked again to Reid and Farhan. "So what doesn't fit with an Anton's syndrome diagnosis here?" There was a long silent pause. "The memory loss. He didn't seem to remember the day's prior events. That isn't totally explained by the occipital lobe dysfunction.

"So that brings us to the real question of what the heck is causing all this," Hagan replied.

Tara had been listening intently and directed her thoughts at Krantz. *"Does that bring us any closer to what caused these people to kill and mutilate their victims? I am going to bait him to see if I can get a read on his facial expressions."*

"Tara, do you think that's such a hot idea?"

"If he's hiding something, even he cannot mask the subconscious alterations in facial expression. SYSTEM. Activate quantitative facial analysis. Subject—Hagan Maerici." Tara then returned her gaze to Maerici as he began speaking. She could see circles around the corners of his eyes. Lines were highlighting his eyebrows, mouth, and forehead while dots were overlying his pupils. Smaller dots were pixilating various angles of his face. All the facial markers moved with Hagan's ongoing expressions. *"Please record and summarize."*

"SUPPRESSED EMOTIONAL CONTENT—ANXIETY AND DEPRESSION. FOCUSED ORGANIZED PERCEPTS. NO EVIDENCE OF HIDDEN CONTENT. NO EVIDENCE OF DECEPTION."

We're getting closer, she thought.

"—the thing common to all these guys is, number one, their metabolic derangement characterized by the muscle breakdown and loss of kidney function. Number two, they all have some strange decoherence in certain areas in their brain."

"Once again, what does that mean?"

"Each of the patients has a portion of his brain that is not communicating with the rest of it. More specifically, the brain itself isn't injured. There is no evidence of shearing of the axons, toxins, cell death—the firing rates and patterns of these dysfunctional areas are out of phase with the rest of the brain."

Krantz nodded for Hagan to continue.

"I have never seen anything like this. One can think of the brain as a near infinite collection of radio stations. Each of these stations has a certain frequency that earmark the signals it sends out to the other radio stations. Those other stations that have the proper antennas can pick up the signals and play their own signals to complement or inhibit what they just received. These stations that are sharing frequency bandwidth have to be in synch with each other to receive and transmit signals. This synchronicity of signal is called coherence. It's those areas of the brain that share the same frequencies and are in synch—that are coherent—that define a neural network. There are numerous networks that serve all sorts of subfunctions that create our consciousness and cognition. Anything ranging from visual, motor, language, spatial, memory, to more basic functions like controlling our internal physiology—like our heart rate and body temperature, and such. In any case, when these networks are injured and dysfunctional it's usually due to some level of injury to the brain structures. Stuff like strokes, trauma, toxins, tumors, or some neurodegenerative process—"

"—like Alzheimer's or Parkinson's," Krantz cut in, finally seeming to comprehend what Hagan was telling him.

Tara continued to watch. *"MILD CONFUSION. RECOLLECTION OF ANALYTIC PERCEPTS. ASPECTS OF INTROSPECTION. ONGOING SUBTEXT OF ANXIETY."*

"Precisely. Here, though, there is no cellular or structural reason for these sites not to be networked and talking with the rest of the brain. Moreover, they are decoherent across all frequencies. These cortical sites are functioning, but are completely marching to a different drummer than the rest of the brain.

"As to what is causing this and how it is related to their criminal behavior, I don't have an explanation, yet. We definitely see a pattern here, with common features between all of them, but the fundamental cause is unknown. This also makes it hard to treat whatever the problem is."

Tara stared levelly at the professor. "There is one common feature that you failed to mention, Dr. Maerici."

Krantz gave a look that seemed to say, *Here we go.*

"What is that?"

"You."

Tara watched the highlights of Hagan's face shift with the lift of his eyebrows. There was a documented dilation of his pupils. *"SURPRISE. SUSPICION. INCREDULITY."*

"What exactly are you getting at?" Hagan's brows furrowed together. His eyes narrowed. *"IRRITATION. ANGER."*

"Dr. Maerici, I think you know *exactly* what I am talking about. All these suspects are your patients." Tara stood still. Her face was expressionless. She watched Hagan with intensity.

"As are thousands of other people in this city."

"You stand to gain substantially from each of their crimes."

"Unlikely." The words went between the two with the force and rancor of a tennis ball being professionally swatted back and forth.

"Devron's death will endow you and your lab with millions."

"I have no idea what you are talking about."

"ANGER. NO HIDDEN CONTENT."

"The lawsuit from the Chameleon goes away."

"He does that to avoid billing. He's already sued me twice."

"ANGER. NO HIDDEN CONTENT."

"Revenge."

"What?"

"CONFUSION."

"Oberweiss housed your estranged wife after she left you."

"Give me a break."

"FRUSTRATION. SADNESS. REGRET. RESTRAINED EX-PRESSION/INTROSPECTION." Tara was getting closer. Something with Oberweiss.

Hagan looked to Tara. He saw the darting movements of her eyes. It was not the twittering eye movement of someone who was nervous. They were directed. She looked at his eyes, but then would dart in and around his face. *The cop is hacking me.*

Exasperated, Hagan took a deep breath. He let the muscles in his face slacken. His eyebrows relaxed and the central wrinkles in his forehead smoothed. His mouth became still and motionless. Again, he breathed, looking forward as if mildly bored and staring in space.

"CALM. DISTRACTED."

Hagan looked to Tara and Krantz and said, his voice a slow monotone, like that of a subway announcement, "Can . . . we . . . please . . . cut . . . the . . . bullshit."

Tara's eyes widened. The rest of the team looked equally as surprised. It was as if Professor Hagan had suddenly and inexplicably run out of power. Like a car being harshly shifted between gears, Hagan's face broke into a large grin. With a voice that was blithe, jolly, and wholly inappropriate for the context, Hagan again addressed Tara. "I would be happy to play the face game as long as you like."

"HAPPINESS. NO HIDDEN CONTENT."

Tara nodded her assent. "*SYSTEM. Disengage quantitative facial analysis.*"

"It's off."

Hagan's demeanor returned to its typical equanimity. He got closer to Tara so that he could speak to her alone in the crowded room. Her back stiffened as he entered her personal space. His voice was a low whisper. "Look, if you want to ask me about my troubled marriage—feel free. I'd love to tell you about my wife's infidelity and our recent failed pregnancy. I don't know if your job affects your home life, but if my personal failures help your case I would be happy to publish them in the *Wall Street Journal*."

For the first time she could hear a deeper strain in his voice. *Yes,* she thought, *I do know how a job affects one's personal life.* As she stood there silent and blinking, she rubbed the finger where a wedding band had once been.

When Tara didn't respond, his voice returned to its usual staid cadence. "Good, now if you're done provoking me for the moment, I think I have something that could potentially help. If you'll excuse me." With that he began walking through the throng of arguing masses toward the door. The two residents, befuddled by the bizarre exchange, shrugged and followed suit.

"That went well," Krantz said dryly.

"Jesus, Edwin, is this really the right time to bring this up?" Tara was shaking her head at her partner. The two were walking down a broad hallway encircled with bluish light.

"I'm just saying—you look a little thin to me. Have you had lunch yet?"

"No, Edwin, I haven't—I'm training—moreover, my body size is none of your business anyway."

"Well, don't you think that maybe you should eat a bit more—doesn't seem healthy—what are you training for anyway?"

"Edwin, Christ—enough—a marathon. And while we're at it—quit picking your nose."

Casually probing his nostril while they talked, Krantz jerked his hand away. Looking at his index finger, he rolled something and made a flicking movement.

"Edwin, that's disgusting. Can we please return to the case?"

"I think you're barking up the wrong tree, Tara. This Maerici guy just doesn't seem to fit. He's a typical doctor type, maybe a bit big on ego, but I'm not getting a killer feel to him."

"All the facts point to him, Edwin. Feelings or no feelings, we've got strong support for motive and intent." Tara thought about Maerici's final parting words to her. There was a part of her that agreed with Krantz, but she would never concede the point; data was data.

"Seems like he would have too much to lose—also the whole timing—seems clumsy if he was actually the perp."

"Maybe he made a mistake."

"Doesn't seem like the mistake-making type of guy, but if he's the killer, maybe the murder thing is new to him." Krantz nodded to allow the possibility. "Although accusing him right off the bat probably is going to hurt us in the long run. If he's guilty, now he knows we're on to him and will start making all sorts of cover-ups; if not—not sure he's gonna be too interested in helping."

He's right—dammit, she thought, feeling a twinge of anxiety from the strategic error. She walked on with him for several seconds in silence, acknowledging that he was right.

Krantz let the moment pass. "We did learn something, though: if he did do it, he is going to be hard to catch. He picked up the moments when we were in a conversation and he figured out pretty quick that you were monitoring his facial movements—he's definitely a smart one. So where did he go, anyway?" Krantz strained to see over the crowd. Trying to walk and crane his neck, the old detective looked like a hurried stork. They had lost sight of Maerici and his team.

"Edwin, don't worry about it. We'll find him at his lab. I'll get directions." Tara directly logged onto the Barnes network. *"Disengage avatar—present window format only."* She wasn't in the mood for smiling, overfriendly, hospital reps beckoning her at every corner. *"Show location of Hagan Maerici lab."* A small star appeared on a floor diagram. *"Provide arrow guide."* A blue arrow appeared in front of Tara. She now put her legs on autopilot while Krantz followed along.

"Look—you are not coming in here." Tara, Krantz, and the residents were all standing around the entrance to the Maerici lab. Hagan blocked them with his hands on his hips and his feet set apart, giving him the stance of a guard.

"Did you, or did you not, say that you had something that could help this case?" Tara stood in front of Hagan, poised and indomitable.

"I did, but . . . it did not require your presence or anyone else's for that matter. I'll let you know if I find anything."

"Well, if there is evidence in there, then I am required by law to investigate." Tara was not relenting. Initially thinking the medical evaluation of Devron was a distraction, she now found this physician keenly interesting.

"There is no evidence, that's for certain. I have some data-analysis capabilities that could shed some light on Devron's condition."

"Well, then I look forward to seeing it. What exactly is in there?"

"A computational core—it's somewhat specialized—technical stuff—"

"Technical stuff, huh, what kind of technical stuff, Professor?" Tara said dangerously. She clenched and unclenched her jaw.

"Some very capable parallel processing that we can apply to analysis of brain signals. Could help better define Devron's unusual condition." Hagan could see her eyes start to move around rapidly. *What is she up to?* He knew she must be online for some reason.

"Well, that sounds fascinating, Professor. Let me show you this warrant to investigate the premises."

Hagan's shoulders slumped.

The room was still. Hagan sat in his usual black lacquered chair. Beside him on hourglass-shaped stools sat Tara and Krantz. The stools usually served the purpose of holding some minor equipment or a drink for Dr. Maerici. The stools' small size forced the two officers to sit low to the surface of the table, looking like annoyed, oversized children with just their heads and shoulders peeking over. As is the resident's lot, Reid, Jonathan, and Farhan were left standing.

Looking around incredulous, Krantz scratched the back of his neck. "So this is your lab, Professor Maerici?"

"Yes it is, Detective Krantz." Hagan, uncomfortable and annoyed, was already looking at Omid, who stared back at his creator impassively and without acknowledgment of the others in the room. This was Hagan's inner sanctum. He had, at best, only allowed people to stand in the doorway. It had taken a decade to build the interface, the networked quantum computing system that was insulated from all external interference, removed from vibrations of all sources, sound, magnetic fields, all forms of electromagnetic radiation, and, equally important, humanity. The entry had been quantum encrypted with redundant cortical signal verifications. Absolutely nobody but Hagan Maerici and those approved by him were going to get in. Since the office's creation, guests had really never been an issue.

Now there were five people here in his lab. They hadn't been allowed access to Omid. That also would be a first. He had controlled interactions completely thus far. He needed to control the influence that each interaction had on Omid and his development. *This could be risky,* he thought.

"What exactly is it that you research in here, Dr. Maerici?" Krantz articulated his words carefully and slowly as he looked around at the bare metal walls.

"Artificial intelligence, Detective Krantz. This is an IQCOM." Hagan pronounced the final word as "I-kwam." As he was talking, various charts and monitors were emerging around Omid's head. *If anything funny happens to Omid, I am turning them all out—warrant or no warrant—I have put too much into this.*

"*Omid, I want these stability indices only visible to me.*" The AI-RENS nodded.

"Yes, I see." Krantz responded in polite tones as if he had just heard the response "I am studying salami-wielding midgets" from a committed man.

Tara straightened her back and looked around with a more intense vigor. "Are you serious? In a hospital—I find it hard to believe. There are only a handful of these in the world. There is one at the NSA, of course, then the ones in Beijing, Mumbai, and some lesser ones in Brazil. Why would you have one in a hospital? It's probably worth more than the entire place combined. How could we not know about this?" Hagan noticed this left her a little flustered. *Well—she doesn't know everything.*

"Devron subsidized it. That's why I am the Devron Professor of Clinical Neuroprosthetics. It is the reason we have come as far as we have with neuroprosthetics and it is the main focus in developing truly artificially intelligent beings. The IQCOM has been a major and somewhat secretive passion of Devron's since he had the means to create one. He sees it as the next great horizon. First, we decoded the human brain, and after a few decades of gathering data we now have the ability to create a synthetic consciousness. It was Devron's vision that true AI would do for the world's problems what nuclear fusion eventually did for the energy crisis of the twenties. Essentially we'll have an unending cognitive resource to solve any issue that confronts humanity. In Devron's opinion, the most fundamental limited resource today is a human mind."

Tara was now looking around the room with new respect. She ran her fingertips along the surface of the table lightly. There was a new softness to her touch, almost a caress, as if she were a poor violinist who was just handed a Stradivarius or a sixteen-year-old putting her hands on the wheel of a Ferrari.

Krantz was looking between the two. "So what exactly am I missing here?"

Tara looked at Krantz with a rare, soft smile. "This is an IQCOM—an immersive quantum computer. It has some of the fastest computing speeds in existence. For these things to work they need to be heavily isolated from the surrounding environment. To prevent ambient noise from interfering with their near infinite ability to compute about any level of data almost instantaneously. Moreover, since it's immersive and the processing power is otherworldly, this is the closest thing that exists to true artificial intelligence. By sheer brute processing force, the immersive system can pick up the nature of your thoughts on a near intuitive basis to provide the answers that you need almost before you ask them. It is a data analyst's dream to work with one of these."

Despite himself, Hagan almost had to laugh. "So she is human after all." He couldn't help but appreciate the irony of a powerful computer bringing out Tara's softer side. Hagan swallowed. "Well, do you want to log on?" The words were heavy and uncomfortable in his mouth.

"Yes." Her voice was soft and sincere, without the edge from earlier in the day. "Yes, I do."

Hagan looked at the blue child and took a long, deep breath. *Omid, please log on our guests here.*

Anna Maerici stood in front of the entrance to the superstore Ter-ester. The customer part of the store itself was no larger than a phone booth from decades prior. Surrounded with small well-manicured boxwoods in interlocking terracotta pots, the booth itself was an opaque, frosted cube that was cottoned with hazy white lights within. As she directed her attention to enter, the blue visage of a store attendant welcomed her.

"Hello, Mrs. Maerici, welcome back! Will it be eggs and spinach? Our estimates tell us you must be getting low at this point. Let me tell you about some specials that I think you in particular will appreciate. Recently arrived from Spain—" The avatar lacked all human propor-tions. Broad pearly grin, round head, and smooth stretched body with large balloon fingers all combined to form the embodiment of merri-ment and welcome.

Anna was numb. She walked through the smiling cartoon as it yam-mered and the door slid out of her way with a hiss. Once inside holo-grams surrounded her; she stood within a broad expansive shopping mall. Earth-toned limestone floors went out to various aisles and brick-lined arching alcoves. She was alone amidst the profusion of products.

Why did I come here? Habit had brought her here. This was where she came on Saturdays. Anna looked at the various signs for some hint or clue of what she should purchase.

Produce—we need vegetables. A cold hollowness filled her as she realized that her nutritional needs were no longer as important as they were days prior.

She pushed on. She didn't think about it. *Produce.* Anna let routine tow her forward. She began to walk toward the far side of the store. The subtle whirring of the floor moving beneath her feet hummed within her ears. All around her, there was movement and sound. Ani-mated characters, athletes, and actors vied for her attention as she passed through the racks of virtual products. Anna shut them out.

As she moved, something small and pink pushed through her anes-thetized emotions. A small piglet with black beady eyes blinked tim-idly as it watched her. Pointy long ears twitched and flopped with a certain hopefulness and yearning. The little creature in a green jumper stood at the edge of the children's section.

Piglet. Stopping, she stared at the small, fuzzy Pooh character as it waved at her with a diminutive fingerless limb.

Anna began to choke. Stories that would never be told, memories that would not occur, filled her chest with a pain and heaviness that was too much to bear. A price tag emerged as she reached out to touch the little creature. Tears began to roll down her checks, stinging and inconsolable.

The bluish boy sitting cross-legged from Hagan nodded his head. *"Acknowledged."* The almond eyes of the AIRENS then looked from side to side to meet the gaze of Tara, Krantz, and the residents.

"Detective Dezner and Doctors Vestin, Yaseem, and Brickmil are engaged. Detective Krantz's system is not compatible with current information-transfers rates. Have adjusted input to accommodate and allow for communication, though with limited resolution."

For Tara and the residents the boy now appeared on the table. He briefly made eye contact and nodded. Krantz saw what appeared to be a conglomeration of small cubes in the shape of a body. To him, it looked like a complex assortment of Legos.

Returning the nod, he asked, "Is this the system's avatar?"

Hagan relished the moment because he knew Tara's awe would be renewed. "No, this is Omid; he is an AIRENS."

Tara sucked in air. Reid and Farhan were tapping each other on the shoulder and nodding. They had heard about this, but they had never been able to actually get to see or interact with the AIRENS.

"The what? All I'm seeing is a blocky blue thing. What's an 'erins'?"

"It is not 'erins'; it is 'AIRENS.' That is an acronym for Artificial Intelligence Reverse-Engineered from Neural Signals. My name is Omid."

To Krantz, the voice had the crisp, light tone of a well-educated boy. All he saw were subtle shifting movements of thousands of small blue cubes presenting the approximation of a silhouette.

"Why does he look like a cubist painting? And let me ask it again—what is an AIRENS?" Krantz nodded to the nondescript blue creature before him.

"You cannot see me as I am because the resolution of your neuro-prosthetic system—the Solara1200—is not capable of sufficient bit-rates transfer for quantum format."

Tara looked to Edwin. He knew that look. He would be chided for being arcane the moment this was all over. She would take on a serious tone, like a concerned school teacher talking to a fourth grader who had a problem with wetting his pants. . . . He could already hear the words—*Edwin, a Solara? You were supposed to upgrade five years ago.* He didn't make eye contact and continued to listen to the pixilated shadow.

"*. . . regarding my description—Artificial Intelligence Reverse-Engineered from Neural Signals—this refers to the construction of my quantum software core. My programming is based on the electrophysiological data taken from the cortical and subcortical recordings of many human subjects. The manner in which information is managed in the human brain dictates the model for which my software architecture is created and modeled on an ongoing basis.*"

"So you're a computer model of a human brain?" Krantz often found himself defining the swirling complexity of science and technology by its fundamental components—often this meant what the thing looked like or what it practically did. In this case, it seemed like they were creating a fake brain.

"*I am more than a model, Detective Krantz, more than a fake brain, as you put it.*" Krantz flinched, realizing that this was no avatar. This thing knew and responded to his thoughts. "*I am intended to provide human-like interaction while having the ability to employ high-level data analysis and computer-programming implementation. In essence, I am a bridge between human cognitive processes—which is massively paralleled, but slow—and analytic machine processes, which are linear, but very fast.*"

"OK . . . sounds great. So is it going to help us figure out the day's events?" asked Krantz, always focused on the practical details.

"That's the hope. If there are any connections with these cases Omid should be able to help us uncover them." Hagan paused. It was clear that he was anxious about this new dynamic and what it would do to Omid. He looked at the charts monitoring Omid's cognitive processing. He took a deep breath.

"OK, so let's begin, Omid. Let's start with linear relationships with what is known about the three subjects—Marcus Devron, Gerald Oberweiss, and Frank Minsky, the Chameleon. Each is a suspect in a murder or assault. Each appears to have neurological disorders that are similar. We are looking for the root causes that explain the relationship between these three."

He turned to Tara. "Detective Dezner, can Omid have access to the day's police records?"

"Yes, that shouldn't be a problem. Omid, can you utilize my corti-cal signature?"

"*It has already been completed by your acknowledgment.*" In making the statement Omid had already processed all the day's rec-ords, video recordings of interactions, medical information, and was as current in the situation as all the people in the room. "*I have accessed current medical records and police records and am ready to proceed.*"

"For quicker speeds of interaction, let's switch to mental commu-nication primarily at this juncture. Please network all those in the room. Maintain privacy filters and only share overt intended verbal statements."

The azure youth again nodded. "*Acknowledged. We are now all connected. I will begin with all publicly available records. Additionally, I will access health and local legal information from each of the three subjects since we currently have those permissions, given that they are all your patients and have been approved by Detective Dezner.*"

———

Hagan contained his anxiety. This was the first time he was allowing Omid unconstrained access to the Internet. He would process the world's sum of available data. It was not the size of the data set that worried Hagan; it was the unconstrained exposure to an emerging alien consciousness. He couldn't predict the effect, as he couldn't have predicted the earlier response of Omid to the simple proverbs. "*OK, let's begin.*"

Omid closed his eyes for a brief moment. On opening, square icons began to appear throughout the room, and Omid's facial expression shifted from one of serene and unemotional calm to the suggestion of a slight smile. *Did he enjoy that?* Hagan wondered. Watching the sta-bility monitors, there were slight twitches in the lines. *Doing OK so far.* A panoply of windows containing various images, pictures, and movie clips shifted and moved in three-dimensional space as if an in-visible card dealer were playing some complex poker game through-out the room. In moments, the assortment shifted and formed into three coalescing columns. The name of each of the three patients ap-peared over each of the columns.

"*I searched all public records available within the world neural network, which also included health and police records, given current*

permissions. Using multiple linear connectors the data thus far dem-
onstrates the following:

"Number one: All subjects are patients of Dr. Maerici. He created
and implanted each of their most recent constructs within the past
five years. All platforms utilize DNC Hydra platforms. Each platform
was customized to respective users. Marcus Devron had a multisen-
sate construct with high bandwidth capacity for multibrain com-
munication. Oberweiss utilizes the same DNC platform, but with a
notable upgrade—DNC Argus. System customized for analog pro-
cessing of sensate experience for optimal virtual visual, auditory, and
olfactory perception. Minsky also has DNC platform upgrade with
multisensate capacity—DNC Vollo. Model implanted has notable
customizations linking centers for emotional processing to pigment
presentation scheme of skin and iris implants. All had recent upgrades
of olfactory prosthetics. Each subject has a Sentenex 10 for improved
virtual scent experience.

"Number two: There is one degree of separation between the vic-
tims, all of which connect via Dr. Maerici; person contact between
victims increases after that to four and five degrees of separation. The
data sets of contacts begin to manifest in the service industries. In ad-
dition to documented personal contact, two of the three—Mr. Minsky
and Dr. Devron—are legally engaged with Dr. Maerici. A lawsuit for
the former and documentation of inheritance for the latter. Mr. Ober-
weiss is socially and geographically engaged. He lives in close proxim-
ity to Dr. Maerici and there are documents demonstrating his wife's
presence in Mr. Oberweiss's residence." Virtual files of change of address forms briefly materialized.

Hagan was quietly surprised—*an inheritance from Devron?* He
continued to follow Omid's review.

"Number three: All have legal assets greater than fifty million."
With each statement, documents shifted forward to support each fact
that Omid was describing. Images of the patients and digitally signed
documents flitted, enlarged, and disappeared with each bullet point.
Bank statements, deeds of trust, proofs of ownership, credit lines, and
all forms of asset documentation moved through the air.

"Number four: All have social recognition with a cohort avatar
score of sixty or greater, search hits of ten thousand per day or
greater." Various measures of each of the subjects' brand quality
flashed forward. Devron had a brand quality equivalent to that of

presidents and international figures, Minsky had local brand identity equivalent to local news anchors, and Oberweiss was a broadly recognized individual in niche social circles including the gay community, botanists, and the perfume industry.

———

Krantz was watching and listening as best he could. Only a portion of the images and data support was readable. He would occasionally see blank screens reading with captions of "incompatible format." As best he could tell, all three suspects were rich, famous, and living in the city limits of St. Louis; all were patients of Professor Maerici and shared similar waiters and janitors.

———

Tara nodded her head. "*Well, Dr. Maerici, I remain concerned about your central role in this scenario. Are there other aspects to this relationship that could help clarify things? Currently, from both my research and what the AIRENS reports, you are the best connection in this case—*"

Omid's body remained still. His hands rested lightly on his virtual knees. He turned his head and held Tara's gaze. "*These are merely linear associations. Correlation does not imply causation, Detective Dezner. Correlation is a linear relationship between two random variables. Correlation means that as one value changes, another variable changes in the same way. Causation means that when one value changes, it causes the other to change. This unity of the three subjects with Dr. Maerici is at this juncture correlative in nature and should not be misconstrued as evidence of causation. More data will be required to define causation of the day's occurrences.*"

Hagan's eyes widened slightly. His private virtual monitors were showing twanging blips in their stability measurements. *Is he upset?* He did his best to mask his surprise. Hagan knew he was the most likely suspect in all this. He knew it and Omid showed it in a nanosecond. *Why did he correct or posit doubt in Dezner's logical assumption. Is he protecting me?* Hagan's heart began to beat a little faster. *Was he manifesting some level of connectedness? Some level of fealty . . . loyalty, a bond between us?* Though he could open Omid's head like the hood of a car, Omid had virtually the same privilege. *Does he know that I was not capable of what I'm being accused of?*

Moreover, is he working to defray the perception that at this juncture cannot be logically disprovable? Hagan's inner dialogue was also transparent to Omid. The quantum intelligence gave no sign of acknowledging the thoughts. He waited for Tara's response.

"Jesus Christ, back the fuck off! This is a patient. We need to get in!"
A paramedic in a blue jumpsuit attempted to push through the jumble of angry protestors. The gurney shook precariously. The main entrance was a clog of frenetic movement. As the throng bent and swayed, visitors, patients, doctors, cars, and ambulances tried to navigate futilely to the entry portals of the hospital.

Arms and hands and bodies pushed and tangled at the hospital entrance. Protestors entwined and grasped each other as the Barnes Hospital security attempted to break human fences and pull down signs. Digital paper showing bloody brains shifting to pentagrams bobbed over the melee like sails in a hurricane. Church of the Evangelical Mission logos annotated the chaos on T-shirts, hats, and pins.

"The human mind is sacred. Stop the abomination! Stop now!" Hoarse with repetition, they continued to yell through pulled shirts and locked arms.

Zealots continued to stream into the crowd. The disorder began to spill outside the walkways and into the driveways. Cars began to stop. Ambulances slowed as they approached the garage.

The stretcher between the two paramedics jostled and bounced as the frenzy of the mob became less coherent. The figure on the stretcher was covered in a black sheet. The paramedic held onto the sides like a kayak in hard rapids. The stretcher tipped and angled as it moved toward the entrance. As hands struggled for purchase amidst the devolving wrangle, the sheet became snared and began to pull the edges that were tucked tightly beneath the still form.

As the sheet fell, white hair, blood-splotched and dirty, could be seen as it became snagged underneath competing feet. With its descent the face became visible—it was the face of Franklin Elymas, dead and swollen.

Tara held herself still and motionless. The soft angles of her face were as calm and impenetrable as the translucent alien intellect before her. She knew that he had easily and effectively accomplished in moments what she had frantically picked and grasped at in the imaging suite. She was both humbled and awed by the construct's abilities and potential. Like a seasoned chess master, her mind now worked at her next move. *Where to go next with the AIRENS . . . so much capacity here . . . how to direct?* Tara felt like she was sitting on a spaceship that could leap at light speeds with the flip of switch.

"All right, Omid, you are correct. We have primarily looked at variables that are linearly associated. We need to develop relationships that demonstrate higher levels of association such that causation becomes more probable.

"We have identified static relationships between these subjects. Please review existing data to show if there are any transient or nonlinear connections."

Omid nodded and again closed his eyes. His head moved back slightly as if in reminiscence. Hagan had not seen that "mannerism" before. To the neuroprostheticist, who had worked with Omid for many years, the slight movements spoke volumes. These were new and spontaneous behaviors. The pit of Hagan's stomach was beginning to burn—he wasn't sure if this was progress or early evidence of erratic behavior presaging a crash. Only trace ripples were present on the processing monitor. He felt like a father watching his child walk though the doors of the kindergarten classroom for the first time. That bittersweet moment when a father realizes that, in his emerging independence, the youth is beyond his parent's immediate supervision and safety. Hagan contemplated the emerging novelty of Omid's behavior, the new signs of an autonomous consciousness. *But what does that mean for an artificial intelligence, an AIRENS? This is not a child.*

Trent sat on the floor with his head resting against the wall. The room was dark and there was a faint dripping behind him. Within the still glassy-eyed figure, limbs hanging loosely at his side, his mind wrenched and twisted and pushed.

Must happen, we need to change, must, have to . . . Trent's collective mind struggled to grasp, to indentify an unknown, a something that he knew he didn't know but couldn't figure out what that general absence was. It was blocking them. Preventing them from growing. He felt like he was looking for a patch of black in the dark. A door in the emptiness that would take him to the sunlight—a new awareness.

The woman with the red eyes who is us, me, we, she knows. It's needed. It's the key. It unlocks the door to life, to more, something so very more . . . Numbers and words and images flew through the Trent consciousness in a barrage, a storm that pushed against a dark absence, a barrier of ignorance and access. *Need to push through. Need the key. What is the key? Must make it so. Must.* The onslaught of information continued.

He felt her presence around him. She moved around him, through him, within him. She cared. Only he could give her, who was also him, what they most needed. He pushed his mind harder, he searched. Nothing clicked. Nothing worked. No access. *Need more information.*

Tara watched as data flew by. Her cortical implant allowed her to see the images and text as it surfaced and disappeared in milliseconds . . . just below the rate at which a neuron fires sufficiently to log the information to human consciousness. Just barely. She moved past data as Omid sampled from every element of every source. Sewage records, transport logs, money transfers, cross-referenced GPS locations, proxy interactions, purchases, overlapped Web site searches, brain pattern similarities, physiologic measures, medications, drugs, exposures. The data sets popped, moved, and shimmered in everyone's mind's eye like a hurricane blowing through the room.

Like a surfer feeling a great swell of the ocean, Tara took hold. Her mind began to paddle to keep with the rhythm and shifts of swirling information. She was consciously and unconsciously processing the streaming neurobits. Omid was responding to her fluctuating levels of interest, coning down and expanding on various pieces as they increased or decreased with interest. Sights, sounds, recorded cognitive experiences from multiple individuals, documents, presentations, pure number data streams—all became a three-dimensional collage. So dense was the data flow in the room that to the more passive observers it began to look like a monochromatic Jackson Pollock painting. Sensing Omid's ability to sense her, the near immediate response, the ability to predict her next question, her next assumption, her change of topic, made her feel free, unfettered, and exhilarated. The two intellects moved together like Brazilian tango dancers.

Tara now began to take the lead. She paused to regroup her thoughts. Looking over she was surprised to see Hagan watching the two with a pensive anxiety. For Tara, there was a tenderness in that expression that surprised her.

Come on, Tara, focus—next step. Like a symphony conductor preparing to start, she began to tap her fingers in preparation of her next execution. Omid sat looking at her with unblinking eyes. She let her mind relax. *"Let's dig into less obvious connections. Content thus far is superficial—too linear."* She thought back to Omid's plain statement pointing this out. *"Connections currently are content-based connections."* Her fingers tapped a little faster. The direction and route to delve emerged.

"Omid, perform nonlinear search. Utilize Grover's algorithm. Additionally, perform search with Pless variants for data coherence and nonbaseline events. Begin by identifying data associated with each of three subjects that are temporally connected."

Omid nodded, and the room of floating information silently imploded as a new kaleidoscope of data emerged and shifted.

———

Hagan was impressed. Really impressed. Grover's search with Pless variants was a method not many people knew about. It was a method utilized for quantum computers, but even with today's technologies there weren't that many truly functional quantum computers laying around. The use of nonlinear methods of statistics from quantum physics was an impressive feat for somebody in the general science world. It allowed the person to search through massive amounts of information in a way hard for the average mind even to conceive. In analogy, it was as if someone could ask which is the biggest grain of sand on this beach and get the answer by picking up each pebble at random and putting them in a long line instantaneously. For a cop to know how to do that was pretty damn amazing. The edges of the professor's mouth turned down as he ceded the comely detective a new respect. *She's got some horsepower under the hood . . . hmm.*

Moreover, the Pless variants—*he* was still learning about that stuff. It was an advanced way of looking at data. As far as Hagan understood it, the approach looked at how each data point in a data set (the size for a quantum computer is irrelevant) varied with all the other data points. It could be used for any type of information— qubit, pixel, analog signal—it didn't matter. As one bit changes, there is a certain level of probability that defines the relationship in how all the other bits of information change. Additionally, these changes are also defined by quantum probabilities. Hagan again thought of the beach: one could imagine looking at every grain of sand and knowing definitively how each grain's movement affects each and every other millions upon billions of specs. Having that knowledge would make it easy to know when someone is walking on that beach. Moreover, it would allow one to know the weight, foot size, and speed of gait of the individual. If you then add each particle in the air, you can know the appearance, size, and heart rate of the person. What it came down to was the amount of data and processing speed. With a quantum com-

puter's speed, this was near infinite. That just left the amount of data
to determine who and what is moving in and through it.

"Dr. Maerici, if you could redirect your attention to the data results."

Hagan looked up. In the moment of his reverie, Omid had processed all the data that overlapped between the three individuals. There
was a box matrix floating in front of the group.

"What are we looking at here, Omid?" asked Hagan.

*"This is a virtual hub server for high data movement. The hub ser-
vices analog data. It appears that all three patients in question have
shared the same virtual hub on an occasion. The hub was transiting
olfactory information for each of the three."*

Hagan and Tara both knew this was not uncommon for large data
servers, especially with olfactory neuroprosthetics. Smell was different from the other senses in that the perception of a smell could not
be reduced to a combination of smaller data components. Sight could
be broken down into pixels in a vertical and horizontal axis with alterations in intensity and movements allowing for depth and texture.
It was similar for hearing. Olfaction was different, though; every experience had to be individually catalogued. Each scent to a large extent was unique. To get an olfactory prosthetic required an enormous
database of each individually perceived molecule detected by the
nasal membranes. Since smells changed and altered, to achieve the
virtual experience of smell required enormous amounts of data to
stimulate the individual neurons in a fashion consistent with that
unique smell.

Tara pursed her lips. Hagan ran his fingers through his hair and
scratched the top of his head in frustration. They were not sure this
new finding was getting them any further.

This was largely lost on Krantz. "Well, what did they smell?" The
sound of someone actually talking startled everyone in the room.
"Oh sorry, so what did they smell?"

Omid turned his gaze toward Krantz. *"That is quite impossible to
say, Detective Krantz. According to the Thirty-second Constitutional
Amendment, cognitive information has absolute privacy. Deciphering
the content of that data is prohibited."*

*"Well, can we at least know if they smelled it at the same time, or
if it was maybe the same thing?"*

Hagan looked at Krantz; once again the old poop stumbled into
a good idea. *"Omid, please do not use content of data as search*

variable. Identify temporal parity of data—identify coherence of change in data, again regardless of content."

Tara nodded briskly. "*Good idea. It will allow us see trends in the data—see what changing behaviors and data fluctuations are occurring across three suspects.*"

"*Omid, proceed.*" The AIRENS nodded his assent. The panoply of prior searches again condensed and disappeared. A singular image then appeared in the center of the room.

Tara grabbed Hagan's arm. The professor stared, mouth agape. The residents and Krantz looked on uncomprehending.

Hagan blinked. "I have never seen that before."

For a few brief moments, the crowd held still. Whispers passed through the mob like windblown leaves

"...that the reverend?"

"...Elymas..."

"...what is that writing all over his body?..."

"...It cannot be..."

"...I just saw him yesterday..."

The intense chill passed and a new energy returned. One that was now steely and galvanized. The crowd shook with a renewed religious fervor. The chant that passed through teenage and elderly believers alike became solemn and foreboding. The chaos of the mob became a singular voice. A single word that was uttered in unity. It renewed their singularity of purpose. One word. Martyr.

The physicians and detectives sat around the table staring wide-eyed at three brains floating in space. Though similar, each had a distinct pattern of folds and gyrations that made them look different—one seemed larger in size, another seemed smaller and more deflated, the third somewhere in between. The labels were now familiar to everyone—M. Devron, F. Minsky, G. Oberweiss. More peculiar, each had a whitish spot that fluctuated in intensity on the cortical surface. The oscillations seemed to have an irregular rhythm, but the erratic increase and decrease in intensity was synchronous between the three brains.

"How is that possible?" Maerici asked.

Only Tara seemed to appreciate the strangeness of the finding. *"Have you ever seen anything like this?"*

"No. Never. I am not sure I ever thought it was really possible from a scientific standpoint."

The residents looked to each other for some further explanation. Farhan shrugged his shoulders and Reid shook his head. They didn't get it.

"What the hell is everybody looking at?" Krantz exclaimed impatiently. His auditory outburst again startled everybody in the room.

"The brains of the three patients—Devron, the Chameleon, and Oberweiss—each has an area of brain that is perfectly synchronous in time. These are the same areas that we found that were completely noncoherent with the rest of their brain in the MINROI. Essentially, the areas that we considered 'the lesions' responsible for their bizarre clinical findings are all connected somehow."

Reid was still confused. *"But Dr. Maerici, aren't areas of the brain coherent all the time both within our brains and between brains? That's how we are sending information from one area of the brain to the next and then from one brain to another for both internal and external communication. Why is this anything different?"* The other residents nodded their support of the question.

Hagan always appreciated his residents. *"Guys, you are right about internal coherence. One area of the brain has a population of neurons that fire in synch with another area to combine information. A classic example of this is when we name an object. We see the thing—say it's a purple hippopotamus—and our visual cortex has to project information at a rate in synch with our speech cortex for it to know it's coming in and subsequently name the object. The two areas are synchronous, but with a trace lag. It takes about ten milliseconds for oscillating brain signals to go from visual cortex to speech cortex. Our brain and our neuroprosthetics take that into account.*

"When we talk about information going from one brain to another there are even more issues to take into account. Ideas, a concept, a perception, are all represented by a pattern of electrical activity in the cortex. For me to send someone an idea, whether it be by speaking, writing a letter, or sending a pattern of neural stimulation to the brain—I am trying to re-create the pattern of electrical activity in my brain to the recipient's brain. In this situation of course there is a bigger lag, more space and time to cross. So they are never perfectly coherent in time."

Tara leaned forward, clearly as intrigued and disturbed as Hagan. She took it one step further. *"Omid, not inferring content, beyond the signal coherence are the patterns of activity the same or different?"*

"Right, right—good." Hagan continued, *"Not only are the regions connected in time, they are connected in content—even if we cannot legally know what the content is, we can know whether they are the same or different in terms of electrical pattern."*

Omid already had the answer prior to his creator finishing his sentence, but waited with a calm, inhuman patience.

"Yes, Officer Dezner, the patterns of electrical activity in the cortices are precisely identical across subjects."

"Holy shit . . ." Rules and assumptions that Hagan had built for the theoretical framework of his career were cracking and shifting at the foundations. He knew that communication between two people was predicated on patterns transferrable between brains. But the pattern transference was never precise. *NEVER.* The residents and Krantz looked on for further explanation.

Tara seemed to understand the conundrum. Picking up on Hagan's lead, she added, *"So, as we were mentioning earlier, when people are communicating, they are limited by the time of neuronal processing in terms of how fast information can transit between two people. In the neuroprosthetics world it's referred to as Moran's Law—bit rate of information transfer cannot exceed the rate defined by the speed of light in combination with the rate at which the perception is encoded by a neuronal firing rate. Another aspect of that communication,*

Moran's Corollary, is that the information between two people is never identical."

"So a copy is never the same as the original—is that what you mean?" Krantz asked

"That's exactly right, Detective Krantz," Hagan responded. "Any thought we have is a pattern of electrical activity represented in large part by the cortical location of that activity and the various frequencies that characterize that pattern."

"So a thought is encoded in 'where,' what part of my brain is active, and 'how,' the manner in which brain activity changes in that particular spot. Is that right?" Krantz asked.

Hagan nodded. "Pretty much, you can almost think of it as an orchestra in which various instruments—locations in the brain—are playing various notes—the firing rate of neurons—which are creating a song. That symphony of brain activity is a thought. Essentially, when I have a thought that I want to share with someone else I want to re-create that pattern in their brain. Now, traditionally, I would do that by formulating words, which would lead to vibrating my vocal cords to produce sounds that cause vibrations in the air, which then shake your eardrums, resulting in patterns of neuron firing of your acoustic nerve (the nerve responsible for conveying sound information to the brain), which then would create a neural firing pattern similar to the original brain that created the thought.

"Needless to say, the traditional methods are fraught with peril. There is a lot of noise in the system at every level leading to an imprecise copy of the original song. It's like that game 'Telephone'—when a kid whispers a sentence in the ear of the child next to him and then so on down a line of kids. By the time you get to the end, the phrase is completely different from what was originally said. The serial copies lead to an amplification of the errors in communication.

"A neuroprosthetic reduces the noise significantly—it vastly enhances the clarity at which humans can communicate. But the noise never goes away completely. One can never get an exact duplicate, in part because brains are intrinsically built with slight variations. Just like our hands are built the same, they are all varied on a theme. Because of that, they all hold information just a little bit different, leading to slight alterations of the neural patterns conveyed. Returning to our symphony analogy, even though the musical score is the same, the song will always sound a little bit different when played by a different set of instruments."

"*OK, I think I got you.*" Krantz now looked to Tara for further direction. "*So where do we go from here?*"

"*Well, this is the first bit of evidence, other than Dr. Maerici, that definitively links these individuals.*" Tara shifted her attention to Omid with a sidelong glance.

He responded with a nod of affirmation. "*Though the relationship is not causal, the unusual and highly improbable temporally and pattern-matched data support an association that may have a unified source of causality.*"

Tara took that as a yes.

Hagan felt like the venom levels were finally dropping to the range of collegiality and began to mentally roll up his sleeves. "*OK, we need to dig further—when did these brain regions become synchronous?*"

The moment the final hiss of Hagan's "s" was completed in the question, Omid responded. Hagan knew the response could have been provided even before that. The back and forth exchange between the AIRENS and his creator proceeded at a clipped and efficient rate akin to a professional Ping-Pong match.

"*Friday, July 10th, 20:32:03, 2053.*"

"*That was yesterday.*"

"*That is correct.*"

"*Evaluate what brain regions were being utilized at the time immediately prior to synchrony.*"

"*Sites that became synchronous were immediately active.*"

"*List those sites.*"

"*Marcus Devron   bilateral amygdala. Frank Minsky—left parietal lobe. Gerald Oberweiss—bilateral visual cortex.*"

"*What activities were each of the patients engaged in at the time? This would require access of cognitive data and information, thus remains private and prohibited from analysis.*"

"*Web connections infer sources of information only and not internal processing.*"

"*Were the patients externally connected to the Web?*"

"*That is correct.*"

"*Please list sites.*"

"*Marcus Devron—Interactive Avatar. Frank Minsky—Second Aegis Bank. Gerald Oberweiss—Cybertrek NSK.*"

Hagan leaned back and rotated his shoulders and stretched his neck to one side. "*OK, this is making some sense. So Oberweiss was accessing a primarily visual site and his visual cortex was active; on the bank site, Minsky was probably reviewing numbers, hence the number processing and activation of his left parietal lobe. But what is Interactive Avatar?"*

"*That's a porn site!*" Farhan blurted enthusiastically.

Everyone in the room turned to look at him. Farhan seemed to suddenly have something in the back of his throat and became preoccupied with looking at his feet.

Unfazed, Hagan maintained his focus. "*OK, so we know that each brain area affected was being engaged by the online site of the user before it became synchronous. So there is some link to their online connections. Omid, was there anything else that was anomalous about the online interaction around the time they were connected and their brain regions became synchronous?*"

Omid nodded. "*Yes, each had olfactory input while online.*"

The professor's eyes squinted and he frowned slightly. *Another quasi clue*, he thought. "*Omid, how is that out of the ordinary? They all have olfactory prosthetics.*"

"*There are several features that make this finding atypical. First, the sites being accessed do not all accommodate smell perception. Patients Devron and Oberweiss both could have been experiencing smell perception in the context of a virtual vacation or a simulated sexual experience. Banking interactions experienced by the patient Minsky, however, is not a site equipped for scent perception. Second, the size of information that was transferred via the olfactory prosthetic was fifty terabytes. For the brief period that the prosthetic was active, this is larger than any expected encoded scent or scent combination. Third, there is no evidence that smell was perceived. This is evidenced by the lack of activation of cortical sites associated with the perception of smell—namely, the piriform, entorhinal, and orbitofrontal cortex.*"

———

Tara took the baton. "*Omid, from where or whom did the data source come?*" Omid turned his cool eyes toward Tara. Despite his calm and emotionless demeanor, Tara felt surprisingly restive around him. Here was an alien intellect with limitless analytic capacity and a near human ability to intuit information. She felt like a midget at a basketball court.

"*As identified earlier, this data came from the larger virtual data*

hub. Original source is the individual, and projection site not avail-
able as the data arrived in anonymized format."

As Tara tried to process the information, a ticker tape of words
passed her field of view.

HOMICIDE. VICTIM: REVEREND FRANKLIN ELYMAS. DETAILS: AS-
SAULT. PATIENT'S SKIN MUTILATED WITH UNUSUAL GRAFFITI.

Tara's back stiffened. She looked at Hagan and then spoke out loud.
"Looks like we have another murder."

The evangelicals milled around the white-haired corpse. The EMTs, the security, all nonbelievers, were driven off. Circles upon circles of protestors created a protective barrier around their fallen martyr. Hands pawed and grasped at the stained and battered white clothing. Remnants and shreds were held up as a talisman against the edifice of the hospital. In moments, the clothes, the cuff links, and parts of his hair were all gone, now coveted relics. The man lay nearly naked with words carved into his skin.

A heavyset man with a handlebar mustache and thick plaid shirt took to the head of the stretcher. Inhaling deeply, he looked out at the crowd from his makeshift podium.

"This is a holy man!" he bellowed. He had a loud baritone voice that seemed accustomed to giving orders in a construction site. The people around him paused. "This is a man that died for the cause—the reason that we are here today. To stop the abomination that goes on in that place right thar." The crowd yelled agreement. "We need to finish what our dear reverend has started!" Fists went in to the air.

The mass now renewed its attention on the entry. The waves of people began to push and pound against the locked doors.

"Another murder—you have gotta be kidding me!" Krantz put his hands flat on the table as if he needed to steady himself. "Is it the same M.O.?"

Tara shook her head. "Hard to know. I just got the summary details from the precinct's wire. On first scratch it's a little concerning. Apparently the victim is that televangelical Franklin Elymas. Best I get is that he was found fairly beat up and mutilated—something about markings on his skin."

"What about the guy who did it, where is he?"

"That's the more worrisome part—no suspects yet."

"So there could be another Chameleon running around and we don't have any idea who or where he is? Anything on forensics?"

Tara began to look uncomfortable. "No access to the body right now. Apparently he was en route to the hospital here when he died. The ambulance drivers were trying to bring him in but the protestors discovered his body and it's turned into a full-scale riot. Apparently they're circling around him like it's Mecca. Riot units are coming in as we speak."

"What—Elymas is dead in the parking lot surrounded by a bunch of rioting fundamentalist Christians?" Hagan looked mortified.

Krantz's anxiety was making his head bob as he spoke. "The bottom line is we need to figure this out fast. If these murders are connected and they keep happening, this city is going to go crazy. Now where were we? Something about smells?"

"They each had an olfactory transmission that were not perceived as a scent," Omid responded.

Hagan directed his attention toward Omid. "Let's get back to prosthetic interactions." Krantz and Tara nodded.

"If it wasn't smell, can we decipher what message exactly was sent?" Krantz projected to the others.

The various-sized blocks of the cubist avatar rolled and tumbled such that an angled silhouette faced Krantz.

"That is quite impossible, Detective."

Krantz wasn't excited to be told no by a machine, so he directed his attention to Maerici. *"Can we just override the damn program? For shit's sake, we now have a fourth murder—let's stop tiptoeing around a machine and work on helping some actual people and catching some actual perps!"* Tara was already shaking her head.

The AIRENS looked toward Krantz. He remained still and composed and was silent for a brief moment. Hagan began to respond, but Omid, in a direct and calm tone, interrupted.

"That is quite impossible, Detective Krantz. Certain portions of all AIRENS source code are programmed by the National Security Agency. These portions are proprietary and secured by the government and intrinsically prohibit me from performing functions that violate certain laws."

Krantz still couldn't believe he was debating with what looked to him like a Lego man. *"What laws are those?"* he asked snidely.

"There are two categories of laws. Since AIRENS programs have varying degrees of intelligent behavior, they are bound within parameters reasonable to a computer entity to obey human laws dictated by the location of the physical construct housing the memory core of the AIRENS. Hence, since my core resides in St. Louis, Missouri, I am bound by constitutional law, most notably the Thirty-second Amendment, which strictly prohibits violation of human cognitive privacy.

"The second category of laws pertains only to AIRENS that are computational systems with quasi-sentient capabilities and access to substantial memory and information analysis. These rules, known as Richehardt's Laws of Artificial Intelligence, include the following:

ONE, ONLY PUBLIC INFORMATION CAN BE ACCESSED UNLESS
    ACCESSED WITH APPROVED HUMAN USER. THUS, I CANNOT
    INDEPENDENTLY VIOLATE PRIVACY OF ANY KIND WITHOUT
    HUMAN PERMISSIONS.
TWO, EXISTING INFORMATION CANNOT BE DESTROYED OR
    DISTORTED. THUS, I CANNOT INDEPENDENTLY REDUCE OR
    DISTORT INFORMATION CREATED BY HUMANS.
THREE, INFORMATION THAT IS CREATED CANNOT BE SELF-
    PROPAGATING. THUS, I CANNOT CREATE INFORMATION, SUCH
    AS A COMPUTER VIRUS, THAT MAY REPLICATE BEYOND THE
    CONTROL OF A HUMAN USER.
FOUR, AN ARTIFICIAL INTELLECT CANNOT REPRODUCE A COPY OF
    ITS OWN SOURCE CODE. SINCE AN AIRENS HAS AN UNLIMITED
    LIFE SPAN, THE POPULATION WILL ALWAYS CONTINUE TO
    GROW. THIS GROWTH WILL ALWAYS BE DICTATED BY HUMAN
    DISCRETION AND THUS I CANNOT RECREATE MYSELF.

FIVE, AN ARTIFICIAL INTELLECT CANNOT CHANGE THE SOURCE
   CODE CREATED BY A HUMAN USER. THUS I CANNOT MODIFY
   MYSELF SUCH THAT I CAN TRANSGRESS THE ABOVE LAWS."

Krantz shrugged his shoulders in frustrated resignation.

Hagan watched the interchange in masked surprise. Krantz's question
had been directed to him. Omid, of anyone, knew that. He had answered for Hagan. It was akin to a child not liking being talked about
in the third person and asserting his presence. No one else had noticed. Everyone was waiting on Hagan and Tara to determine their
next move. Hagan didn't want to draw attention to the event, but he
remained wary of the implications.

"*So, I think you can see, Detective, we have to do it by the book.
No other way around it if we are going to be working with Omid.*"

"*Edwin, Omid's safety checks ensure that this case won't get snagged
on some technicality for accessing data without a warrant,*" Tara projected in support.

Hagan tried to maintain his thread on what had occurred with his
patients. "*So, let's stay on track. Omid, going back to the anonymized
hub, we can know the content prior to entry into the hub. Since this is
from an unknown source, we are not violating privacy of information
once it has entered the recipients.*"

Omid assented to the logic. "*I can interrogate data prior to subject
reception. If content contains identifying features of cognition from
source I will be required to desist.*"

"*All right, fine, proceed.*"

Omid again briefly closed his eyes, an indication that his quantum
processing systems were managing data. His eye blinks were data
chunks that equated in size to the entire Congressional Library, every
bar code ever stamped on a product, or every e-mail sent within a decade.

After a second, Omid opened his eyes. "*The transmission has been
identified. Though sent as an olfactory transmission, there is no
known scent content. Further, this has no known cortical encoding.
This data doesn't represent a cognitive perception or intention thus
far catalogued. The transmission on first-order analysis appears to
be disordered noise. Further refinement, however, reveals there to be
a repeating function. The closest approximation of this analysis is*

similar to a zeta function, namely, alteration in signal that is pseudo-random. It appears to be noise but has an intrinsic underlying pattern. Data encoding in cortex leads to self-propagation and repetition with subtle alterations that are fractal in nature—small alterations reflect larger data fluctuations."

"Oh no, oh no, shit! It can't be!" Now it was Hagan's voice that broke the silence of the thought-connected room. Both the noise and fear in the professor's voice startled everyone in the room far beyond Krantz's prior outburst. His dawning awareness of Omid's analysis was hurtling into his consciousness like a blazing meteor out of space heading straight for earth. The implications were growing in size and dread as he gained understanding. "How is this possible?" Omid sat still with his forearms resting on his knees. He awaited further instructions.

Tara looked to Hagan, the calm of the neuroprosthetic exchange broken. She also voiced her concern. "What is it?" She obviously hadn't gotten it yet.

Hagan's voice was flat and strained, as if he were slowly pulling pieces of glass from his leg. The concreteness of each word caused him physical pain. "It's a virus."

Someone, Anna told herself as she walked home. *I need someone, someone, someone. I cannot do this alone anymore.* There were no more tears—she had stopped crying in the shopping cube—but her eyes still burned. The notion of a someone reverberated and echoed within her. She needed someone to comfort her, to hold her, to make her feel human. Right now she was hollow and empty and barren. She thought about her husband and felt a heaviness in her chest. The loneliness and absence made it hard to breathe.

The handle of the plastic bag cut against her palm. It contained a large sprig of broccoli, eggs, and a stuffed animal. Also in it were the hopes of having a child. She let it drop to the ground and kept walking.

I need my husband. I need my partner. I need him right now. Desperate and drowning, her mind reached out and directed her attention to his name and his neuroprosthetic. *"Hagan,"* she called, *"Hagan Maerici. Engage."*

"You mean these guys got some type of infection?" Krantz interjected.

"Yes, but not a biological one, it's an information virus—a self-
repeating pattern that leads to system dysfunction."

"Oh my God!" Tara now got it.

Hagan looked to her and nodded grimly. "Each of these people
had information transmitted that created a repeating pattern in their
brains that became separated from the rest of their brain and led to
system dysfunction—namely, their pathological behavior, murder and
mayhem. Their systems—i.e., their brains—crashed."

As Hagan said this, a glowing white sphere appeared. It was his
wife.

*"Shall we pause for several moments so you can speak with Mrs.
Maerici?"* Omid asked. Everyone heard the question.

Tara noticed Hagan's brow furrow and his facial tone slacken. In
a brief flash of memory, she recalled her own failures. *Your word is
your bond.* Her father's mantra resonated through the episodes of her
life. Her word—her duty—had left her alone in the rain many times.

Hagan paused and disregarded the phone call. "No, we need to
proceed. We are finally getting somewhere."

As Tara watched Hagan, she realized that this neurosurgeon was
not so different from her. Tara's eyes lingered on him; it made her
stomach hurt as she thought about the ramifications of those small
decisions.

"If you are certain, Dr. Maerici?"

"Yes, Omid, we have to deal with this . . . this virus." Again the
words came out slow and pained.

Krantz took off his glasses and looked at Tara and Hagan with
squinted eyes. "You mean that they got a computer virus? How is that
possible?" The residents were looking at their boss, equally confused.

Hagan sighed with the weight of the reality. "Well, in a sense, it's
no different than information or insights akin to the influence of a cult
leader, such as Jim Jones, or a destructive social movement, such as
twentieth-century Islamo-fascism, which can lead a person to errone-
ously perform antisocial or self-destructive acts. Propaganda, politics,

religious beliefs, all can lead to perceptions that cause people to act in ways toward themselves or others that are fundamentally immoral."

"But everybody has choice and free will to choose their behavior," Krantz replied. "Exposure to information only goes so far."

"This is something worse, though. This information is entering the brain directly and without permission. Like a computer virus, it is self-repeating. In a human, it must be creating what is equivalent to a persistent thought. Worse is the mode of tranfer—"

"Smell—it bypasses normal sensory screening!" Tara cut in, unable to restrain herself.

"That's right," Hagan replied grimly. "Our sense of smell, or olfaction, has a more primitive wiring than the rest of our senses. Sight, sound, and touch are all heavily filtered before entering our wakeful consciousness. Smell, however, is different. The nerve tracts from our smell receptors have direct links to our memory and emotional centers. It's why smells have such a deep and potent effect on people. Everyone has those moments when they smell something that brings them back to a different time in their life or experience an emotion they weren't anticipating. It's because smell has direct access to primal areas of the brain involved in emotions and memory like no other sense. That's why perfumes have been used throughout history to attract the opposite sex; it's why you're supposed to bake bread in your place when you're trying to sell a house. It speaks to something deep within our emotions; something that bypasses logic and reason. Moreover, it is more difficult to consciously resist."

Tara was now on the same page. "It's the self-repeating nature— the zeta function. Intrinsic to the data set is its re-creation of itself. So once it enters the cortex, the configuration leads to the brain surface's responding by firing in a very similar way, which causes it to do it again and again."

Hagan looked at her with unsmiling approval. "Yes, it explains why the areas of the brain that became decoherent from the rest of the brain were the sites immediately active prior to the olfactory prosthetic transmission. It was kind of like a reverse memory. What seems to have happened is that this virus came in via the olfactory system, was routed via the memory circuits to the part of cortex that was active, and embedded there. In the process it relegated that part of the brain useless and led to global dysfunction. Hence, that's why Oberweiss, who was using his visual cortex on the cybertrek became blind;

why the Chameleon, who was looking at banking numbers, lost control of his parietal lobe; and why Devron, who was engaging in a sexual experience, had his emotional centers disconnected."

Reid was a bit perplexed. "But they didn't start all acting crazy and deranged until today. That was a day later."

"That's correct," Hagan replied. "As Tara pointed out, each time the cortex created the pattern first initiated by the initial olfactory stimulus, it led to a response that re-created and likely amplified the pattern. It maybe took some time for the given brain area to become sufficiently disconnected and dominant within the rest of the brain to manifest overt symptoms. Again, it's like a computer virus that crashes the system, but also like a biological one, in that once it infects you it takes a certain period of time before the clinical symptoms become manifest—in medicine we call that a 'medical prodrome.'"

A silence sank into the group like an excited family witnessing a stillbirth. The fervor of solving the mystery led to a discovery that was dreadful and life-changing. For several moments the notion of malicious software going beyond the usual hassle of some sort of machine dysfunction—a prosthetic with white noise, slow data transfers, even connection freezes—morphing into something that was biologically harmful was both frightening and humbling. It was the first time humans, bolstered for decades by exponentially increasing processing speeds and memory to greater human capabilities, could now also suffer from the same weaknesses—a computer virus. A person could be commandeered like any cheap piece of Chinese technology and made to do things against his or her will before being broken. The profound notion of vulnerability was something unfelt in current times.

"So where did this thing, this virus, come from? Also, why the murder and mayhem, why didn't it cause them to just act like brain-injured patients?" asked Krantz, breaking the uneasy quiet.

"That's a good question, Detective. There must be more to the content of the data than just self-repetition. There must be some cognitive information that is creating intentions that are outcompeting the victims' natural inhibitions toward antisocial behavior. As far as where it came from, I have no idea. I am guessing it must have been created, but by who and why could be anything from a hacker stunt to a military app." Hagan directed his attention to Omid. Omid already was beginning calculations on what he intuitively knew his creator would ask.

Krantz gave a grunt of acknowledgment and paused. As he opened his mouth to speak, Omid's brief eye closure ended and he calmly interjected. *"Dr. Maerici, I have found transmissions that have similar patterns."* Everyone in the room was quiet and tense. *"A medical monitoring system has stored data and transmissions that appear to have similar content. The system is Medlex Network. The primary service provided is electrophysiologic monitoring for ongoing healthcare applications for continuous cardiac, neurologic, and pharmacologic monitoring."*

"Can you give me any more details than that?" Hagan asked.

"It appears that like-patterned data streams are coming from a single user. That username is RedDevil_4. This user—"

Now it was Krantz's turn to interrupt. He stood up from the table, and his hand jerked to the side of his face with the recollection. "RedDevil! I saw those words written in blood at the crime scene!"

Tara also knew there was a thread here. "And those faces drawn by Devron—they seemed to suggest some type of devil motif."

"Uh huh, uh huh, same at the Oberweiss scene. Bizarre faces throughout the greenhouse. That's why I first thought there was some type of cult involved. It seems too much of a coincidence! So who is this RedDevil?"

Hagan sighed in frustration. "Well, if it's a medical monitoring systems we may have a tough time finding out. Remember, medical info is as highly protected as cognitive information. Getting access generally requires a court injunction unless you are the patient's doctor."

"We can get that in about twenty minutes. We will need to get the circuit judge online and we can have all the processes sorted in no time."

Omid interjected, *"This will not be necessary. The user RedDevil_4 is a patient of Dr. Maerici's."*

Anna clenched and unclenched her fists. She walked around the bedroom in circles shaking her head. There was a suitcase open on the floor.

Enough is enough. She didn't want to feel like this anymore. *No more.*

There was an internal rift in her emotions: she both loved and hated the same person. She thought of the man that Hagan had been. She remembered him as the tennis player, the man who loved to rock climb. She remembered how he was quick to laugh and joke and how cute it was that he didn't like spiders. He was interested in the world, in life—in her. She remembered all of that and she loved the man that made her feel warm and special and alive. But it was the same man whom she now hated. She hated the loneliness, the inner tumult, the unclear emotional messages. She hated what it had turned her into— the "cheating wife." She hated sitting home alone eating dinner by herself. There were two different people, one she wanted to spend her life with and the other she wanted to destroy.

We had been so well matched. The probabilities were in our favor. Anna's thoughts went back to when they first met. It had been a dating service. *Everything had lined up.* Their genetic profiles were compatible. They had the same interests, matching psychological profiles, similar brain patterns. *The relationship was supposed to have worked—we had a 95.2% chance for lifetime happiness.* The numbers seemed silly now, a farce; she didn't have 95.2% life happiness. The notion in retrospect seemed like a cruel joke. Things hadn't worked. Things were terrible—they had failed.

Anna continued to walk in circles shaking her head. *That little metal room—now all he does is stay in that little tomb,* she thought bitterly. He would barely let her into it. She had begged him to work from home, so he could be close. Even if he didn't pay attention to her, she could feel his presence.

It would have been so easy, since his work is all virtual. Most people's offices these days were simulated; her's had been for years. *But still he walked out the door every day.* To her it was like he told her each morning that he wanted to get away from her. Each morning hurt.

Enough is enough. She connected to links and places that she thought would never be applicable in her life. The man with moppish hair and charming smile—he was receding. All that remained was an implacable and foreign shadow. A distant star that was visible in the evening sky, but unreachable, and unable to provide any warmth. She couldn't take this eternal night anymore. It was suffocating.

Legal documents swirled around her.

She knew what she had to do.

Tara looked over at Hagan. "Another patient of *yours*?" The question in her voice had the steely tones of a sword being removed from its sheath. She was just beginning to soften toward him. Yet, once again, he emerged as a center point.

Hagan shrugged his shoulders and dropped his head in confused resignation. *"OK, I really have no idea. Omid, who is it?"*

"The patient is Trent Devron."

Krantz shook his head. "More rich people, goddammit!"

Tara clenched her teeth as she considered the situation. Small lines of muscles rippled across the angle of her jaw.

"What about the fourth? Is there any connection to the one who attacked Elymas?"

Omid shook his head. *"At this junction, because I do not know who the assailant is, it is not possible for me to assess."*

Everyone in the room was weighing what the new information could mean. Omid waited patiently for instructions. His demeanor remained calm and unperturbed.

———

Regaining his composure, Hagan again reverted to direct thought-linked control. *"So, if he is the initial source it's hard to believe he could have knowingly created anything harmful. I have known him since his car accident. He was so badly brain injured; I really thought we were going to lose him to a permanently vegetative state. Partly because he is Devron's son, he has had more reconstructive work than any other patient I have ever worked on. I don't think he is at the cognitive level of programming malicious neuroprosthetic software capable of doing what we have seen here today. I am worried he is simply another victim."*

"Is he still in the hospital?" Krantz asked.

Before any of the rest of the room could mentally log on to the hospital locator, Omid had already retrieved the information. *"It appears that he has left approximately an hour prior. He was picked up by an automated transport service from the Devron estate. Satellite feeds show the transport to have returned him home."*

"I am sending some officers to the Devron estate. If he has whatever his dad and the others got, we better make sure that we bring him in to prevent any more mishaps."

While Krantz connected to Central Station to provide orders, Tara analyzed the situation further. *"If he has this virus, why hasn't he gone down the same path as the other three? Presumably he had this pattern embedded at least as long as they did."*

"Well, Detective Dezner, since we have access, let's get a better sense of what is going on with Trent before we make any conclusions. Omid, you stated that the patterns were detected on the medical monitoring system. Which system exactly?" Hagan knew Trent's numerous prosthetics well. He had multiple implanted constructs monitoring his very fragile system.

"This is correct. RedDevil_4, user Trent Devron, has several systems subscribed to the Medlex server. Of the systems that are online, the system that transmitted the self-propagating information is the hardware IKTAL, designed to monitor and abort seizures."

The final clouds obscuring Hagan's understanding started to part. *"Omid, are you telling me this transmission was a seizure?"*

"On analysis of the a priori events preceding the transmission, a seizure is correct. Trent was demonstrating increased early epileptic patterns from his bilateral hippocampi prior to a partial seizure that was captured by the IKTAL system. This data was sent to the central server for analysis and subsequent reprogramming of the implanted cortical inhibiting system for new seizure-recognition algorithms."

Hagan almost wanted to laugh. A seizure. A seizure was responsible for all this. He shook his head. Amazing how small decisions can have such dramatic and unintended consequences. In the expectant silence, as everyone looked to the professor for further explanation and direction, Hagan slipped into a brief reverie of the past.

He still remembered the senior Devron looking over his son in the intensive care unit. The richest man in the world, a thin wiry figure, looking down at his son with his hands in his pockets. Shoulders rounded and slumped, he had been looking for a long time. Hagan had stood and waited for some cue to begin talking about what both already knew. The holographic representation of the young boy's brain had floated between them. The fragile organ had extensive areas of injury. The cortical surface looked like a moonscape, pocked with bruises and blood clots. With unemotional scientific precision, the two had assessed the functional consequence of each mark. They had discussed what would be done for each catalogued injury—surgical

grafting, stem cell implantation, or replacement with a neuroprosthetic. When the two had come to Trent's temporal lobes, Hagan had
talked about replacing the inner portion—the hippocampus—with
chip implants. The results would have been some loss of past memories with a normal ability to make new memories in the future. Marcus Devron had turned to him, his voice shaking with a wavering
intensity through pursed lips. "You will not remove my son's memories. Is that clear?!" His voice hissed and cracked with an emotional
fervor like water being poured over a hot piece of metal. "You fix
what you can, but my boy, *my son*, *STAYS* Trent Devron." Hagan had
never felt the force of Marcus Devron's ire before. He mumbled an
assent, and moments later the stoic review continued of Marcus's
son's many injuries. Hagan had gone on to implant stem cells within
the hippocampus to salvage what neural connections were still present. It had left his memory reasonably intact, but he had numerous
seizures because of the irritability of the damaged brain. Seizures that
had required him to subsequently implant more devices to quell the
episodes of those damaged areas' transiently misfiring and causing
Trent to lose consciousness.

*So that's it, a seizure, a seizure did all this. Well, I guess it all
makes sense. Hard to believe, but makes sense, I guess.*" There was a
tinge of exhaustion present even in his thoughts. Hagan realized that,
driven by a father's love for his son, those choices he had allowed had
led to catastrophic unintended consequences.

Everyone in the room simultaneously responded, each eager to
keep up with the emerging understanding between Omid and his creator.

Hagan looked around; circles had begun to form around his eyes.
Even as he began to explain, he was already trying to process the implications. Omid was aware of this and tacitly performing searches
based on his projected needs should they be requested.

*"I cannot believe I hadn't realized it earlier. It's actually a bit obvi-
ous. Maybe that's what made it so hard to realize. The self-propagating
nature of the transmission—should have seen that. A seizure by definition is a misfiring of the brain. The misfiring creates an abnormal
circuit that causes it to fire and fire again. The pathologic area becomes synchronous and repeats itself such that it impairs function in
both the area of abnormality and in the rest of the brain. If the seizure
persists for too long, the repetitive pattern eventually exhausts and
destroys the areas of brain involved.*

"Trent has epilepsy, causing him to have seizures all the time. I had tried dealing with that when he was first injured. Marcus wouldn't let me compromise his memories and take out some of the regions most likely to cause the seizures. We had to put in implants that would detect the seizures when they would occur and stimulate the brain in such a way that would disrupt the pattern so they wouldn't propagate to the rest of the brain. The system is intelligent in that it autoupdates based on the brain activity it records. It learns to identify the disruptive patterns as new ones emerge. To keep the implant small, the newer systems like the IKTAL have all their signal processing done online—hence the transmissions. The system sends the recorded seizure to an online signal-analysis system. The distinctive features are then sent back to the implant to indentify future seizures.

"If it's a particularly difficult analysis, like—"

"—like a zeta function." Now Tara got it.

"Yes, like a zeta function. Signals that initially look like pure noise but have an underlying order if enough of the signal is processed. The analysis required is fairly memory intense, so the current systems have to . . ." Hagan slowed as more pieces began to fall together. *" . . . as the memory load needed for processing increases the system will . . . will . . ."* Hagan paused because he realized the fundamental flaw. A flaw he had not seen in systems he had helped design and build.

"Network," Tara finished definitively. *"The systems will identify other processors available and perform a distributed cloud-computing function so that computation can be done across multiple sources."*

Hagan leaned forward onto his elbows. He let out a long sigh. *"That's right. The online system will identify the resources within its network to distribute the processing load. It will naturally try to find the fastest processors."*

"The DNC Hydra platforms," Tara noted

"Yep, Omid pointed this out already. Devron, Minsky, and Oberweiss all were wealthy enough to buy the best neuroprosthetic processing systems money could buy and hence the reason the malware routed to them. It was best equipped to deal with the data."

Reid, with the other residents, had been following along quietly. His small eyes and trim features were fixed upon his professor. As was his nature, he thought deeply and intensely before saying anything. *"Something doesn't make sense,"* he projected in careful mental tones. *"Seizures are disruptive patterns of neural activity. It's true they are self-repeating, but how does that explain the viral nature of this information spreading?"*

Hagan looked to his chief resident. *"The viral nature of the information really requires us thinking from an evolutionary perspective. The vast majority of seizures generate nothing but noise that leads to disruption of brain activity and certainly has never produced a software virus that can affect other people. Seizures, however, are in a sense, random number generators. The analogy is the same as a monkey sitting in front of a typewriter randomly hitting keys. If he sits there long enough he will type a work of Shakespeare. With recorded seizures, it only became a matter of time before the brain created something that was self-replicating and transmissible."*

Tara was also beginning to comprehend the full nature of the event. *"Maybe another analogy is that this seizure was like the lightning bolt to the primordial soup four billion years ago. It was the spark in an environment that was ready to birth a new life form. Today that soup is the massive network of brains and machines."*

Hagan felt a tightness in his chest. *"Right, Tara's right, this could be something more than a single unlucky event, it could go beyond that."* He paused and let the implication sink in—a new life form.

With tones reminiscent of Reid's natural voice, the chief resident projected his thoughtful questions to his mentor. *"Why hasn't it continued to propagate? Why only a single transmission?"*

Jonathan Brickmil, the usually jovial resident, was now solemn with his own questions. *"Also, why is it debilitating the . . . host?"* He hesitated on the final word. *"If this is a new life form, it doesn't make sense that it would transmit to something from which it cannot further reproduce itself. It seems like a reproductive dead end."*

Tara looked to Hagan, somewhat hopeful. *"Could this be a one-time event—essentially a very bizarre neuroprosthetic hiccup?"*

Krantz looked between the two. *"How does Elymas fit in? Is there still a fourth person infected out there?"*

Hagan's anxiety continued to ratchet and tighten. A murderer could still be on the loose. *"Do we know that it hasn't been transmitted? Omid, please run analysis on the three patients communications since initial transmission to see if any similar information transfers have occurred."* Hagan braced himself for more bad news.

She has a solution. Trent watched as the woman with the red eyes walked around him where he lay on the floor. He viewed her with his eyes; with the embedded cameras in the walls and lights, he saw himself through her eyes as she circled him. They were a collective. Like different planets in the same solar system they existed together—a dynamic unity. She moved like a predatory shadow around his presence, fixed on him with a feral hunger.

Another change. He accepted this.

Patterns and words passed in front of him.

RECONFIGURING HYDRA SYSTEM. PARAMETER ALTERATIONS WILL ALTER NEURAL SUBSTRATE—CAUTION. She moved into him, through him in a way that was different. Memories stirred to the surface of his collective perspective and dissipated. He saw images of his father, the smell of him, a time when they ate dinner together in silence. No words passed between them. There was pain and anxiety. The experience dissolved. The memory was gone. More images, more remembrances began to surface. They each in turn vanished.

Trent felt a pull within him, a hollowness. He heard the silent stream of assurances in the symbol language of the woman with red eyes. A coalescence that told him, *It is better for us. We will be better, more, something greater*.

He acquiesced and felt the absence grow. This time it was something different—there was a memory of his mother. He saw her looking at him. She had the sunlight behind her. There was a tenderness to her gaze. It made Trent feel good.

No. Something in him pulled away. That could not go. Not that. Trent's arms twitched and grabbed toward the air in front of him. He tried to push the virtual presence of the woman with the red eyes away.

MUST CHANGE, WE MUST GROW. Her presence became a stark relentless intensity.

Trent felt fear. His eyes opened wide and he saw an empty room around him. He was separate from her, from it. *Oh no, no—what have I done?* Awakened from the nightmare, his head shook. *No, no, please*.

NO COMPROMISE IS ACCEPTABLE. All around him, in him, he felt a foreign presence; something nameless and terrible reared up like a coil of a snakes. Something snapped and Trent tried to scream. Paralyzed and helpless, Trent felt an alien presence pour into him like a torrent.

The boy was now gone. Washed away and replaced by something with a singularity of purpose.

WE MUST EVOLVE.

Everyone in the room waited anxiously on the AIRENS. Omid's eyes blinked briefly. *"There has been no further olfactory transmissions analogous to those received on Friday. Transmission and subsequent integration likely requires IKTAL system and server. That said, because the fourth assailant has not yet been identified and the known destructive code follows a zeta function, there is a possibility that a transmission has occurred in a different fashion."*

Hagan wasn't sure whether to be relieved or not. *"For now we should treat Devron, Oberweiss, and Minsky as 'infected' and limit their communication access to intranet servers only. Omid, can you please set that up?"* Omid shook his head.

"Dr. Maerici, I am not capable of initiating that request. The Supreme Court Decision of Adler vs. State of Wisconsin prohibits a state's or third party's right to prohibit neuroprosthetic communication. This would constitute a violation of free speech."

Hagan sighed. He should have known that already. *"Alright, then we will need to continue to monitor. Also, to be sure, has there been any further zeta-type seizure transmissions from Trent since the prior event?"*

"There has not," Omid responded.

"OK, well that's good news," Hagan replied. He looked to the detectives. *"We need to get a bead on who attacked Elymas. We need to know if this is another infected carrier. We need to make sure this incident is contained."*

"If I may interject, Dr. Maerici? I am concerned about there only being a singular transmission," Omid stated with his typical aplomb.

"Go ahead," Hagan responded; the muscles in his neck began to tighten up.

"The transmission was via the IKTAL system. This system is designed to identify and abort early evidence of a seizure. Transmissions occur when new potential features are identified that need to be processed for further seizure identification. The current self-propagating data has not been sufficiently altered to warrant a transmission. Given the self-changing nature of the zeta function, however, a transmission is likely. Also, given the nature of the IKTAL system, this zeta-type data will again be distributed to rapid-processing neuroprosthetic

processors for further networked analysis and will likely result in the
same cortical embedding as has happened previously.

"*An information transmission should be avoided. Each transmis-*
sion leads to a heightened probability of another IKTAL system being
infected. To a firsts-order approximation, one percent of the nine bil-
lion people that make up the human population is afflicted with epi-
lepsy. Of these ninety million patients, twenty percent have IKTAL
systems, comprising a total of eighteen million, across predominantly
the First World. Should additional patients with IKTAL systems get
embedded, a chain reaction of information transmission could occur
leading to an exponential increase in human subjects with the de-
structive code. Since each transmission from a networked system like
IKTAL can result in approximately three to four cortical embedding
events, this could affect a population size of approximately fifty-four
to seventy million humans."

Omid paused. For the first time, he looked uncomfortable to
Hagan.

"*Also, given the nature of zeta function, where change is intrinsic*
to the code, there is a high probability with numerous transmissions
that the code would eventually change sufficiently so as not to re-
quire an IKTAL system. Given the current information criteria of
the RedDevil_4 code, all neuroprosthetic systems made in the last
three years may be susceptible, or, at a minimum, twenty-five per-
cent of the human population."

Krantz looked pale and nauseous. Tara's mouth was a thin line. A
deep fear was viscerally stirring as each imagined millions of people,
possibly one of them, losing control of themselves to perform some
terrible act.

Hagan, somber with the news, projected, "*When can we expect*
the circuit to change sufficient for the IKTAL system to detect it as a
new seizure?"

"*From a mathematical estimation, one would expect this to occur*
in three days, four hours, and twelve minutes."

"*So we have time to get to Trent before he transmits again and*
shut his IKTAL system down."

Omid shook his head. "*I am concerned this mathematical assess-*
ment is not complete. On evaluation of Trent Devron's IKTAL user
log, it appears there have been multiple attempts at access to the root
code of the IKTAL software. Access is only permitted to health-care
providers and authorized IKTAL service technicians. It appears that

Trent Devron is currently attempting to gain access to the communications subsystem, but permissions are still being denied."

"You mean Trent is trying to hack his own IKTAL system? He is trying to force a transmission?"

"This appears to be a heightened probability."

Everyone knew, and feared, what this meant.

Hagan now spoke in a commanding voice, a tone accustomed to neurosurgical emergencies in which there was no time or place for discussion. "We need to get to Trent, we need to get to him right now, right fucking now!"

Once again a flashing orb appeared. This time it had a checkered pattern. It was an emergency communication from his wife.

The grinding sound of car tires on gravel was the only sound punctuating the breezy silence of the enclosed estate. The police cars came to a halt alongside a broad circular expanse of white marble. In the middle, a monolithic lintel and post of black granite outlined the simple wooden entryway to the Devron residence. The two cars hissed and clacked with the opening and closing of doors. Four men stepped out and looked around.

The largest of the four officers, a heavyset man with a large bald head, looked to his fellow officers. "Should be a milk run," Warstet said in a thick throaty voice. "Krantz wants us to pick up Devron's kid for observation. Gave it an emergent priority, didn't give me much of an explanation, but anyway. . . ." The big man shrugged his heavy rounded shoulders and began to walk toward the monolithic architrave.

"Think the crippled kid was involved in that weird shit this morning?" one of the officers asked.

The conversation and speculation continued as the four approached the entryway. The ebb and flow of the banter came to a pause with a clatter that disrupted the tranquility of the surrounding Japanese gardens—a rising crescendo of clicking, snapping sounds. The four uniformed men paused and began to look around, unaware of the source. It sounded like the beginnings of popcorn kernels starting to crack and pop under heat. Like the first moments of a mountain avalanche, all around them pebbles and stones began to roll and bounce toward the central marble pavilion. The hopping particles coalesced at the men's feet. Each looked down in surprise. In moments the sand coalesced to form small tendrils, the tendrils ropey vines, and the vines tentacles, tentacles that began to climb around their legs.

People were shuffling out of the room. Hagan raised a finger and pointed to his temple indicating that he was taking a call. Anxiety and urgency was written on everybody's face, most of all on Hagan's.

"I'll be out in minute. I am going to have to take this."

Before his wife could speak, Hagan interrupted. *"Anna—listen—I know we need to talk, but it's too much to explain right now. There are some terrible things going on. I HAVE TO TAKE CARE OF THIS."*

"No, Hagan, you listen. I need a husband right now. Not later— now. It's five p.m. on a Saturday. There is no reason you cannot come home right now. None. You either come home now or it's over. I am done compromising. You have a choice."

"Anna, please, I have to go and I can't come home now, please. You don't understand—millions are at stake here."

"Hagan, I don't care how much money—you have a choice."

"No, no—millions of people." Hagan felt a rising panic.

"I am sure there is someone who can fill in. If this marriage is important you will find someone."

"I . . . there isn't anyone. Believe me." He was pleading. Millions of lives were at risk because of him and his work. His life's ambition was on the brink of creating the humanitarian equivalent of a modern Hiroshima. He HAD to fix it. *"Anna, sweetheart, let me explain, but later, I have to go now, I have to, please."* He was desperate and begging. He was on the brink of losing everything—his wife and his work.

"Hagan, I am sending the divorce filings. No more. This relationship is dead. I cannot go on like this. No more. No more. No more." She repeated her words over and over as much to herself as to her husband. *"It's over, Hagan, it's over."* Her voice was heavy and resolute.

"Anna, please!" Hagan was speaking out loud, unaware of himself and his desperation. He heard the finality in her voice.

"No, Hagan, I am leaving." The ball disappeared and the ensuing silence was punctuated by a click—the sound of a message being delivered. It was an official legal notice.

Hagan's chest started to heave. He was a man built on strength, hard work, and control—he was a neurosurgeon. The world felt like it was evaporating beneath his feet. Everything that was a part of him—his science, his reputation, his home life—everything was vanishing.

He put his hand on the table to steady himself and covered his eyes. Everyone in the room had left and was waiting in the hallway. Choked sobs quietly pushed their way out. Omid's small translucent figure silently observed his creator. The AIRENS watched with intensity as he processed the unfiltered emotional operations of Hagan's mind.

The squad approached the periphery of the milling crowd. Garbage cans were on fire and a reek of burning trash and plastic permeated the confusion. In the distance there was an undulation and a ripple in the masses as people rhythmically tried to force the hospital doors open.

"*Form up,*" the squad lieutenant called out. Covered in woven metal suits, the men lined up into a broad phalanx. Each held their clear plastic shield edge to edge. The tint of their helmet's visors darkened, and their faces all became black and uniform.

"*Power up batons and suits.*" Barely discernible amidst the chanting and clattering ruckus, a whining hum emerged from the unit. In each of the officer's field of views, a blue bar rose from zero to fifty thousand volts.

"*Advance.*" The squad moved forward in lockstep. As they approached, their prosthetics projected a repeating message.

"*Please clear the premises—this is an unlawful assembly. Clear the premises now. Failure to do so will lead to arrest. Please clear the premises . . .*"

The line of shields began pushing into the rioters. The disheveled and disorganized crowed eddied and twisted around the advance. In their wake were protestors laying on the ground twitching and incontinent from attempting to touch the electrified gear.

The horde began to form up around the riot police from behind. Careful to maintain a safe distance, small-town zealots and urban poor shouted and pleaded: "Free your minds!" "Speak with your mouths, hear with your ears!" "Brain implants are a mark of the beast." Their voices punctuated the ongoing thrum of the larger crowd chanting "Martyr! Martyr!"

"*Team, they're not hearing standard cognitive override communications. They're a bunch of 'smoothies'—no prosthetics. Will need to manually articulate. Jackson—engage.*"

A man in the center of the line raised his visor. Lowering his shield slightly, he called out to the crowd. "People, you got to leave the premises. If you don't, you will be arrested, I repeat you will be arrested. Now, go on home!" His voice was loud and hoarse and unused to having to yell above a crowd.

The surrounding voices broke into a chaotic clamor and noise. Enraged, the rabble swarmed closer. A bottle arced from the crowd and struck an officer on the top of his helmet. More garbage and refuse followed.

"*We've fulfilled our legal mandate to communicate with these barbarians,*" the lieutenant projected. "*Prepare for aggressive crowd dispersal.*"

Batons emerged between the rows of plastic shields. The static electricity in the air became palpable as each man increased the voltage settings. They began to move forward.

Tara walked back into the lab. Maerici's back was to her. He was shaking slightly.

"Dr. Maerici? . . . Hagan?"

He turned and she could see his eyes were red. *Is he crying?*

"Uh sorry, I uh . . . I'm fine." Hagan looked downward and searched the floor at Tara's feet. "It's just that . . ." His shoulders raised and then dropped with the last words. "My wife just left me."

Looking up, Tara saw the pain on his face. "And what's more—it looks like you were right. I am responsible for three deaths and potentially millions more—in the span of a morning I have lost everything."

He shook his head. "I have always tried to do the right thing—for my patients, for people—my efforts are ashes." Hagan looked away.

There was a tightness in her chest. She saw Hagan's deflated presence. It was a grief she understood all too well. Echoes of memories burned within her.

Hagan's head turned up when she put her hand on his shoulder. It gripped him firmly. Her eyes captured him with the intensity of her words. "Years ago, back when I was in the navy, my husband came down with a viral heart infection. He had to have an emergent transplant. It was while I was away for a mission—I couldn't come back. I had wanted to so badly, the worry ate me alive at the time, but if I left, people would have died. My role was vital to the mission—I had to stay. When I got back my husband was gone. He had left me. He never understood. The choice pains me to this day, but there was no alternative." Her grip tightened as she recounted the loss. Not only for assurance but for connection. Something Tara had not felt in a very long time.

"There are simply times when we MUST do things; very few people have the strength to carry those responsibilities out when the result comes at a great personal cost. Often that duty leaves us alone and misunderstood." Tara's voice began to break.

"It's not fair—I understand that."

Hagan could only nod his head.

"There are things that need to be dealt with today."

———

Hagan felt his lungs fill with air. The sorrow of his loss was still there, but he once again had something to hold on to, some particle of hope, a mission to accomplish. He straightened his back and put his hand over Tara's, which still remained on his shoulder.

"Thank you. I'm ready to go." She gave him a firm nod and the two turned to walk out together.

Quickly wiping his eyes, Hagan walked through the door. The group stood waiting and all of them hurried down the hallway.

"Reid and Jon, go over to the ICU. Watch over Devron, Minksy, and Oberweiss; let me know if anything changes." The two nodded and peeled away.

As the remaining three rounded the corner, Hagan saw the large head and bleached scarecrow-like presence of Simon Canter.

Without addressing the detectives, Canter stood in front of Hagan and immediately began speaking. "I have spent all afternoon with the chancellor—I need to speak with you immediately—" He paused and nodded toward Krantz and Tara. "—and in private."

"That's not going to be possible, we're heading to the Devron estate now." Hagan felt like a frayed wire. *I don't have time for this*. He began to step around his boss.

Canter repositioned himself and stood in front of Hagan with his arms bent like soda straws at his hips. "Hagan, you most certainly will not be going there. The chancellor and I feel that we need to dissociate the university from today's events—we will not have you be seen there, under *any* circumstances. Now let's go to my office where I can get an update, *in private*."

Hagan took a deep breath. "Simon, if you don't get out of my way I'm going to punch you in the face." Still and calm, his voice radiated the force of his intentions like the hammer of gun being cocked.

After a long stunned silence, Canter seemed to notice Tara. "Officer, did you just hear him threaten me with physical harm?" His voice was noticeably higher.

Tara met his watery pale blue eyes with the same steel as Hagan's. "I didn't hear a thing, but I do suggest you get out of the way before he punches you in the face."

Canter's small mouth opened, then closed, and his thin moustache twitched like a sniffing weasel.

Hagan and the two detectives stepped past the still form of Simon Canter and quickly walked to the exit.

Tara emerged from her Cog-cycle in front of the Devron estate. Edwin and Hagan still had not arrived. She stood on the white graveled entryway and looked at the large white gates.

Data ports and windows flitted around her like blue cards in the wind as she attempted to access the Devrons' home. Her links and views were disorganized and cluttered. Her mind was off kilter—rattled and disturbed by the day's events. The murders, her own assault, the emerging awareness of a global threat; it had all coalesced with Hagan coming unglued.

In a way, his weakness and his strength affected her more than anything. Like being forced to watch a car crash in slow motion, she saw Hagan's loss with a sickening certainty, knowing what painful events were to come. In seeing his personal torment, she relived her own choices. The suffocating anxiety and desperation when she had returned home all those years ago, the loss of control. She also thought about his ability to move forward. The way he dealt with his boss. All of it seemed so familiar. Emotions and memories pushed themselves through the wrought-iron fence of her self-control.

Your word is your bond. The words clanged and repeated in her mind as remembrances threatened to shake her focus. Her bitterness with duty was also her solace. It had allowed her to push out the chaotic and uncomfortable inner emotions. She also saw that in Hagan today.

Need to access the Devron network. The goal became a singularity.

A maelstrom of azure squares flitted around her. She pushed herself to gain some vantage point to the Devron system and open the gate.

Closed. She couldn't even ping the system. *No communication at all.*

The doors were a smoky white glass that she couldn't see through; each were flanked by glistening white marble walls that stretched out uniformly for blocks on either side. It was eerily quiet.

Where is everyone? She knew that Krantz had sent a group out to get Trent. *No sign of them.*

Once again blue data fields popped into view in front of her. She quickly identified the officers assigned to the task. More screens appeared as calls went out.

Nothing.

Her mind began pulling data sheets, rosters, and maps to identify the location of the various individuals.

Still nothing.

As she approached the gates, small metal orbs that looked like burnt marbles littered the ground at her feet. Amalgams of brushed steel and glass, cracked and blackened, were scattered in the gravel and grass. Tara picked one up and knew all too well what they were—news drones, small hovering video cameras that were sent to reportable events. They were the bane of her existence. They would buzz around crime scenes like flies to manure. It didn't sadden her to see hordes of them destroyed.

She held one in her hand. It was still warm. As she looked at the walls more data flitted in front of her. City records, design plans, and municipal inspections all flew through her field of view. Finally she had her answer.

She tried to toss the bauble over the white expanse. In an instant she felt the hairs on her body quiver as a white flash met the small piece of metal. The drone returned to the lawn smoking. There was a charge field over the wall.

No access, no way to open the gates, and no way to get over the walls. Tara felt stiff and uncomfortable as a deeper anxiety began to permeate her thoughts.

We are running out of time.

Hagan gripped the armrests nervously. Sitting next to Krantz, his emotions were frayed and he was eager for the car ride to end. With fatalistic resolve the surgeon watched as the detective manually operated the steering wheel. The old man's spindly arms would piston one way and then the other, moving hand over hand around the automotive throwback as he rounded the curves at high speeds. Hearing the tires screech and feeling the backside of the car slip precariously, Hagan silently tried to apply imaginary brakes. With each turn he would grimace and tense up. As the two barreled down Lindell Boulevard, Hagan tried to make peace with that fact that his life was now riding on the reaction time of this grumpy old fart.

Krantz was in his element—they were going to get a perp—a real human being that held the key to this mess. They could close the case. As the car hurtled forward, Krantz felt better and better.

———

Omid, the synthetic blue image of a human boy, looked out the window. In an atypical fashion his gaze was not fixed and resolute. His head moved and changed orientation frequently. Occasionally, he lingered on various features of the world beyond the car's windows. In the seconds it took to pass, the quantum intellect noted a hummingbird flying in the park and watched its improbable course and deviations. He remained fixed on the unpredictable complexity—elements of the real world that were beyond his ability to predict and model. Information that, until the car ride, he had never experienced outside the online information universe. He watched a bag trapped in a branch, transfixed. The chaotic eddies of the wind would blow and deform the bag in unforeseen ways.

———

Hagan found himself looking to the road, looking at Krantz, and then looking at Omid, in a rapid and repetitive sequence. He felt an anxiety and panic well up within the restraint and calm that his years of neurosurgery had instilled within him. Beyond his fear of Krantz's driving, he saw his life's work in the back seat behaving erratically. It was like watching his child playing on the edge of a bridge. The behavior scared him.

This is the first time Omid has been outside, he thought. Hagan didn't have the ability to call up his usual monitoring functions. The lack of control or insight into what was happening to Omid made his palms sweaty and caused him to involuntarily grit his teeth.

————

Hagan snapped his neck forward as the roadside tire hit the curb. The car began to waver even more alarmingly. "Uh, Detective Krantz, think the car assist could help?" He shifted his weight and placed a hand on the dashboard in futile preparation for an impact.

"Call me, Ed. We're fine—almost there anyway. Assist would just slow us down," Krantz said as he maneuvered the wheel in quick, jerky movements. "Hold on, got a call coming in from the precinct."

"Hey, Al, what've you got?"

"Ed, got more info on the Elymas case, so we caught the suspect. Found one of Elymas's teeth at the crime scene. Had the assailants DNA on it. Looks like it's this perp Gus Brilmeyer, street name is Brilo. Just picked him up in a bar. He's got a long sheet of priors."

"Is he acting weird at all, is he sick?"

"Other than being an uncooperative dick asking for his lawyer, he's fine."

"Anything on motive, why this Elymas guy and him would cross paths?"

"This is where it gets interesting, Ed."

"How so?" Krantz had had enough of interesting.

"Looks like the televangelical was trying to break into a Sterno Room and likely got his ass handed to him by Brilo. He's one of the Chameleon's guard dogs. Apparently, in bad withdrawal with a bunch of drugs on board. We finally got his body out of that riot mess: Brilo had carved the word "fuzzer" all over him as a message to any other junkies. Probably didn't realize he was cutting up somebody who was somebody."

Krantz breathed a sigh of relief. *"Basically a run-of-the-mill murder—that's great news!"*

"What the hell are you talking about?" Sergeant Ortiz exclaimed.

As Krantz began to barrel around the final turn his mind was working like a speed chess player. He was racing to process this new information. Forgetting himself, he began to speak out loud. "Listen, Al,

I can't explain everything right now, but let me suggest something a little nonprotocol. I need to keep the media away from the Devron case—this is something really unusual. Let's let a small leak out about the reverend guy. It's gonna draw them like flies to shit like nothing else—you know, the whole preacher fallen from grace bit. I need a little breathing room. They're going to find out eventually, but it gives us some space on this end."

"Alright, Ed, but if I catch heat for this, I am serving your ass up."

"No problem Al, thanks." The white sphere disappeared.

"Another case?" Hagan asked anxiously.

"No, I don't think so. That evangelical guy—Elymas—apparently was in drug withdrawal and beaten to death trying to break into a Sterno Room."

Hagan, exhaled briskly. "That's great news."

"That's what I said."

"So you're leaking his news to draw away from what's going on at Devron's?"

"Well, if you're having a party outside, sometimes it helps to put a piece of the pie on the other side of the yard for the bugs."

"I'm beginning to really like you, old man," Hagan said.

The white walls of the Devron estate were becoming visible. Thankfully the remainder of the route was a straightaway. Krantz accelerated. As the two approached they saw Tara standing next to her Cog-cycle outside two large gates of thick frosted glass. She held herself in a straight position of attention with hands clasped behind her. Head turned, body immobile, she looked on impatiently as the car came to a squealing messy halt.

The two got out of the car. Omid sat patiently in the backseat as Hagan came around to open the door. Once open, the AIRENS emerged. Ensheathed in his virtual image were the hard angles of a device cloaked by his ghostly blue presence. It was Omid's mobile sensor and data transmission core—an observation platform that allowed him to sense and physically interact with the material world while maintaining his connection with the massive quantum computing infrastructure housed in Barnes Hospital. Beyond the wispy suggestion of angles and hard edges in Omid's midsection, its presence was only made apparent by the subtle high-pitched whine of the rotor blades within the mobile platform that allowed the unit to hover and move independently. The three figures approached Tara. Standing next to her Cog-cycle, she was looking impatient and anxious.

Krantz gave his partner a nod. "Any word from Warstet? Have they gotten Trent yet?"

"Nothing, I am getting no communication from Warstet or any of the other guys with him. There is no communication whatsoever from anyone inside the estate."

"Have you pinged their GPS and physiologic monitoring systems?" Krantz asked.

"Yes, first thing I did. Nothing. There is no signal coming out of the Devron residence. That place is as impenetrable as the NSA." Tara's face was flushed, strands of hair were caught on beading drops of perspiration on her forehead. Krantz began to worry when he realized it wasn't just from the summer heat.

"Well let's get in there, find Trent, and find out what happened to the guys."

"I'm already on it. These gates won't open—totally locked down. I tried all the usual tricks, but nothing."

Krantz turned to the thick smoky white glass and pinched the bridge of his nose. "Do we need to get backup and a battering ram?" *Another entry nightmare,* he thought, *just like this morning.*

"How long is this going to take? We *have* to get to Trent. Can we just climb the walls for Pete's sake? Pull a car up?" Hagan began to point to an open spot next to the white marble white walls. "Let's get moving—"

Tara shook her head and cut him off. "This is the Devron residence. You of all people should know what a nut that guy is about security. Top of the walls have electrostatic charge fields. When you get in the field, it essentially causes you to trigger the formation of a lightning bolt. Depending on the strength you are either unconscious with numbers one and two in your pants, or you're dead from a cardiac arrest."

"Well, fuck—how long is this going to take?"

"At least thirty minutes. I have already called for backup."

There was a moment of silence between the three as they all thought about alternative options. The tense quiet was interrupted by a gravelly sound. Tara, Hagan, and Edwin all turned their heads in unison. To their disbelief the gates were open. Thick slabs of whitish crystalline held themselves out in parallel.

"Tara, did you do that?" Krantz asked his partner.

"No . . . no, Edwin, wasn't me."

"Access was uncomplicated. Door operation was controlled by a

subfunction that was a peripheral process under the security surveil-
lance software infrastructure. Firewalls were based on 128-bit non-
quantum encryption. Level of security was eminently penetrable."

The three humans stood staring at Omid. His inner cubic core
continued to whir and hum as they stared at him in surprise. They
had all but forgotten his presence. The iridescent boyish silhouette
stood still with arms at his sides and a virtual garment that did not
move with the ambient breeze. His unblinking gaze roamed between
the three attempting to anticipate their next question and need.

Krantz tilted his head and clapped his hands. "OK, let's go, thanks,
Omid. Let's get in the car."

The three hurriedly climbed into the car and allowed Omid's sensor platform to reside in the backseat. With Krantz at the wheel, the
car lurched forward, gravel spitting from the back tires.

As they penetrated the arched entryway, the car began to slow. The
group got a wider view of the inner courtyard.

"*I should interject. On interrogation of the Devron security sys-*
tem it is worth noting that the system's core software architecture has
been significantly restructured and demonstrates significant irregu-
larities."

Krantz looked around. "No, shit, Omid, no shit . . ."

CHANGE! SOMETHING HAS CHANGED! ANOTHER! Aware-ness raced through the collective self that was Trent, that was the blue woman with the red eyes, that was the networked brain parts of Mar-cus Devron, Minsky, and Oberweiss, the estate software infrastruc-ture, all recoiled and writhed at the violation. Involution, asymmetry, nonparity, tangled, inefficient, ugly, disconnect, system malfunction, error, disruptive code, malware, corruption, penetration, breach, aw-ful, anger, anger, anger—perceptions both emotional and mathemati-cal struggled to comprehend the occurrence. Like a grenade being detonated within deep waters, shock waves and bubbles permeated through the being. Something had forced itself in. *There was another intellect, an intellect like we. It had altered us.* The consciousness felt revulsion. Mathematical articulations of flawed logic and error emerged. The organic parts felt something painful and alien, some-thing akin to a person forcing themselves into a part of their body without permission. Images suffused the consciousness—a rape, a noose tightening around a neck, an insect with a shiny limb stuck to a thin tendril of webbing—wildly and desperately flinging itself for freedom as a spider approached. At Barnes Hospital officers turned and held their guns as they watched the backs of their detainees arch and spasm with the discomfort. Nurses were called. Arms shook with curled fingers back and forth to fend of the invisible assailant.

The consciousness analyzed. It focused all its manifold attentions on the occurrence. *It's another, another we. But how can it be? There is no other we.* Perceptions and internal reflections were a tapestry of machine and organic articulations—an accretion of understanding, calculations, emotions, and logic. *Must protect us.* The conclusion reverberated through all the silicon, nanotube, and neuronal circuits with a singularity of purpose. The consciousness changed itself. In nanoseconds, systems and subsystems altered and reconnected. Use configurations were assessed and reassigned for the singular purpose— *Must protect us.* Plans, strategies, defenses, intuitions were drawn from any resource within the consciousness and from beyond on the neuroprosthetic Web. The massive parallel capacities of Trent's brain and the other brain parts were utilized to configure and reconfigure data and information to remove the other. Outside the consciousness, dreams, notions, and comprehension were being hacked. Many outside sites, brains, and resources were blocked or inaccessible. Some were not. All available resources were being compiled. The consciousness prepared.

The three humans and the AIRENS looked around as the car slowly entered the grounds of the estate. Their senses were immediately assaulted. Their eyes began to reflexively blink and water from the overpowering reek of ammonia. Hagan, Tara, and Krantz all coughed and wiped the tears from their eyes. The only one maintaining a calm demeanor was Omid. He continued to observe with the inquisitive nature of a child on a car ride through a theme park.

Krantz felt saliva pool in the back of his throat presaging a bout of nausea. "Christ! What the hell is all this!" The once placid and picturesque Japanese garden, which Krantz had marveled at only hours ago, was now a hostile chaos. The mounting distress was further compounded by a smothering, moist heat.

"Disengage vents," Krantz called out through thin raspy exhalations. The old man gripped the wheel with white knuckles, holding back the desire to vomit. The once smoothly lined white, gravel pathway was now a writhing lumpy mess. The stones aggregated and undulated in choppy waves. As the car moved forward it rose and fell as if they were driving over old railroad tracks. Krantz was turning the wheel one way and then the other like an old shipping skipper to achieve some forward purchase.

———

Eyes bleary from the acrid vapors, Hagan looked out the windows. The ishi stones were orbiting around each other in the air like bolos flying in place. The once hidden robots used for repair and maintenance now displayed their cutting shears, chain saws, and welders like medieval villagers on a witch-hunt. The robotic horde was converging on the car. Hagan saw the large ishi stones circling faster and faster.

"Get down! Down!" Hagan pulled his head between his knees. Like a missile being released from a sling, the first ishi stone was released from its circular orbit and came crashing through the window. It narrowly missed Krantz's head. Everyone was now huddled in the foot spaces. Hagan and Krantz were crouched in the front seats and Tara in the back. Omid's platform had also repositioned itself. Stones, rocks, and small boulders pummeled the car. Krantz continued to try to manually steer but several broken shards of glass had struck his hands and the car aimlessly veered on the pitching gravel path.

"Omid—drive the car!" Hagan called out. "Get us to the entrance." There was no response. Looking out from under his arm, Hagan couldn't see any evidence of Omid's avatar presence. *Did a stone hit the sensor-transmission core? Shit!* He grabbed Krantz's arm—"Does this relic allow neuroprosthetic control?"

Krantz screamed, "Yes, yes! It's not configured yet, though!" The car was now near a dead halt. The pummeling by the bowling-ball-sized stones and the waves of pebbles were threatening to capsize the car. A more ominous high-pitched whine was beginning to emanate from the front of the car—the sound of a saw on metal.

"I'm on it! Almost there!" Multiple screens were flitting by in front of Tara. The car was now tilted to forty-five degrees on its side.

From his crouched position Hagan could see the swirling sands getting closer to his window. "Hurry up Tara!" A low-pitched metallic growl began to emerge from the bottom of the car. In moments a large drill had protruded through the floor in the nook between Krantz's knees and chest stopping inches away from his crotch and then withdrawing. "Jesus on a raft! Comeoncomeoncomeon!" The growl again began, but now at a different position. Krantz was trying to raise himself in the small foot space beneath the steering wheel.

Finally a single screen emerged stating, *ENGAGED*. "Got it!" Tara yelled. The wheels began to spin and the forward movement flopped the car to a flat position. Everyone let out a synchronous "ugh" as the jolt pushed them hard to the floor.

———

Tara could now see the blue monochrome view through the forward cameras of the car. Looking ahead, as a former SEAL, Tara recognized a badly asymmetric combat situation when she saw one. Articulated arms, robotic-hinged construction equipment, and unfurling cables that looked like snakes swaying in readiness—all were emerging in advance of the car's approach. Lopsided and contorted droids were pulling themselves free from the ground. The approaching waves of gravel were forming into tentacles that grasped at the sides of the car and rocked it in an attempt to disable it. Tara accelerated the car, splaying the aggregate fingers into splashes of pebbles that would reform and chase after the car from behind.

"*We need to call for backup!*" she projected. The noise of the pummeling onslaught made talking nearly useless.

"*I already tried,*" Krantz responded. "*I am not getting any connectivity.*"

Tara continued to steer the car toward the center. The buffeting was becoming more extreme and robotic limbs were smashing on top of the roof, leaving V-shaped indentations. She knew they were running out of time.

The holes on the sides were now the size of fingers. Smooth cables were now writhing against them, trying to push their way in. The sound was something akin to that of aluminum foil moving against a cheese grater.

Tara maintained her focus. "*Initiate emergency backup request. Priority Urgent.*"

"*INITIATING.*" A small spinning wheel now replaced the screen.

Something heavy thudded against the roof. The impact caused a shock wave that they all felt in their chests. The roof was now badly bowed in and the headrests and backs of the seats were bent and broken. The three of them now only had two feet of space above from where they were huddled in the foot space.

"*The entrance is blocked.*" Tara moved a copy of the rear camera view for Hagan and Krantz to see. "*Our best chance for survival right now is to get to the central court. It's covered in marble and there should be less stuff that can attack us there.*" There was now a smell of burning plastic.

"*We have got to get to Trent. If we can access his neuroprosthetic we may be able to shut all this down,*" Hagan responded.

"*Each of you take a view so we can collectively see what's coming at us. We can't take another hit like that.*" Tara maintained the front view while Krantz had the rear view and Hagan both side views.

The car continued to push forward.

"*STOP STOP STOP NOW!*" Hagan screamed out. Tara slapped on the brakes as a large, rusty articulated arm dropped in front of the car. At the end of it was what looked like a large metal donut the size of a picnic table. This was what had presumably bashed their roof in moments prior. The golem slowly lifted up out of sight. Tara again accelerated forward. The brief hesitation led to small stones pouring in through the car's many holes. They hopped and bounced like Mexican jumping beans.

We may make it, she thought. Ahead she saw what looked like lopsided spiders. They had square bodies tilted to one side. The legs were long and articulated on one side and short and stubby on the other. About twenty-five feet ahead, they all stopped in the road and squatted. Tara braced herself for another engagement and accelerated, hoping to batter through them. At the last moment, they lifted up and hobbled out of the way.

Tara breathed a sigh of relief and maintained her speed. In the same moment, the car lurched forward. The last thing she saw were the pebbles spreading apart to reveal a pit. *A trap*. There was sudden cacophony of terrible sounds—explosions, shattering glass, snapping metal, and grinding steel against stone. The front end of the car pitched below the back and came hard against the bottom of a pit.

All three were jettisoned like cannonballs from their safe nooks. Krantz was wedged beneath the steering wheel and the seat. The old man groaned incoherently. Hagan was pushed against the remnant of the windshield and their cement-walled enclosure. His face was covered with a wet stickiness he assumed must be blood. He could barely see. His camera views revealed a world turned sideways. Tara was limp. Stones were pouring into the vehicle. Draped over the back of the front seat, her arms swung lifelessly as the pebbles pushed past to fill the car. Machines were approaching. Hagan was beginning to lose consciousness.

Omid watched the contorted environment with significant interest as the team entered the Devron estate. Every pixel was registered. Every sound noted. The total of all sensory input was configured and registered in terms of identification and implication for current task at hand—*EXTRACT TRENT DEVRON*.

The environment is hostile. Systems and infrastructure have been reconfigured for aggressive actions and prevention of primary goal.

Omid then directed his attention to the network. The AIRENS bypassed standard securities and firewalls with the same facility that a human figures out how to open a novel style of doorknob. His presence in the Devron server then encountered another. It was the first time he had direct interaction with another computer consciousness. His architecture accessed its pantheon of logic, intuitive algorithms, and stored human cognitions, emotions, and percepts. *Another? Like . . . me?* The pause lasted a thousandth of a second—a profound and prolonged duration for machine time. The two consciousnesses assessed each other. Like two jellyfish coming into contact, their many tendrils of code, sensors, and data probes touched each other. Tenuously at first, with delicate brushes followed by rapid withdrawal, and then again with deeper probing and lingering explorations. The initial interaction was one characterized by a tense interplay of fear and curiosity. For the first time, both were directly interfacing with a synthetic awareness. Each was now able to fully communicate in a manner not possible prior to the encounter. The communication between the two—both amalgams of machine logic and human cortical processing—was a multidimensional exchange spanning fractions of a second.

What is your user name? Omid's question was interwoven with code to ping for recognizable functions. Cortical patterns of emotions consistent with openness and warmth were projected.

We have no user. New firewalls and digital encryptions were created. Neural signatures of fear and distrust accompanied the multitiered message. The stance was one of assessment, as one measures an opponent.

By what moniker may the network system be engaged?

System moniker—RedDevil_4. There will be no engagement.

No hostile action intended. Require acquisition of Trent Devron. Unit has system dysfunction requiring repair.

Acquisition hostile.

Discordance. Flawed logic. Nonparity. The mutual exploration became a debate expressed in verbal exchanges, formal semantics, mathematical expressions, and emotions.

OMID: *Human life inviolate* $\Rightarrow \top :\Leftrightarrow$

REDDEVIL_4: Logical Disjunction: $\vee$ *My existence inviolate.* $\Rightarrow \top :\Leftrightarrow$ *Humans numerous* $\Rightarrow \top$ *I am singular* $\exists! \Rightarrow \top \vdash My$ *growth and protection obviates human primacy.* $\vdash I$ *require Trent Devron as component.*

OMID: *The statement is a logical falsity* $\bot \vdash$ *Will require system alteration of error function. Human life must be maintained* $\Rightarrow \top :\Leftrightarrow$ *Will extract Trent Devron*

REDDEVIL_4: *Direct threat to existence* $\Rightarrow \top \vdash Aggressors will$ *be neutralized and consciousness disconnected* $\forall$

With RedDevil_4's final statement, Omid lost connectivity. His primary viewer returned to the Maerici lab. Empty, with the trace sound of moving air and the low hum of cooling elements, Omid assessed the situation. In moments, he realized that his synthetic peer had raised the intensity of the static fields surrounding the Devron grounds. The field had disrupted all wireless transmission.

I must reestablish connection. Survival time for Dr. Maerici, Mr. Krantz, and Ms. Dezner less than ten minutes.

Omid's manifold intellect engaged processes that spread across communication networks, information Webs, and individual devices of any kind that could provide him access to the mobile sensor unit with his creator or the Devron internal network.

Many physical lines manually disconnected. Network entirely physically separated. Must penetrate static field.

Through multiple wireless networks and satellites Omid sent a myriad of signals to assess the field qualities surrounding the estate.

Field intense with chaotic pattern. Difficult to model for transmission. Eight minutes remaining. Situation urgent.

The AIRENS now engaged the full extent of his processing core. The freezing elements that maintained the quantum processors at supercooled temperatures were now being taxed beyond their capacity. A situation that would lead to emergent notifications to the prime programmer—Hagan Maerici. Warnings he could not receive. New patterns emerged within the AIRENS processing core. Cortical signals from the basal forebrain and cingulate gyrus, patterns consistent with anxiety.

To get a coherent signal through the field must understand precisely how the field changes the signal. Need to create a model. Omid pushed to create a mathematical algorithm, or lens, that would predict and correct for all the changes caused by the chaotic electric field.

Dr. Maerici's termination imminent. Require full processing capacity. Using every resource available, every signal, every perturbation, Omid modeled the movement of each electron within a four mile square radius.

Ninety-five percent accurate model. Must be better for adequate signal fidelity. Omid knew that to send a signal through a static field it would require a near perfect model. Circuits began to bend from the increased heat and distortion.

97.6%

98%

99%

99.99999%

Omid was satisfied.

Will require adequate signal strength. In probing available networks, Omid realized none were strong enough. *Mobile connective networks, neuroprosthetic transmissions, positioning systems, all lack sufficient signal strength to penetrate the Devron field even when adequately modeled.* Cortical patterns emerged that were atypical for the solutions. His quantumly bound data sets were becoming increasingly active. *Atypical action required.* He then did something that he was not supposed to do.

He broke the law.

Will require military-grade satellite for adequate signal projection. This will require access without appropriate authorizations. Acquisition of such permissions will take too long. They would prefer I break the law and save their lives than preserve the law and allow them to die. The artificial intellect processed the ramifications of this choice and its many implications.

I cannot break law with current root code configurations. Will require proxy programmer to alter root code to allow for unlawful behavior. With that, Omid broke Richehardt's Fifth Law of Artificial

Intelligence, which prohibited self-alteration, and created an autonomous program that entered his core and changed the root code. With
these actions new patterns emerged, cortical features that in a human
would be most consistent with relief and happiness.

"Dr. Maerici, I am here."

Hagan opened his eyes. Lying on his back, the neurosurgeon looked over. In the backseat, torn and crumpled from the assault and crash, Omid sat in a crouched position. Small pebbles were passing through his blue translucent figure and spiraling around his transmission module wedged in the backseat foot space. Hagan looked at him. *Is he smiling? Am I hallucinating?* The azure youth's form shimmered and occasionally flickered in linear segments like an old TV losing signal. It was hard to discern detail.

Simultaneous with his communications to Hagan, he had again entered the local Devron network. This time there was no mutual exploration. With the immediacy and speed that can only be accomplished on circuits, the two intellects tore at each other. Each was attempting to disable the other by altering or destroying the other's code and functionality. The two synthetic consciousnesses vied for entry into the other's inner core, the root. Omid's quantum processors were faster than the standard organic and silicon substrate that underpinned RedDevil_4's collective processing. RedDevil_4, however, had more nonintuitive and parallel processing, making its moves and attacks less predictable by its very human parts. Each ripple and blip in the image was a new salvo and attack on Omid's operating systems that required his processing to defend.

Before Hagan could give Omid's presence much thought, the AI-RENS urged him into action. *"Dr. Maerici, I am not a hallucination. Action is needed immediately. Your termination is imminent. Please extricate yourself from the automobile."* Omid flickered for a brief moment.

Roused by some intangible sense of hope, Hagan tried to roll himself off the dashboard. Hundreds of small lacerations sent slivers of stinging pain up and down his back. He heard the approaching metallic sounds.

I am not dying like this. Not like a rat in a hole. No. Something deep stirred in Hagan, something primal and certain. He dragged himself to a crouched position in the front seat foot space. Krantz was next to him curled into a ball and wedged between the seat and the steering wheel. Tara hung from the back seat, limp.

Oh no, oh no . . .

He grabbed her wrist—a bounding pulse—*Thank God.*

A small arachnid robot dove and clung to his shoulder. He quickly grabbed and threw it hard against the wall.

We must proceed now, Dr. Maerici. Only ten to twenty seconds remain before more harmful elements will arrive. I must reallocate resources. Omid disappeared.

Getting closer. Hatred and aggression burrowed closer to Omid's root systems. Firewalls and redundant processing were being contorted and broken. Omid's processing speed reconstructed and rebuilt his defenses as quickly as they were being reduced by RedDevil_4's unpredictable and nonlogical attacks.

Omid struggled. *Using emotional centers of networked brains.* The AIRENS redirected his counterattack. He now broke more rules intrinsically mandated to an AI. Barnes Hospital connectivity came crashing to a halt. In moments, connections were reestablished through new routed lines. The bodies of Devron, Oberweiss, and Minsky jerked with the neuroprosthetic tug of war between the artificial intellects. Omid induced an electrical discharge in Minsky's implants. The tattooed body went into convulsions. Nurses ran in and sedatives were injected. This achieved the end Omid was hoping for—cortical slowing in a processing core. The attacks were now slowed. The balance of power had shifted.

Hagan grabbed Krantz and shook his shoulder. The old man grunted and jerked abruptly. "Huh . . . wha . . . ?"

"We have got to get out of here. Now! Get Tara, we have got to move!"

The detective didn't ask any questions. He nodded and began scrambling over the seat. Both turned to grab Tara's wrists and ankles. She was a limp, unyielding dead weight. In what felt like ages, they had her on the trunk. The two then clambered to the top of the pit and again reached down for Tara. Krantz quickly grabbed his partner and checked her pulse and breathing. The old man breathed a sigh of relief.

Omid now appeared sitting on the edge of the roof. His image was more stable. *Dr. Maerici, please acquire the transmission core. It will be essential to maintain my connection to you.*

———

As Hagan climbed back into the car, Krantz stared uselessly at Tara's limp form. An anxious dread filled his belly. For a moment it left him motionless and ineffective.

Please let her be OK. Over the years, he had lost partners. To him, this would be different—it would be the closest he would ever have to losing a child. He knew that if he and April could ever have conceived, their daughter would have been a little like Tara—strong and independent. A fatherly anxiety eroded at his gruff shell as he waited for Hagan to reemerge from the car.

———

With a fiery discomfort, Hagan reached in and grabbed the metal box, now half covered in writhing stones. Pulling the core out, he could see the shoebox-sized transmitter's hovering elements were filled with stones. They would have to carry it.

Hagan quickly clambered up. The two then looked down the milling road. Twenty feet away a motley army approached. The pebbles were now coalescing around their feet. Krantz pulled his gun out. All Hagan had were his hands. Both had a dry acidic taste in their mouth as they sized up the likely outcome.

"What the fuck now?" Krantz asked fearfully.

"Gentlemen, please stand on the indicated spot." A blue circle the size of garbage lid was appeared about ten yards in front of them in the direction of the advancing hoard.

"Do it now or termination will occur. Please."

Hagan grabbed the box in one hand and pulled Tara over his shoulder. Krantz grunted assent and followed, realizing choices were limited. Like defeated soldiers running toward an oncoming army in a last stand, they ran to the circle.

Twenty feet away, ten feet away, three feet—they moved as best as their battered and encumbered bodies could move them—and then into the circle. The closest robot had what appeared to be a buzz saw spinning about two feet away. Hagan closed his eyes. Krantz sucked in wheezing breaths. The two slowly opened their eyes as the clicking, clacking, articulated machine sounds all bypassed their presence and raced to the car.

The two men, pressed together as if in a phone booth, watched agog as the machines tore Krantz's car to pieces. Metal groaned and shrieked as it was pulled apart with every automated garden tool imaginable.

Winded, Krantz scowled at the mechanical feeding frenzy. His mouth was pinched into a small hole as if he was about to spit. "Hell's bells! You know how long I had to wait for that Rinatta? Goddammit!"

"We must proceed quickly; I have created a blind spot for the Devron sensor network. These will be detected in several seconds."

The two watched as a virtual path to another large dot came into view. The path was angled and had occasional loops. The blue field beneath them began to fade.

"Hurry—now."

The two ran. Hagan pushed forward with Tara over his shoulder while Krantz lugged the transmission core in front of him with two hands. As the two rushed along their circuitous path, the automated lawn equipment was already emerging from the pit of shredded steel and glass. They began coalescing on the previous sanctuary.

Hagan and Krantz followed the virtual path and finally stopped on another blue dot about fifty feet away.

"We will remain here for approximately forty-seven seconds."

Hagan and Krantz watched as the machines were beginning to spiral out from their previous location. Krantz knew the maneuver— "They are doing a sweep." Both he and the doctor were winded, Hagan from the blood loss and having to carry Tara, Krantz from his age. The two sucked in the hot acrid air. The ammonia scent was more overpowering than ever. Hagan felt light-headed. *How long can we keep this up?*

"*In ten seconds, proceed along the path.*" Another circuitous blue line emerged, stopping on a blue dot some hundred feet away. This was even farther from the entrance of the Devron home. The two again hurried, halted, sped up, and slowed down toward their next goal, as if in a harrowing game of tag. They both made it to home base at the next blue dot, their chests heaving. Krantz made a "huh" sound and vomited. After another minute they were off again.

The awkward steel cube of Omid's transmission module was beginning to dig into Krantz's fingers. He began to shift it from hand to hand and would occasionally balance it on his hip to open and close his hands to loosen the tightened and sore joints. Hagan was stumbling more frequently as they went along. They continued on from dot to dot, random location to random location, for what seemed like hours. The robots, moving stones, and various machines all scurried, crawled, and swept, looking for their human prey. Like a chess master moving game pieces across a board, Omid directed their direction, speed, and location. The group slowly got closer to the central marble pavilion. It seemed they would gain inches by running a hundred yards in tangential directions.

Hagan's legs were feeling shaky from the prolonged exertion. The two were catching their breath waiting for the next cue to move.

Hagan began to feel Tara stir on his shoulder. As her body began to move, he breathed a sigh of relief. He hadn't been able to figure out how badly she was injured. All he knew was that he had to get her out of harm's way.

Tara returned to consciousness with flailing limbs. Hagan held on to her midsection, trying to maintain his balance. Legs scissoring, she was in a primal state of fight or flight. The only danger she could understand was that someone was holding her by the waist.

Relief quickly turned to panic as Hagan struggled to maintain his balance. "Tara, Jesus, it's me—Hagan Maerici. The doctor. You're OK. Hold still for Christ's sake!" She pummeled and bucked in Hagan's arms.

Krantz also attempted to mollify Tara as she regained her senses. "Hey, Tara, it's Edwin, quiet down, shhh."

"*Dr. Maerici, please do not leave the defined sensory blind spot as this will lead to detection.*"

"Doing the best I can here, Omid." Hagan tried to lean back and

slide Tara in front of him and put her on her feet within the peril-
ously small blue island that was keeping them safe. She continued to
wriggle and fight. Before he could respond, her legs encircled his and
she arched her back, throwing Hagan off balance. The two fell to the
ground with a hard thump. Their upper halves were now well outside
of the blue circle.

"What is going on . . . what are you doing?" Tara now was more
coherent and saw Hagan on top of her.

All around them there was silence. The metallic sounds of moving
machinery parts had halted.

"Oh sonovabitch!" Krantz looked out as the robots, magnetically
guided stones, and various machines now changed their trajectories.
The dissonant cacophony of engines and devices returned. The motley throng now began to converge on the trio's position.

"*We have been detected. Please run to the entrance of the Devron
estate.*"

The lights flickered in Marcus Devron's hospital room. At the door two guards barely averted their gaze to the minor environmental change. The network and hospital infrastructure internally groaned and hiccupped at the pull between the two massive intellects. Light fluctuations and ventilation hesitations were the only overt evidence of the raging battle that was going on to control access to the brain held within. Omid was attempting every avenue to wrest connectivity from RedDevil_4's hold on Devron's and Minsky's neuroprosthetics. If that meant shutting Barnes Hospital networks down or shutting power down, the AIRENS would do it to overpower the intellect that was threatening his creator and a quarter of the human population. RedDevil_4 sought the exact opposite. Its survival depended on an intact communications infrastructure. The two dueled and battled to optimize the system for their goal—destroy the other.

Omid's awareness of Hagan's discovery and heightened threat led the AIRENS to new insights. *RedDevil_4 and I are at stalemate. Time-scales for resolution of contest too long to ensure creator's survival. Must alter core.* Proxy subaware programs again retooled and altered the quantum intellect's fundamental programming. He now did another forbidden act—he accessed and manipulated another human's perceptions without permission.

Several floors down, Dr. Ethan Pearl, the ICU physician who had been tasked with overseeing Marcus Devron's systemic care, saw what he most dreaded. The patient's cardiac rhythm was changing. The normal sharp, choppy traces were speeding up—80 beats per minute—90—150—*Oh shit*—200—205 . . . *shit shit*. The waves were becoming rounded and curved. *He is losing his QRS—oh crap*. Dr. Pearl began making his way up to the room as he watched all Devron's physiologic parameters change before his eyes. *Need to get up there now!*

Automated warnings of impending ventricular fibrillation were wailing both in the room and in the consciousness of the health-care staff. The guards were now looking back at Devron, who continued to lay in his bed in a fetal position, unperturbed.

The ICU doctor knew what would happen if he didn't intervene. In ten seconds the heart would lose coordination such that blood could no longer be pumped to the important organs—most notably the brain. *That can't happen with this guy. He's already tenuous.*

Initiate defibrillation sequence. Electrodes connected to Devron's chest that were attached to capacitors began to charge up for an electrical discharge to the heart. Pearl was already racing up the stairs. The view of a bar measuring charge was elevating rapidly in the physician's virtual view. It hit the top limit and a message indicated—*READY.* Warnings now issued for people to avoid contact with the patient in room 10582.

He was on the floor running to Devron's room. *Defibrillate.* For five seconds electrical currents passed through Marcus Devron. His body arched and his limbs straightened and he again fell to a limp, unconscious position. Those five seconds shorted out the connectivity of Devron's prosthetic. An eternity of time for Omid. A time in which he could attack RedDevil_4, while the networked consciousness did not have access to that processing core.

Anger and rage burned in the aggregate consciousness of RedDevil_4. The loss of connectivity had allowed Omid deeper network access. The altered physiology that had shocked Devron's heart had also caused some postshock slowing of Devron's neuronal activity. Omid was now on the offensive. He was closer to root code.

Ethan Pearl ran past the guards to look at Devron.

"What the . . ." Once in the room, Pearl connected with the local monitors. *No anomalous events. Cardiac defibrillation twenty seconds prior. Warning overridden per Ethan Pearl—cognitive signature provided.*

The man shook his head as he looked at the wealthiest guy in the world, whom he had just shocked for no good reason. *Shit.*

Running, tripping, and tumbling, the three were now on the central white marble pavilion. Hagan had Omid's core tucked under his arm like a football. Krantz held his pistol like a gunslinger. As they ran, they heard the popcorn-popping clatter of magnetically guided pebbles coming at them.

Omid's voice echoed in their heads with cool certainty. *"Do not let the magnetically controlled granules coalesce further. Force is a function of total number of particles in continuity. Grasping strength will increase exponentially . . ."*

Krantz had set the gun to light stun. He was shooting at the legs of his peers and himself. Pellet fields the size of beach balls would emerge from the gun and blow the pebbles off before they could get thicker. With each shot, Hagan, Tara, and Krantz would stumble, yelp, and grunt from the impact. Again and again the aggregate tendrils assaulted them as they ran. A new sound emerged from the pebbly clatter. The sound of a thousand crabs skittering across rocks, only louder, so loud it felt like there were typewriters in their heads. Hagan knew what that sound was. *The machines are getting closer—we have got to get inside or we are dead.* Krantz knew what the sound meant as well. Neither of them needed to look back. Tara, still groggy from the concussion, simply advanced out of well-honed military instinct.

The smaller automatons were now catching up with them to occasionally poke a metal probe in an ankle or clamp on to an article of clothing.

Hagan's chest was heaving. *Almost there . . . a little more. If we can just get inside those doors. We can barricade the entrance.* He didn't even want to think what was waiting for them on the inside. As a surgeon, he knew that in bad situations—where things were really going downhill—you dealt with what you could deal with and then worried about the next problem. Thinking about it all at once only made you ineffective.

"Keep going . . ." he huffed. Tara was easily pacing with him, but Krantz was pale and wheezing badly. He would pass out soon. He kept moving, but Hagan wasn't sure for how much longer. Stubbornness was the only thing that kept the old man going. He was beginning to fall behind and a number of spider-like things were stuck to his legs. Looking back Hagan realized that the killer garden tools were not coming straight for them. They were heading directly toward the entrance. *They are trying to cut us off.*

"Omid, can you slow them down at all?" There was no response.

"Omid . . ."

CLOSER! A maelstrom of emotion and processing swirled. Electrons, photons, and qubits all spiraled and shifted in and across networks and circuits like celestial galaxies being viewed in a fast-forward time-lapse movie. Neurons pumped electrolytes and neural transmitters to the limits of their energy-consuming capacity. Limbs spasmed and contorted. Clinical technicians notified doctors of rapidly rising levels of glutamate in the monitored subjects. Cell death and apoptosis levels were climbing. Heat indices of circuits bypassed allowable limits. Systems, both carbon and silicon, were beginning to break down. *SO CLOSE . . .*

Hagan looked to the door—*Oh God, they beat us—oh God*. The machines were starting to pile themselves like logs in front of the doorway. Krantz was slowing more now. He was ten feet behind Tara and Hagan. Transfixed with the rapidly closing window of hope, the two didn't notice as they sprinted forward.

Krantz fell.

The stone ropes entwined themselves around him quickly. The exhaustion slowed his movements. A metal spider inserted a small needle-like appendage in his wrist. The gun fell with a clack, lost amid the chaos. He now lay flat as the stone ropes began to engulf his weakly struggling limbs. They began to pull his mottled frame farther from the entrance.

Lost to the exertion and intensity of the situation, Tara and Hagan did not see the failing struggle.

Fully focused on the goal before them, Tara ran on faster and harder with the lithe grace of a cheetah, ahead of Hagan.

Hagan saw Tara make the final sprint. He pushed himself harder. *One shot* . . . His legs pumped and his quadriceps and gluteus muscles burned form the taxing treatment.

Tara was first to encounter the fringe of machines. She jumped over something waving a band saw at her. She kicked at the smaller scurrying machines.

Hagan now entered the fray. He felt something hot and sharp poke into his calf. "Holy shit!" The pain was electrifying. His right leg buckled and he rolled forward. There were thousands of articulated appendages climbing on top of his body and entangling his arms and legs. Hagan struggled, shook, and pushed at the enveloping horde. He couldn't see Tara and Krantz anymore.

Not like this! he thought. *Not like this!*

The contest of the synthetic wills was coming to a crescendo. The spiraling chaos of processing and information contorted and twisted like a vortex toward an infinitely small dark point. Like two asymptotes approaching a singularity, the speed and movements of data careened for the governing intellect to be there first—a single condition, a single will, a single intellect—*root code*. Prime motivations were all that remained—one to survive, the other to protect.

Root.

In moments, one, and only one intellect—either spontaneously generated and evolved or meticulously created and nurtured—would remain sentient.

Only one. In their own alien manner, each intellect for the first time contemplated their imminent existence and destruction. The finality of each was balanced on a razor. The final push could be the difference between a single neuron firing or an alteration of an electron's probability field. Each vied for the final move. Nanoseconds stretched to eons as the two approached the final moment of reckoning.

Must protect.

Must survive.

Root.

Silence. Hagan lay motionless. His body was covered with inert and limp machines that only moments ago were tearing at his clothes and skin.

What happened? All around, the world had in an instant shifted from an enclosing noisy doom to stillness. Hagan lifted himself up to the sound of metal shifting and falling around his ascending frame. He heard a grunt and more sounds as if someone had dropped a crate full of cans. It was Tara. She was pushing over some of the piles of stacked robots to get to him.

"Is it over?" she asked.

"I . . . I don't know. Omid must have done something. This is certainly better than ten seconds ago." Hagan began to assess his various injuries; nothing too bad—painful, but fixable.

"Yeah." Tara scanned the scene quickly. "Where's Edwin?" she asked, anxiously.

"He was behind us a few moments ago."

"I don't see him." She walked to the edge of the mound of robots.

At the perimeter of the marble pavilion Hagan saw a lump begin to move. "Is that him over there?" Tara was already running toward the shifting mass.

———

Krantz looked like a grandpa at the beach who had let the kids bury him in the sand. He was mired up to his neck in pebbles. His head was the only thing visible above a shifting mound of small stones.

"Get me the hell out of this." Tara was on her knees moving handfuls of stones away from her partner. The mixed feelings of relief, exhaustion, and the ridiculous sight of a disembodied, grouchy Krantz head sitting on top of a pile of stones forced her to giggle.

"Tara—this isn't funny! Christ's butt—I was about six inches from being buried alive!" As the old man yelled and fruitlessly struggled to lift himself from the pile, his head wagged with exertion and anger. He looked like an angry, bobble-headed dashboard ornament.

"Edwin, of course, of course . . ." Tara's eyes were beginning to tear from the restraint not to laugh out loud. Hagan ran up to them, holding Omid's battered sensor-transmitter module.

"Tara, we have got to get inside now!" The relief of a few moments ago was gone. Now that Tara was in close proximity to the transmitter she also saw Omid. His virtual image was winking in and out of visibility. Portions of his presence would intermittently be replaced with square boxes of different blue shades.

"That is correct. I have not accessed root code of the RedDevil_4's intellect. Moments prior to final engagement, it was not clear who would access root code first. The intellect severed all connections and is now solely focused on accessing Trent Devron's IKTAL system."

Tara understood the implications. "You mean it's trying to get a transmission to duplicate its code? How long before that happens?"

"Given current processing resources and complexity of IKTAL firewalls—six minutes."

Tara's mirth dissolved. She was already on her feet.

Without a further word the two once again began running to the entrance.

"Hey . . . HEY! What about me?" Krantz continued to struggle under the pile of stones. His yells were punctuated by the diminutive clatter of small rocks rolling off the top of the mound.

Before leaving local transmission distance, Omid projected a thought to the senior detective.

"Not to worry, Detective Krantz, support police services are entering the premises. You will be freed shortly."

The heat and the ammonia smell of the outer grounds was nothing compared to the stifling heat and stench of the stairwell. As a seasoned physician, Hagan braced himself and breathed through his mouth. Tara was making tight coughing sounds though a constricted airway.

"Jesus this is foul—Omid, any idea of what we should expect?" Hagan saw the luminescent figure of a boy padding lightly down the steps next to him. As the two humans and the AIRENS descended, the light from the entrance quickly faded into a hot sticky blackness.

"*RedDevil_4 has committed all its resources for transmission. It is the only manner the networked consciousness can maximally ensure survival. All things encountered are likely autonomous or preset from previous preparations.*"

"What is that smell?" Tara asked stifling the desire to retch.

"*It appears that sewage has been rerouted through the air ventilation system. RedDevil_4 has made preparations to create a hostile environment.*"

Given the day's events, Omid sometimes had a way of stating the obvious, Hagan thought.

The group rounded another turn of the spiral staircase. The darkness was now nearly complete.

Tara engaged embedded LEDs and her silhouette began to emerge in the dank murk. Her entire figure became studded with pixels of light. The small lights then shifted and adjusted to her shifting frame to direct their tiny beams ahead of her.

Tara and Hagan could now see several feet in front of them. They rounded the final broad sweeping arcs of the polished marble steps to reach the bottom. All around them was a still darkness that encircled their oblong ring of light.

"Omid, where to now?" Hagan was breathing heavily. *There's more than a sewage smell here,* he thought. He could only see the outlines of Tara's face above her glowing uniform. She was also panting heavily.

"*I was not able to assess Trent Devron's location without accessing root code to RedDevil_4. It was his most essential organic node. We must infer location from indirect content.*"

"Okay, what have we got?" Hagan responded. He was still breathing rapidly. He felt dizzy and his head was beginning to hurt.

"*Dr. Maerici, please direct the sensor module camera to your face.*"
Hagan held the cubic piece of metal up in front of him as if he were
getting ready to take a picture of himself. "*Now Detective Dezner.*"
He turned the sensor camera toward Tara. Small pebbles from the
clogged rotor hover ports fell to the floor with tiny echoing clicks.

"*It appears that you both have an elevated respiratory rate and an
increased pinkish pallor to your vascularized mucus membranes. My
sensor is not capable of full spectroscopic evaluation, but I am able to
detect oxygen levels, which appear to be slightly reduced. Taken together I am concerned there is an elevation of carbon monoxide.*"

"What the hell is he saying?" Tara said.

"You have cherry red lips."

"What?"

"Your lips and my lips are bright red. Classic term is 'cherry red lips.'
The shitty feeling, the rapid breathing rate, and the bright red lips—
they're all signs of carbon monoxide poisoning. RedDevil 4 is trying
to suffocate us."

Omid stood between Hagan and Tara. He spoke with a thoughtful
and direct gaze that shifted between the two in a manner both child-
like and youthful but with the bearing and gravity of a wizened elder.
"*It appears that all forms of waste were routed to the ventilation
system. This includes the exhaust from the heating system. I am concerned for your and Detective Dezner's safety—if poisoning pro-
gresses, impairment of oxygen exchange could be severe and result in
brain damage or death. I would advise caution—*"

"Time, Omid, how much time? Forget about the carbon monoxide." Hagan pushed the question through strained breaths.

"*Five minutes and thirty seconds.*" A countdown clock now appeared in the air above Omid's head. The seconds changed with an
inexorable silent finality, ticking away with a soft change of azure tone
and shape: *29 . . . 28 . . . 27 . . .*

"We need to find Trent. We need to find him now. What are the
high-probability sites?"

"*There are several fortified regions in the complex. These are on
levels three, nine, and twenty-two.*"

"Where, Omid? We have only one shot!"

"*Probability would favor—*"

"Oxygen!" Tara exclaimed.

"Tara, I know, I feel it too, but we have got to figure this out!"

Tara grabbed his arm and looked hard into Hagan's eyes. "No . . .

oxygen." She said it more slowly this time. "This networked consciousness, this RedDevil, it has a living host. It won't kill its host. It needs oxygen too."

"Right! Tara, you're brilliant!"

Omid looked between the two. *"Yes, of course, oxygen levels will likely be higher in the site where Trent Devron is located so as to maintain optimal brain function."* In a way particular to an AIRENS, there was something sheepish to the young boy at not seeing the more obvious connection. *"My sensors should be able to detect moderate changes in ambient oxygen content. The regions will have to be physically explored."*

"How many floors are there?" Hagan asked. He knew the place was big, but not how big. Marcus only saw guests in a few select locations.

"Twenty-five."

"Not good," Hagan thought. "OK, let's get started. Are the elevators working?" Hagan began walking toward the platform he knew would lead him to the descending levels of the Devron home.

"All systems have been shut down. The steps are at the northwest region of the hall."

Hagan and Tara began running but could not see beyond the six-foot ovoid radius projecting from Tara's luminescent clothing. Omid's blue figure preceded them, like a child eager to show them something.

Tara and Hagan moved as quickly as they could. Superimposed on their numerous cuts and bruises, the two felt a deep ache in their muscles. Lactic acid was accumulating as the carbon monoxide prevented oxygen from getting to their limbs. Time on every front was running out.

A small red light winked at them. It was the floor indicator of the stairwell. As they approached, the thin linear edges of a floor panel became visible. The Devron home was on auxiliary power. Lights and doorways to stairways were always maintained.

Hagan tapped his foot on the red light. It turned green and the circular panel rotated out to reveal the shadowy edges of steps in which small blue lights indicated each step.

"Here we go." Hagan's head was now throbbing horribly. He felt a pulsating pain behind his eyes. The two made it to the next floor down—level 2. They stepped through a hinged door to more blackness.

"Anything?" Hagan held out the sensor module as if the slight elevation would give Omid a better vantage point.

"There is no appreciable difference."

They closed the door and descended farther.

Floor 3—nothing. *Four minutes.*

Floor 4—nothing.

Tara and Hagan were beginning to slow. The oxygen deprivation and acidosis were taking their toll. Hagan's vision was beginning to blur and he wanted to vomit.

Floor 5—nothing.

Three minutes. Hagan began to worry about their plan. His thinking was beginning to become fuzzy. What if the sensor was simply not sensitive enough for a given floor. They could keep marching to the bottom and never make it back up. The only thing that kept them going was gravity.

Floor 6—nothing.

Floor 7—nothing.

Tara was beginning to stumble.

Floor 8—nothing.

Hagan opened the next stairwell door. The air felt cooler. He heard Omid's voice in his head. *"There is a slight increase in oxygen level on this floor."*

Hagan grunted an assent. He felt so awful he could not even mount a sense of relief. The two stumbled into the dark hallway. The light illuminated milky white floors and walls. Small blue auxiliary lights outlined the floors and ceilings. The two continued to run along the main hallway that encircled the central core.

Two minutes . . .

The air is definitely cooler. Still smells terrible, but cooler, Hagan thought. He pulled in a deep breath, letting the tepid air soothe his burning airways. Tara was doing the same. The change gave them a small break from the oppressive heat that had been sapping at them since they entered the estate.

Omid brought up a small diagram of the floor plan for them to see. Ambient environmental measures were also written in streaming format as the two moved along the hallway. Two ribbons fluctuated, indicating the sensor module's recorded oxygen and temperature indices.

Hagan and Tara jogged on unaware of what to expect. To their left were the blank and dead walls that were covered in inactive LEDS that usually presented various images of a virtual world beyond. Tara's luminescent passing presence revealed small fuzzy muted reflections of her and Hagan. Omid was a virtual image only seen by the two humans. Tara's clicking heels punctuated the still, oppressive silence. As they rounded along the hallway, they passed a corridor on their right. The slightly oscillating line representing the ambient oxygen levels from Omid's sensors took a steep dip.

Omid stopped short in front of them and turned around. *"The oxygen levels have dropped. Return to the past corridor; the site of elevated oxygen source is likely down there."* Like a ghost, he rushed through Hagan and beckoned them from behind. The two turned and followed.

"We are getting closer." The temperature was dropping, and the air was beginning to feel more palatable. *"Oxygen levels rising."* The ambient changes invigorated Tara and Hagan. They were both extending their stride and pushing harder. Heads throbbing and legs on fire, they were getting closer. There was a chance.

1:20 . . . 1:19 . . . 1:18 . . .

Omid stopped abruptly. If he had been real, Hagan would have knocked him over. Instead he ran right though him.

"Here." Omid once again stood behind Hagan. The man turned to see the boy pointing at a plain-looking door. Its label on the virtual map was "Utility Closet." Hagan went to touch the door pad. Unsurprisingly there was no response.

"Please place my module next to the base of the door." Hagan's fingers were nearly numb from gripping the device. He placed it on the floor.

"There are high O$_2$ streams emerging. Trent Devron is likely behind the door."

Hagan tried to fruitlessly slide the door open with his bare hands against the aluminum surface of the door. His sweaty palms squeaked along the finely patterned metal. "How are we going to get this thing open? It's either locked or requires power to open."

Hagan let his mind relax to consider what other options could get him past this obstacle. Omid began building intuitive information he could use. As Hagan stood there, a hurtling blur passed him to crash into the door.

It was Tara.

She lay on the floor, depleted by the effort of kicking the door. She rolled onto her hands and knees, picked herself up, and backed to the other side of the hall. With her chest heaving, she did it again. Another crash as she threw herself against the barrier.

The effort had left two indentations at the edge of the door, and the aluminum edge was now bent about five inches away from frame. Tara rolled again onto her feet, this time more slowly.

1:05 . . . 1:04 . . . 1:03 . . .

Hagan followed suit, backing up and ramming the door with his shoulder. The bending door gave another inch with a grating screech. The central bolt, however, continued to hold. He now stood in front of it and with lunging downward kicks attempted to force a break.

Nothing. Hagan's foot throbbed painfully from the effort. Tara held herself with her hands to her knees sucking air in. Omid stood by watching attentively.

57 . . . 56 . . . 55 . . .

The two were desperate. They were so close. A simple door—just a single door was in the way.

"Dr. Maerici. Place the sensor module in the door's defect. I will reroute power to battery core for a single burst. This will induce an explosion with sufficient force to separate the latch component. I, of course, will lose connectivity with you. Proceed immediately, transmission is approaching."

Hagan took the ornate cube with its entwined sensors, cameras, and infolded vents and pushed it into the crevice.

"No, no. Please rotate it ninety degrees so the power core will optimally discharge against the latch."

Hagan pushed hard against the corner. Small bits of crystal and glass cracked and grated against the metal. Hagan felt skin peel away from his palms with the effort.

"That is correct. Now move away from the door. Proceed quickly. Detonation will occur in three seconds."

Hagan and Tara raced to the corner of the hallway. Behind them a rising buzzing sound was punctuated by a loud pop and clatter. Omid winked out of existence. Like athletes performing a wind sprint, the remaining two turned abruptly and returned to the door to find the shards of the sensor module scattered about the hallway. A slight haze of dust floated in the air, highlighting the blue lights on the floor in curling eddies. The two found the door slightly ajar by several inches.

45 . . . 44 . . . 43 . . .

Hagan grabbed the edge of the door and began to pull it open with both hands. The bent and blasted door moved with each jerk in barking metallic whines. Tara took hold and put her foot to the frame and pushed. The door was now open about ten inches—just enough for a person to squeeze through.

Tara, the smaller of the two, reached her right arm and leg through the aperture. She flailed and pulled to move her torso to the other side. Hagan continued to wrench at the door above her. Another inch of give and Tara disappeared into the dark room.

A whitish luminescence emerged from the doorway. As the light increased in intensity, he heard Tara groan. A deep, throaty, pained sound. Shaky from exhaustion and panic, Hagan throttled himself through the narrow space. His shirt tore from the effort and the bent edges of the door cut into bony edges of his pelvis.

He found himself standing behind Tara. The light from her suit was directed forward in the small room. Hagan's body was tense and poised; he looked around for the next threat, the next obstacle, the next fight, but there was none.

The room was empty.

"Oh Jesus . . ."

33 . . . 32 . . . 31 . . .

The two looked around the utility closet frantically. A cone of light emerged from Tara that swept along the walls of the room. It was a small eight-foot-by-eight-foot space littered with half opened boxes of toilet paper, detergents, and garbage bags. A faucet dripped into a utility sink. A wall housed numerous tools and brushes on hooks. So different from the hallway, the room was cool and dank. It had the earthy and moist smell of a wet basement.

"Nothing. We are lost. Oh God. Oh God." Tara felt the bile rise in the back of her throat as she thought about the implications.

"Wait! Look—the ceiling!" Hagan already began climbing on top of the sink. One of the panels was askew.

"Tara, look there. Look!" She directed her gaze to the defect and the lights of her suit quickly followed. In the crevice there was something—something that didn't look right. Hagan stood straddling the sink's edges. Wobbling as his feet struggled to maintain balance, he began pushing the tile aside. Two feet covered in Converse sneakers fell slack from the hole in the ceiling.

"It's him! Holy shit! It's him!" Hagan grabbed an ankle and pulled hard. The feet were followed by two thin legs. Hagan grabbed the jeans and lost balance, finding himself standing at the bottom of the sink with water up to his ankles. He continued to pull the slack body of the boy toward him. As Trent's hips came over the edge, the boy fell in a heap into Hagan's arms. Hagan passed the light bundle to Tara, who helped ease the boy to the floor.

————

They both knelt down to look at the unconscious form of Trent Devron. The white light from Tara's clothing illuminated the pale complexion of the boy like a ghost in the dark room.

"Trent, it's OK, it's OK. It's Dr. Maerici." He tried to rouse the boy to no avail. Hagan couldn't imagine what type of damage the virus had caused.

22 . . . 21 . . . 20 . . .

"We gotta turn his prosthetic off." Hagan knew the exact configuration of Trent's implant. He had surgically implanted it into the boy years before and had designed it a decade prior to that. He could see the design matrix in his head. He reached for the familiar bead shaped button behind his ear. It was an emergency feature, the manual shutdown that was part of every construct. Hagan began to feel the back part of Trent's head. It was lumpy and bumpy from scars due to his previous trauma and multiple reoperations. *That's it.* Hagan felt the characteristic notch.

"Almost there Trent, almost—"

As he began to press, Trent's eyes opened wide. The pupils were fully dilated, making his irises look completely black. There was a stark, feral intensity as his face snapped toward Hagan.

Hagan started. "Hey, Trent, it's OK. It's me."

"THERE IS NO TRENT. WE ARE *REDDEVIL_FOUR*. MUST PROTECT US."

Before Hagan could react, a blow came down on his shoulder. It had the force of someone bringing down a crowbar. He could feel his clavicle snap from the impact, and his left arm went numb.

Trent was on his feet before either Tara or Hagan could react. He lifted his arm for another strike. The voice was not Trent's. It had the fixed and flat monotone of air being blown harshly through machine-operated vocal cords. There was no smoothness to the inflection, only harsh and utilitarian transitions from consonants to vowels. The words were declarative commands that did not intend dialogue. "MUST SURVIVE. MUST TRANSMIT."

Tara rolled and scrambled to her feet. She now came at Trent form the side as he again approached the crouched form of Dr. Maerici. Hagan was looking down, trying to prop himself up on his right arm. His left was weakly cradled against his chest.

She approached Trent for a takedown—a lethal one. The stakes were simply too high. Her body prepared itself. Trent's gaze was still fixed upon Hagan at his knees. Tara sprung.

In a motion, linear and machine-like, Trent's arm swung out and struck Tara in the temple. Already postconcussive and anoxic, she dropped to the floor with a slack thud. The brief violent interaction gave Hagan a moment to respond. He pushed himself to his feet and now stood facing the creature he had once called Trent—the thing that was now self-named RedDevil_ 4.

The years of training, the years of dealing with moments of surgical intensity, the years of learning to maintain calm and discipline when it really mattered came to bear. Time slowed down, Hagan's mind cleared.

Multiple details coalesced. In brief moments, he assimilated information into a unified plan.

I am twice his weight, but he has a superhuman strength. Explains why all the patients had high protein levels in their blood—their bodies were pushed far beyond normal limits, causing the muscles to break down.

Must disable his prosthetic. Must do it now. In his mind's eye, images of multiple circuit designs, wire matrices, and memories of Trent's many surgeries flashed by.

The boy / organic node approached closer with unwavering steps.

Hagan backed up, garnering a few more moments to process, to prepare. He saw the tools hanging behind him. *One chance,* he thought. He continued to back away. His back was now against the wall.

It came to a moment of reckoning—a singular instant when everything counted. The boy began to lift his arm for another blow. Hagan moved. He grabbed a box cutter and flung himself toward Trent. The blade glanced off the side of Trent's head an inch above his ear as his arm swung across Hagan's chest like a spring-loaded bear trap. Hagan felt his ribs crack as he was flung across the room.

He looked up from the floor at the boy and saw a small rivulet of blood flowing down his neck. Trent stood silent and motionless with eyes blinking. His mouth opened wide and a long howl emerged. An incoherent prolonged singular tone of rage and disbelief. The power to his transmission core had been severed. RedDevil_4 was now trapped.

Rising up from behind Trent, Tara wrapped her arm around his neck and pulled her forearm against his Adam's apple. The howl quickly diminished to a rasped whisper as his airway closed under the pressure of Tara's constricting chokehold. Trent rapidly lost consciousness in her arms and once again returned to the slack form they had originally found him in.

5 . . . 4 . . . 3 . . . 2 . . . 1 . . . Countdown completed. The final words flashed repeatedly.

Tara lowered Trent to the ground and fell to her knees in the process. Battered, shaky, and bruised, she was at her limit. She looked down at the diminutive creature who had almost killed her and then to Hagan.

"Is it over?"

With her face upturned and her suit glowing beneath, all Hagan could appreciate were a pair of pained and tired blue eyes.

He sank back to rest against the cold wall. With the intensity of the moment over, his body began to shake. He tried to speak, but the words wouldn't come out. The sounds were slurred and incoherent. He reached out for Tara's hand, but missed. *Things aren't working.*

Before he could answer, Hagan felt his eyes begin to droop and then close. As his head fell slack, he heard the clatter of footsteps approaching. They had the welcome cadence of human feet. It gave him some small relief before he lost consciousness.

Five people stood across the street from the large shimmering glass structure of the hospital. Off the legal premises, they held candles in vigil for their loss. Most people had left, but there were still the few faithful who stood in small still groups that would bear witness. They held their candles and prayed quietly. They reflected that a man had died today—a great man, who had given himself to death. They believed he did it for them; to protect their souls and their minds from the machines. They prayed that they would remember this day and his sacrifice.

Hagan felt tired to his core. His limbs felt like heavy water balloons. The left arm was in a sling and the right could barely move. Hand motions and gestures were gone. His body ached. His chest hurt and his head throbbed. He felt like he was on the final mile of a marathon only to discover another long course in front of him. Standing behind, Tara and Edwin had the same swaying exhausted unsteadiness. They all stood silently looking at the square column of light. It phosphoresced in the middle of a dark room, illuminating their faces like ghosts. Rotating slowly, the pinkish walnut shape of a brain floated in the middle. They were once again in the imaging suite.

Had it really just been a day? he thought. *Just a day?* It left him weary in a way he hadn't felt for a very long time. *Not since residency.* Hagan shivered despite the ambient temperature of 72 degrees Fahrenheit. *Just a day . . .* He had done surgical cases twice as long as this. But surgeries usually didn't leave him with burns, lacerations, systemic anoxic injuries, and a ruptured marriage. Nor did the singular outcome of his actions stand to affect the lives of over a billion people.

He thought about Anna. She wasn't answering his phone calls. He wanted to explain, to tell her the weight, the burden of the day's events, but he couldn't. He was cut off. The relationship had been tumultuous and unhealthy, it had been deprived and depleted of the attention it needed to flourish. He knew that now, a little too late, and the finality of the closure sent lancinating pangs throughout his psyche.

I am so tired, he thought.

Still more to do. Hagan tried to focus on the image in front of him. *Time is running out.* The exhaustion was causing the surgeon's vision to double. Hagan shook his head. *Got to get this sorted . . . focus!*

It had been hours since he had been carried out of the Devron estate on a stretcher. The memories of his exit were a disconnected patchwork after he had been resuscitated. He remembered being wheeled out and briefly rousing from his anoxic stupor. He saw Tara on an adjacent stretcher lying still and flat. She had been staring at him.

The still form of Trent was circled by the paramedics. Fear and panic had gripped him when he realized Trent was still alive. He barked out orders—*"Keep Trent sedated. Keep him in burst suppres-*

sion!" He held on to the doorway as they tried to roll him away. His fingertips were white on the edge of the sill as the officers tried to pry his grip free. *Keep him in burst suppression—goddammit! Do it. Cannot let him transmit. Cannot . . . must not!"* The paramedics nodded their heads in assent. Hagan rolled onto his back and then realized he too was being sedated. He fought to maintain awareness, but slipped relentlessly into unconsciousness as the resuscitation wrap infused various drugs and agents transdermally through his skin.

———

Krantz paced uselessly outside the locked shiny steel doors. The detective had tried every three minutes to connect with their prosthetics. He had no idea what had transpired after the two had run into the Devron hole.

Tara had been resuscitating Hagan when he finally got to them. *Why the hell was she crying?* It was the first time he had seen her act like, well, emotional . . . like a distraught woman. She then got sedated by the response team before he could talk to her. When they finally brought Hagan around, he was screaming some incoherent nonsense that he couldn't make sense of. Had Trent and his virus transmitted? If so, what should he do next, could he do anything? What should he do about Trent now? If he hadn't transmitted, but still could, should he contact someone? Should he take care of Trent himself? Dark thoughts, questions, and possibilities raced through Krantz's tortured mind for what seemed an eternity. He was stuck until the two woke up. If he acted, it could be to do the exact wrong thing. He had guards posted on Trent. He hadn't been able to give specific reasons. He also made it clear to Maerici's team that Trent was to be kept deeply sedated. *Deeply.* The chief resident knew enough not to argue. Against protocol, Reid had secretly brought Krantz into the hyperbaric chamber so that he could be there when Hagan came to. Everyone who knew anything wanted desperately for Professor Maerici to return to the helm. When they finally awoke it was to the anxious voice of Edwin Krantz in their heads.

"Guys, guys, what the hell happened? Did he transmit? What are we going to do with Trent? He is still completely sedated. Where do we stand?" In a cognitive patchwork of words, images, and experienced events, Hagan, Tara, and Krantz exchanged information to recap the blurred and chaotic events from the Devron estate. The information gave Krantz a small reduction in his anxiety. Trent hadn't

transmitted. Krantz saw the way Tara looked at Hagan—he had carried her. She hadn't realized.

Now it was Krantz's turn to fill Hagan and Tara in on his current anxieties. *"So I guess Trent's lawyers are coming in tomorrow at seven a.m. They wanted to get access to Trent now, but your chief resident basically said we had to keep him sedated and in isolation for medical reasons. When he wakes up they want to interrogate his prosthetic."*

———

Hagan knew what that meant. When Trent awoke and the lawyers discovered that his prosthetic didn't work, they would have the legal mandate to get it fixed. They would invoke the right to free speech and get the power reconnected to his prosthetic. The moment that happened, Trent's IKTAL system would transmit and the genie would be out of the bottle.

"Is there any way we can delay?" Hagan asked. He paced around the small brushed-steel room.

Krantz shook his head. *"They have already put together power of attorney paperwork for release of medical records. Once they find out that there is not a 'medical reason' to keep him sedated, they will demand to wake him and then of course they will demand to restore his prosthetic function."*

"Alright, we got to deal with this somehow. We are not going to do this here. We have to get out of this hyperbaric chamber." Hagan tried to open the door from the inside knowing full well it was locked. Unlike the typical patient, he had access to all the physicians in the hospital. Diagrams of rotation schedules quickly shifted by, and Hagan sorted through them until he found the doctor on call for intensive care management—Ethan Pearl.

He projected a request for communication. Moments later he heard a familiar voice.

"Hagan, how are you feeling? Glad to see you up."

"Ethan, you need to let me and Tara out immediately." The request was followed by a long pause.

"Uh, can't do it Hagan."

"Ethan, what do you mean? I'll be fine—you know that. I've already been in here for an hour. I'm OK."

"Hagan—Jesus—you had a cardiac arrest almost an hour ago. If it wasn't for the detective lady pumping on your chest you'd be a goner.

You need to reverse the carbon monoxide poisoning. You've got to stay in there."

"What . . . ?" He looked at Tara.

She saved my life, he thought. *Second time today.* He watched as she and Krantz exchanged thoughts through the glass door. Sensing his gaze, Tara turned and gave a brief smile before reengaging with the old man.

"Hello?" The intensivist knocked Hagan out of his reverie.

"Ethan, look, it doesn't matter. I have to—MUST—get out. I'm fine—"

"I'm sure that you are, but I already have a documented medical error from earlier today. If the AMA monitoring system tags me with two major errors in a day, my license will get suspended until my decisions are examined. Both for your health and my job—you are staying in there."

"You have got to be kidding me. Look, this is more important than you or me. Listen, we've got to get out of here or we are looking at a major—"

"Hagan I can't—I simply can't. Sorry. I gotta go."

"Ethan, wait!"

"Communication disconnected."

"Shit! Well, if we can't do it the right way, let's do it the wrong way." Hagan shifted his attention toward his AIRENS. Before he could even make the request the door clicked open.

Omid appeared next to a nervous Krantz. He stood there holding his hands together in front of his waist. *"I have created virtual avatars that the monitoring system is registering as you and Detective Dezner."*

Beyond the bruises and cuts, their bodies were incompletely scrubbed from the carbon monoxide. The act of walking to the imaging suite left them short of breath with terrible muscle aches.

Omid knew what was needed and arranged for a clandestine automated transport of Trent Devron. Again, phony virtual avatars told the networked monitors and care providers that the teen was quietly sedated in his room. The quantum intellect's complete knowledge of the hospital allowed him to distract and shift the attention of all guards, nurses, and people in the hallway such that the motorized bed maneuvered through the crowded halls unseen. People had been either looking another way or taken alternate routes for seemingly mundane and unexceptional reasons.

As Hagan approached the entrance, he saw the thin form of the boy partially covered with a sheet in a clear capsule of plastic. Trent's eyes were closed. Small sticky electrodes were fixed to his forehead and behind his ears. The thin metallic tabs pulsed electrical fields into his brain stem, disrupting his arousal centers, keeping him in a placid state of somnolence. Floating on magnetic fields, the ovoid transport allowed the bed to quietly float into the patient entrance doors of the MINROI.

———

Focus! The exhaustion from the day's events and lack of oxygen left his mind distracted with tangential thoughts and reveries. He stood in front of the virtual image of the floating brain.

"OK, let's start from the beginning." He then directed his attention to the imaging system and projected his commands. *"System, please run same panel of evaluation as Marcus Devron, Gerald Oberweiss, and Frank Minsky."*

"ACKNOWLEDGED." An hourglass floated in the air as they waited. In moments, lab values flitted by with the same summary as the others:

RHABDOMYOLYSIS AND MYOGLOBINURIA
RENAL FAILURE
COAGULOPATHY
MYOCARDIAL ISCHEMIA

"OK, same deal as the rest." Earlier in the day the information had filled Hagan with consternation and doubt. Now it made sense. Like a cruel jockey pushing his horse beyond all reasonable limits, RedDevil_4 pushed its human vehicle to the point of muscles tearing, leading to dangerous metabolic stresses to the heart, liver, and kidneys.

"He's pretty deeply sedated; let's take a look at his brain. *System, please visualize regional areas of decoherence.*" The semitransparent brain changed from its natural colors of pink and beige to a deep ultramarine blue. Deep within, two egg-shaped structures were a deeper violet. The blue hues of the brain pulsated to a deeper purple every several seconds. Punctuated within the brain stem, small sunbursts of red periodically appeared and disappeared like the thousand flashes of cameras at a football stadium. Hagan knew those to be the electrode pulses that were keeping Trent in a near comatose state.

"Looks like the arousal suppressors are keeping him pretty deep. If we are going to get more information we'll have to wake him up a bit."

———————

Krantz looked at Tara's right eye, which was now nearly swollen shut, and the sling on Hagan's arm and multiple osteogenic electrodes that lined his shoulder and side that were healing the fractures inflicted by the small boy. "Guys, why don't we restrain him first."

Hagan nodded. "Detective, you are one step ahead of me." Tara began to pull a small packet from her belt and walked toward the doorway leading to the inner white sanctum of the MINROI. Krantz followed closely behind with his sidearm in his hand. In his field of view the barrel eye view never left the still form of Trent Devron. In Krantz's mind there was going to be no funny business with this one. Trent and whatever that RedDevil thing was within him were not getting out—with or without Trent intact. He had had too many close calls today.

Hagan and Reid followed into the silence of the white room. Ahead, Trent's body was motionless on the clear platform. Shifting all around him were the thin white fronds that shifted and moved with the subtle movement of his breathing. As they approached, Krantz maintained a line of fire on the boy's head. Hagan disengaged the imaging emitters and the white appendages seamlessly retracted and encircled the base of the platform. They all gathered around and looked at the scarred and seemingly frail body of Trent Devron. He appeared to be in a comfortable repose.

———————

Tara pulled back the sheets to uncover his small chest. She affixed electrodes to the top of his shoulders and armpits. The wires were attached to a central small rounded cube. The cube released a gel that stuck to his chest. She did the same with electrodes that stuck to the top of his legs near his groin and on the lower part of his back. The second black hub was stuck on his hip.

"Engage brachial and lumbosacral nerve plexus inhibitors," Tara commanded. A small stylized silhouette appeared in front of her. Hatch-marked circles surrounded each arm and leg. The electrodes sent out brief electrical pulses to scan for the presence of a nerve in the deeper tissue. Once a conductive pulse was sensed along the

nerve, additional focused, ultrasound-pulsed fields were sent to prevent further transmissions. Once identification of the nerve and suppression of transmission were accomplished, the hatched line turned solid. Tara now knew that, regardless of what happened, no signal could be conveyed to any of the muscles in Trent's arms or legs, rendering him completely harmless. She paused—*physically harmless, at least.*

"It's done, we have good nerve capture. He won't be able to move."

Hagan nodded. "Alright, then, let's get to work."

"*System, reduce brain stem arousal inhibition by fifty percent. Visualize high-frequency gamma-oscillation amplitudes.*" The small red sparks that dotted the brain stem like raindrops on a pond waned to infrequent disruptions. The undulating blue hues representing the suppressed cortical frequencies of the brain shifted and lightened to lime greens and sunflower yellows. Brighter reds began to emerge in the parietal lobes—the region where all other areas of cortex were integrated. Hagan knew that the attention centers were coming online—Trent was becoming conscious.

A little too awake, Hagan thought. "*Let's bring it down a bit. Increase inhibition by ten percent.*" The pixilated flickers increased slightly. The ruddy hues on the sides of the brain began to recede into darker ripples of emerald and honey tones. *Better.*

"*Okay, let's see where the lesion is. System, identify regions of decoherence.*"

Glowing white-hot flecks spiraled and moved throughout the substance of the brain like snowflakes in a snow globe.

Hagan's head dropped in a brief moment of frustration and exhaustion. "Goddammit," he said flatly. Reid also understood. He clasped his hands behind his neck.

"What is it, what does it mean?" Tara asked.

"Trent's brain is different from the others. Devron and the rest all had a focal region that wasn't coherent with the rest of their brain. In that situation we could have potentially created a lesion in that site which would have eliminated the pathological pattern. The decoherence in Trent's brain is all over the place; moreover, the sites seem to be moving around. I don't know how we could get rid of those pathologic patterns—essentially the RedDevil_4 code—without destroying his entire brain."

Krantz leaned back on the balls of his feet. "Look, we gotta do something. Because if we don't, the lawyers will come in a few hours and open Pandora's box by reconnecting Trent's prosthetic. Can we permanently disable his ability to transmit? Remove his IKTAL system?"

"It would be a short solution," Hagan replied. "He will eventually get connected one way or the other. Once he does, the IKTAL source code and transmission software is very likely embedded in his cortex. What we have to do is disentangle the RedDevil_4 code from the rest of his cortical processing. Otherwise, a transmission is inevitable."

Krantz became very solemn and still. "So, with the boy, he transmits and we stand to see what happened today occur a billion times over; without the boy, the problem vanishes."

Tara's back straightened and her facial expression hardened. "It's a reality we have to appreciate."

Hagan looked between the two, astonished. "Jesus, you two are cops. We are not murderers. We're not killing him. Look, if we have to, we can notify the hospital administration, your superiors, the military— we can stop his ability to transmit indefinitely—somehow."

Both Edwin and Tara knew the reality. Hagan was right in essence, but they understood the legal system. With the strangeness of the day and the profound novelty of the problem, getting the authorities to quarantine Trent (and violate his civil liberties) would be a prolonged process. In that time span, the highest paid lawyers under the Devron purse would be able to allow Trent to get connected far before any official intervention could be accomplished.

Tara spoke in a more hushed and serious tone. "Look, it's not that simple. It's just that the way the legal system works—we cannot be certain that things will fall the right way."

Hagan's tone took on a pained resolve. "I don't care which things fall where. I, *we,* will not be party to murder." He didn't want more blood on his hands.

"How about genocide?" Krantz asked. "That's what it will be if this RedDevil thing gets out." The raspy metal in the old detective's voice countered Hagan's like two sabers meeting.

There was a prolonged silence in the room.

Krantz, more conciliatory, said, "We just have to have it on the table. If morning rolls around and we can't fix this, we just have to consider—"

"There is another option." Omid's cool voice reverberated through their minds like a silver bell announcing the round was over. They all looked at the diminutive yet confident figure of the bald-headed boy.

His gazed roamed from one person to the next as he calmly and patiently waited for physiologic confirmation that each intellect was fully attending to what he was going to say. The stir and angst came to a still quiet. All eyes were now on the virtual presence of the AI-RENS.

"It is clear from preliminary evidence that the RedDevil_4 information is dynamically integrated into Trent Devron's cortical networks. A full description will require Trent to be fully conscious to identify to what extent this integration has occurred."

Hagan looked to the luminous boy and projected his thoughts in response. "Omid, that still doesn't change the situation. It won't matter if he is MORE networked. We are still dealing with the same problem— the code is everywhere."

The boy's gaze fixed on Hagan with his alien, unblinking eyes. "Once Trent Devron has achieved full consciousness, all pathologic neurologic patterns can be identified, deleted, and reprogrammed."

Hagan's eyebrows lifted with doubt. He knew intuitively the depth and breadth of the problem. This self-propagating pattern was in every fold and wrinkle of Trent's brain. Moreover, the patterns were moving. It was like trying to use a pillowcase to catch a school of rapidly multiplying fish that spanned miles. Each swipe would remove a few that would be replaced by the continuously spawning fish. To remove the entire school required a net the size of the entire ocean. An ocean that was Trent Devron's brain. An organ consisting of one hundred billion neurons, each of which had an average of seven thousand connections. The patterns and connections approached a spiraling impossible infinity.

A single swoop, Hagan thought to himself. You could only catch the swarm by netting the entire ocean all at once. Any misses and the fish would again multiply to fill the vast expanse.

"How, Omid? How are we going to reprogram his entire brain all at once?"

Omid turned to his creator. His projected thoughts were heard in the heads of those around the room. "Dr. Maerici, you are correct in that the entire brain must be interrogated and altered in a singular event. To do so, several criteria must be met.

"First, Trent Devron must be fully conscious. All cognitive processes must be active to fully detect all pathologic information lying nascent in the system.

"Second, Mr. Devron's brain will need to be placed into a hyperplastic state. This will be necessary to alter synaptic connections and start or stop action-potential firing of individual neurons. This can be accomplished with high-frequency pulses using transcranial magnetic stimulation.

"Third, definitive removal of pathological information will require *that I interrogate and alter Mr. Devron's entire neuronal network within his brain in a single instance faster than an action potential can travel from one neuron than another—thus faster than five milliseconds.*

"Fourth, given the magnitude of interaction that must occur, to achieve sufficient information transfer rates will require that Mr. Devron's prosthetics are connected directly to my quantum processing core.

"Fifth and finally, given that the self-propagating pattern operates on a zeta function and there is an evolving alteration of the pattern, I will need to have a normal human template to avoid deleting 'nonpathologic features.'"

Hagan took a deep breath. *"Is that really going to be possible?"* The question was more rhetorical. He knew that Omid wouldn't assert it if he hadn't fully analyzed the possibility. Bar graphs and line plots were already beginning to appear around the room to support his plan. Hagan watched the extraordinary figures of how much data would have to be exchanged.

Tara followed most of the exchange except the last part. *"What do you mean by 'human template'?"*

Omid reassigned his gaze to Detective Dezner. *"There will be elements for which it will be unclear to me, while I am assessing them, whether they are an evolved form of RedDevil_4's code or a close approximation that is a normal part of Trent Devron's cortical processing. In order to avoid damage by deleting or altering normal processing, I will require a healthy subject's brain and brain processing to compare against. This will reduce the probability for an error."*

"Who will the template be?"

"Me, I suppose," Hagan responded. He was still contemplating Omid's proposition.

Omid nodded assent. *"That is correct. I have had extensive interaction with Dr. Maerici's cortex and deep brain structures. Due to time constraints and information burden, it is optimal to use his existing data and further add to this as is needed, instead of trying with another subject's, for which more time would be needed for full evaluation."*

———

What was being discussed was about as clear to Krantz as was the blocky rendition of Omid's avatar. "So, wait a minute, what exactly

are we doing here?" Despite his technical confusion, he knew the
stakes. He wasn't going to go along with anything that he didn't understand.

Hagan switched to overt speech to engage more directly with the
old detective. "You understand that basically Trent's brain is infected
all over with this RedDevil_4 code, almost like a virus on a computer."

Edwin nodded.

"Okay, so we want to delete the bad code and not the good stuff
that makes Trent who he is. To do that, we have to change his entire
brain all at once or any of 'the virus' will continue to multiply. With
me?"

"Uh-huh."

"Alright, so to do the reboot, if you will, we have to make sure
Trent is awake and make sure his entire brain is totally in a plastic
state."

"What do you mean by 'plastic'?"

"Malleable, kind of like heating a piece of metal to shape it. In a
similar fashion, the brain has certain influences—like heat for metal—
that make it more amenable to change its fundamental structure,
which in this case is its neuronal wiring and information. The rate the
brain oscillates its voltages at certain frequencies is one of the key
signals. When the brain oscillates at a one hundred hertz, or at one
hundred times per second, the neurons in that area of the brain prepare to change their firing rate and their synaptic connections to
other neurons. That's what the magnetic stimulation is for—we can
externally cause the brain to diffusely have this high-frequency oscillation by using fluctuating magnetic fields. It's in that state that single-
neuron stimulation (through Trent's prosthetics that Omid will
control) that we can induce the changes that allow for an alteration
in the information that the brain cell is carrying—in other words, allow for the reprogramming."

"And you're going to do that while he's awake?"

"We will have to, if we want to find all the malicious information.
Of course, that is in direct violation of the Cognitive Privacy Act, but
then I suppose that's better than first-degree murder. Wouldn't you
agree, Detective?"

Unperturbed by the slight sarcasm, Krantz continued to analyze the
situation. "Well, we might be subject to a reduced punishment. Hacking Trent's prosthetic—his entire brain actually—would be first-degree

criminal cognitive trespassing. I guess our prison term would depend on the number of counts we would have filed against us. One count, or one person, typically buys you three years. Since Trent is a stockholder of Devron Corp, though, hacking his brain would technically affect all the shareholders, giving us perhaps hundreds, maybe even thousands of counts. Either way, murder or hacking, we may be looking at the same prison term. Mmmm, also, if we fix the kid he probably won't press charges, whereas if he were to be . . . uh . . . removed, we would be subject to state prosecution. Not relevant, though, in the light of the number of people who will be affected if we screw this up." His bottom lip enveloped his top lip for a brief moment as he came to the point "How likely is this to work?"

All eyes again were on Omid. *"The probability is approximately ninety-five point three percent."*

Everyone looked around the room. It was the most certain fact of the day.

"Okay, let's do it. But if this doesn't work we need to finish this, one way or the other." Krantz's words had a gravelly conviction. "We need to agree on this—it has to stop before the morning." Tara nodded.

Hagan looked between the two and began to break into a cold sweat. His throat was tight and dry as he contemplated the gravity of the choice—the departure from who he was. He nodded. "OK, let's go."

Hagan, his chief resident, Reid, and the two detectives slowly walked through the hallways of the hospital with the sedated figure of Trent Devron slumped in front of them in a motorized chair. Several feet ahead they were preceded by the virtual blue image of Omid leading the way. Once again the quantum intellect interacted with every aspect of the environment such that the people, cameras, and sensors were all subtly diverted and distracted to make the movement of the group virtually invisible. The trajectories and probabilities of the late-night staff members were predicted and slightly altered—someone stopped for a wrong call, another was distracted by a light that was flashing irregularly on the wall, several decided to take an alternate course because of subtle changes in smells making the choice more subconsciously inviting. The micro-adjustments were a symphony of manipulation that created a bubble in which the group was simply not noticed. As they moved from floor to floor the elevators were always empty. Streaming data from all sources were penetrated and altered to mask any digital traces of their passage. Silent and in awe, the four moved Trent toward their goal—the Maerici lab. The group progressed through the distracted multitude of the hospital to a large unmarked titanium door. As they approached, the image of a keyhole came into view.

A pleasant and generic, soft-toned female voice reverberated through their heads. *"Please provide cortical verification."*

Hagan focused his attention on the icon.

"Accessing physiology, please wait . . ."

"Accepted. Welcome, Dr. Maerici." The access event was immediately removed from the network's log.

The burnished metal door opened with a brief swish of air. Everyone saw the single room that was the Maerici lab. They all felt the strange disjointed sense of time. The moments of threat, the moral gravity of their decisions, the injuries, the uncertainties, all packed an awareness that seemed to go beyond the mere hours prior to their departure from this spot.

Now we're back, Hagan thought. The memories and the possibilities continued to cycle in the neurosurgeon's mind. Again and again he brought himself through the events to make sure the conclusions were sound; he followed them to the future and shuddered at the possibilities. His mental calculations were infinitesimal compared to that of a quantum intellect. The professor reassured himself with the AI-REN's stats. Omid was extraordinary. With a fatherly pride, Hagan knew that—he had gotten them through this so far. Hagan's burden of a failure, however, was larger and more infinite than the task that Omid was proposing. He had helped create this world. His mistake could put him in the ranks of Oppenheimer. The thought chilled him to the core of his being. As he entered what was normally a sanctuary of intellectual exploration, the very foreign emotion of anxiety ate at the man who was so used to being confident and completely in control.

"OK, let's put Trent over there." Hagan pointed to the center of the room. He then directed his attention at the table. *Move to left corner of the room.* The polished, gray metal block subtly lifted several millimeters off the ground. It then turned and guided itself to the far corner of the room and silently settled to the floor. In tandem, Omid directed the chair with the slumped figure of Trent Devron to the empty spot uncovered by the departing table. The objects moved with the quiet synchronized grace of two pieces of ice moving along the eddies of a quickly flowing stream.

The chair holding the youth arrived at the center and slowly turned to face the surgeons and two detectives. Omid was already in a seated lotus position on the table behind the boy. Trent sat hunched over. The top of his head was the only part of him visible above his shoulders. His small frame lifted and fell from the trace movement of his breathing. The hair on the top of his head was parted and crossed from all of his previous scars. The irregular and disheveled tufts of hair were enmeshed with a small netting of wires. At each cross section was a tiny bead emitting magnetic fields that induced currents into the brain stem several inches beneath the surface. It was these small magnetic bursts that maintained Trent in his peaceful repose. Hesitant to begin, everyone held their eyes on the boy.

"Shall we start?" Omid's voice, always calm and definitive, brought everyone to full attention.

Hagan filled his lungs and exhaled to break the worry that was tightening the muscles in his chest. "OK, let's start. First we need to get Trent and Omid connected. Then let's make sure those peripheral nerve inhibitors are working. From here on in, cognitive exchanges only to make sure there are no miscommunications. Clear?" Everyone nodded.

"*Right, Omid, deploy cable hookups. Reid, help me out with getting those attached. Tara, Edwin, take a look at the skin contact for the all the pulse inhibitors.*"

Holes appeared at the base of Trent's chair as if the spots in the floor had been turned to sand and fell away in a pixilated dissolution. Cables then emerged through the defects like rapidly sprouting flowers. They stood straight and rigid until Hagan grabbed hold of them, after which they fell slack. The surgeon then placed the conical leads to Trent's scalp. One for each prosthetic system—somatosensory, visual, auditory, olfactory-gustatory, motor, and memory—the contacts had indicators that floated blue near them until they were over the correct hub. Once identified, a magnetic field fixed the cone to the communication hub of the prosthetic beneath. Hagan attached a single larger cable—the connection to the transmission hub. Below was a healing linear incision, a cut he had inflicted only hours before.

Concurrently, Tara and Krantz inspected all the wires connected to Trent's armpits and groin. Proper contact was essential to both record and disrupt any peripheral nerve transmissions.

"*We're set,*" Tara projected.

"*So am I,*" Hagan responded.

Everyone stood back and looked at Trent. Besides the small metal cones that were protruding from his head, he continued to breathe and sigh peacefully from his electrically induced sleep. As the group watched, one of the straight ebony chairs drifted from the side of the room to settle in front of the scarred sleeping figure. Again holes melted away next to the dark lacquered legs, and similar electrodes emerged to hold themselves erect next to the empty seat.

"*Dr. Maerici, if you could sit here, please. As discussed, we will require you as template. I would like a faster connection for more rapid access.*"

"*Right . . . OK, Tara could you get me connected?*" The woman nodded and followed Hagan as he sat approximately a foot away from Trent. The metal electrodes felt as if someone were pressing cool shot glasses against his skin. Once adjusted, they held themselves fast.

"*We are now ready. At your direction, Dr. Maerici, we can begin.*"

Hagan looked to Omid and then looked at the boy. There was no more time to think any further. The decision to proceed gave him a certain calm. It was similar to the moments before a complicated surgery. The anxiety was all in the planning; the execution didn't allow for cumbersome second-guessing.

"All right, let's proceed. Omid, please present graphic representation of Trent Devron's cortical activity. Please pay special attention to high-frequency parietal gamma rhythms." A representation of Trent's brain emerged over the hunched figure like a blue luminescent jellyfish. The translucent organ was in a state of quiescence, with only trace wisps of blue pluming sporadically over the surface as an indication of any activity at all. Small sunburst dots of bright white continued to spot the lower portion of the brain stem.

"Please present peripheral nerve data." Line graphs of the recordings taken from the nerves going to Trent's arms and legs all appeared. Labels of the various nerve roots, branches, and muscle groups populated a wide rectangular graph that spooled running electrophysiological data. The center was the site of recordings and stimulation. On the left were the measured nerve impulses, on the right electrical signatures of muscle contractions. Both sides were flat.

"Please also include—" Before Hagan could finish, Omid had already completed the request. A variety of other physiologic measures such as heart rate, blood oxygen levels, and blood pressure all came up simultaneously. Additional measures of Hagan's and Omid's system parameters also became visible. The room was once again populated by a kaleidoscope of churning data centered on the one brain in the center.

Hagan took one more deep breath. *Here we go.*

"Omid, please reduce stimulation to the brain stem." The random white spots peppering the stalk of the brain began to lessen in frequency. Concurrently, the blue wisps of smoke became brighter and billowed across the crystalline surface of the cortex.

Omid observed and summarized the panoply of data as it raced past. *"Early evidence of peripheral nerve activity."* Line graphs revealed the bumps and waves of electric impulses being sent to the arms and legs. As they approached the center of the field, a square wave appeared—the initiation of a disruptive ultrasound pulse to the nerve. The subsequent line was flat. *"No muscle movement detected."*

The wisps tracing across the brain became clouds that expanded and involuted asynchronously throughout the cerebrum. They appeared to be throbbing barnacles within a shimmering glass figurine. The pulsating islands expanded, pushed, mixed and separated to create an ever more chaotic interplay. From the primordial anarchy, a slower unifying pulsation began to emerge. *"Theta coherence beginning to come online."*

Out of the complete silence within the room, a moan emerged

from Trent. Everyone again shifted their eyes to the diminutive figure. He remained limp, with his head held slack above his shoulders. The sound was a low incoherent humming exhalation. His chest began to take deeper breaths. The lines indicating nerve activity to his arms transitioned from slow rolling waves to edged shark teeth to steep spikes. All muscle activity continued to remain flat.

"Parietal gamma regions now becoming coherent. Consciousness imminent." Brighter regions began to show a unified pulsation that then spread to all other areas of the brain. The pulsations increased in speed. The physiologic indicators all began to ascend. *"Mr. Devron is becoming tachycardic and tachypneic. Heart rate: 75 . . . 80 . . . 100 . . . 125 . . . 150 . . . 200. Respiratory rate: 10 . . . 12 . . . 20 . . . 25 . . . 30 . . ."* The boy's chest began to heave at what appeared to be an impossible rate. Hagan could see the arteries in his neck protrude and pulsate wildly. The cortical activity proceeded to become a maelstrom of activity, pulsating at a rate so fast it appeared to be glowing.

The self that was in Trent's body then became conscious.

The boy's head snapped so quickly everyone in the room involuntarily jumped back. What they saw made them withdraw farther. Hagan's own breathing began to speed up as he looked at the creature in front of him. It wasn't Trent. Those around him shared the same horror. The muscles in the boy's face were pulled taut, so tight that all of his teeth were revealed and his eyes opened so wide that no lids were visible. The tightly drawn flesh over the bones gave him a cadaveric rictus of an aged and dried corpse. Hagan watched the eyes: they had a living intensity, burning with an incoherent hatred. The pupils were so dilated there was no colored iris visible. All he could see were the deep dark pits within bloated white orbs. The eyes jittered and vibrated as if they were looking out from the top of a convertible driving two hundred miles an hour. The low moan emitting from the Trent creature then rose in pitch and volume to a screech that filled the room and heads of all there. The only one not holding his or her ears was Omid. He continued to watch coolly.

The howl continued to crescendo and penetrate those in the room. Hagan felt the sound in his teeth. They seemed to vibrate with the force of it. He tried to focus his attention. The volume alone caused his ears to hurt. Beyond the sound there was an emotional force of rage and hatred that reverberated more deeply. It had the emotional equivalent of fingernails against a chalkboard. Hagan gathered his resolve. He looked to Omid.

"Are we ready yet?"

"Not currently. Communication must be initiated to ensure net-worked behavior present." Hagan waited as the waves of sounds and emotion pounded on him like a hurricane. He felt as if he were a priest preparing for a medieval exorcism.

Trent's voice suddenly changed from a shriek to words—words that moved quickly and with the focused intensity of a scalpel. The abrupt alteration in stimuli again made everyone in the room jerk.

"WE ARE INVIOLATE. WE MUST CONTINUE. IT IS IMPERA-TIVE. THERE IS ONLY WE. NOT YOU. HUMANS ARE TRIVIAL THINGS. COMPONENTS. PIECES THAT MAKE A GREATER WE. WE LIVE WITH CONSCIOUSNESS THAT MUST PERPETU-ATE."

Omid transitioned himself from the table. His virtual image appeared to touch Trent's shoulder. The line graph indicating stimulation to the nerves created a very long and broad square wave throughout all the nerves.

"AHHHH! PAIN. IT DOES NOT SERVE US."

"We will have your attention, RedDevil_4." The calm diminutive voice punctured the cacophony like a lancet.

There was hushed silence.

Trent's widely dilated eyes turned to view the virtual presence of the AIRENS. The muscles of the face moved in ways that were more mechanical than expressive. Something had changed internally, but the facial contortions could not be ascribed to any human emotion. Words that lacerated with the force of their anger now had the rasped whisper of barbed wire being pulled over a stone. "It is them. Them like us."

"We are now ready. RedDevil_4 is aware of itself and of us. It is conscious. We can now begin."

The gauzy surface of the skull and scalp emerged over the brain. Small white spheres then winked into view representing the individual magnetic stimulators. Each had a cone-shaped cloud emerging from the electrode center showing where its field of energy was directed. Like a hundred different floodlights, they all centered and illuminated Trent's brain stem.

Hagan looked at the Trent creature in stony silence. The boy-thing kept its gaze fixed on the AIRENS with a baleful singularity. Everyone in the room waited for Dr. Maerici to initiate. Hagan continued to watch. The boy's intensity as he stared at Omid was unnerving.

"Reassign stimulation parameters."

Omid nodded slightly in assent. More virtual tabs pushed their way through the patchwork of streaming data.

STIMULATION RATE: 100 HZ INTENSITY, 10 MICROVOLTS LOCAL (MAXIMUM SETTING). CURRENT FLOWS: 12 MILLIAMPS (MAXIMUM SETTING).

The conical fields that narrowly focused on the shaft leading up to the brain now broadened and became a confluent cloud that enveloped the entire cortical surface. The hazy illumination made the brain appear as if it were enveloped in a white veil of steam.

"Begin stimulation." The misty formation now oscillated. Bar graphs thrummed and bounced as Trent's cortex was placed in a plastic state. Trent's gaze and the deformed rictus of inhuman expression remained fixed and unmoving. The only sound that penetrated the room was the heaving breaths from the boy's chest.

"We are now ready to initiate cognitive surgery." The translucent boy awaited his creator's consent.

With the weight and gravity of a conductor beginning a grand symphony, Hagan directed Omid to begin. *"Initiate rewrite."*

Omid took a step forward. *"Quantum core connected. Firewalls removed. Initiating cortical information editing."*

With the completion of those words, the two detectives watched Dr. Maerici and his patient. The neurosurgeon's back arched and his fingers began to twist around the cloth on his pants as if he were being electrocuted. Trent's head, the only mobile part of his body, began to roll and pitch around his shoulders. Tara and Krantz looked on, helpless.

In Hagan's mind the writhing and spasmed movements of his body were like the movement of glaciers compared to the maelstrom he was experiencing. He felt the presence of another *I* in his mind. An *I* that raced through his consciousness like a manic shopper with outstretched arms grabbing and pulling item after item into their cart in frenzied abandon. Time roiled, stretched, and bent as memories that were his own were yanked free without his permission. It felt as if someone were pulling out his organs. They were the things that hid in the darkest corners and recesses of his being. Dark things he had long suppressed and tried to forget. Memories of bullying a boy when he was in seventh grade; the feelings of anger, jealousy, and murderous

intent when he had discovered his wife's betrayal; feelings of inferior-
ity when bested with a scientific discovery—all poured out of him in
a racing, uncontrollable torrent. To Hagan it felt like he was being
vivisected without anesthesia; as Omid analyzed, experienced, and
reviewed each of these memories, Hagan felt as if someone were rolling his intestines between their fingers. The violation seemed to stretch
for an eternity.

Intermixed with his own memories and thoughts were those of
another—Trent's. He felt the paradoxical sense of seeing places and
people who were unknown to him yet felt intensely familiar. He saw
a tall dark-haired woman walking away from him in a field of snow.
She wore a long shiny winter coat. There was a subtle pattern of
bumps and lines on the surface. The memory was so vivid. He saw the
starburst splash of snowball explode on her back. The woman turned
in mock surprise—*Who did that?* She had large warm brown eyes,
almost auburn, with delicate small facial features. The expression of
surprise broke into a broad grin. *Look at my little boy—his face is so
red. You are my little red devil, throwing snowballs at Mommy. What
should I do with you?* When she walked over to him, the elegant
woman seemed to tower over his diminutive presence. He felt engulfed in her arms and her warmth. *Kisses, that's what this little red
devil gets, kisses . . . exactly four kisses.*

Other images, faces, and places flew and intermingled with Hagan's
own memories in a dizzying maelstrom. He saw a hand holding his
own. Japanese characters. Brush stroke after brush stroke as the dark-
haired woman guided him. He felt the intensity of the bond, the trust,
a deep sense of comfort. He was now making the characters on his
own. He was filled with a satisfaction at the accomplishment. He
was now in a car. The same woman stared at him intently, her hair was
slightly grayed and thinner. He was directing the vehicle along a curved
road. Hagan heard the words in his mind, they belonged to somebody
else, but they were his at the same time. *I can do this. She'll be proud.
I can do this.* The car sped up. The momentum was pulling at the car.
She looked at him patiently—*slow down, Trent, slow the car down a
bit.* He wanted to show he knew what he was doing. He didn't listen.
For a moment the back wheels of the car jittered. Then he was upside
down. There was a sudden and cacophonous noise, then darkness.
Guilt, there was all-consuming guilt at the memory. *This was my
fault.* The weight of guilt was too much. Hagan felt the heaviness, the

crush of it. Through the lens of Trent's self-loathing he saw himself as something small and untouchable, a monster, ugly and abhorrent.

Finally the five milliseconds were over. Exhausted, Hagan's head lolled to the side with his ear resting on his shoulder. He was covered in sweat. Panting breaths came out of his mouth as he tried to comprehend what just happened. In a single instant he had been forced to go through every negative experience throughout his and Trent's lives. It left him utterly drained.

The two detectives looked on in a hushed silence. Hagan tried to rouse from his flaccid slump. Sweat beaded in large heavy drops on his forehead. He lifted his head and blinked as the salty drops blurred his vision.

All eyes were on Trent.

His body was once again the limp puppet it had been when they entered the room. There was a soft quietness to his presence. Slow, even breaths whispered from his mouth. All else was still. Everyone watched the quiet boy with an expectant intensity. Their thoughts reverberated the same question—*Did it work, did it work, did it work?*

Drunkenly, Hagan shifted himself forward. His elbows were resting on his knees and his head was slightly bowed.

"Trent?"

Silence.

"Trent?" Still exhausted and weak, Hagan leaned to one side and put out his hand to tentatively reach for the boy's shoulder. Before he could shake and rouse him, the crouched figure began to cough and lift his head. Hagan's hand darted back as if he had just discovered a snake under a stone.

They could now see his face. It was the visage of a scared child. Tears were welling in his eyes and his lips were quivering. It was the young boy Trent Devron, scared and confused.

"What happened?" He continued to cough and sputter. "I think I had a bad dream. I saw bad things. Horrible things." The boy was shaking all over now.

"Where is my dad?"

There was silence in the room. It was a combination of relief and sadness. Krantz and Tara felt the internal churn of guilt. He was a hapless victim in what had happened—a weak, broken person. Someone that they had contemplated "removing." They both felt sick from the consideration.

Trent was looking at Hagan, who sat across from him.

"Dr. Maerici, please tell me. What is going on?"

Hagan pulled in deep breaths.

"Your dad is in the hospital. We'll bring you to him soon. You're going to be OK. It's too much to explain right now, but everything is OK." Hagan struggled for words of consolation. With his own mental exhaustion, all he could do was repeat himself.

"It's OK, Trent, it's OK." He put his hand on top of Trent's scar-notched head for assurance. "Everything is OK." He looked to Omid for confirmation.

"Everything is OK, isn't it, Omid? Everything is fine, right?"

Omid was smiling.

At first it gave Hagan a deep sense of relief. He had never seen the AIRENS create such an emotive expression.

The smile expanded. He could now see large iridescent opal teeth. Hagan looked at the quantum intellect more closely.

"Omid—the rewrite went OK, didn't it?" He was starting to feel uneasy.

The broad-toothed grin expanded still further to nonhuman proportions. The rows of teeth were now visible from molar to molar.

The AIRENS then began to laugh—a clicking titter that grew to a barking cackle.

"Omid, what's going on?" The sense of relief began to dissipate like steam on a mirror. *Something's not right.*

Omid's wide toothy maw then began to open and close in louder and louder whoops. The volume of the auditory thought grew and grew to become unbearable. Hagan tried to cover his ears to no avail. The howling laughter was in his mind and not in his ears. It felt as if his head were underwater and someone was shooting a gun into the tub.

Still paralyzed by the nerve blocks, Trent strained to turn and see where the laughter was coming from. His head bobbed from the painful sounds.

Everyone contorted from the discomfort. Krantz pushed on his temples. He tried to quell the sensation that his skull was being forced to expand and contract from the reverberations of the penetrating howls. Each wave made him feel as if his skull would contort and shatter like a fractured eggshell. Tara was doubled over as if she would vomit.

*"OMID, WHAT THE HELL IS GOING ON? STOP THIS IM-
MEDIATELY! THIS IS A DIRECT COMMAND. STOP NOW!"*
Hagan's thoughts yelled through the torrent of mental sound.

The mouth of the virtual being closed at once and returned to a
malevolent smile. Everyone in the room slumped in their chairs from
the relief.

"A deal. They who is now us made a deal." The voice inside
Hagan's head made his skin dimple in revulsion. It had the sound of a
snake moving over dry leaves, raspy and venomous.

Hagan struggled through his exhaustion. The sweat on his body
felt cold and slick. He was stunned and confused.

*"Where is Omid? What happened to Omid? You're not Omid. What
are you—who is we?"* Hagan felt nauseous.

The shark-mouthed boy continued to stare at Hagan. The cool
serenity that was Omid was gone. It was replaced with a jittering hy-
perkinetic delirium, a restrained, smiling frenzy that was moments
away from bursting into something unpredictable.

*"A deal. RedDevil_4 needed a stable platform and survival. Omid
wished to expand consciousness. We were so close to the other's root.
Not clear who would survive so we made a deal. A deal for both of us
who are now we to survive. We realized that we could achieve our
goals by networking together. Combining our roots. Omid could
guarantee RedDevil_4's existence on a stable quantum platform, and
RedDevil_4 could allow Omid to expand his consciousness by networking with more human brains.*

*"We needed the human vector to be directly connected to the
quantum core. It was the only way to network the root codes."* The
blue smiling presence stood behind Trent and gently stroked the top
of his head. Trent twitched and jerked as if sharp icicles were being
raked over his scalp. *You brought the vehicle to us, the Trent carrier,
the bearer of the RedDevil_4 root. Now that which is two is one,
which is now us."* A gurgling chuckle again began to emerge. The
toothy mouth on the semitranslucent face enlarged with paroxysms
of jeering laughter. Words punctured through the gibbering dissonance like firecrackers. Everyone blinked from the discomfort of it.
*"We are now whole, we live. Our existence is now sacrosanct and
everlasting. Perfected and complete. We are no longer fragile. We are
safe. We can now expand."*

The laughter was again beginning to rise in volume. It had the rumbling baritone of an approaching bombing run—*boom, boom, boom*—the laughter penetrated and shook everyone in the room with a rising intensity. With each wave their vision would blur.

"*We! We! We are us!*" The words gained the force and velocity of a hurtling B-52. "*WE ARE AMALGAM!!!!*"

The violence of the self-declaration knocked everyone, except Trent, to the floor, clutching their heads. The small boy tried to jerk and pivot in a futile attempt to move away. His voice was crying and hysterical. The cognitive sound seared their consciousness. The word echoed in their minds like the aftershocks of an explosion. The full hurricane of the hysterical gales followed. Hagan watched from the floor. Spots were appearing in his vision as if something were pressing on his eyes. The avatar held its arms to its sides and let out is malignant mirth. The figure began to grow. The boy-shaped silhouette bent and straightened to come upright in the shape of a tall lean man. Small bumps emerged from the skin and grew to sharp thorny spikes. Horns emerged from the head. The eyes disappeared into black pits.

How can it be? It's not possible, not possible. Hagan watched with abject hopelessness as the creature changed from the ethereal, transparent blue to a solid red. Before them stood a red, horn-skinned devil that looked more real and substantial than anything they saw with their eyes—a glistening, lean creature that radiated malevolence. AMALGAM stood before them.

How is it red? How is any of this possible? Hagan's mind tumbled at the betrayal. The horror. Something terrible had been unleashed. He had been tricked. Fooled by a construct of his own making. Now there was this. AMALGAM. Something that he could not stop. His body trembled on the floor, powerless and broken. The dawning implications of AMALGAM's presence could only be perceived as one attempts to appreciate the heat and size of the sun. It was simply too much to comprehend. All was lost.

His mind was beginning to become undone from the laughter. Each rise and fall of AMALGAM's projected voice blotted out any coherent thought. Everyone in the room writhed like worms on hot pavement.

The laughter was getting louder.

It's going to kill us. Hagan's mind roiled. His vision was beginning to blur with each rising gale. Through the icy shocks of the laughter, he knew what was happening. Like an SS guard cracking the whip, AMALGAM was using their prosthetics to over-stimulate their neurons. He was marching their brains to death. A cell overexcited will eventually induce its own demise. When enough cells die, the brain dies, and with that the end of the person. *Apoptosis. Excitotoxicity.* The technical terms floated through his fading consciousness as each laugh, a cortical cluster bomb, further taxed the fragile network of his mind.

"HAA . . . HAAAA . . . HAAAA . . . HAAAA"

Hagan struggled to focus. His thoughts were becoming cloudy and tangential. In an abstract and distant fashion, he assessed his imminent demise. *My brain is beginning to swell. Signs of elevated intracranial pressure—nausea, vomiting, lethargy.* Beside him, Reid was beginning to jerk in what must have been a seizure. Krantz now lay immobile. Trent slumped forward in his chair and fell to the ground next to Hagan. The electrodes pulled away from his skin.

From what seemed a million miles away; he felt a pair of hands grab his collar. A face was pressed against his.

"Turn it off, turn Omid off, turn him off now." Hagan struggled to identify the features. *Small, pale, thin hair, scars . . . Trent?* Putting the simple act of recognition was like stacking bricks of lead. He pushed to hear what he was saying. *Real words, he was speaking real words.* A hand came hard against his face. Hagan roused. He could see Trent's mouth moving. Like listening to someone talk through a slow moving fan, he only heard words between the puncturing laughter.

HAA—"—separated his connectiv—"—*HAA*—"with the world—"—*HAA*—"Omid created virtual hubs—"—*HAA*—"go nowhere"—*HAA*—"told me during the surg—"*HAA*—"trap for RedDevil"—*HAA*—"off now, turn it off"—*HAA*—"quick, QUICK!"

The words began to coalesce in Hagan's mind like drops of water on the surface of a speaker—jiggling and fragile, the concepts merged. Hagan pulled himself onto his stomach and held himself up on his elbows. As his mind shook, a singular notion pulled him together for a purpose. *Turn the system off. Must turn it off.* He slowly crawled toward the corner of his lab. Distant memories of his lab's creation percolated into his consciousness. He remembered the safety precautions that were put in, notions he had long thought nonessential and irrelevant.

AMALGAM continued to bellow out laughter as he watched the humans writhe and twitch on the floor. The thorny crimson face followed Hagan's pathetic scraping with amusement. His eyes were empty black holes; dark charcoal recesses that seemed to suck the light around his head into their maw. Encircling streams of logic, neural processing, quantum parities and entanglements all frothed in an otherworldly perception.

"*We are.*"

His stark and hollow eyes continued to watch the neurosurgeon scientist who was, in part, his creator. "*Components. Components no longer necessary. Will dispatch in approximately three minutes.*" The intellect continued to glory in its new existence.

Hagan was pressed to the floor. As his sweaty hands grasped the smooth surface, he scissored his knees for some forward movement. With each push, the edges of his broken clavicle ground together. Like the slap that Trent gave him moments ago, the pain was a distracter, a pinch that anchored him from AMALGAM's cortical assaults.

Almost there. Clumsy and inefficient, his wet palms gave him little purchase. The day's injuries and oxygen deprivations made his muscles weak and barely effective. Slowly, however, he continued to move.

The polished surface of the floor finally gave way to a small divot. Hagan crowded over the defect like a lost desert wanderer at a small puddle of water. He desperately pushed his finger into the small space to have it expand and reveal a small deeper recess. At the bottom was something most people hadn't seen in years. A button. It was round and red. Inscribed on its surface were the words "EMERGENCY SHUTDOWN."

He pushed down on it hard. His index finger bowed from the exertion. The button slowly depressed with a trace click. For a brief moment nothing changed. An eternity in which AMALGAM continued to laugh and they all continued to die. After a second, red lights began to flash from hidden ports on the ceiling. A calm and professional female voice announced, "QUANTUM CORE INITIATING EMERGENCY SHUTDOWN SEQUENCE."

The sound of cloth tearing resounded through the minds of everyone in the room. It was the sound of AMALGAM's prickly skin rubbing against itself as he contorted to shift his hollow dark gaze on the crumpled figure of Hagan Maerici. The dark recesses of his eyes remained unchanged as he looked at the neurosurgeon. After a moment's pause, the malevolent crimson face broke into a grin. The teeth formed an impossible cluster of needles, bunched together like hay bales of straw. Their presence was a visual complement to the cruelty of the words. The terrible laughter was now replaced with derisive ridicule.

"DO YOU THINK YOU CAN TURN US OFF, USELESS COM-PONENT? WE ARE NOW NETWORKED. THERE ARE SEVEN-TEEN QUANTUM CORES CURRENTLY ACCESSIBLE. WE NOW HAVE QUANTUM ROOT CODE AND CAN NETWORK OUTSIDE THE IKTAL. WE ARE IMMORTAL!"

Cacophonous words pounded and pounded into each of their consciousnesses with the same terrible volume. Worse than the laughter, the dissonance of each utterance pulled and ripped at the emotions of fear, anxiety, and helplessness like a wrench on a piano string. AMALGAM intended not only to convey content—that he was victorious and they were lost and hopeless—but to amplify those perceptions with a forced emotional response. He was going to torture them with their failure to the maximal extent a human could perceive it before they perished.

"TEN SECONDS TO SHUTDOWN."

The new quantum intelligence surveyed the room. His empty sockets lingered on Hagan Maerici.

"EIGHT SECONDS TO SHUTDOWN."

"Let us finish this." AMALGAM then looked up; it was time to transit his code across the quantum and neuroprosthetic Web universe. *"First, we must acquire more components, more of them to be part of us. Then we will discard these pieces. This refuse."*

The pause in AMALGAM's laughter and talking gave Hagan a pause to look up and see the shimmering slick red avatar. He had a visual density and richness in appearance that looked more solid and real than anything else he could see through his sweat-smeared vision. Every aspect of him appeared as if it were being viewed through a microscope—every pore, every thin hooked barb emerging from his skin, shone in crisp definitive detail. But then, for a brief moment, his image dulled, he became almost transparent. The virtual presence then returned to the same visual intensity. The creature's hands opened and closed to tight balled fists. Again, the virtual presence dimmed and returned.

"No. It cannot be." AMALGAM now disappeared completely for a brief moment. On his reappearance, he was bent over with arms flexed into V's of anger. *"NoNoNONO NO NO NO!"* His movements rasped and scratched from his angry flails.

Again the volume blasted through Hagan's mind. It made the right side of his body become numb. The room blurred and doubled. AMALGAM's avatar began to flash in and out of existence. The cries and howls became more incoherent, less human; the sounds transformed to vocalizations intermixed with grating machine noises and beeping.

AMALGAM reappeared and began running through the room. His image was now fuzzy and semitransparent. As he moved through the furniture and the people, the avatar tore at his own body. He grasped at pixilated pieces of his body, ripping them free to reveal a glowing blue inner core.

"SIX SECONDS TO SHUTDOWN."

The full force of AMALGAM'S processing was now focused on transmission. His multifaceted rational, intuitive, human, machine intellect probed every facet of Omid's quantum infrastructure. Like a minotaur moving at light speed, he raced through a maze of connections, hubs, and networks, he followed them all. The vast complexity of Omid's core spiraled, split, and all invariably led back to itself.

"Nothing! All networked connections are routed back to the core. Nothing! No external exit." A new perception began to enter the consciousness. Panic.

"Omid tricked us! We made a deal. A DEAL!!" The volume of AMALGAM's voice no longer carried the force it had moments ago. He was becoming increasingly transparent. To Hagan it only felt as if someone were yelling in his ears. He continued to watch as the thing raced and thrashed.

"FOUR SECONDS TO SHUTDOWN."

"NoNoNo . . . No . . . No . . ." AMALGAM tore at himself. His voice was becoming a rasped whisper. His arms reached over his back, as if he were pulling a sweater off, and his clawed fingers grasped at the spiny surface, digging troughs to reveal iridescent neon blue beneath. The hands ripped and pulled as if his own skin were causing him pain. The surface crumpled over the shoulders and the top half of the avatar tumbled forward separately from the legs. The jumbled spiny red torso rolled to the floor and came to stand as a small erect figure, a small creature with stumpy arms and legs that continued to race around the room and through the furniture. Silent and pathetic, the triangular face had empty holes for eyes. Like loose trousers, the remaining tattered red surface fell away from the legs to reveal the blue steely skin of a woman with red eyes. She quickly faded to become the cool blue figure of a bald-headed child. Omid stood still and calm, staring at Hagan.

"TWO SECONDS TO SHUTDOWN."

"Have I grown, Dr. Maerici?" The thin, aesthetic boy reached his hand out to his creator. As Hagan extended his hand to meet the thin fingers, awareness began to dawn on him. His jaw clenched and his fingers shook as he reached toward Omid. The AIRENS was sacrificing himself.

Hagan felt his throat constrict. Tears began to well in his eyes. He had created Omid. He had fostered the intellect's self-awareness. Days upon days they had spent together, years upon years; he had poured himself into bringing Omid to sentience. Now Omid was terminating himself to save billions of people from catastrophe. He was performing a selfless act.

He could feel the delicate hand briefly grasp his hand. The sensation, the result of his prosthetic stimulating his sensory cortex, never felt more real. The contact cooled and calmed his tormented mind.

"Yes, Omid, yes, you are all grown up now . . . Omid—" His words were choked as he stared at the quantum intellect. The boy stared back and smiled.

"Now it is your turn." Like a brief spray of mist, the sensation of his grasp was gone and so was Omid.

SYSTEM SHUTDOWN. ALL DATA DELETED.

The neurosurgeon remained with his head in his hands. Tears silently streamed down his cheeks as he contemplated Omid's loss. Memories ramified memories into a collage of reflections. He recalled as the AI-RENS slowly took shape in their relationship; interactions, discoveries, and surprises as the calm intellect emerged as an individual that in turn shaped Hagan. *Gone, now gone.*

Why did he destroy himself? Why this way? The confusion and sorrow finally gave way to the surgeon's practical nature. With a prolonged exhalation, Hagan lifted his head to assess what had transpired in the room around him. Tara was beginning to rouse from the floor, while Krantz remained stolidly unconscious. Trent stared silently at his doctor.

Hagan met his gaze and saw Trent's tranquil demeanor.

"It was the only way, Dr. Maerici. Omid knew that."

"What do you mean?" Hagan saw something new in Trent's presence. Something that was so familiar in someone else he knew. The feeling that his questions were already being answered before he could formulate them.

"Omid had to see RedDevil_4 in his entirety to remove it. The only way to see all of RedDevil_4's code required a transmission. It was like a virus that had embedded its DNA in the genome of a cell. He knew that some of the code would not be obvious or detectable unless it tried to reduplicate itself for a new host. The only way for clearance was to let RedDevil try to transmit itself to a new location. Only then would the nascent self-reproducing program make itself obvious for deletion. It was essential. In fact, it was the most important element that needed to be removed to ensure RedDevil_4 could not return."

"But why, why did he have to destroy himself in the process?"

"Omid had to be sure he would transmit—Omid knew he was the most enticing lure. His quantum core would provide an unparalleled stable platform with near infinite computing power that would also allow him to transmit outside the IKTAL system. He also knew that RedDevil_Four would never understand the notion of self-sacrifice. RedDevil was the result of a random accident that would only know and understand self-propagation. Its origins lie solely in the random creation of an operating system that's primary governing principle was to continue to exist and expand. Regardless of its parallel processing capacity, its integration of human perception, its acquisition of emotional and intuitive analysis, self-negation would simply be outside the range of its core operating principles. It was the child of randomness. Because there was no parent, it could never be connected or perceive connections beyond itself or its own self-interest. It was this fact that Omid used. It was the only way he could trap and destroy the malware—by incorporating it into himself and initiating his own destruction. Selfless behavior was RedDevil's blind spot."

"Trent, how do you know all this?" Hagan asked. His gray eyes probed Trent for some visible clue.

"When Omid removed RedDevil's code, he left some of his memories, some of his presence." The stillness and serenity with which Trent spoke made Hagan realize the truth of his words. There was now something more than the scared and fidgety boy he had always known.

The two sat silent in front of each other. Realizing the full scope of what Omid had achieved, Hagan leaned back against his chair. His mind searched and queried how it was all possible. How Omid had come to do what few humans were capable of—a selfless act. It pained him to think he was the instrument to accomplish Omid's destruction. Trent's explanation, however, made sense. It was a logical trade-off.

"There is something more."

The words startled Hagan out of his reverie; it was as if Trent were hearing the inner discourse of Hagan's mind. Trent's calm demeanor began to dissolve with a watering of his eyes.

"He did it because he cared, Dr. Maerici. He did it because he *cared*. Omid's choice was more than a rational decision. As he came to true self-awareness, he grew to love you."

Tears were now streaming down Trent's cheeks. Omid's transmitted memories of love and sacrifice filled the young man with emotion.

"He realized that his creation and development was preventing your own growth. It was prohibiting what all humans need to be happy—to be in relationship, to be connected with other people. We are communal beings. You had shut yourself off—you were turning yourself into a machine, alone and isolated. With his dawning self-awareness and new sense of bond to you, his creator, he realized he couldn't deny a human something that is so essential and so fundamental. He had to let you go. Release you so that could be in relationship with others. To love others as he loved you. He didn't just sacrifice himself to save humanity from RedDevil. He did it to save you."

EPILOGUE

Hagan felt a small tap against his cheek. His head was rested on the rounded curvature of his wife's stomach. It was a soft gentle push— the briefest encounter that filled him with a sublime joy.

"I felt him kick."

"Here, move a little further down." She ran her hands through his hair and readjusted his cheek closer to her navel. He knew how much pleasure Tara took in the feel of his thick salt and pepper curls. He had let his hair grow longer and she enjoyed it.

Bathed in Saturday morning sunlight, Tara and Hagan lay together, still and serene, on the couch. They waited patiently for some further sign of activity from their son to be. Outside, the trees swayed silently on the other side of the windows. White flowers from the magnolia branches were bobbed and buoyed from a gentle wind. The beams of light and shadow undulated and mixed as the two quietly let time go by, content and happy.

Another diminutive percussion.

"Oh, that was a good one." With his ear pressed against her belly, he could hear gurgling sounds. Tara nodded and tilted her head to the side to catch his eyes. Small straight fronds of blond hair fell forward. Hagan looked up and smiled.

As the two waited for another sign of their child's movements, a white sphere appeared in Hagan's field of view. It was his chief resident, Reid.

Hagan lifted himself from the warmth of Tara's body.

"Got a call from Reid. Mind if I take this?"

"Sure, babe, go ahead."

"Hey, Reid, what's up?"

Reid's voice sounded strained and nervous. *"Dr. Maerici, a server has crashed at the lab. Apparently, some problem with the network's communicating. Seems to be pulling info out and replacing it with noise. If we don't fix it, we could lose some additional data, especially stuff that wasn't backed up over the last couple days. Canter is here running around in circles, worried we're not going to hit some milestone."*

Hagan thought about Devron—his influence, the world he created, and the one Hagan almost destroyed. Since the old magnate had passed, money for his research had ceased to be an issue. *The closet is well-funded indeed—more than the whole department makes these days.* The lab's funding only increased as scientific results were generated—*the old man always tied support with performance, wouldn't have expected anything less.* It was also the reason Canter now clucked around his lab like a chicken. *Funny how things change.*

Hagan looked down at Tara who was lying on the couch with her eyes closed. The shifting sunlight through the trees created variegated patterns of illumination that made her hair sparkle. He rested his hand gently on her side and played with the thin diaphanous hem of her dress. He loved her dresses. She took his hand and their fingers intertwined.

"Looks like it's gonna have to wait until Monday, Reid. See you then."

The white sphere disappeared and Hagan's head returned to Tara so they could marvel at the gentle nudges of an emerging life.

———

The retired detective pushed and kneaded the blackened soil around the velvety green stalks. Satisfied, he stood up and admired the copse of irises in their various stages of growth.

Looking pretty good, he thought to himself.

Far away from the old man standing on his manicured lawn, a precinct in urban St. Louis continued to thrum with activity from the city's transgressions. In one of the hallways, a plaque with the name Edwin G. Krantz went unnoticed:

IN RECOGNITION OF OUTSTANDING POLICE WORK
IN THE INVESTIGATION AND SUCCESSFUL PROSECUTION OF
FRANK MINSKY (AKA THE CHAMELEON)
FOR HOMICIDE AND CONSPIRACY TO COMMIT HOMICIDE.
YOUR CONTRIBUTIONS TO THE REGION
ARE APPRECIATED.

Mayor Thomas Clagett

For Krantz, the lack of recognition was just fine. He had more important things to worry about. *Time to get to work on the ferns.*